TOIL &
TROUBLE

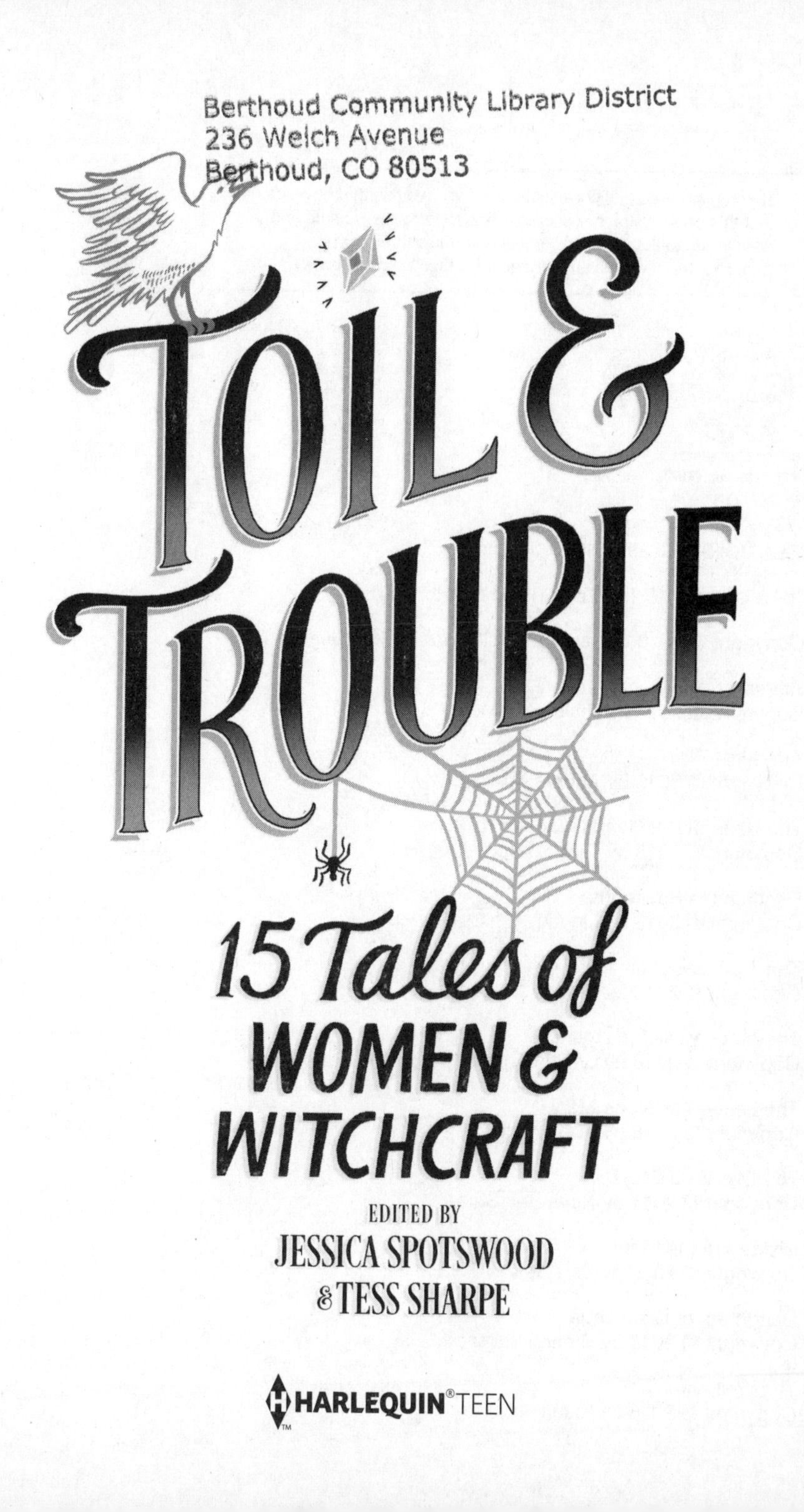

TOIL & TROUBLE

15 Tales of WOMEN & WITCHCRAFT

EDITED BY

JESSICA SPOTSWOOD

& TESS SHARPE

HARLEQUIN® TEEN

ISBN-13: 978-1-335-01627-0

This edition published by arrangement with Harlequin Books S.A.

For questions and comments about the quality of this book, please contact us at CustomerService@Harlequin.com.

Printed in U.S.A.

CONTENTS

For all the troublemakers
and everyone who needs a little magic

STARSONG

by

Tehlor Kay Mejia

THERE'S A CALM THAT COMES OVER ME WHEN I'm painting. The same one the stars bring out.

During the day, I'm high-maintenance like my mamí says. Face contoured and flawless, brows fierce, lips popping. My nails are perfection in whatever shade my tía whispers from her photo on the top of my bookshelf. Amethyst, for emotional balance. Rose, for an open heart. Obsidian to ward against people who look at me with envy—and trust me, there are plenty of them.

Last week, when the comments got too petty, I painted a red-and-yellow eye in the center of each middle finger and posted it on my Instagram account—@delasEstrellas.

I see you, said the caption. *And you can't touch me.*

That one got 38k likes. It's still being reblogged on Tumblr hundreds of times a day.

People call me magic in the comments, but that's not magic, and I should know.

Because when I sacrifice my custom ringtone to the vibration gods and sit down at my desk, the scent of the stars blowing across the Santa Anas and into my open window, I feel it wake up. The real magic. The kind that's bound to blood and culture. To history. To violence I say a thousand thanks a day for never knowing.

It's a hum, and a whisper; it's a guiding hand. At least, that's what my mom always used to say when I was a little girl, still clean-faced and wide-eyed. Before Tía went through a guardrail in a rock band's tour bus on a dark, winding highway. Before I was admitted to the West Hills Hospital last year, full of vodka and pills and the strange ramblings of the boy who fed them to me. Before I knew I was born to hear the song of the stars.

Tonight, the moon is just visible beyond the waving palm trees, and I can hear the ocean. My mamí is long asleep, a brown seed planted in that big bed in this giant house beside Bruce-the-life-coach, who says she has the purest soul of anyone he's ever known.

He says it like I should be so lucky, and he's probably right. But let's face it, purity isn't really my aesthetic. At least, it didn't used to be.

I pad over to my altar, eggplant toenails almost disappearing in the plush of my rug. Pink. A little girl's dream. I'm sixteen now, not that little girl anymore. But she missed out on a lot. I try to throw her a bone every once in a while.

Mamí and I have come a long way since the trailer I grew up in with the peeling paint. The closeness and the noise. The neighbors fighting. The thuds against the walls that I hid from in the little closet where we kept the recycling, counting my fingers and toes again and again until it went quiet.

I'm not there anymore, I tell myself now. The waves crash outside, the only sound apart from the stars.

Inhale. Exhale.

It's more important than ever that I stay grounded.

I light one candle, holding my intentions clear. A bubble of white light around my body. Around the house. Around Mamí and sure, even Bruce. *Keep me safe. Keep us all safe.* From what's out there. From ourselves.

The next candle is for Tía Jasmin. She's back with the source now. The place our magic comes from.

Inhale. Exhale.

Mamí says I'm just like her. My tía. That our magic is restless and wild and trouble-bound. But I don't know if I agree. Maybe we were just two people chasing numbness because we didn't know what the stardust inside us was for.

Maybe Tía Jasmin got on that bus the same way I went to that party. Maybe she was tired of feeling different. Tired of the magic and the way it made everything seem so significant. Tired of the way someone was always watching, waiting to see what we would become.

My fingers shake around the last match. This one, I close my eyes for. When the wick catches, I picture the open sky above my second-story room, the clear darkness that gets even clearer as I project myself above the haze of LA smog.

I shake, because the first time it happened was that night, my back against the cold desert ground, the oil-can fire so far away. I was just looking for a little oblivion. A little normal. A little of the dead-eyed shimmer the girls at school wore through the cafeteria after a night in the desert—the kind that made people look at them like they were women.

But in that moment, the distance expanding and contracting before my hazy eyes, I found something so much more. Despite the spinning that had sent me to the ground in search of something that wouldn't give way, I'd never been as sober as I was when the pinpricks of the stars grew larger, taking on color spectrums I'd never seen.

That's when a voice somewhere deep down whispered that I belonged. And not among the scattered crowds clutching red Solo cups and scuffing their shoes in the sand. I, Luna Mendoza, was part of the swirling color and dancing light of a sky that had never seemed so close.

After they pumped my stomach, the hospital shrink said those hallucinations would fade, but I just smiled. Even the emptiness in my veins couldn't take away what I knew.

Back home, I finally approached the altar Mamí set up for me on my fifteenth birthday, the one that had done nothing but gather dust while I tried and failed to forget it. To fit in. That day, I lit the candles, and sober as I was from forty-eight hours in the hospital and a tube down my throat, the path to the skies was wide open, like I'd only needed to find my way once.

That's the journey I take tonight, through the mistakes and the heartache and the new circles beneath Mamí's eyes. The ones that have a hint of Tía Jasmin in them. Poor Mamí, doomed to love two girls who followed their magic down the wrong roads. But at least I have a chance to make it right.

I'm alive, I remind myself. *Alive.* I drift up to the stars, repeating it until the magic is tingling in my palms and I can't feel the rug beneath my feet anymore. Until the Instagram haters, the wannabes, and my mom's disapproving clucks when I wear NYX Pin-Up Pout in Rebel Soul are all thirty light-years below me and falling.

The match still in my hand, I clear the path between my grounded body and the unbound stars. I whisper to Tía Jasmin, and the Water Bearer of Aquarius, and the moon's pale-faced diosa to send their own inspiration down.

By the time I open my eyes, I'm not Esperanza Luna Mendoza Stevens anymore. I'm a star-child. A bruja with magic sparking from my perfect pedicure to my massive barrel curls and everywhere in between.

I haven't taken a drink or a pill since I came home from the hospital. Why would I? I know exactly what I was looking for in those bottles, and that it can't be found there.

But now, I know where it can.

Tonight's chart is a tricky one. Jonah and Jess and Bree, a poly trio new to each other and madly in love. Jess sent the email, sugar sweet. She knows they're soul mates, she just wants proof for the living room wall of their first apartment together.

It's not the first three-way I've done. Sometimes it's other poly kids, sometimes new parents and a baby. In one very strange case a single woman and her dog and cat. It's not my place to judge, but on the low I bet that Leo dog was the absolute worst.

People find me when they need to see the beauty they feel. They find me when they want to be sure, and when they can't be. They want a little star magic to tell them it's gonna be okay. What they get is something so far removed from the newspaper horoscopes they're barely even related. And after all the ugliness I've seen? The funerals and the shaking walls and the beeping monitors of my own hospital room? I like to give people that magic. Maybe it's my penance for all the heartache I caused.

My phone buzzes. It doesn't happen as often these days, but the text makes me smile in a nostalgic sort of way. Party in the hills, it says. Everyone's going. Pick you up?

I don't even bother to text *nah* anymore. They know. They're still looking for the Luna I was. The life of the party. The girl who would say anything. They miss her.

But I don't.

I have the math aspect of this chart open on the Mac screen in front of me, neat black-and-white columns of times, degrees. They wouldn't mean much to anyone else—certainly not to the girls trying to coax me out tonight. When I look at them, though, they take on new significance. Magic and the starsong and the guiding hands of my girls in the sky spin stories in the cozy angles, draw glittering threads from the anchor points that will build the foundation of their life together.

My hand does the rest, led by the music my magic lets in. A giant sheet of thick watercolor paper covers my desk, and I close my eyes. The breeze plays across my face, and that trine intersection of Jonah's sun and Bree's Saturn is so beautiful and I'm flying higher than anything synthetic has ever taken me...

I don't look up 'til my neck is stiff, and when I do, there are the bones. Lacking shading and nuance, just bright blots of color and spidery black veins connecting it all. Their own personal constellation.

"M'ija, it's late," comes my mama's voice, along with a tap at the door. The stardust scatters, returning to the night sky. The blue candle that holds my connection to the ethereal skies snuffs out in a serpent of white smoke.

"Mamí!" The rug swallows my footsteps, and I open the door. "Why aren't you in bed?"

"I saw the light," she says, the familiar mixture of concern and disapproval deepening her wrinkles. I've ordered her like, five BioRepublic sheet masks and I swear she's never used one. It's a tragedy, really. With her genes? She could look twenty-five.

"Stars stay up late," I say.

"You're not a star," she bites back. "You're a girl up at three in the morning with your face painted like a calavera." Disapproval is winning the battle. "You're chatting all day and night with these sinvergüenzas from that Instagram, probably all perverts pretending to be teenagers."

"That's not even a thing anymore," I say with an irritated twitch of my mane. "You're old, Mamí."

Her eyes flash, and I know what's coming next. But like, honestly, how can she not know MTV blew that catfishing thing wide open before I was even old enough to annoy my primos on Facebook? I almost feel bad. I know where her worry comes from. The scent of disinfected hospital hallway she probably still wakes up smelling.

"You think I'm just a superstitious old woman, huh?" she asks, drawing up to her full height of five feet nothing. "You think I don't know what's waiting out there when you and those friends of yours…when your Tía Jasmin…" Her sentences fracture when she gets upset, the rift of two languages springing up like a chasm between them.

She's too proud to speak Spanish, even when she's mad and the English slips away on the tide of anger or fear. But sometimes I wish she would let down her guard. Show me who she really is.

"I'm safe in my room," I say. Again. "I don't go to parties. I don't drink. I don't do drugs. I sit in here at this desk, and I use the gift *you* passed down to me, and sometimes I stay up late. That's it!" But there's more to it than that. The *anymore* I don't put at the ends of my sentences now. Like I'm hoping she'll forget.

Like I'm hoping I will.

She can't possibly know that I'm scared too; it'll only make it worse. She doesn't know how I feel that cold against my back, spreading through my body as the sky faded in and out. The rough arms that lifted me. The way the pickup bounced with me in the back on the way to the hospital.

The way they left me on the sidewalk outside, not wanting to get in trouble because I was underage.

She doesn't know about the white aura I draw around myself when I light my candles, or the way it's flickering now. Dying. Her fear creeping in like a black tongue.

"You think I've forgotten so easily?" she asks, her voice too low now, the rumble of earth before a flood. She's a Virgo, but her deep, earthy channels are prone to flash floods. *Damn Cancer moon.* "You think I'm stupid," she says. "Behind the times. But you're looking for glamour, just like she was. That's why I had to pick you up at the hospital, full of booze and—"

"Mamí," I try to interrupt, but she's not done.

"Listen, maybe this *tumbler* is the new party. The new backstage pass. Maybe these *snack chats* are the new tour bus. But how long, m'ija, until you find the new overdose?"

I huff, irritated at the way she always draws us together. The twins of Tía Jasmin's Gemini twining between the watery blue waves and curls of my Aquarius. Both air signs, sure, both a little strange. But so different… Why can't I make her see? It's like the moment she walked into that hospital room I was Jasmin all over again, the little sister she had to identify by one mal de ojo tattoo.

"You need to stay close, Esperanza Luna," she says. "You're not ready."

Of course, the dreaded first name. Everyone who values their lives or my opinion calls me Luna, but she won't quit.

I can't even be annoyed, though, because I'm swimming in it again. The reason I can barely breathe outside this ridiculous house. The reason I didn't speak at an astrologers' conference last summer, when I was totally invited. The reason my stomach twists into knots whenever I think of meeting a friend for coffee, going to the beach.

Never mind going on a date, holding hands, kissing…

If I stray too far, I'll end up back on that desert ground, too far from the fire, the cold eating through everything. I'll end up like Tía Jasmin, alone in the wreckage of a bus after everyone else woke up.

I'm trying to move on. To embrace my gift. To let go of what I was and become who I want to be. But my mom's fear is making nests in my chest, and if I don't stop her now I'll never remember how far I've come.

"Stop," I say, my voice no longer sparking, my Aries waning as her Cancer waxes and waxes. "You have to stop."

Her eyes tear up. Harvest moon. "Bringing in strangers. Showing them our world. Giving them a taste. That's how she got pulled out to sea. Those pinche rock stars wanted to see the future. They wanted to use her, have her trace the lines of their palms until they understood. And they want the same things from you. To read the stars. To give them one piece and then another until there's nothing left. You think I don't look at these Instagrams? The things people say? We just got you back, Lunita," she says. "Don't go chasing another grave so soon."

I roll my eyes, I can't help it. "You think I *talk* to these people? Please. They're lucky if they get a heart-eye emoji. I don't talk to anyone! I don't meet up! I don't have a single friend, do you know that?"

The tides are pulling at us both now, our shared Mars in Scorpio. Like fighting your own shadow. "And this is my fault?" she asks. "Because I remember what happened? Because I want you to be safe?"

"Because I'm not Tía Jasmin!" I shout, secure in the knowledge that no one can hear. "And I'm not who I was last year! I learned my lesson. I changed my life. I'm looking inside instead of outside and I'm healing, but you're making me afraid to *live*, Mamí." The tears are there, just out of sight. I can't cry, though, not now when I've finally made her speechless. "I'm proud of myself, and how far I've come, and what I can do," I say. "I like who I am."

She opens her mouth, but I'm not done.

"…I just wish you did, too."

The fight goes out of her, her shoulders slumping, and I almost feel bad. But there's a galaxy of spirit sisters and grieving ancestors and a million intersections of stars between us, unreadable even to me.

For a second, I think she'll raise her face, smooth my hair back, look me in the eyes, and build a bridge with her words. Isn't that what mothers are supposed to do?

Instead, she turns away. "Do what you want," she tells the floor. "Just don't stay up too late." And then the door is closed between us, and I can hear her padding down the hall. Back to Bruce. Away from me.

I swipe at my lower eyelids with my ring fingers. Some of these girls are into that raccoon-rings, mascara-tracks, nervous-breakdown-chic look, but I have a reputation to uphold. My hand is only trembling slightly when I snap a selfie, making sure to get my latest chart in the background:

@delasEstrellas: when mamí says it's bedtime pero like, you're communing with diosas

The first comments start before I even close the app. Normally I don't read them. What's the point? It's not like I'm gonna reply. Talk. Make friends. I can't, or I'll end up back on my back in the desert, right? Or worse—on the side of the road in the wreckage.

But I haven't closed the window yet, and the next comment pops up before I can:

@futureNASAqueen: Your art is dope, but please tell me you don't actually believe this stuff! You look smarter than that.

I'm clicking through before I can rein it in. I'm angry at Mamí and my dead tía, and fifteen-year-old me. I'm so sick of the tiny life I've been living in all of their shadows. And now this?

This hater's avi shows a heart-shaped face, freckles scattered across skin the color of my favorite sun stone. She wears these square glasses that could be awful but are actually cute. Ugh, why does she have to be pretty? This flip-flopping in my stomach is distracting from my rage.

What am I doing? I shake myself when the hat reminds me. It's pink, but there's a super official-looking NASA logo across the front. This girl is not interested in me or anything I have to say, so why am I still reading her bio?

"Future stellar astronomer of your dreams. Flat-Earthers need not apply."

She's local. "Location: City of Angels." But something small and sad is already closing in my chest.

@delasEstrellas: @futureNASAqueen you look smart, too, but life's too short for debates with closed-minded folks. She doesn't deserve the peace sign emoji, but I add it anyway, followed by the nail-painting one that reminds me I'm too good to let people make me small.

The reply is almost instant:

@futureNASAqueen: Am I though? DMs are open if you're brave enough.

My heart kicks into nervous rhythm, the amethyst cluster on my necklace twitching along with it. I shouldn't. What good can it possibly do? A good night's sleep is the frontline of skin care, and I've had these debates before. Science vs. Magic. No one ever wins.

But my mamí's accusations are still ringing in my ears, fresh again after tonight's latest throw down. I'm wild, right? I'm reckless. I'll never be anything but a stupid sophomore who said "yes" too many times.

And compared to tour busses and parties in the hills, a debate between haters feels almost tame—even after all the shutting-myself-in I've done this year.

Plus, this girl is *cute*.

The devotion candle I lit to Tía Jasmin is burning high, flame nearly clearing its glass cylinder, dancing, jumping for attention. She's egging me on, and it feels good. Plus, it's not like I'm *going* anywhere, right? Just a friendly chat.

I roll my eyes. If this chat is *friendly* I'll say yes to the next nervous dude that asks me out at school. *That's* how sure I am that this is gonna end in a mess of blocks and hurt feelings.

So why am I clicking that little message icon? And what's up with these sparks?

@delasEstrellas: I'm doing this against my better judgment, but hey

Almost at once, the message switches from "sent" to "seen," but she doesn't reply. A minute passes, then two, then three. This girl is *not* about to leave me on read. Five minutes. I'm legit about to start chewing on my hundred-dollar manicure when that ellipsis finally starts blinking.

@futureNASAqueen: Ha! Hey, didn't think I'd hear from you. Cool.

@delasEstrellas: what can I say? I don't intimidate easy

@futureNASAqueen: See? We already have something in common.

She ends it with a wink. My heart dips. I'm biting my lip. It's ridiculous. Not that you'd know it from the comments on my photos, but I've never been on a date. Never so much as held hands, let alone kissed someone. Mamí says love and magic get mixed up, that they make it harder to trust your instincts, easier to get lost.

So even when I was partying, it was never about that. It was about glowing up and getting high with my girls and being seen in all the right places.

Even with all that baggage, though, I have to admit, this heat in my cheeks isn't half bad. Plus, I confirm with a glance at my selfie camera, it looks *good* with this contour.

@delasEstrellas: so, isn't this the part where you tell me everything I believe is wrong?

The reply doesn't take so long this time.

@futureNASAqueen: Isn't this the part where you ask me my birthday and tell me all about myself? A cry-laughing emoji. The nerve.

I force myself to wait sixty seconds. I start fidgeting around eight.

@delasEstrellas: if you want a chart done you can pay like everyone else. The brown-girl-shrugging emoji completes it. I won't be so easily ruffled, it says. I do this all the time.

@futureNASAqueen: Ha! Ice cold, I like it. Look, I don't doubt you'd say some shit that resonates, that's how this stuff works! I'm not here to call you stupid, I've just done a lot of research.

@delasEstrellas: and I haven't, right? can you tell because I don't wear geek glasses? *Simmer*, I tell that lunar Aries flash. Don't be defensive. You have nothing to prove.

@futureNASAqueen: Haha, hey, that's not what I said. The science just disproves your theory. The stars don't know anything about us, and that's the way it should be.

The wind chime of starsong is answer enough to that one; the answer I discovered that night when I got too close to the edge of nothingness and something bigger kept me from falling.

I wish I could record it for her, send her the file. That song is filled with knowledge, with care, with the distant but benevolent spirit of a universe that knows every heart beating and flower blooming within its boundaries. I was chosen to hear that song, and to interpret it for people who can't.

But I interpret through art, not words, and I can hardly answer in watercolor now.

I start typing as I cross to my bed, not looking up, almost wiping out on the corner of my shag rug and laughing at myself. The exchange picks up speed, but it doesn't get ugly like I predicted. She's drawing the cold, clear lines of logic. Math. Science. This is where she lives, and there's beauty in the order of it all. In her passion for it. But between those inexorable lines, I'm filling in the color. The blues and greens of nebulae. Solar flares refracting against frozen metals we can't name.

It feels like dancing. It feels like painting.

It feels like magic.

An hour passes like a few heartbeats, then another. I barely notice the time until we've been through Mercury retrograde and string theory and are just getting started on the phrase *pseudoscience.*

The sky is turning periwinkle along the horizon when I finally get her:

@delasEstrellas: the place y'all get tripped up is thinking about it as a competition. like we made up another science to cancel yours out

@futureNASAqueen: Okay, so what's astrology then?

I actually do it. I chew on a nail. Barb is gonna roll her eyes when I come in a week early for my fill. For a minute, I set the phone down, closing my eyes, letting the song fill my head and the fading constellations dance behind my lids.

@delasEstrellas: art. faith. something between the two

She's quiet for a long time, almost six minutes, but this time I know she's there and it makes me smile.

@futureNASAqueen: Tell me more.

The smile widens. I run a hand through my hair without thinking of my curls.

@delasEstrellas: it's like...say someone writes a poem about you, okay? is it a list of your height and weight and address and birth date and social security number?

@futureNASAqueen: Haha, I hope not. Wouldn't be a very interesting poem.

I'm up off my bed again, pacing. The starsong is louder now, swelling in a way that says something's coming. Something bigger than just tonight. But maybe something steady. Something that doesn't have to make me feel afraid.

@delasEstrellas: exactly. but does that mean it's not true? someone paints a picture of you. it's not a photo. your hair is more blue than black, your eyes more gold, but does that mean it can't tell you anything about yourself?

Another long pause. Four minutes this time.

@futureNASAqueen. Wow.

@delasEstrellas: 'wow' I'm so uneducated you're gonna have to spend an extra hour with your telescope tomorrow just to cleanse the memory of this conversation from your neat and tidy brain? A smirk emoji. Is this flirting? I think it's flirting. I don't wait for her reply, instead clicking back to her profile and scrolling down.

I tell myself I'm not looking for what I'm looking for.

There are no pictures of parties. Of red cups or powder or pills, of slitted eyes or lazy whiskey smiles. She's selfie-ing on a college visit to MIT. And here's a picture with her brothers, one of them in a white doctor's coat. There are a few pictures of food, which I'll overlook because her freckles are so cute, and then, fifty-three pictures in, a photo dated two years ago. Another selfie, this time cheek-to-cheek with a redheaded girl. Her eyes are closed. They're both smiling.

There's no caption, because the universe is cruel, but it looks like something different than friends.

@futureNASAqueen: More like "wow" you just blew my mind. That doesn't happen very often, girl. I'm reeling a little over here. That laugh-cry emoji again. Adorable.

@delasEstrellas: I'm putting that in the testimonials on my website, jsyk. Another smirk.

The pause now is comfortable; I don't mind it. The sky outside my window is going slowly pink, a sight I remember from a dozen parties past. It never looked like it does tonight, though. Never once.

@futureNASAqueen: What's your real name?

For the first time all night, my blood's warning is back, siren-loud. This girl is local. And beautiful. And smart and interesting and *cool*. And look, my Mars is in Scorpio like I said—when I find something I want, it can get a little intense.

Intense is the opposite of what I've been chasing since I walked out those hospital doors. And love? Even *like*? Forget about it.

I never really understood how Tía Jasmin could get on that bus. Follow some guy she just met backstage even though it was dangerous as hell.

But tonight, I'm getting a first taste of how it might have felt.

@delasEstrellas: you first

@futureNASAqueen: My name's Mari.

@delasEstrellas: Luna

@futureNASAqueen: Four-letter names. Something else we have in common I guess. The wide, smug-smile emoji makes me wonder what her actual smile looks like. Not just in a selfie where she's trying to look cute, but for real, when it stretches her cheeks out and makes her eyes go slitty.

@delasEstrellas: so, when's your birthday? I send the same smile back. It's the one on my goofy face anyway, might as well be honest.

Eight minutes before her reply. Eight. The ellipsis comes and goes a dozen times as she types and deletes. Types and deletes.

@futureNASAqueen: Look, this is ridiculous and I would normally NEVER but like, you're beautiful and I swear I'm not a serial killer and I'd really like to tell you my birthday in person. Somewhere public and well-lit. With plenty of people aware of where we'll be just in case.

The starsong has never been so loud, swelling and changing, growing more and less complex. She treats me like a girl who hasn't ever taken a risk worse than this one. Like a girl who needs to be reassured that something is safe before she leaps.

She treats me like the girl I've been trying to be.

I close my eyes again, surrendering to this feeling, the influence of a new constellation pulling at me. Every one of my candle flames is blazing, casting warbling gemstone lights and streaky glass-shadows on the wall.

In her photo on the mantel, Tía Jasmin seems to be smiling brighter than usual.

When I open my eyes there's another message:

@futureNASAqueen: The suspense is killing me, girl, I gotta log off. But here's the link to my Facebook. I have parents and I go to school and I have a couple ex-girlfriends and you can learn all about them before 2pm when I'll be at Dinosaur Coffee on Sunset really, really hoping you show up. The peace sign emoji. The nervous sweating emoji.

I'm nervous. I might float right off my bed.

Am I gonna go?

The stars are trying to answer for me, but isn't this what got Tía Jasmin in so much trouble? Is it new-crush bliss? Is it magic? Is it both?

I set my alarm for ten. I can't believe I'm about to fall asleep without taking my makeup off. Moisturizing. Braiding my hair. But I do, the past and present playing tug-of-war in my head, dreaming of buses and dinosaurs and rocket ships blasting off, the stars' symphony guiding me like a promise.

It turns out I don't need that alarm after all. When I wake up a few minutes before it, there's something peaceful in my chest, settled like a purring cat. All the candles on my altar have gone out except my Tía Jasmin's, which is burning steady and clear.

Saturday morning, I think. No school. Nowhere I *have* to be.

But the fear-shadows that have darkened the doorways of Bruce's massive mansion since Mamí brought me home from the hospital are gone, and outside, that honey-drop sunshine beckons instead of warning. It's a gorgeous day, and even though I was up till sunrise I find myself bouncing out of bed with a cheesy catalogue smile on my face.

That is, until I see my hair. The smudged eyeliner. The contour gone horribly wrong against the creases of my pillow. After a seriously less-than-chill shrieking sound, I'm locked in my bathroom, hoping there's enough time.

I have a date today, after all.

By twelve-thirty I'm descending, miracles performed. I've changed my clothes four times, finally settling on black skinnies and my ironic Ouija Board tank, bright red Converse for a color pop. My hair is natural, all mismatched waves and curls.

My nail still has a bite mark in it, and there's no time to get it filled. I wouldn't be surprised if I'm wearing two different shoes.

But I'm not. Please, even nervous I'm still on my game. Even first-date, palm-sweating, butterflies nervous. Even almost-unable-to-put-one-foot-in-front-of-the-other nervous.

Those freckles, I remind myself. *In person*. The resulting blush gets me the rest of the way.

In the kitchen, Mamí and Bruce are cooking something time-consuming. He's chopping onions and looking at her like the sun rises and sets behind her eyes. It's cute. I never noticed before.

When she sees me with my purse on a Saturday, Mamí's eyes widen, then settle.

My smile is an unnatural thing, the shadows of last night's fight in its creases, layering over the darker ones I put there when I let myself get lost.

"Where are we off to?" she asks, and I take a deep breath.

"To meet a...friend."

I feel it in the air between us. The earthy skepticism of her Virgo giving way to the nervous eddies and swirls of an Aquarius letting down their guard.

"Be careful," she says, her eyes saying more than her words.

"I will." An automatic response. But there's something cold and sharp pulling from the other direction, like the breeze off the ocean in December, and I'm not sure *careful* is in the stars.

Whatever's out there, though, it'll be me going to meet it, not my ghosts.

And I have a feeling it's gonna be out of this world.

★ ★ ★ ★ ★

AFTERBIRTH

by Andrea Cremer

"And see how the wisdome of God fitted this judgment to her sinne every way, for looke as she had vented misshapen opinions, so she must bring forth deformed monsters."

—Thomas Weld on Anne Hutchinson
in the preface to *A Short Story of the Rise, Reign and Ruine of the Antinomians Familists and Libertines*, 1644

New England, 1650

DESPITE THE PAIN, SARAH COOKE CAN NO longer scream. Her voice is used up. Sounds spill from her throat, but they are rasping and raw. Whispers of agony. The cries of a ghost.

"Change the cloths, Deliverance. And bring more water," Midwife Ley orders.

I gather the sodden linens I tucked around Sarah's body no more than an hour ago. They were clean when I placed them between her thighs. Now they are heavy with blood and mucus. The odors of impending birth seep from the cloths into the air. It is a perfume I have come to know well: a scent that is life and death mixed together. Alpha and Omega. Creation itself.

Midwife Ley measures herbs into a mortar, then sets to crushing them with a pestle, murmuring under her breath all the while.

Goodwife Prower, who cradles the whimpering Sarah's head and shoulders in her lap, shifts her gaze to Midwife Ley and purses her lips. I do not like the way Goodwife Prower's eyes have narrowed or how her face has pinched with judgment, sour as curdling milk.

But it is not my place to object. Goodwife Prower is the mistress of this house, and Sarah is her servant. A new mother couldn't want for a better place to birth a child. The village came together to build this home for Judge Prower and his wife. A house of stout timbers and windows with glass and a wide stone fireplace, large enough for a spit and a copper kettle. There are even walls to separate two bedrooms from the main living space. I am certain it must be the finest house in the colony.

"Now is the time, Sarah," Goodwife Prower urges. "Speak the name. Give us the name of the father."

"This is a difficult enough birth, Mistress Prower." It is Midwife Ley's turn to frown. "Do not trouble her further."

Goodwife Prower sniffs. "Confession will serve her better than any of your medicines, Midwife Ley. God will be merciful should she speak her sin now."

She turns her attention back to the laboring woman. "The name, child, the name!"

Sarah moans again, sweat beading on her brow. Her upper arms rest on Goodwife Prower's thighs, her hands white and bloodless with how tightly she grips the Goodwife's fingers.

"Master..." Sarah whispers.

I look at Midwife Ley, whose frown has deepened. "What did she say?"

"Set your mind upon God." Goodwife Prower raises her voice as if Sarah did not speak at all. "Be steadfast in faith, for your suffering is His miraculous will. Forget not that 'Unto the woman He said, I will greatly multiply thy sorrow and thy conception; in sorrow thou shalt bring forth children.'"

Whimpering, Sarah turns her head from side to side. She has no strength left, or she would be thrashing. Goodwife Prower means to fortify Sarah's body through faith, but I do not think Sarah hears the words. She is lost to a fever dream, or on the edge of a revelation more profound. I have heard it said that childbirth brings women closer to the Spirit than even the most devout man could hope to be. Because it is a Christlike suffering, because it demands passing so close to death.

I do not want to doubt God's great works, nor question His mysteries, but I would that Sarah Cooke's suffering might be less. In all the years of my apprenticeship to Midwife Ley, I have never witnessed a birthing so torturous as this one. I struggle to see anything miraculous about it. My own silent prayer is that after a full day's and most of the night's labor pains, this birth will soon be over.

Excerpt from the trial of Miriam Ley
August, 1650

Mr. Smyth: And you bear witness that the babe was stillborn? It did not draw breath? Neither did it utter a single cry?

Deliverance Pond: It had not drawn breath before I went to fetch Midwife Ley's nanny goat. Nor did I hear it cry.

Mr. Smyth: Did you find it strange that Midwife Ley failed to ask for your help? That she asked you to leave rather than aid her in ministering to the child?

Deliverance Pond: Midwife Ley told me to fetch the nanny goat, in case the child should need it.

Mr. Smyth: Yet you testify that the child was dead.

Deliverance Pond: Midwife Ley believed the child might yet be saved.

Mr. Smyth: What of Sarah Cooke? Had she passed on?

Deliverance Pond: Sarah Cooke still lived when I went to fetch the goat.

Mr. Smyth: Did Midwife Ley tell you why a new mother would not be able to nurse her child? Why did she believe a nanny goat would be needed?

Deliverance Pond: She did not tell me, sir. Only that it was urgent and I must fetch the goat with haste.

Mr. Smyth: And when you returned, the child was revived?

Deliverance Pond: Yes.

Mr. Smyth: And Sarah Cooke?

Deliverance Pond: She died while I was absent, sir.

I did not witness the moment that Sarah Cooke passed from this world into the next. When her mortal being expired, neither Goodwife Prower nor I were present. But had death visited the birthing room at the climax of her struggle, I doubt any of us would have known. Our eyes were all fixed upon the babe Sarah had issued forth. The babe and what came with it.

After hours of straining, the final moments of her labor passed with impossible swiftness. Her body, so unwilling to open, suddenly thrust forth the tiny body. Head, shoulders, arms, hands, fingers, stomach, sex, legs, feet, toes. A girl. She came into the world in mere seconds. Silent, slippery, and gray.

Midwife Ley bent to clear fluids from the child's nose and mouth. I waited for the baby's first, vital cry and for the midwife's next orders. When neither came, I looked to the babe and saw that she had not shed the purplish, gray cast of birth for the rosy shade of new life. I also watched as Sarah's body continued to empty itself.

At first I thought what was wrapped around the infant's ankle was the length of the umbilical cord and the additional flesh spilling out of Sarah was the afterbirth. But I was mistaken.

Mr. Hammond: What caused you to flee your own home?

Mrs. Prower: I required the counsel of Reverend Alcott.

Mr. Hammond: Did Sarah Cooke still live when you left Midwife Ley?

Mrs. Prower: She had fainted, and did not speak, but she did yet live.

Mr. Hammond: You are certain the child was dead?

Mrs. Prower: Yes. The babe neither drew breath nor cried out after leaving the womb.

Mr. Hammond: And for that reason you summoned Reverend Alcott? To pray for the child's soul?

Mrs. Prower: Yes. And because of the second issue of Goodwife Cooke's womb. Because of that other...

"We must summon Revered Alcott at once." Goodwife Prower lifts Sarah's head and shoulders, easing them off her lap and onto a folded quilt. "There is evil in this house."

Sarah's body has gone limp. I think I see her chest rise and fall with breath, but she does not otherwise stir.

"Do what you must," Midwife Ley tells her. "But both mother and child are in peril and will suffer more in your absence."

"The peril of the soul is greater than that of the body." Goodwife Prower draws herself up imperiously. "I will return anon with Reverend Alcott."

Mr. Smyth: Do you bear witness that this creature had form?

Mrs. Prower: It grasped the babe's ankle with one of its clawed hands.

Mr. Smyth: The dead babe dragged the creature from the womb into this world?

Mrs. Prower: Yes.

Mr. Smyth: What else can you tell us of this creature?

Mrs. Prower: Wings, like a bat's wings, wrapped around its body. It had two tails. On its body I saw both fur and scales. And eyes. Many, many eyes.

"Is it the Devil?" I ask Midwife Ley in a whisper.

I have never been a fearful girl, but my limbs are shaking like branches in a tempest.

Midwife Ley's face is drawn in concentration. "That is not for me to say."

The babe that came forth first is still mottled shades of gray and blue, but otherwise well-formed. Midwife Ley extricates the infant from the flesh of the other that is wrapped around its ankle and foot.

In my mistress's books I have read of twins joined together, two bodies connected by flesh and organs, but nothing I have studied prepared me for this sight. Even the words to describe it are difficult to choose: Is it a mound of flesh, or globs? Does it have enough shape to be called a body? Are the stubs and nubs and outgrowths from the center truly limbs? Had I spotted an eye, perhaps two? Did I see fingers or toes?

I keep averting my eyes, as if looking too closely at it will pollute my soul. As if this unnameable thing, though obviously devoid of life, may still endanger any who linger too closely.

But another part of me—the thinking, reasoning part—craves to examine the unnatural thing, because that small voice inside me murmurs that it came from the mother. That it is of her, of the human body and thus must be, somehow, natural. Only study of it can explain how and why it came forth and what it truly is.

I am about to sneak a long look at it when Midwife Ley's voice commands my attention instead.

"Deliverance, I must ask something of you. It must be done before the Reverend Alcott arrives."

She cradles the infant girl against her chest and begins to clear mucus from the babe's nose and mouth. I wonder why, for it seems too late to save this child who has shown no signs of having the strength or will to draw breath. Perhaps Midwife Ley cannot give up after toiling so many hours. Her face is careworn as she ministers to the babe. Strands of silver and brown have escaped from her braided hair.

When at last Midwife Ley turns to me, I see fear in her gaze. "Go to the house. Hide the book. Hide it well."

Mr. Smyth: Reverend Alcott, what did you witness at the Prower house?

Reverend Alcott: Upon my arrival, I witnessed Midwife Ley tending to a living babe. Sarah Cooke lay dead, the monster beside her.

Mr. Smyth: You found Midwife Ley alone with the babe, Sarah Cooke, and the monster?

Reverend Alcott: Yes. Her apprentice, Deliverance Pond, returned to the Prower house moments later, with the nanny goat.

Midwife Ley keeps the book in a small wooden box beneath her bed. All of Midwife Ley's other books reside on a low shelf that sits between her bed and mine. My mistress has thirteen books to her name: a rare collection that I coveted even before she taught me how to make sense of the shapes scrawled upon their pages. When I first came to live with Midwife Ley, I would take a book from the shelf and sit on my straw-stuffed mattress with the book open in my lap. My fingers walked across the pages, tracing the lines, swoops, and squiggles. It mattered not that the writing held no meaning for me; whenever I opened a book, any book, I became mesmerized.

When I became Midwife Ley's apprentice, she explained that in order to practice her craft I must learn to read and to write and that she would teach me. When she asked if I was amenable to that, I began to cry. She did not ask if I cried from fear and frustration or from joy and gratitude. She looked upon my tear-streaked face, and I understood that she already knew my mind, and possibly my heart.

I take the book from the box, holding it carefully, tenderly. I know its worth.

Hide it well.

There is a hole in the cover of my mattress that I have been meaning to mend. Now, I rip the cloth until it is wide enough to slide the book inside. I wiggle it deep into the straw. When I pull my hand free, I press the mattress, making sure the shape of the book is indiscernible. There is no time to sew the opening closed, but I pray there will be soon.

Mr. Hammond: How did you bring the child to life?

Miriam Ley: The child was not dead. It had not drawn breath because of an obstruction in its throat. I cleared a path so the babe could breathe.

Mr. Smyth: Yet while you ministered to the infant, Sarah Cooke expired. Was there not hope for the mother's life?

Miriam Ley: I am grieved to admit that Sarah Cooke's

injuries were beyond my skill. She could not be saved. Thus, I gave my attention to the child, who could yet be saved.

Mr. Smyth: Do you know what caused Sarah Cooke's death?

Miriam Ley: The birth was difficult and caused great bleeding within her womb. The bleeding could not be stopped.

Mr. Hammond: Was this bleeding caused by the monster? Did its claws rend Sarah Cooke's womb?

Miriam Ley: I saw no monster, but I did witness a long, difficult birth. Such births can cause bleeding that leads to death.

Mr. Hammond: Goodwife Prower and Reverend Alcott have both given testimony to the birth of a monster following that of the infant. Both have described the monster as having claws.

Miriam Ley: The Reverend Alcott and Goodwife Prower chose their words as I choose mine. I saw no claws, nor did I witness the birth of a monster.

Mr. Hammond: If not a monster, then what was brought forth from Sarah Cooke's womb?

Miriam Ley: A second infant, a twin, not fully formed.

Mr. Hammond: Do you reject Reverend Alcott's understanding that God sent His judgment through this

monster? That its presence is a sign of the Devil's work in our village?

Miriam Ley: I am no minister, only a midwife. I can but speak of that which I know.

I hear the babe's howling before I open the door to the Prower house. The first cries of an infant have become my favorite sound. Lusty, hungry screams that resound with life. With hope and possibility.

Midwife Ley has swaddled the child, who is no longer blue and gray, but flushed. The colors of death belong now to its mother. Sarah Cooke's glassy eyes stare at the roof beams. The strange mass of flesh lies in a pool of her blood, unmoved.

Weariness lines Midwife Ley's face, and there is crimson splashed on her cheeks now as well as her arms, but she offers me a little smile.

"We will need the nanny goat."

Mr. Hammond: In your time apprenticing with Midwife Ley, have there been signs that she consorts with the Wicked One?

Deliverance Pond: I have seen no such signs.

Mr. Hammond: Has Midwife Ley been known to use poppets in her healing craft? Have you witnessed Midwife Ley making poppets or asking others to make poppets for her?

Deliverance Pond: No, sir.

Mr. Hammond: From whence does Midwife Ley's knowledge of the body and spirit come?

Deliverance Pond: She apprenticed to her mother, who was also a midwife, as was her grandmother and her great-grandmother.

Mr. Hammond: Midwife Ley is skilled in both reading and writing, is she not?

Deliverance Pond: Yes. It was she who taught me to read and to write.

Mr. Hammond: Are there many books in her house?

Deliverance Pond: She does have books on medicine. Some that were her mother's, others that she has collected.

Mr. Hammond: Among these volumes, have you ever seen an unusual book?

Deliverance Pond: I beg your pardon, sir?

Mr. Hammond: It is well-known that the Deceiver requires his helpers to sign their name in his black book. Have you seen a black book among Midwife Ley's books? A book unlike the others?

Deliverance Pond: No, sir.

Mr. Hammond: Are you certain?

Deliverance Pond: Excepting her Bible, sir. Her Bible is bound in black.

★ ★ ★

I first learned of the book amid the weeks that fever ravaged our village. Burnished leaves hinted at autumn, but a close, weighty heat smothered the land as if it were yet high summer. Fifty of our number collapsed with burning skin and twitching limbs. Thirty-two of those souls were carried away.

The sickness spared me, but in the midst of our work, Midwife Ley fell ill. By God's mercy, the height of the illness had passed, else I am certain I would have collapsed under the strain of treating my mistress as well as those in the town still suffering.

"Study it, consult it, but never let it be seen," Midwife Ley told me, even as her body shook with fever. "It must never be seen."

She pressed the book into my hands. The pages I needed, those that gave instructions on our village malady, she had marked with a thin strip of cloth.

Study it, consult it.

Now I wonder if Midwife Ley meant for my eyes to wander beyond those marked passages. My devotion to her drove me to interpret her admonition more broadly, for there is no person in the village I admire more than my mistress. In her hour of need, I wanted to prove my love, to demonstrate how much I had learned since she took me on as her apprentice. Before Midwife Ley intervened, I had little hope of bettering my station save through marriage. At the age of ten I was orphaned, my parents carried off by one of the many sicknesses that preyed on our village during the harsh winter months. My mother and father were still working off their indentures. The labor still owed their masters was the only inheritance left me.

It would be falsehood were I to deny that fear drove me

also. Fear of losing this woman who had seen something in me, something that signaled I should be more than a servant. That I should be taught to read and to write, to identify sicknesses and tend wounds. That I would be sought after and deferred to at one of life's most miraculous and dangerous episodes: the welcoming of a new soul into this world.

The first time I picked up the book, its weight surprised me. It felt heavy despite its slenderness: a volume of no more than one hundred pages. The first page was filled with names. Each name was followed by two dates, the year of birth and the year of death. Unlike other family histories I had seen, the sort recorded in massive, gilded Bibles like that belonging to Judge Prower, this page held only the names of women. The last name written was:

Miriam Ley b. 1610

The book was well used, well loved. Some pages were loose, on the verge of slipping free of the binding from overuse. Most were filled, but there were some empty pages at the back of the book, waiting for notes, new recipes for unctions, poultices, tonics, and elixirs.

Or.

Dare I think it?

New spells.

Midwife Ley's magicks could only be discovered by careful searching. They were disguised, hidden within otherwise benign formulas.

I only happened upon these arcane writings when I read the book cover to cover. Had I limited my selections to common ailments, those I was already familiar with or had at least heard of, I would have remained ignorant of the book's secrets.

There have been many nights since the birth of Sarah

Cooke's monster that I have wished I had preserved my innocence.

My eyelids had begun to droop, weighted by exhaustion, when I came across Covington's Folly—a strange condition that seemed to be no more than a tingling in one's toenails. How easy it would have been to dismiss the entry as irrelevant, to stop reading. Instead I pushed away sleep and read on. Halfway through the entry, the sentences stopped making sense. Cut off mid-phrase, the next line on the page would be something entirely unrelated. I thought I must have dozed off and lost my place, but upon re-reading it was clear I had not.

> If the smallest toe of the right foot is longer than the smallest toe of the left foot
> *When the moon waxes break an egg into the water of a stream or pond bathed in its light*
> An odor should not be present, but hair may sprout from the heel
> *Speak the name of your mother three times*
> A paste of water, flour, and mustard rubbed on the nail with a freshly cut onion
> *Collect a cup of the water, drink it immediately after you know the man whose seed you desire*
> Soak the afflicted toes in a bowl of water and oak leaves
> *"On the Bearing of Desired Fruit"*

Instructions for getting with child, buried within sentences about another remedy. Wide awake with curiosity, I continued to read. The next several pages contained nothing unusual, but then I came upon The Shadow of Mary, another odd malady I'd never encountered, this one to address the numbness of earlobes. Again, halfway through the recipe were sentences out of place. This time they described a method for finding someone who is lost.

I did not sleep the rest of that night. When dawn crept through the window, I had collected a treasure of hidden gems and stowed them in my mind.

Mr. Smyth: Who is the father of Sarah Cooke's babe?

Mrs. Prower: I do not know.

Mr. Smyth: Did you ask for the name of the father while she labored, as is custom?

Mrs. Prower: Yes. I asked for the name.

Mr. Smyth: But she did not give a name?

Mrs. Prower: She gave no name...but she did speak. She spoke one word.

Mr. Smyth: What word did she speak?

Mrs. Prower: *Master.*

Mr. Smyth: Did you take any meaning from this word?

Mrs. Prower: At first, I did not understand. But when I saw the monster she had birthed and after I had consulted with Reverend Alcott, the signs became clearer. She named the father, her true master. The Deceiver. The Devil.

Mr. Smyth: Why do you believe the Devil to be Sarah Cooke's master?

Mrs. Prower: Because she kept company with no man in the village, but took long walks alone in the wilderness. And the Devil resides in the wilderness, so Reverend Alcott has taught us.

Midwife Ley and I are toiling in the garden when the four men arrive: Reverend Alcott, Judge Prower, and Magistrates Smyth and Hammond. We carry the crib outside and the babe sleeps between us as we pull weeds and the nanny goat grazes nearby. For a child borne of such violence, she is astonishingly peaceful, rarely crying or even fussing. She does not yet have a name, nor is there any certainty as to her future. She is an orphan, like me.

I stay on my knees, gazing up at the men while my fingers dig into the earth, needing its steadiness. Midwife Ley rises, brushes the dirt from her hands, and faces the visitors.

Magistrate Smyth speaks first. "Midwife Ley, you have been accused of consorting with the Devil, of the practice of witchcraft, and of murder."

"I am innocent." My mistress is straight-backed, her face calm.

My fingers have clawed so deep into the ground that my hands are buried to the wrist. Beside me, the baby stirs and makes a small, mewling sound of distress. The nanny goat lifts her head and bleats.

"You will answer these accusations at your trial," says Judge Prower. "Through the course of which, you shall be confined to the stockade."

"If it must be so," Midwife Ley replies. "I will come with you."

I pull my hands from the garden, soil raining down on my skirts as I stand. I must speak for my mistress. I must tell them she has done no wrong. They cannot take her away.

But Midwife Ley silences me with a look. Her face shows not fear, only resolve, and I marvel at her courage, though my heart is rent in two.

Reverend Alcott's attention is drawn to the infant, who has begun to cry.

"Has your apprentice the skills needed to care for this child?" he asks as I take the babe from her crib and try to soothe her.

"She does," Midwife Ley tells him. "Moreover, she has skill enough to tend to any sickness in the village and to aid with any birth."

I can do nothing but hold the child close to me as they lead my mistress away.

Mr. Hammond: You accuse Judge Prower of adultery? A man of upstanding character and great esteem in our village. A man who cannot defend himself because he has traveled to Boston on business.

Miriam Ley: I make no accusation, sir, only offer another interpretation of the word *master*. For Judge Prower was Sarah Cooke's master, and she could have named him thus.

Mr. Hammond: Can you bring forth a witness to corroborate this testimony? Have you evidence that Judge Prower had carnal knowledge of his servant Sarah Cooke?

Miriam Ley: Goodwife Prower and Deliverance Pond

heard her utterance in the birthing room. I give no testimony except to question the meaning of her word.

I am present when they search my mistress's house. I stand aside and think on the things that make this house my home. The single room with hearth and chimney against one wall, a square table and two chairs near the door, two narrow beds at the far side of the room. Always it smells of drying herbs. When I first stepped through the door, I was overwhelmed by the marvelous unction. Now I can separate and identify each plant and its properties by scent alone. While the baby girl squirms and fusses in my arms—something she never does when we are alone—Magistrates Hammond and Smyth empty the cupboard and the chests. They unfold quilts and blankets. They lift the mattresses and hunt beneath the beds and find the empty wooden box. Twelve books are confiscated.

I close my eyes and catalog the herbs that hang along the walls, remembering what is missing and should be gathered soon from garden or forest.

Judge Prower: Midwife Ley, you have been found guilty of consorting with the Devil, of the practice of witchcraft, and of the murder of Sarah Cooke. Should you confess your crimes now, the court may show mercy in passing your sentence.

Miriam Ley: I have committed no crimes.

The stockade is damp, the heated summer air close. No good for any person, but especially not for an infant. I know I cannot linger.

Midwife Ley turns her face away from the small, square

opening in the cell door. I do not like the hacking sound that spills from her lungs.

"I will bring you a tonic for your cough," I tell her. "Do you have a fever, as well?"

"It does not matter," Midwife Ley says after the coughing fit has passed. "Nor should you bring me a tonic. You must stay away from this place, Deliverance. You must shun my company."

The hot air does not keep me from shivering at her words. "I will not abandon you."

"I will be gone soon enough." Midwife Ley does not sound afraid, but I wish she would not sound so certain. "I am condemned and will hang, though perhaps not before this sickness takes me."

"Do not speak thusly," I argue. "You have done nothing wrong."

Midwife Ley coughs again, then smiles sadly. "In my mind and yours I have done no wrong. But my words contradicted those of our minister and the judge's wife. I alone raised the possibility that the judge got a child by his servant. In the eyes of the village, my truths cannot be suffered to live."

"Let me go before the magistrates again. I could do more to affirm your testimony." I lower my voice. "What if...what if I showed them the book?"

Midwife Ley hisses, and then the hiss becomes another fit of coughing that lasts and lasts. When it finally ceases, she shakes her head.

"To show them the book would only mean you swing from a noose beside me," she says.

"But there is no devil in the book," I whisper. "No evil."

"Deliverance, they will see the Devil in those pages because they will choose to." Her gray gaze shifts to the babe in my arms. "She looks well."

"She is healthy and strong." Despite my sorrow, I cannot stop my smile when I look down at her little face. "And very greedy for goat's milk."

"Good," says Midwife Ley. "She is fortunate to have a skilled midwife to care for her."

I look at my mistress. "I am only an apprentice."

"No more," Midwife Ley tells me. "Deliverance, you have honored me with your love and loyalty, but you cannot save me."

"But—"

"Save yourself," she continues. "Save the child. You are free of suspicion now, but I do not know for how long. And that babe, so innocent…the shadow of her birth will haunt her all the days of her life, as will the whispers of cruel, sharp tongues. That is…if she remains here."

I turn my eyes to the child again, my fingers gently touching her cheek. She is asleep, safe from the sorrows and horrors of this stockade.

"She does not have a name," I murmur. The tears gathering on my cheeks threaten to spill onto the peaceful infant.

"You will find one for her." Midwife Ley smiles at me, but her eyes are glistening, too.

Mr. Hammond: An examination of Midwife Ley's body was made by the leading women of this village?

Mrs. Prower: Myself, Goodwife Smyth, Goodwife Hammond, and Goodwife Alcott examined Midwife Ley as ordered by the magistrates.

Mr. Hammond: Upon your examination, what did you discover?

Mrs. Prower: We discovered a witch's teat upon her right thigh and a birthmark upon her left breast in the shape of horns.

Mr. Hammond: Were your discoveries confirmed by a second examination?

Mrs. Prower: A second examination was attended by Reverend Alcott, who confirmed our discoveries and their interpretation as signs of the Deceiver.

The last thing I do before leaving Midwife Ley's house is to open the book to its first page.

To:
Miriam Ley b. 1610
I add:
d. 1650
Then, just below, I write:
Deliverance Pond b. 1634

To the north, along the coast, there are fishing settlements where English, Dutch, and Algonquin peoples live and trade together, shirking the fastidious rules of Boston, Plymouth, and like-minded colonies. Or I could go east, into the woods more dense and dark, where I might live with Papists and their priests, whom Reverend Alcott denounces as just as devilish as any witch. In his mind my soul would be imperiled, but among the Jesuits I would be safe from this village's judgments. I would have to learn French, but I have a quick mind and a willing spirit.

I know not where this journey will end, only that it will be a place in want of a midwife and healer. Somewhere that welcomes a young mother, named Deliverance, and her daughter, called Miriam.

★★★★★

THE HEART IN HER HANDS

by Tess Sharpe

BETTINA CLARKE HAS NEVER HAD MUCH TIME for destiny.

She's sixteen when she feels the burn of the soulmark work its way to the surface of her skin. She's in the tea shop alone when she feels it, but instead of lifting her shirt eagerly to see the words emblazoned on her hip, she shifts behind the counter, trying to ignore the pain. Her fingers clench around the canister she's filling, and she has to uncurl them and breathe deep. Still she does not look.

Not all acolytes of Lady Fate feel the burn of the mark, but the Clarke witches have followed Her longer than most. Every witch in her family for generations has carried Lady Fate's mark. It is the Clarke way.

She thought she'd have more time.

Later that night as she undresses for bed, she finally looks down on the mark embedded in her skin. Her fingers trace the letters on her hip, a dreadful tightness gripping her chest.

Bette, huh? Not Betty?

The first words her soul mate will speak to her.

The mark means they're coming. And soon.

Bette wants nothing to do with them.

She tells no one. Not Brenna. Not her mother. Not even Auggie, who shows up the next morning. Her ever-present bandanna—to keep her curls in check when she bakes—has rainbow skulls on it today. It's one of the sixteen carefully chosen ones Bette got her for her last birthday. A bandanna for each year.

"Jasmine water and honey," Auggie says, thrusting a scone, wrapped in a vintage handkerchief, at Bette.

Bette takes an obedient bite, her lips almost brushing against Auggie's thumb. The scone's crisscrossed with golden icing and the sugar flakes just so as the taste sweeps through her senses, the delicate jasmine floating through the deeper notes of the honey.

Auggie looks at her expectantly, and Bette wipes the crumbs off the corner of her mouth. "Really good," she says.

"Better than the rosewater ones from last week?"

Bette tries not to smile. Auggie is her own biggest critic. "The ones from last week had candied ginger chunks. You know I'm biased when it comes to anything ginger."

"You and your spicy things," Auggie says, making it almost sound like a scolding. "Come on." She hands her the rest of the scone and takes the travel mug of tea out of Bette's hand without asking if it's hers. "We need to get going."

"Wild grapes again?" Bette asks, as they get into Auggie's VW van. They spend hours in the woods this time of year, gathering the forest's bounty long forgotten by anyone who doesn't know the hidden paths.

"Violets," Auggie says. "I'm making flavored sugar and your sister needs some for a new tea blend."

They hike deep into the woods to gather the violets that grow in the shadow of Castella, and Bette lies on the forest floor, her head in Auggie's lap, as Auggie weaves wild sweet peas and braids into her red hair.

As the sun begins to set, they head back out of the forest, and before they part, Bette squeezes Auggie's hand. "I'm not going anywhere, okay?"

Auggie laughs at her and asks, "Where would you go, weirdo?" and tells her to go get ready for Circle.

Bette tries to ignore the burn of the mark against her skin.

This is the thing about Bette: She will never let anyone control her again. Not even Fate Herself.

She wears gold plaited around each of her wrists, a series of delicate chains twisted together in nine-stranded braids. When she was five and her power blossomed, her wrists were snapped into leather cuffs crafted by the Elders. They were butter soft, but the magic in them was itchy and uncomfortable. They were spelled so that only her mother's touch released her from them. Only then would she be allowed to use her power—when her mother or the Elders deemed it.

It was for her own good, they said. Healing Hands are dangerous when they belong to a young witch. Her magic might go wild, racing to heal everything she touched before anyone stopped her. It could drain her, leave her a lifeless husk before anyone had time to intervene. She needed to learn control, they said. By being controlled.

When she was eleven, her father took her on a hike. Just the two of them.

She came back. Her father didn't.

It hadn't been quick. The rock slide had pinned them both, and he'd used whatever magic he had left to move the rocks off of her.

She'd been helpless. Trapped not by the rocks, but by the Elders' spell. She'd watched her father die because she couldn't heal her broken leg and go get help.

When the search party had finally found them, nearly a day later, Bette refused to let the Elders come near his body at first. She had hissed and screamed and spat at them while her mother made sounds Bette had never heard a human make, and it was the first time she'd looked at her and actually hated someone.

Even then, after all of that, after the pain and the nightmares and the grief that still sits heavy in her heart, the Elders refused to release her.

It was not the way things were done. Even after such a tragedy.

Fate takes us when She chooses, Bettina, they said.

That was the first time Bette thought: *Screw Fate.*

It took months to craft the spell. But she was patient. She gathered the ingredients when her mother wasn't paying attention. Her sister was too deep in her own grief to see that Bette's had turned to rage, but she could hardly blame Brenna for that. When Bette was finally ready, she slipped out during the full moon to venture deep into the forest at Castella's base, where a ring of thirteen volcanic stones lay, long forgotten: a perfect circle of power.

She'd plaited the chains under the light of the harvest moon, sitting cross-legged in the center of the stone circle, stripped down to her skin and shivering in the autumn air. With each loop and twist of the chains in her fingers, she hummed a tuneless song, drawing the heat buried deep in the stones to the surface and into the braid. The gold glowed hot and red and then orange as she continued to hum.

Her magic, a dark green twist, was like springtime, and roots thrusting through the soil, and the soft brush of a girl's hand against her own. The feeling twined around her veins and muscles and bones, settling there. She sealed the braids with her blood, grave dirt, and three tears collected from grieving hearts, and when she wrapped the chains around her wrists, they burned the leather—and the Elders' spell—to ash.

She blew the soot gently off her skin, away from the gold braids, and for the first time since her power had blossomed as a child, she felt free.

When she saw Bette's chains and felt the old magic of Castella in them, her mother was furious. "What were you thinking?" she demanded, her violet eyes sparking with power.

"It's my choice," Bette replied.

"You're a healer, Bettina," her mother spat out. "There is no choice. We belong to the Lady, to our Circle. As healers, our lives are theirs; we are integral to the health and bounty of the Circle."

Her mother had done everything right in her life. Growing up, she had obeyed the Elders. Her Hands had been bound until she was twenty-one, and it would have never occurred to her to burn herself free. She had helped grow the Circle by having daughters, she had taken her mother's place among the Elders when Gran finally passed through the veil, and even now, with her husband dead and her child at war with her, she stood tall.

She had done everything right.

Except she had birthed a daughter who had her Hands, but not her temperament.

Bette is not sweetness and goodness, all bright calm and white light, willing to sacrifice her life for the good of the Circle. She is prickly and defiant, and willing to use blood and tears and the dirt of the dead to break free.

Refusing to look at her mother she ran a finger over the chains, and with her words never wavering, she said: "I didn't have a choice before. Now, I do."

"Bettina—" her mother started, but Bette met her eyes, and something in them made her mother stop, her own eyes flickering, suddenly uncertain.

In that moment, Bette realized her mother was scared of her. Scared of her potential. Scared of her power. Scared of the spell she crafted that burnt decades of magic from her skin as if it were nothing. And Bette was angry enough—her grief a gushing wound inside her—to like it.

Now they know better than to cage her.

Bette gets to the tea shop late. The sign's flipped to *Closed*, and she locks the door behind her, turning the key three times to activate the wards. Sometimes tourists come tapping on the windows, wondering why they close so early on full moon nights—or seeking them out for less mundane reasons than tea.

The shop is quiet, and it smells like herbs, like earth, like home. Tins line the shelves, and little glass jars of tea samples are scattered everywhere. Rows of teapots take up a far wall, everything from fine china to cast iron and even a few bamboo pieces her mother has been pushing.

"Bette? Is that you?" Brenna's voice floats out from the back.

"Yeah, sorry I'm late." She sets her bag on the counter and

ventures into the storage room. There's water boiling on the stove. Brenna has drawn it from their spring at the base of Castella and brought it to the shop for this occasion.

There is old magic in the mountain, and if She blesses you with Her attention, there is much to be gained.

Bette knows that better than most.

"Did you and Auggie get the violets?" Brenna asks, pushing a strand of dark hair off her forehead. Brenna looks like their mother, with delicate features and a small nose and big eyes. Bette is all their father: wide mouth, freckles everywhere, hair that's more carrot than red. Sometimes it hurts more than maybe it should, looking at her reflection and seeing what's left of him in her.

"Auggie has them at the bakery. She said she'd put a batch in the dehydrator for you."

"Good. Come help with the trays." Brenna points at the stack of them across from the stove.

"Auggie said Ronnie was asking about you," Bette says over her shoulder. "Something about running into you on a hike? He's nice, you know. He takes care of all the stray cats behind the bakery."

"Don't, Bette," Brenna says, her voice sharpening, and Bette sighs, because Brenna's cheeks are turning red and she *knows* Brenna likes Ronnie. She also knows Brenna won't ever do anything about it.

This is the thing about Fate: She takes your choices away.

Four years ago, Brenna's soulmark appeared. A week later, the two sisters were driving down the road that curved up Castella when they came across an accident. The driver had spun off and hit a tree. And when the man saw them come running, he slurred, "I didn't think anyone would come"—the exact words that twisted around Brenna's arm like a cat's tail.

Brenna's screams as she begged Bette to heal his wounds still haunt her. But he was too far gone by then. All she could do was make it painless.

Brenna had spent years waiting for this man who'd spoken just six words to her, words that were carved into her skin like an inky reminder of what she'd never have.

Brenna doesn't really live anymore. She exists. She tends to her garden and mixes up tinctures for the Elders, as she always has. She works in the tea shop but rarely ventures out of the back room, leaving Bette to deal with the customers. She takes long walks in the woods alone, never letting Bette join her no matter how many times she asks. Brenna always hangs on the edges during dinners and gatherings, disappearing as soon as she can.

She had surrendered herself to Lady Fate, to the idea that her soulmark would bring her not only love, but answers to all that ailed her.

It was supposed to make her whole in a way nothing else could. Instead, it withered her to a heart beating persistently, but dully, without its mate.

Bette knows pushing Brenna about Ronnie won't help, so she turns back to arrange the fine china cups, hand-painted with runes and sigils that shimmer in the sunlight. Her phone buzzes in her pocket, and she puts the cup down to grab it and see the text from Auggie.

Ronnie called in sick. Gotta get the bread made so I'll miss tonight. Come over after?

"Is the tea ready?" Brenna asks.

Bette looks up from Auggie's text. "Almost." She puts her phone down and turns back to the tray.

The Elders always meet at the shop before heading out to the woods. It's considered an honor to be invited to take tea with them before Circle. Today, there's a handful of witches in the back garden, the caws of magpies in the old oaks blending with the snatches of conversation Bette hears floating through the open window. She pours hot water into each cast-iron pot, swirling it around to heat the metal before dumping it in the sink. Brenna hands her a silver container and a spoon, and Bette scoops out the fragrant leaves and herbs, adding a measure to each pot. It's a mix of ginger, honeysuckle, and rose hips—a blend made for luck, for light, for success. It's one of the teas they don't sell to the tourists who come into the shop, giggling about witches.

"Which one is for the Elders?" Brenna asks, and Bette points.

Her sister moves her hands over the pot in a complicated dance, sketching sigils in the air over the herbs. Bette can taste flowers and dirt on her tongue. She feels a frisson in the air as the boiling water hits the herbs, releasing Brenna's spell.

When the tea has steeped, they carry the pots out to the garden. There are people Bette doesn't recognize—guests, she realizes, as she sets the last of the trays on the long table at the end of the garden.

"Bettina," says Elder Lee, a gray-haired woman with arthritis in both hands and a fondness for velvet dresses. Bette goes to her home twice a week to work on the woman's hands and knees, drawing out the pain—the deep, troubling kind that makes her own bones ache for hours after—as much as she can. "How are you?"

"I'm fine," Bette replies, handing her a cup of tea poured from the pot spelled for the Elders. She thinks, for a moment, about giving her tea from one of the other pots. A small defiance, but she decides it's petty. There are guests. And she doesn't need to give her mother more reasons to be angry with her.

Elder Lee's eyes fall to the gold plaits. Bette tilts her wrist slightly so they slide against her skin, catching the light. Elder Lee's lips purse, and Bette smiles innocently at her.

They had tried to bind her hands a second time, after she'd cast her spell and burnt theirs to a crisp. Elder Lee had led that particular charge. But every time the Elders tried to get close to the chains with their chanting and sigils, the metal would spark, the magic of Castella wild and a little angry at being disturbed by anyone but Bette.

Sometimes, during her twice-weekly healings for Elder Lee, when Bette brushes her fingers over the braids and the metal slithers in an almost liquid coil into her palm, she wonders how many of them see her as a tool first and a girl second.

"Thank you, Bettina," Elder Lee says before going back to her group, the half a dozen Elders who watch Bette with wary eyes.

"Sweetheart!" her mother calls, and Bette looks from the Elders to see her approaching across the garden, towing a boy Bette's age by her side. "You were late," she says.

"I'm sorry."

"We have guests." Her mother gestures to the boy. "A friend from college and her son. Grayson, this is my younger daughter, Bettina." Her mother touches her on the shoulder, and then Elder Lee calls her name. "Just a moment, you two." She hurries off.

"It's actually Bette," Bette says to the guy once her mother's out of earshot.

"Bette, huh?" he asks, flashing a smile at her. "Not Betty?"

She doesn't go hot. Or cold. She doesn't shiver or shake.

Her heart doesn't start thumping too fast, and there are no butterflies. The mark glows in recognition against her skin, the energy flowing through her like a river, speeding toward her heart.

But it won't find a home there.

She can feel it, this razor-thin wire starting in her chest, reaching out, wanting to touch him. And she knows he must feel it too, because his eyes widen in confusion.

She considers him carefully now, assessing, thoughtful. It's as if she's outside of her body as she looks at him. Tall, blue eyes, shock of blond hair dipping across his forehead. He's beautiful, and he'd smiled at her bashfully before, in that way boys do when they see a pretty girl. When they know their smile twists girls up into knots.

If she reaches out and touches him, the energy will spark and flow between them, and everyone will be able to sense it. Everyone will know.

If she doesn't touch him, Lady Fate will intervene. He'll start showing up where Bette is, pulled toward her, and he'll figure out she has the mark after the first or second time, and then he'll be invested, Lady Fate's magic and whatever commonalities they have drawing him in, mixing him up, getting him attached.

It'll hurt more, then. And she doesn't want that.

She could run. She could hide. She could try to deny it.

But she isn't a runner and denial isn't her style and she is *tired* of hiding.

She reaches out and touches his arm, and the heat bursts between them. It makes him gasp, and her mother's head whips toward them. A hush washes over the gathered witches. Even the Elders fall silent.

Bette folds her arms across her chest and taps her foot.

"So," she says. "Grayson, was it?"

He nods, clearly dumbfounded. He must not be soul-marked. She's not surprised; it's not one of Lady Fate's common blessings. Maybe it'll make it easier, that he didn't know she was coming?

Her stomach clenches. She feels bad for him. She feels bad for her mother, whom she can see out of the corner of her eye, smiling, *beaming*, like all her wishes have come true.

"I'm sure you're a very nice person," Bette says. "And I'm truly sorry. But this? You and me? It isn't going to work."

Her mother drags her from the garden and into the tea shop, Brenna trailing after them, her eyes round with worry.

"What is wrong with you?" her mother hisses. She's furious. The frown lines on her elegant face are worn to deep grooves as ire takes over. "What are you thinking?"

Bette loves her mother. And she knows her mother loves her.

But her mother hasn't ever bothered to get to know her. She's never asked and she certainly hasn't seen and she's never listened and Bette's never corrected her, but now she has to.

"It's not going to happen," Bette says. "I'm not interested."

Her mother's eyes bug out at her words. Energy crackles in the air, and thunder rumbles in the distance. "This is not like your Hands, Bettina! He is your soul mate. This is not denying the Elders…this is denying *Her.* We do not deny Her blessings. There are *consequences.*"

Bette swallows. She knows the consequences. She's heard the stories. Her throat's dry and her fingers knot together, but all she can think of is how her heart slipped into Auggie's hands one day and never left.

"Bette," Brenna says, and there's a light in her eyes. A bittersweet sympathy that tells Bette she *knows.*

God, for how long? Bette can't help but feel a twinge of guilt for hiding from Brenna. They are sisters, but they seem to have lost grip on that in the space between them that holds their grief and Brenna's regret and Bette's secrets and all of Lady Fate's choices for them both.

"I can't love Grayson," Bette says to her mother.

"You can't?" Her mother repeats it, and then her brows scrunch together. "Bettina…" she begins, and there's not only warning in her voice, there's begging.

"I love someone else," Bette says, even though she knows she's breaking her mother's heart and sparking fear in it. By denying the person chosen for her, she's spitting in Lady Fate's face, and no disciple denies the Lady without punishment.

But she's been making her own choices for a long time now. And that's not about to stop because of a boy.

"Who?" her mother demands.

"Auggie, Mom," Bette says, like it should be obvious, because it *should*.

Bette doesn't remember a time where she didn't love Auggie. She doesn't remember a time where Auggie wasn't there. They were born three weeks apart, and that was the longest time they'd ever gone without seeing each other.

Isn't it nice our girls are such good friends? their mothers say, with the self-satisfied smiles of women who see only the surface.

Augusta Bell has never been Bette's friend.

Augusta Bell is the love of Bette's life.

And Bette isn't giving her up for anything.

Not even Fate Herself.

This is the thing about falling: It's tricky. Sometimes you're tumbling down into love before you realize your feet have left the ground. But it's a choice, too.

Bette could have ignored how Auggie made her feel. She could have pulled her hand away the first time Auggie's brushed against hers. She could have resisted kissing her at thirteen, quick and nervous and about to lose her nerve if she didn't do it *right then*.

She didn't lose her nerve, though, then or now. Every time she could have backed away, she moved forward instead. And now she's here, driving away from her mother and her soul mate, toward a girl she chose for herself.

The bakery's at the edge of town, right where it fades back into wilderness. There's an oak tree in the front yard that's older than any building for miles, with wrought-iron tables set around it for the morning customers. The picket fence that surrounds the garden changes color each year—right now it's dark blue. Last year it was yellow. Bette helped Auggie paint it each time.

The lights in the back are on, but Bette can't bring herself to knock on the door. So she stands outside the fence and waits.

It takes exactly ninety-three seconds. She counts in her head. And then the bakery door swings open, and Auggie steps out. Looking at her is a relief. Looking at her is terrifying. Bette has no idea what to say. Where to begin.

But Auggie, as always, does.

"I heard you had a big day." There's a smudge of flour on the high curve of her cheekbone and a dark curl escaping from the gingham bandanna that holds her hair back, and Bette wants to reach out, to touch her, to remind herself that she is real...that *they* are real.

"I should have told you."

"That would've been nice," Auggie says, her mouth—that

wicked, sharp, beautiful mouth—twisting. "Look, it's not like I didn't know this was going to happen eventually."

Bette appreciates the out, but she's acted like an ass, and she's woman enough to admit it. "I still should've told you. It showed up a few days ago."

"I figured, considering I didn't see it anywhere last time we..." Auggie trails off, and Bette knows they're both thinking about the last time: kissing in the water, all cascading droplets and naked skin, the curve of her against her fingertips.

Auggie sighs, looking up at the sky like she's lost. Bette wants her to yell, to be angry, to be *anything.*

"What's he like?" Auggie asks, finally.

Bette blinks. She actually has to snap her mouth shut, because out of all the questions she thought Auggie would be asking, that wasn't the one she would've picked.

"I have no idea," she answers. "Blond, I guess?"

Auggie's eyebrows knit together. "You didn't talk to him?"

"He said the words, and I realized who he was. So I told him I was sure he was very nice, but this wasn't going to work. And then my mother lost it and dragged me away to yell at me...and now I'm here."

"What?" Now Auggie's the one gaping at *her,* and it hits Bette all at once.

Auggie thinks Bette's come here to break it off. She expects her to prance over and be all, *Sorry, we're done, I found my soul mate! It's been fun!* And then lose herself in Fate-approved bliss, like she's supposed to.

Bette would be horrified if she weren't so damn relieved that Auggie's upset about something that isn't going to happen.

She walks through the gate, down the winding stone path

that leads to the bakery stairs. "Why would I be interested in him?" she asks. "I have *you*."

Then Bette sees a terrible kind of hope spring up in Auggie's blue eyes, and it's like a broken bone that didn't heal right, the ache that fills her.

"But he was chosen for you. He's your other half," Auggie forces out.

Bette's never felt like any of her was missing, let alone *half*. She certainly wasn't made complete when Grayson's eyes met hers.

He can't fill the empty spaces in her because there are none. There is no emptiness in a devoted heart.

"Screw that," Bette says, and it startles a laugh out of Auggie. It's a clear, resonant sound, ringing across the empty sidewalk like her last name.

"You hear me?" Bette tilts her head up to the starry sky, raising her voice. "I'm talking to you, Lady Fate! Screw you and your soulmark. Screw your rock slides and your Elders. I chose before, and I'm choosing now." She looks at Auggie, standing at the top of the porch, just steps away from her. "I love *you*," she says, and it's far from the first time she's said it, but she knows it's different now.

Because now Auggie knows for sure that she's not second best. She's first and only and the best damn thing that's ever happened to Bette.

"I will *always* love you," Bette goes on, and it's more than a promise in that moment as she looks at Auggie, all the love, all the fight, all the power sparking between them like a cut wire.

It's a spell, the purest kind of magic. Born from love and truth and unshakable belief.

Thunder rumbles around them, clouds forming in the sky that was clear seconds ago. All the hairs on Bette's arms rise, and her stomach tilts like she's slipped on a ledge with no foothold.

Neither of them is causing this.

"She knows," Auggie says quietly, staring up at the sky.

Lightning crackles across the darkening clouds, and the chains wrapped around Bette's wrists begin to heat. She starts to say Auggie's name, but it dissolves into a gritted yell because the chains are melting into her skin, burning her flesh away, trickles of gold and blood dripping down her hand. She falls to her knees, and she's screaming as Auggie rushes to her.

But it's too late. The magic of the mountain, the ancient energy from the stones that Castella once spit out in volcanic fury, that Bette harnessed in the gold centuries later, flies free. Castella's magic, once safely contained in the chains, courses through Bette's body, tearing it up in places she didn't even know she had. She can feel her organs shudder against the rush of it, and her ears ring, a shriek of laughter echoing in them as her teeth clatter and her eyes roll back in her head.

This is the thing about Lady Fate: She takes with a vengeance when crossed.

When Bette wakes, she's alone, in her bed at home. Her wrists ache, despite the strips of muslin soaked in an herbal balm wrapped around them, and her head feels swollen as she struggles to sit up.

There's a voice outside her door. She closes her eyes, focusing.

Elder Lee.

She gets up. It takes two tries, but she manages to get to the door. When she jerks it open, the air shimmers. Her eyes dart down to see a solid line of herbs and crystals across the doorway.

Wards. To keep her in here and away from Auggie.

A slow slug of fear moves through her, the dread strong enough to distract her from the pain burning her entire body. Her eyes narrow as they meet Elder Lee's calm, righteous gaze.

"Bettina," she says, her silver braid slipping over one velvet-clad shoulder as she steps forward, her hands steepled in front of her like a warning.

"Where's my mother?"

"The Elders believe it's better that I handle this."

So her mother had run away rather than face the terrible disappointment Bette had become.

She can't even bring herself to be surprised. She'd feel sad, but she has more important things to worry about.

"Let me out," she tells Elder Lee. Sweat's popping across her forehead; she can feel it dripping down the bridge of her nose. She forces herself to stay upright. She has to stand tall. She has to show the Elders they still can't win when it comes to her.

"I can't let you out," Elder Lee replies quietly. "I don't yet know what punishment the Lady has wrought on you, what magic was unleashed when She..." She trails off, looking down at Bette's wrists in distaste. "You were a child, crafting a spell you had no business casting. You never learned to be humble. You never learned to sacrifice. Your Hands should've been tied to your mother for *years* yet. This will be the end of you, Bettina."

Bette slams her palms against the wards, her hands bouncing off the invisible wall of energy. Elder Lee's eyes widen, and she shifts from foot to foot.

Lady Fate is powerful, but Castella is something more. Castella's magic had always been contained in the chains, working in harmony *with* her, rather than *within* her.

Lady Fate tore that protection away, thinking it would weaken her.

But Bette can feel the mountain in her veins now…a terrifying rush of power that sings through her like water crashing from the falls at its peak. In the thrill of it, she can barely remember what *weak* ever felt like.

"Where's Auggie?" she asks.

Elder Lee's lips press together tight. "She isn't here. You won't be seeing each other for a long time."

"You're really wrong about that." A voice rings out behind them.

Elder Lee whirls, and it's Auggie, stepping to the top of the stairs, like a warrior queen with a skillet instead of a spear. She walks forward, swinging the pan back and forth, her agile fingers so clever, so skilled, twisting and turning against the gleaming black metal.

"Are you okay?" she asks Bette, and Bette licks her dry lips and nods.

"You are not needed here, Augusta," Elder Lee says, her thin mouth flattening as Auggie comes to a stop just three feet away from her. The upstairs hallway is narrow, and Elder Lee plants herself in the middle so Auggie will have to shove past her. "Go home. Your mother will be worried."

"My mother knows I'm here," Auggie says. "And Brenna is the one who told me what you were up to."

Bette's stomach clenches. "Really?"

Auggie beams. "Really," she says. "I have their blessing," she adds, looking at Elder Lee pointedly as she twirls the pan in her hand. Elder Lee can't keep her eyes off it.

Some witches use wands to focus their power. Crystals. Jewelry. Herbs.

Auggie has a one-hundred-year-old cast-iron skillet that's been seasoned to perfection.

Only a fool underestimates a kitchen witch—and Elder Lee is no fool.

"Augusta, it's time to go," she says firmly.

"It's time for *you* to go," Auggie answers.

A shiver floats through the hallway, and Elder Lee's hands twitch.

But Auggie's too fast. She snaps her fingers. Blue fire sprouts at her call, a greedy line leaping across the floor to Elder Lee's feet. She scrambles back and Auggie snaps again, more fire blossoming like a flower along the worn oak floorboards, boxing Elder Lee in, keeping her from reaching Bette. She's trapped…for now.

Elder Lee's eyes widen with rage, and she begins to mutter, her fingers sketching sigils in the air, but Auggie's fire holds.

She darts over to Bette, staring at the line of herbs dividing them. She holds her hand inches away from it. It sparks when Auggie pushes at it with her power, the air rippling and singeing, and the smell of burnt flesh—like before, when her chains melted—makes Bette's stomach turn. Auggie straightens up. "Stand back," she says, and Bette scrambles to obey, her heart in her throat.

"This is not the way, Augusta!" Elder Lee shouts.

"Your way sucks, Katherine." Auggie shoots her a disgusted look, deliberately ignoring her title—a precise verbal blow before the real strike.

Auggie swings her arm—and the skillet—back, and the air tastes different as Bette breathes it in—like rising bread and caramelized onions and bacon as it hits a hot pan. The skillet strikes the wards and they flicker, but they don't fall.

Elder Lee's feeding power into them…that's what the muttering's about. Auggie's eyes narrow and she snaps her fingers again, the flames leaping higher, the temperature in the room rising.

Auggie swings her arm in three full circles, like a pitcher winding up to throw, and the skillet leaves her hand in a graceful arc, spinning in the air before its wide, flat bottom crashes against Elder Lee's wards.

They shatter, sparks of light dancing across the floor, and Elder Lee sags to the ground unconscious as Auggie's fire dies out.

"Come on," Auggie says, picking up the skillet with one hand and reaching out to Bette with the other.

Bette doesn't take it. Who knows what will happen if she does? Who knows what magic is loose in her...what punishment Lady Fate has wrought?

"I'm scared," she whispers.

"Sweets, we can be scared together," Auggie says. "But we can't be scared here. Not anymore."

She's right. They need to go. Elder Lee will come to before long. Then she'll call the rest of them. She'll call Bette's mother. And the Elders will come for them.

Bette still doesn't take her hand, but she follows Auggie down the stairs and through the halls of her childhood home, knowing she likely won't be back.

Auggie's Westfalia is sitting in the driveway, and she tucks the skillet away in the little kitchen in the back of the camper before getting into the driver's seat.

"Where to?" she asks Bette.

"The mountain," Bette says.

Castella helped her once. She prays the mountain will answer her call again.

She has never returned to the circle of stones, not once since that night she burnt herself free. She's never given out the location; never drawn so much as a crude map or scribbled down hasty directions.

The Elders had demanded she do so. By then, she had learned she could say *no.* They had searched without Bette's help, but Castella only reveals Her secrets to the worthy.

Bette can feel the power rising as she steps inside the ring, Auggie at her side. Standing with her in the center of the circle feels both secret and sacred. Bette's fingers itch to reach out and stroke the end of the gingham scarf knotted over Auggie's hair, but she resists the urge.

"Wow," Auggie says, her voice hushed. The air around the volcanic stones ripples at the sound of her voice, like the fire in them recognizes the burning in Auggie. "You told me, but..." She holds her palms out, her eyes closed. "These stones have stories," she whispers, sending chills down Bette's back.

Bette looks down, terrified that her own story is about to end. She'd ignored her fear on the drive and the hike through the forest. But now she's here, in this special place, in Castella's shadow, and she must face what Fate has done.

With a shaking hand, Bette presses her fingers against the burnt skin on her wrists, searching within herself.

Before, her magic had been bright, rushing through her like dawn racing across a field at daybreak. It had been tough and always trying to climb free, like wild grapevines twining up trees in the deep, cool parts of the forest.

But now, her power is not bright. There's a slick bubble of heat rising in her where light and forest should be. It is gummy and too hot, sticking to her bones like scorched jam, and her skin burns as blisters spread up her arm, swelling by the second.

She's making it worse.

She snatches her hand away with a soft cry, and Auggie moves toward her.

"No!" Bette stumbles back. "Don't touch me. We can't. We—" She looks down at her hands, and deep down, she *knows*. She has heard stories. Stories of what Lady Fate does to the disciples who reject Her gifts. Yet she's still defiant as she reaches out and grasps a single stalk of the lupine that grows in clusters at the foot of the stones.

She doesn't even need to reach for her power. It's there in her grasp, like it's an old friend instead of a terrible punishment. The moment her skin makes contact with the flower, it wilts, the vivid purple fading to gray, and then there's nothing but ash so fine it floats off in a breath.

"I don't understand," Auggie whispers.

"If you take from Fate, She takes from you." Bette recites one of the edicts of their childhood, meant to keep naughty little witches in line, just like the leather cuffs and the Elders' pursed lips and her mother's disapproving stare.

She looks down at her fingers, bitten nails and spidery knuckle hair. There's a smudge of flower ash on her pinky.

Before, her hands gave life.

Now, they take it.

This is the thing about Augusta Bell: She never gives up.

Bette's numb as they sit in the circle of stones. Trying to settle into this fuzzy new reality of *don't touch anything or anyone ever* and *what am I going to do; who am I going to be?*

She has never been the kind of healer her mother was, never the kind of healer the Elders wanted to mold, but she had been a healer all the same. To have it taken from her, to have it replaced with *this*…

Everyone knew of witches who were either born or cursed

with the touch of death, but they were always spoken of in hushed, nervous tones. *They are the very opposite of us*, her mother once said, shaking her head as if the mere thought troubled her.

Is Bette the opposite of herself now? Or is she who she's always been: someone who chose the right path, not the easy one?

Maybe those choices made her grow to a woman in a breath. They surely made her heart battle-worn and ready. But they made her *her.*

They also made her Auggie's.

"We just need to think about this from another angle," Auggie says, sitting down on one of the stones just feet away from her.

Bette stares at her and then looks back at her hands. It's like she's naked without the weight of the chains. The metal fused to her skin feels strange. The gold doesn't hurt, though the blistering around the metal does, and what's left of her braids is cooler than the rest of her skin. She supposes she'll get used to it.

She'll have to.

"What angle?" she asks dully. "My hands kill things. What other angle can there be?"

"Well, that's what I'm trying to think about!" Auggie says, her eyebrows snapping together as the air flares with irritated heat. She has that look on her face. That *I'm going to solve this with food or fury* face, and any other time, it'd make Bette's stomach flip and her cheeks flush, because she loves that look.

Her cheeks do flush a little, but it's not from the heat Auggie's giving off. She wants to touch her so badly it hurts, and for the first time since...*everything*, Bette's eyes well with tears.

"Oh, sweets," Auggie says. "We can figure this out."

"How?" Bette asks, because she wants to believe it, but she can't *see* it. "What good is there in killing?"

"I don't know," Auggie replies after a moment.

"There isn't any," Bette says softly. "That's why Lady Fate did this. It's a curse. My punishment."

"No!" Auggie cries out, rising, forever restless. She's always moving, kneading bread dough and Bette's sore muscles, her fingers stronger than anyone's. Will she ever get to entwine those fingers with Bette's again?

"This is *not* going to be a punishment!" Auggie declares, like just saying it will make it so.

She tilts her face up to the sky, and Bette is so familiar with the curve of her neck, she could write an essay on the baby-fine curls at the nape that always escape her bandannas. But she has never seen her like this. Auggie raises her hands to the north, toward Castella's peak.

The air in the circle of stones ripples, the smell of rising bread and fury ripening around Bette as the stone she's sitting on heats to the point that she scrambles off it.

"Auggie," she says, stepping back to the center of the circle. She hears it then—the laughter from before, when she cursed Lady Fate—and Auggie's fingers clench, because Lady Fate's mocking echoes in her ears, too. But instead of backing off, Auggie's mulish expression grows even more determined.

Bette's eyes widen as the stones around them begin to glow red and the laughter in the air catches, just for a moment, as if in surprise.

Lady Fate did not come expecting a fight. Not with something bigger and older than Her.

Castella may have chosen to help Bette once, but Auggie is fire and warmth; she is hearth and home; provider and protector. And like recognizes like.

Auggie is Castella's true child. She has walked Her forest paths and bathed in Her waters. She has never, ever forsaken Her or used Her ill.

When Auggie lowers her gaze from the sky, in her eyes are the reflections of the fires of old: the eruptions that carved this valley and these mountains and their home millennia ago. The laughter fades, leaving a hovering sort of silence in the air, as if Lady Fate is waiting, holding back to see if they'll swing first.

"Come here," Auggie says, and, as she did before when she broke Bette free, she holds out her hand.

"I can't," Bette says.

Auggie's mouth twists. "Trust me."

Trust me. Love me. Choose me.

She puts her heart and her self and her hands in Auggie's.

Auggie bends her head, and Bette's stomach swoops as she feels Auggie's lips against the gold chains fused to her skin, a sweet kiss dropped on each wrist. A sudden fizziness spreads from the touch, and something twirls awake inside her, something bright and holy. That dark bubble of heat in her chest does not roar to life, but instead, stirs, like a cat mildly interested in being petted. Bette looks down at her wrists, shocked to see that the blisters are fading, and the gold—rough and puckered before—has shifted, the edges now sloping and sharp, like a mountain range.

Bette's power has been contained. She can feel it. She knows it, because Auggie's not turning to ash in front of her.

Once again, Castella has freed her.

It is a curse only if you let it be one.

The voice is like the roaring echo of the water from Castella's falls, like the dull breaking of a branch in the darkest, wettest part of Her forests. It sets Bette's teeth on edge and soothes her like a hug.

You broke free of their petty ideas before, my child. Are you strong enough to do it again?

Bette takes Auggie's hand, pressing their entwined fingers to her hip, where the soulmark is etched. "I love you," she says solemnly. "More than anything."

Auggie gasps as the mark beneath their hands begins to burn, but she does not withdraw. Not until Bette pulls their hands away.

Grayson's words are no longer there.

In their place, the words *I like Hippo!* are forming on her skin, in a clumsy, crayon-thick scrawl.

They may not be the first actual words Auggie ever spoke to her, but they are the first she remembers, sitting on a blanket in the backyard as toddlers, a well-loved stuffed hippopotamus toy between them.

A shrieking sound lances through the forest, sending needles and pinecones raining down from the trees as Lady Fate flees.

This time, Castella is the one laughing.

It makes Bette's bones rattle.

Her hands clear fields of prickly grass now. They fell trees rotting from the inside, and send off beloved pets peacefully and painlessly. She rids ponds and lakes of harmful algae and orchards of blight. And she's single-handedly responsible for taking care of the pine beetle epidemic in Colorado—not that she likes to brag or anything.

The day she finally figures out how to kill disease is a good day. Flesh-eating bacteria, necrosis of the liver, kidney failure, even some forms of cancer. It is not like healing...it's different.

It is *more*. Her entire life is so much more.

Her touch is light and sure. Her touch is deadly, but she has found many uses for it. She has found a way to hate it some and love it more and make good with all of it.

Her touch is not a curse, as the Elders would think. But it is not a gift, either.

It is simply who she is, in a way that nothing else has ever been.

Some witches fear her and others shun her, but even more make the journey to the little house half hidden in the trees at the very top of Castella. Auggie serves them rosewater scones and Bette pours tea at their big wooden table and says, *Tell me your troubles.*

Lady Fate never darkens their door again.

She has learned Her lesson when it comes to Castella's witches.

★★★★★

DEATH IN THE SAWTOOTHS

by Lindsay Smith

A PERSON CAN TELL YOU ANYTHING, BUT bones—those tell the truth.

I've seen warlocks swear on their mama's graves that they found the secret to immortality, and they'll sure behave that way, too. But when they get their heads blown off mixing glamour magic with curses, or goad the wrong foul-tempered War wizard into a knife fight, I'm the one left with their bones. People want to think they can outrun death, but she's the surest patron there is. Success rate of 100 percent.

I get it. Everyone fears my Lady, Xosia, the Lady of Slumber. When you're all dolled up with glamours from Firenzi or getting your wounds mended by a Hypnos witch, you don't want to be reminded about the Lady waiting for you.

I didn't ask for her to be my patron. It just worked out that way. Every time I was around a dead thing—when our dog got after a bird, or we drove by the slaughterhouse down

Highway 11, or even when my ma dragged me to some other witch's wake—I heard the whispers in their bones. Somebody's gotta do something with those whispers; somebody's got to settle their affairs. And the Lady, she picked me.

Most the time, I don't mind. I've made my peace with the Lady, for sure, and I feel like I work her magic well. It's the rest of the folks out here in the Sawtooths I've gotta worry about. The ones that don't like how I'm a living reminder of their imminent demise. Slashed tires, spray paint on my granny's antique front door, death threats slipped under the door of the morgue (irony, I know), and I ain't never once gotten the locals' discount on pancakes at Jenny's. But I lived through way worse when I was at the Conservatory of Advanced Magics. Most the time, I get by just fine.

The night's already thick when I reach the county morgue—my own personal workshop, tucked into the scrub pines at the end of State Route 5. Used to be situated in the basement of the State High Warlock's offices, but folks complained. Buzzbugs saw away around me as I unlock the place—another nasty note's taped to the door, but I crumple it up and pitch it the minute I see the angry, jagged handwriting. Once I'm inside, magicked lights humming overhead, I check the logs. Just one body to work over tonight.

The body before me is kind of like a piece of artwork I don't understand—I respect it for what it is, but it doesn't hold any special meaning to me. My system, though, that's what I respect. Wash. Pray. Rest my shaking hands on the cool flesh, fingers laced through clammy fingers, until I go calm and still. The other witches at the Conservatory never really understood the need for all the ritual when it's just a dead body and not some customer paying for the show, but

I guess they don't have to understand. Someday, we'll all go through it. If we're lucky, I suppose.

Next comes the cutting—long slits along each limb, down the belly, down both cheeks, and across the brow. The cuts are narrow, but deep. I sink my ornamented blade in until it scrapes bone.

"Xosia, Lady of Slumber." I close my eyes, let my heart rate slow, and will the soul to rise. The air in the morgue is cold, but feels as dense as a held breath around me. The silence presses in. "Grant me this soul's secrets, and I'll commend the soul to you."

When I open my eyes, the cloud of energy is already forming above the body, thickening up like a roux. I reach out for it, fingers stretched wide. Carefully, like picking up a frightened rabbit, I curl my fingers around it—

My son, the soul sings. *My son. I never got to tell him what he meant to me. I forgive him—tell him I forgive him—show him everything I left behind—*

And my sister, I didn't mean that stuff I said. She's as good a witch as any. Please, tell her for me—

Secret after secret, task after task, what's left of this person's soul cries and sobs with all the things they left undone. It's not for me to judge them for it. I'm just the messenger, the medium, putting it all down on paper. And when I've written the last note—the soul is Xosia's now.

I take a moment to catch my breath and shake out all their secrets from my head. Then I begin to stitch up the cuts, mumbling the Lady's prayers to myself while I work. The dead are safe now. No one else can steal their soul, or use their body against their will. Folks can hate me, shun me, fear me all they want, but I'll lay their bones to rest. In the end, they come to me with their dead, because as much as they fear death, they fear the alternative so much more. Better to let their loved ones rest in peace, all their business tended to, than wonder what might have been left undone.

Tires churn up gravel outside my door, and I catch myself cringing. Dealing with the living is my least favorite part of this work. "Mattie?" someone calls, banging against the rusty metal front door. "Mattie, are you in there?"

I spread a drop cloth over the body, but don't have time to shuttle it back into the freezer. "Yeah, I'm here." I flip the switch on the front door's lock, but realize too late I'm still gripping my ceremonial knife. Considering the threat I received earlier, maybe that's not such a bad instinct.

"Oh. Hi." Savannah, the Priestess of Glamours, stands in my doorway, wearing strappy-heeled sandals and a sequined skintight evening gown that drapes to the floor. "Hope I'm not interrupting anything," she drawls.

I take a step back, folding my arms across my ratty T-shirt advertising Fred's Funeral Home. "I was just finishing up."

She's glamoured head to toe, from the glimmer on her lips to the gold-leaf highlights in her chignon. A bronzed leg peeks out of the dress's slit. She looks like she's come here straight from some High Warlock's ball at the state capitol, and with a pang, I realize she probably did. Pretty much all the Priests I went to the Conservatory with are in the capital now, venturing deeper into the Sawtooths only on official business, when their magic is needed to keep things running smooth. I wonder what wrinkle has dragged her out here tonight.

"Well. Looks just like your old workshop at the Conservatory." Her gaze roams the scattered herbs and metal shavings spilled across one of my countertops, and the dirty instruments piled up in the basin, waiting to be washed. "Guess things haven't changed much for you, huh?"

My shoulders tighten. “Don’t fix what ain’t broke.” I reach out to right a jar of shells that’s fallen over, but then decide to leave it.

“You don’t get lonely out here?” she asks. “You never come to any of the covens, the alumni rituals, none of it. It’s not healthy, you know. And the High Warlock would love to meet with you more. Make sure everything’s going well.”

As if the other witches, warlocks, and wizards want anything to do with me and my patron. “I’m happy as I am. Where I am.” I position myself so the body on the slab is between us. “Is there something you need, Priestess?”

She clucks her tongue. “Well, excuse me for making pleasantries.” She steps toward me, but then cuts her eyes toward the figure on the slab, and seems to think better of it. “I’m afraid the High Coven has need of your…services.”

I lean back against the slab, eyebrows high. I’m surprised the High Coven has any use for me and the Lady, and I’m none too thrilled they sent Savannah of all people to fetch me. We’re older now, but every time I see her, all those old feelings come rushing back, as sharp and bitter as they ever were. My skin feels too tight, like I’m squeezing back into the girl I was, angry, unbound. “Must be pretty urgent to send you out here in the middle of the night. What, did one of the High Priests die or something?”

Savannah presses her lips together. She bobs toward the body, then away from it, like she wants to prove she’s not bothered. “Oh, I’m sure you’d love that. No, this isn’t so easy.”

Her usual wry grin has vanished. In all our time at the Conservatory, I don’t think I ever saw her without the armor of that smirk, but with it gone, she looks impossibly young. Savannah was always the girl blazing a trail on sheer force of will and cold-bloodedness, and it served her well. At age sixteen, she became the youngest Priestess of Glamours in the state.

Of course, if the state still handed out the title Priestess of Slumber to Xosia's servants, I'd be there with her. But I should've known that was never gonna happen. The High Warlock himself told me so, sitting at his heavy oak desk with the portrait of the High Warlock who stopped the Pall glaring down at me from behind him. *Just think it might send the wrong message, is all,* he said. *Folks still get a little jumpy about us treating Xosia like she's got a seat at the table. And really, who can blame 'em, after what her followers did?*

"All right." I shove off of the slab. "What do you need my help with?"

"Well...it's a bit difficult to explain," Savannah says. "In fact, we were hoping that maybe *you* could explain it to *us*."

"Either someone's dead and y'all need me to deliver them to Xosia—" Savannah winces when I say the Lady's name out loud "—or they aren't. Don't see what's so difficult about that."

Savannah shakes her head, knocking loose a few locks from her chignon. "I think you're just gonna have to see for yourself."

Savannah takes one look at me when I try to hop on my bike and sighs. "Put that damn thing in my truck bed, Mattie." I make a fuss, but ultimately comply. As we crunch across the gravel, her heel spikes into the threatening note I'd crumpled up earlier, and she smooths it out against her truck window and starts to read.

"We got no need for none of That Lady's folk down here or anywhere else. Go spread your hateful magic somewhere else, you—" Savannah clucks her tongue. "Get this a lot, do you?"

I stare at her in disbelief. "Do you not remember a damn thing about our time at the Conservatory? You—your friends—"

She shrugs as she climbs into the driver's seat, looking right at home as the massive engine growls to life. "Oh, we were just bein' kids, you know? We didn't mean nothing by it."

"You trapped me in the girls' bathroom by erasing the door," I say as I buckle my seat belt. Anger pulses, hot and jagged, under my breastbone. "For three days."

She titters to herself. "Was it really that long? My goodness." She angles the rearview mirror to check her teeth, then points it back. "Well, we all turned out all right, didn't we?"

I stare at the window and don't reply. There's nothing I can say to erase the past, and it's far too late to demand apologies. Maybe someday it'll be her body on my slab, and in her last wishes she'll tell me her regrets. There was a time I wanted that sooner than later. Being this close to her again, I remember it a little too well.

The Sawtooths sprawl like an invasive vine across the southern half of the union. Swampland lows alternate with ridgeline highs, up and down, all of it magicked up to yield crops and fish and scenic vistas galore. We don't want for much down in the Sawtooths, but like everywhere, we took a pretty bad hit during the Pall, and half a century of magic hasn't been enough to heal up that wound. Roadside temples mix with bait shops, glamour stores mix with bars, and produce stands mix with Hypnos healers' stalls.

Twenty miles on, Savannah turns off the state road and heads for the town square that surrounds the Capitol. I don't mean to, but I hold my breath; my whole body goes tight. Maybe she won't look at it. Maybe she won't say anything—

"Huh." Savannah glances toward the memorial in the center of the plaza, the granite stone pillar ensorcelled with swirling lights. "That's gotta be weird for you, ain't it, to go past that all the time?"

IN MEMORIAM

THE BRAVE WIZARDS WHO FOUGHT
AGAINST THE WICKED FORCES
OF THE DARK LADY
MAY THE PALL NEVER CROSS US AGAIN

"I don't come to town often," I say, and look the other way.

Savannah has the good sense to stay quiet for the next few minutes as we wind our way through town. When she does talk again, it's in a softer tone. "Things are different now. At the Conservatory, I mean."

"They aren't different much anywhere else," I say.

"Your thesis, though—it did a lot. I know you don't see it yet, but it's true. There are even a few others studying your old research now. Nobody with your gifts, of course, but at least it's happening."

I'm not sure if I feel comforted by that or not. She's just buttering me up, most like, but I'm not some biscuit at Jenny's.

"It takes time. Took me a while to accept, and I'm sorry for that," she says. "But your Xosia won't be forgotten just yet."

She turns us on the access road that runs around the hulking Capitol. I expect her to pull into her VIP spot around the side entrance, but she continues on past the compound entirely and turns into the parking lot for the Starlight Club. Seriously? I've got nothing against the Starlight Club, if you're the kind of person who likes to drink enchanted beer and rub elbows with Priests and maybe hop onto the dance floor for a tune or two, but I didn't crawl out of the back roads for this.

"You pullin' my leg?" I ask as she kills the engine.

"You got something against the Starlight?" She grins as she says it, but I'm always looking for the knife hidden under her pretty words.

I shake my head and break eye contact. I feel it again, that dark itch, the one that always begged me to scratch it back in school. Xosia's magic can get you all turned around, if you don't care what Xosia thinks. I remember all the times I thought of ways to twist it just so. "Just remembering, is all."

One time at the Conservatory, Savannah's pals told me the High Warlock wanted to meet me at the Starlight Club. They said he wanted to talk to me, real quiet-like, about making me a Priestess of Slumber, but he had to do it on the sly because folks wouldn't understand. So I barged in, all bubbling over with hope, and sat myself right down at his private booth like I owned the damn place. The look on his face could've melted blessed glass.

"Wait." Savannah laughs. "Are you talkin' about the time—"

I whip my head around to glare at her. I've got some glass-melting glares up my sleeve, too.

She flicks away the whole episode with a wave of her glamoured nails. "No prank this time, I promise."

My body is buzzing, a pinprick mixture of shame and rage. How can she write it off so easily? Again, I hear those old urges calling me back. The desire to reach out and take hold of my magic, my gift. Snatch someone's energy—take it for myself—make it into something more.

Instead, I take a deep breath and close my hand around Xosia's pendant until the buzzing fades.

I let Savannah lead me into the Starlight Club. Luz Alvado croons on the speakers overhead, asking if her lover will still love her when all the glamours fade. The dimly lit club is full, but not overwhelming; people keep their conversations at polite enough levels, and the dampening spells help. Worn-velvet booths cluster around parqueted wood tables under enchanted lights that dazzle like constellations, a classic but accessible look. The Starlight lets anyone believe that they deserve to live in the orbit of the Priests and the High Warlock; I certainly bought into it for a time. Conservatory students giggle and laugh at one table while a group of Mending wizards hold court at another booth. I trail behind Savannah as she waves and coos over them all, and do my best not to meet anyone's eyes.

Naveen, the Starlight's manager, rushes up to us as soon as he spots us. He's impeccably dressed and beautifully glamoured as always, gold linework painted across his dark arms, but I know his patron's Vantissa, the Lady of Vengeance. I've seen him call on her a few times to pitch unruly patrons out of the club. A halo of galaxies swirls around his head, throwing strange shadows across his face as he scowls at me.

"You didn't say you were bringing *her*," he snaps at Savannah. "She serves the Wicked Lady."

"Xosia isn't wicked," I protest, probably too quickly.

"Of course *you* don't think so." He turns toward Savannah. "We need a mender here, not some backwoods necromancer."

Savannah keeps her stance neutral, her expression cool. "The High Warlock's already sent our best menders to work on one of these poor souls, and they weren't able to do a damn thing. This calls for special measures. I've got permission from the High Warlock himself." She drops her arms to her sides and storms past Naveen. "So let's get on with it."

"On with what? What poor souls?" I ask. Dread creeps up my spine like a frosty hand.

Naveen huffs and turns to follow Savannah. "See for yourself."

I follow them into the back rooms, past the shelves of bottled spells and charms, to the storeroom full of untapped kegs. A burly woman stands guard, marked with the same Lady of Vengeance lines as Naveen—gold on her walnut skin. Beside her, in the dim light, sits a figure: a dark-haired, bronze-skinned boy, maybe a year younger than Savannah and myself. He stares right at me with cold steel eyes. He's not glaring, exactly—I know a glare when I see one, but this is more a lifeless stare, like the creepy dolls in the antiques shop off 12. His chest rises and falls with calm, even breath, but otherwise he's perfectly still. Expressionless. Empty.

The cold dread wraps around my throat and squeezes.

"He closed up last night, or was supposed to," Naveen says. "When I came back this morning, though, the whole place was wide open. Unlocked, unswept, chairs still down. I came back here to see if we'd been robbed, and found him standing in the corner, staring at the wall."

I swallow down the lump in my throat. "Has he done… well, anything at all? Since then?"

"Not really. Mostly, he's completely motionless. We pushed him into the chair, and he sat. Except…" His voice cracks. "Well, when I tried to check the—the cuts on his arms and face. That's when he went wild, swinging his arms and snapping at me. But the moment I backed off, he went right back to this."

I squint into the darkness. I'd missed the cuts at first, but now, they're practically screaming at me. One across his forehead. One down each cheek. One on each arm. And with a sickening twist to my gut, I already know what we'd find on his legs, too.

A long slit, clean but deep down to the bone. Stitched back up with Xosia's blessings. Only this is no blessing at all.

"The Pall's come back for us, hasn't it?" the guard mutters. "The Lady's cultists are tryin' to kill us all."

Anger blooms inside me, white-hot and scorching. I'm already fingering the pendant dangling from my neck as I step toward her. All the dark curses I never used, all the ugly spells I'd scraped together at the Conservatory—they sit on my tongue, ready to be unleashed.

But I can't. I can't betray Xosia that way and lose control. Even if it's just what they expect me to do. Maybe *because* that's what they expect. And with that thought, the anger simmers rather than flares.

Savannah raises her hand like she's going to hold me back, but I won't give her the satisfaction. "The High Warlock thanks you for bringing this to our attention," she says, all syrup-sweet and diplomatic as hell. "But it's a matter for the Priests now. We'll need to take him with us, if you don't mind."

"Why?" Naveen asks, eyes wide. "What are you going to do with him? I mean—if he isn't really dead—"

"Oh, we'll bring him around," Savannah says quickly. Then turning to me, her smile sharpens. "I'm sure you can find some way to undo this, can't you, Mattie?"

"That," I say, "is for Xosia to decide."

I want to take the boy back to my morgue—it's where I feel safest, after all, my own little fief. But Savannah insists we take him to one of the labs in the Capitol's basement. The High Warlock wants a full accounting of my work soon as it's done, no matter the hour. Judging by what little Savannah's told me, this isn't an isolated case. What that means for the Sawtooths—what it means for *me*—has me knotted up inside.

"Holler if you need anything," Savannah says, her voice echoing off the gleaming marble floor and walls. "I'll be just around the corner."

I lock the lab's door as securely as I can and rub my pendant until my mind runs clear.

I pull my ceremonial knife out of my belt loop and start examining the boy. The more I look, though, the more that seed of dread takes root. Whoever's done this to him, they're deeply familiar with my work, that much is clear. Except my method's meant to usher the dead into the Lady's embrace—protect their energy so it can't be used for anything else.

This, it would appear, is just the "anything else" I feared.

It looks like they drugged him first, or so the streaks of purple at the corners of his lips would suggest. Then came the cuts—deep but thin, scraping to the bone. One on each limb, on his brow, and on each cheek. Whoever did this put a lot of effort into stemming the bleeding, and keeping each cut nice and clean.

And then—

I remember standing in the Conservatory hall, the air thick with adrenaline and stale perfume, presenting my graduation project to the Priests. There hasn't been a Priest of Slumber since the Pall, of course, but they were treating me like I was the closest thing to it, and I wanted to prove that I was worthy. After having to piece together the works of former Xosia servants from mildewy, half-censored records and pages clipped from journals, I'd forged my own way to carry out the Lady of Slumber's works. And for my project, ironically, I'd aimed at *preventing* another Pall.

The souls are the key, I'd said, standing over a corpse, ceremonial knife still in hand. *We draw them out and lay their business to rest. Their souls go on to the Lady, and no one else can make use of them once they're in her embrace. A new practice—but one that will keep us all safe from that ancient threat.*

But someone's done made use of these souls after all. They've sliced into this boy and teased his soul right out of his bones. Problem is, they've done it while he's still alive.

Humming along to the Luz Alvado song from the Starlight Club, I pick up the ceremonial knife and move toward the boy's feet. It doesn't feel right doing this here instead of my morgue, but I'll make do with what I've got. I can't commend his soul to Xosia while he's still alive—or whatever state he's in right now—but if I examine it closely, then maybe I can determine who did this to him, and how.

The boy lies unmoving on the workbench before me, limp and oblivious. But the moment I reach out for the stitches along his calf, he lurches up.

"Hrrphhh, mrrrphhh," he says, or something like it. I'm not really paying attention, because he wraps his hands around my throat and digs his thumbs into the underside of my jaw.

I drop the knife and try to hold my hands up in surrender. "Sorry! I'm sorry—"

The minute I let go, he sighs, eases his grip, and slumps back onto the workbench, lifeless once more.

And no one else can make use of them...

I swear under my breath, then stick my head out the door to call for Savannah.

Savannah brings in a library cart brimming with dusty folios and cracked leather journals. "Looks like some of the ones on your list were checked out, so I guess we'll have to make do with these."

"Thanks." I pick up one of the old notebooks I used extensively for my project, then glance nervously toward Savannah. I'd never put up with her or anyone else saying it, but there was certainly truth in what Naveen at the Starlight Club had said—the Lady's gifts can be used for malice. The Pall was proof enough of that. And in the darkness of a ruined laboratory, or amidst the flickering embers of my school notes that someone burned, or in the crushing silence of the bathroom when they sealed me inside—I surely dreamed of using them that way.

I flip through the pages but keep them close to my chest. The truth is right there, between the lines: all the spells I could have worked, if I'd changed my process just a hair. If I'd used it on live subjects, instead.

The dark root of my old urges spreads. It coils around my limbs, my neck, my thoughts. *I* could have worked this spell—snatching control of someone's soul and making them dance on my strings. Assign them a task—guarding the stitches on their limbs, for instance—and leave them to carry it out. Because that's exactly what it looks like they've done to this boy. Just like the Pall, when the old cultists turned half the Sawtooths into their servants. I could squeeze the very essence of someone like Savannah out of her and force her to do as I like.

The dark root whispers: *I could do it still.*

"Find something?" she asks, looking up from the records she's poring through.

I shrink back, shame flaring on my cheeks. Does she know what I was thinking? Is it written all over me like the Dark Lady's prayers? It's been a long time since I entertained those thoughts, but being around Savannah again makes them come rushing back. I shake my head to clear it. "I was just thinking how—"

A shadow stirs behind her, beyond the doorway to the lab. Then, like an echo, the boy on the slab lurches to his feet.

Savannah swears. "Now hang on, we aren't finished with you—"

He shoves her back with force. I jump up and reach for one of the basic spells from our Conservatory days—an air-thickening spell—but my tongue's clumsy with it. I haven't used any spells not meant for Xosia's ears in a while. Savannah reacts faster, trying to weave a net across the doorway to keep the boy from leaving.

But he brushes it off like there isn't even anything there, and takes off down the hall.

"There was someone down there," I say. "Just a minute ago."

"Do you think it's whoever's controlling him?" She takes off at a sprint, strappy heels clacking against the marble floors, and I shuffle after her in my high-tops.

"Could be. Where's he going?"

We both skid around a corner, nearly crashing into each other and the wall. We're just in time to see him disappear down a stairwell.

Savannah swears under her breath. "He's headed for the tunnels."

The tunnels connect the Capitol to the Conservatory, plus a few other administrative offices. I grab her by the arm and pull her with me toward the stairwell. "Come on. He could lose us quick down there."

We reach the bottom of the staircase, but it's anyone's guess which direction he went in the honeycomb of tunnels that stretch beneath the town. Savannah fixes me with a determined stare. "This way," she says. "The paths beneath the Conservatory."

I nod, my pulse pounding. The Conservatory is about the last place in the Sawtooths I ever want to be. But we don't have a choice. I've got to stop whoever's done this to him—and whatever else I fear they have planned.

Cold sweat drips down my spine as I head deeper into the bowels of the tunnel complex. Any minute now, I should be surfacing into the labs and study rooms underneath the Conservatory. The same rooms where I first designed my work. If someone's perverted my designs—if they're trying to create another Pall—

Something throbs in the back of my skull, a dense sound that's too low to hear. Xosia's sigil grows warm where it rests against my sternum, underneath my T-shirt. Someone's working the Dark Lady's spells nearby. Someone who isn't me.

I skid to a stop as a turn brings us over a stonework ledge, overlooking a narrow channel of water far below. We're in some kind of chamber far beneath the Sawtooths, the Capitol and the Conservatory somewhere far above us. But down here is a different world, one I'm betting has escaped the High Warlock's notice. Probably all the rest of the Priests', too.

"Where'd he go?" Savannah whispers. She's trying to be quiet, but her words bounce off the rounded chamber.

"Only one way to go." I point toward the narrow staircase that wraps around the chamber's lip.

Savannah eyes it warily. She's still in her evening gown and strappy pumps. "Um...you go first."

I follow the staircase down toward the next chamber with my heart in my throat. When I step inside, though, I see why.

Sparks of light—dozens of them—twist together and seethe in the heart of the round chamber, coiling like ropes. They aren't just any lights, though, I realize as the sigil practically burns into my flesh. I know these strands of energy too well.

The souls harvested from the dead.

Except these aren't from the dead—or from the living. They're from people trapped in between. Shucked out of still-living bodies and leashed up like attack dogs, ready to obey a wizard's command. Was this how the cultists of the Pall enslaved thousands to their will so long ago?

But I already know the answer to that. This is the dark usage of the Lady's gift that, in my darkest moments, I thought of seizing for myself. And now that I'm asking the question once more—of what *other* ways the Lady's magic could be used—I feel that pull again.

We obey, a voice whispers—a sparkling strand of energy dancing toward me. *We are meant to obey.*

But this isn't what Xosia wants. Death is her final gift, not a holding cell. Only she can claim these souls and shape them to her own purpose—it's not for me or anyone else to decide.

"Mattie..." Savannah whispers, but she trails off.

The energy swirls around me—whispering, crying, screaming, shouting the secrets of the not-living and the not-dead alike. It shouts the secrets in my own heart.

The dark curses that sat sour on my tongue every time the other Conservatory students taunted me.

The Dark Lady's forgotten teachings itching in my fingertips whenever the High Warlock disparaged me, disparaged my work.

The cold hunger in my chest when I look out at the Sawtooths, the lands I aim to protect, and see only distrust and suspicion looking back.

You could do this. You have this power, they sing. They caress my cheeks like silk ribbons; they lift my hair and make it dance in their breeze. *You could hold our leash. You could make them all believe.*

You could make them all understand.

"I found your notes," someone says.

A boy steps forward from the far side of the chamber. Amber and violet and teal lights dance across his face, obscuring his features, but he looks young—young as Savannah and me when we studied at the Conservatory. Young enough to be one of the new Xosia acolytes Savannah mentioned. He reaches toward the mass of energy and snatches a fistful of it with an angry curl to his lips.

"Your research was so helpful. Far better than those useless old tomes in the archives. But you didn't go far enough—not nearly."

I grip the sigil around my neck, even though it feels molten hot. Savannah's not standing behind me any longer. Where the hell did she go? "This isn't how the Lady's gifts are meant to be used. Those souls belong to their bodies, or to her—not you."

"No? And why should they have their souls, these cowards, these wicked people? They hated you too at the academy—I know they did. And they hate and fear you now."

"I don't need them to love me," I say. "I serve Xosia, the Lady of Slumber. She's enough."

"Not for me." He twists the strands of souls in his hand, and I feel a tug deep in my gut.

The souls crackle, seething, angry. Their whispers turn to shouts; their words shred into sharp consonants, lashing and stinging at me.

Lady of Eternal Slumber, guide me, I pray. *These souls aren't ready for your embrace. Give me the strength I need to stop him—let me return these souls to where they belong—*

"They hate and fear us because they hate and fear Xosia. They know she'll come for them someday. But with all our spells, our glamours, our magic—no one wants to admit it. They think they can keep puttin' her off."

Footsteps sound all around us; slowly, people begin to file into the room. Not just any people—they're the ones whose souls he's currently wrangled. Some I recognize, like the lady down at Jenny's diner who's always got a stack of pancakes towering over her. One of the guys from our class at the Conservatory. He never made it to Priest, but he sells some healing stones and quick fixes down off the interstate.

Just people from the Sawtooths, people like any other—fearful but hopeful, capable of hate and love. I've seen their best and their worst. As long as the people of the Sawtooths are in love with life, they'll always dread Xosia's coming. Though I'm content with the company of bones, even I feel the teeth of loneliness and distrust every day. I felt far worse at the academy. I feel far worse sometimes still.

"You think they deserve your pity? You know what they do with that fear. They take it out on us—Xosia's faithful servants. But it doesn't have to be this way." He tugs at the souls, and the husks of people surround him, slack-faced and waiting. "We can make the Sawtooths a land for the Lady—a land of the dead. Life only for those who deserve it, for those who serve the Lady true. And for the rest—they'll serve *us*. They must earn the chance to pass into her embrace."

Give me strength, my Lady. But my grip on the sigil falters.

"You know I'm right." He laughs, a hollow, scraping sound, like nails dragging against stone. "Xosia wouldn't have let me build this army if not."

Behind him, Savannah's eyes—dead, empty—stare back at me. And I know what I have to do.

I close my eyes. No use in pretending I didn't once think these same things. I probably did when I wrote those papers he's used. But the Lady doesn't mean us to use her gifts this way. Because if she did—

Lady of Slumber. I've given you my life, and in death, I look forward to your embrace. A calmness drifts around me, soothing as a blanket. *I'll always harvest the souls, and I'll always gather their secrets so they can be put to rest.*

"No more fear," he says. "Only obedience."

I shake my head. *But my Lady, these souls aren't yours just yet.* The dark vines of dread pull taut. *If I'm right, then give me your gifts to set them free.*

It happens in an instant. With one hand, I seize hold of the pulsing mass of souls, gripping it like a tangible thing. The light compresses in my fist, warm, screaming. The energy fuels me; it propels me forward. And in my other hand, I unsheathe my knife.

Savannah lunges forward, her glamour dropping, and pounces on him. He throws up his arms to block her, but the Lady guides me: I slash open his cheek. He turns to fend Savannah off, but it's too late. The Lady's got him now. *I've* got him now, with the ritual I perfected. The one he corrupted. With my other fist wrapped around his minions' souls, I take hold of his and move to block his exit.

His soul trickles toward me as his scream dries out. "Stop," he wheezes. "You can't do this. I carry out her will!"

I shake my head. "No. I do."

I thrust my left hand forward, releasing the knotted strands of souls as Savannah weaves a quick air spell to wrestle him to the ground. The souls slam back into their bodies, some screaming, some crying, some simply looking around dazed;

slowly, I can see the light coming back into their eyes. They're safe from Xosia for now.

"The High Warlock's gonna have a good time talking to you," Savannah says, grinning, as she draws on elemental spells to bind the boy's hands behind his back.

"Just kill me," he sobs. "Let me be with the Lady, at least."

I stand over him. "The Lady deserves better than the likes of you."

Savannah and I take him to the holding cells in the jail, attached to the Capitol compound, as I pull his strings. Once he's in custody, I release my hold on his soul. The High Warlock can deal with him as he wills.

Savannah and I stop off at Jenny's for some pancakes before she takes me back to the morgue. We're quite a pair, her all disheveled in her evening wear and me scuffed up and battered from the long night, but we both dig in to the pancake stacks. I keep expecting her to lecture me, or blame me somehow for what the student did. But when she finishes up, she just wipes the syrup from her mouth and regards me with a smile.

"You did all right," she says. "The High Warlock will be very pleased."

"You don't think he'll blame me? Blame all the Dark Lady's followers?"

She shrugs. "Some people will. But you were right, you know—what he was doing, that ain't the Dark Lady's way. I'd say as servants go, you're about the best she could possibly ask for."

I shove another bite of pancake into my mouth to hide my smile.

"I'm sorry for the way I acted back in school. It's true, how easy it is to be scared. Plus, I think something about being a wizard just makes you feel better than everyone else. Not the best combination." She lowers her gaze. "We need all kinds to run the Sawtooths right, though. You don't have to stay away from the Capitol if you don't want."

"When the Lady needs me to speak for her at the Capitol, I'll speak. You don't need me for the day-to-day."

It's only back at the morgue that I let myself slump forward, heart aching. Maybe that's the worst of it—not the fear and suspicion the boy's actions are sure to spark. No, the worst is that I feel for him, at least somewhat. On dark nights, in cold rooms that echo with too much quiet, I've thought the same as him.

But I know my purpose, and the Priests all know it, too. Bones speak the truth, but the living—they're the ones who need to hear it. I was given the Lady's blessing to speak those truths, and protect every last one of us from the likes of him. The Lady has no use for a life that hasn't been lived in full.

So I'll serve her—and all the Sawtooths—in mine.

★ ★ ★ ★ ★

THE TRUTH ABOUT QUEENIE

by Brandy Colbert

SOMETIMES IF YOU PRETEND LIKE A PART OF you simply doesn't exist, you can will it away.

I'm not talking about physical attributes, like my eyebrows, which are a bit too thick for my liking. I mean on the inside. Like how I've been scared of tall staircases and sky-high balconies my entire life, but last year, I hiked to the top of a steep, narrow trail with my field hockey teammates without launching into a full-blown panic attack. Maybe part of it was because it was too late to turn back, but I like to think it's because the whole way up, I repeated out loud that I was no longer afraid of heights.

I'm pretty sure my best friend, Webb, is one of the bravest people I know. He's a skateboarder; he went pro last year, when we were fifteen. Webb has been banging around on his board for as long as I can remember, his long limbs always sporting bruises and gross scabs and a fresh wound or two.

The first couple of years after he got a board he messed around close to home, practicing tricks in our neighborhood. But the more courageous he got, the uglier and more dramatic his falls became, and neighbors started to complain about watching his stunts go down in front of their houses. He moved his operation to the skate park, and I went with him a few times a week. I felt like I was living vicariously through him, like his fearlessness rubbed off on me as he sailed through the air on his board.

Now I barely see him. He travels so much that his parents had to hire a tutor.

My sister and I are sprawled out in the family room, doing our homework after dinner, when my phone buzzes with a new text. I put my finger on the paragraph I'm reading and glance at my phone.

I smile as soon as I see who it is. I sit straight up when I read it.

Coming home for a few weeks, back Sunday

Sunday. That's only three days away.

Nia looks up from her laptop where she's furiously typing an essay on James Baldwin. Her temporarily idle fingers twirl around the end of one long cornrow as she squints at me. "Why do you look like that?"

"Like what?"

But I can't stop smiling, and before I know it, Nia is leaning over my shoulder, staring at the screen.

She shakes her head as she retreats back to her laptop, as if the effort wasn't worth it. "You are so in love with him."

I know what she really wanted to say. She thinks I'm wasting my time missing him when I could be having fun with guys we see at school every day.

But the truth is, none of them measures up to Webb, and no amount of distance between us can change that.

I wake at six-thirty on Sunday morning.

It's way too early for the weekend, but it's like my body knows something exciting is happening today. I check my phone, but there aren't any new messages. Webb is probably still on the plane. He didn't give me any details, just said that he'll get ahold of me when he lands.

It's strange being best friends with a famous person. Well, famous-ish. He's well-known in the skating world, but he's not a household name. Not yet. It's weird thinking he used to just be the quiet kid with an Afro who'd rather fool around on his skateboard for hours than hang with the kids from school.

He doesn't post a lot of pictures or videos himself, but he's always showing up in photos with celebrities and other skaters and fans. Webb has *fans*. He had a decent following before he went pro, but he has a legit fan base now, and I'm still not used to it. Once, I spent a whole afternoon reading posts online from people who were crushing on him.

My life is so normal. I live in a normal house with my normal parents and my normal sister in Pasadena. We try so very hard to be normal it hurts.

I flip to the photo album of Webb and me on my phone. Nia thinks it's creepy, but now I can go to one place to look at the two of us when I'm missing him. Which seems to be more and more often, because he's gone longer and longer each time he leaves. I guess I should be used to it by now.

I scroll through the pictures a couple of times before my eyes start to get heavy. Eventually I doze off, and then I guess

I completely fall back to sleep, because I wake up to a hand shaking my shoulder. I swat it away and roll over, feeling my phone lodge under my ribs.

Then the covers vanish from my body. My eyes fly open. I yelp, ready to scream at Nia, when my gaze lands on him.

"Webb, come on. It's cold!"

"It is not cold. It's April in L.A. and it's seventy degrees outside."

"I'm always cold," I mutter, grabbing the blankets back from him.

"Good morning to you, too," he says with the grin that shows his dimple. I always feel validated when I see him in photos that aren't showing his dimple because it means that he reserves his real smile for people who know him. He once said he thinks it makes him look too young. "What kind of welcome is that?"

I sit up and rub my eyes. "Welcome." I yawn, then remember I'm still wearing my satin sleep cap. Oh god. I touch the edge where it meets my ear and cringe, but Webb doesn't even mention it. "What time did you get in?"

"Just now. I had the car drop me off here from the airport."

I raise my eyebrows, trying to ignore the way my stomach jumps. "You didn't stop at *your* house?"

He's only a couple of blocks over, but I know how much his parents miss him, too.

Webb shrugs and then smiles again. "I wanted to see you first."

I busy myself with pulling the covers up over my legs and pretending to search for my phone because I am embarrassed by how happy this makes me. My cheeks burn.

Suddenly Webb backs up and takes a running leap onto my bed, crashing just a few inches from me with a huge thud.

He bounces up and down a couple of times on his butt, like a little kid.

"Where are we going for breakfast?"

I look at my phone. "It's eight-thirty."

"Exactly. Have you heard of breakfast? People usually eat it before noon?"

"I hate you." I shove him away, but Webb wraps his arms around me in a bear hug. He pushes his nose into my neck and exhales a long whoosh of breath. Webb being so close to me warms me from the inside out, and I am so glad he's here. Giving me shit in person and not over text.

"Come on, Your Highness. I'm hungry. And I haven't seen you in a long time."

Your Highness. That nickname used to annoy me—I get plenty of teasing with a name like Queenie; I don't need it from my best friend, too—but now I crave it. I allow myself to relax in his arms for a moment, even though it probably doesn't mean the same thing to him. Even though it's just a reminder that if I told him how I felt, maybe things *could* be different with us.

But I don't think I'd ever be that brave. And besides, what if I did tell him and it changed things for the worse?

"Fine," I say. "But you're paying."

We drive to our favorite family-run Mexican restaurant because Webb says it's been nearly impossible to get good Mexican food on the road. The place has only three booths and a single table in the middle, and it smells amazing, like fresh tortillas.

We order our usual: chilaquiles for me and huevos rancheros for Webb, mango agua frescas for us both. Then we slide into the free booth by the window.

Webb leans his head back and groans. “Fuck, I’m tired.”

“Still can’t sleep on planes?”

“Nah.” He cracks his knuckles. “And I only got, like, two hours of sleep last night. There was this party at the hotel—” He stops, like he wonders if he should be telling me this.

I stare at him. “Yeah?”

“It just got kind of weird. Paolo invited all these girls, and some of them were serious fans and, like, crying because they were in the same room with him. They wouldn’t stop taking pictures of us. Then some of them got wasted and started doing body shots. It was…intense.”

“Body shots?” I seriously can’t believe I’m talking to the same Webb. He used to be so shy, and the couple of times he’s tried alcohol, he said he didn’t like the way it made him feel out of control. Those rules don’t seem to apply when he’s on the road. I always wonder if he’s hooking up with any of the girls he meets, but I never ask; I have a feeling I wouldn’t like the answer.

“Yeah, well. That’s what ends up happening when Paolo’s around. What’s going on here?”

I sip my agua fresca, pretending to think. “Nothing, nothing, and nothing.”

“Come on, Queenie. You gotta have *something* going on.”

But I don’t, really. Nothing as exciting as what he’s doing. I shrug. “It’s pretty much been school and family. And field hockey back in the fall.”

“You still killing it out there on the field?”

“*Killing it* might be an overstatement.” Coach likes me, but I think it’s mostly because I can run fast and think quick on my feet. Which is kind of a requirement when you’re a midfielder. “We did all right this year, though. We got to the play-offs, so Coach was happy.”

"How's your grandma?"

"She's good. A lot better…thanks." I give him a small smile. "She'll want to see you before you go again."

"Damn, I just got here, and you're already talking about me leaving?" Webb shakes his head, but he grins back at me.

"Always." I look away. It's harder to stare in his eyes and act like I don't care about how often he's gone.

"Of course I'm gonna go see Ms. Armstrong." He pauses and I know what he's going to say and I wish he wouldn't. "Any more…instances?"

Instance. Such a generic word for something so big. It's so big that I don't like to think about it, let alone talk about it.

"Nope."

"I just thought…since she's better…and you said Big Queenie was around…"

My shoulders tense. "Big Queenie has been gone for almost two months."

"Okay, okay." He holds up his hands as if in surrender. "But if *I* came from a family of witches, I sure wouldn't be hiding it like you do."

I kick him under the table just as a guy our age brings breakfast over. Webb stares at me with a fake-wounded look as he rubs his shins. "These legs are precious goods."

"Can I, uh, get you anything else?" the guy asks, wiping his hands on the towel hanging from his belt.

"Nah, man, we're good, thanks." Webb rubs his hands together in delight as he looks at his plate.

The guy is still hanging around, though, and when I look up, his neck is turning red. He's staring at Webb. "You, uh… you're Webb Johnston?"

I see the change in Webb's face. It's subtle, but almost like he slips on an invisible mask—something to shield him from the public.

"Yeah, man." He nods at him. "What's up?"

"Uh, big fan of yours. I, ah, used to watch you at competitions around here...before you went pro."

"Hey, thanks. What's your name?"

"Miguel." He pauses and the color on his neck darkens, traveling up to his face. "Think I could get a picture?"

"Yeah, sure. Of course."

Miguel pulls a phone from his pocket and snaps a few shots of them himself, then asks me to take a couple. He does one of those complicated handshakes with Webb, then says, "It's real dope to see more brown skaters out there."

Webb nods and gives him his public smile. "Appreciate that, man. Thanks for the grub."

Miguel retreats to the kitchen, and Webb immediately stuffs a huge bite of egg and tortilla into his mouth. I take a tentative bite of my chilaquiles, waiting for him to bring up our previous conversation. But he's fixated on the food now, already eyeing mine. The routine is that we each eat half of our meal and then switch plates.

"Fuck, this is good. I missed this," he says after a few moments, pushing his plate away so he won't devour the whole thing in one go. He looks at me with a lopsided smile, dimple in full effect. "Missed you, too, Queenie."

"Yeah, yeah," I say before I take another bite, pretending his words don't make my heart crack wide open.

After breakfast, Webb says he needs to go home and sleep. I drop him and his bags off, then hop on the freeway and head to Hollywood.

Relief ripples through me as I spot Grandma Anita working in the flower beds that border her porch. She's been well for a few weeks now, but I never know what to expect when I come to see her. A part of me still worries she'll get sick again. I can't deny that my aunt, Big Queenie, has a gift, but I know better than anyone that having a gift doesn't mean you're infallible.

"Hi, baby," Grandma Anita says as I walk up the front path. She's wearing a big straw hat to shield her from the sun. Beautiful, brightly patterned head scarves have been her go-to for the past six months or so, but ever since her soft curls started growing back, she's been wearing her short new 'do with pride. She does whatever she can to protect her skin, though. It's a gorgeous deep umber, completely free of wrinkles.

"Hi, Grandma Anita." I bend to kiss her on the cheek, steering clear of the hat's wide brim. "Want some help?"

"Like I'd let that brown thumb get anywhere near these beauties." She shakes her head. "No, baby, I'm just finishing up. Go get something to drink."

I'd be offended by that comment if it weren't true. I've lost count of how many plants have died on my watch. Which I maintain is further proof that my "gift" isn't really a gift at all.

I love my grandmother's bungalow. It's small, but the perfect size for her. The stucco is painted a cheery vibrant blue, and the front porch is a colorful array of hanging and potted plants with a white wooden bench near the door.

Inside, the windows fill the rooms with sun. My feet creak along the familiar hardwood path to her kitchen, where I've spent hours watching her cook and bake. For a while, this room felt off-limits, because she was too sick to leave her bedroom. Meals came from our house or her friends and neighbors; her kitchen was used only to heat up the food that she couldn't eat.

There's a pitcher of fresh lemonade, made with lemons from her backyard tree. I pour a glass and sit at the table just as the front door opens. Grandma Anita heads straight to the sink to wash her hands.

"Webb is back in town," I say.

"And he hasn't stopped by to see me?" She flicks the dripping water off her hands and dries them with the towel folded neatly on the counter.

"He just got in this morning. He said he doesn't want to see you until he's all rested up, but he'll stop by soon."

"He'd better." She pours a glass of lemonade and joins me at the table. "When are you two finally going to get together?"

"Grandma Anita!"

"Girl, don't you 'Grandma Anita' me." She shakes her head. "That boy might be the only one too stupid to see what's going on here."

"He said he missed me...but you're supposed to miss your best friend." I shrug. "That doesn't really mean anything."

She rubs my hand. "Baby, it means he cares about you."

Grandma Anita is right about most things, but if Webb liked me back—*really* liked me—wouldn't he have confessed or made a move by now?

"Big Queenie called this morning," she says. "Told me to tell you hello."

"Where is she?"

"Barcelona. Heading over to the Canary Islands tomorrow to stay with friends."

"I hope I get to travel someday like Big Queenie."

"Work hard and save your money like she does, and you can do it, baby."

I bite my lip for a moment before I ask my next question. We don't talk directly about this stuff, not even among family members. But I have to know. "Are you worried that—you know..."

She raises an eyebrow. "Use your words."

"Are you ever worried that what she did won't work forever?" I blurt, then cast my eyes down to the wooden table.

Aren't you worried that the cancer will come back?

Grandma Anita stiffens. "I'm thinking ahead to the future," she says evenly. "Enjoying the present. It wouldn't hurt you to do the same, Queenie."

"Yes, ma'am." I choke down the urge to tell her I might never stop worrying. That I was so scared we were going to lose her. That even if Big Queenie is good at what she does, I was terrified that her methods would backfire and none of us would be able to forgive her. And now, even as Grandma Anita sits in front of me, healthy and happy, I am worried that the cancer will come back.

Grandma Anita smiles when I look up. "You like the lemonade?"

"I love it."

"Good. After we finish, let's take a walk. It's jacaranda season; the neighborhood has never looked prettier."

Webb picks me up after school on Tuesday.

He's meeting a friend at Union Station and wants me to go with him. I don't know who it is, but other skaters are always stopping through L.A. on their way somewhere, wanting to meet up with him for a day or two.

Webb has his mom's minivan, and he looks ridiculous behind the wheel. He's decidedly not tired anymore, practically springing up and down in his seat as we weave through traffic.

"Nice of you to pick up your friend," I say as we pull up.

"Yeah, well...she's kind of special." He puts the car in

park and looks at me shyly. "I can't wait for you to meet her, Queenie."

She? Her?

But it doesn't matter what Webb said, because everything I need to know is shining in his eyes. My breath catches in my throat. I always hoped I'd see that look from Webb—I just never thought it would be meant for someone else.

He glances past me to the front of the train station, where people are streaming out of the doors. His whole face lights up when he spots her. I don't look. Not until he's out of the car.

I can't see much—just long arms wrapped around his back. They finally pull away, but before I can avert my eyes, they're kissing. Not just a quick peck on the lips, but a real kiss. The way I've thought about kissing Webb so many times.

I pretend to look at my phone until the door behind me slides open. Webb tosses her duffel bag into the back, then she gets in, settling behind me. She's light-skinned with super-thick Marley twists piled on top of her head in a voluminous bun, and she's somehow completely glamorous, even though she's wearing cutoffs and a cropped sweatshirt.

"Queenie, this is Blythe," Webb says with a smile so wide I think his dimple will never disappear. "One of the dopest female skateboarders you'll ever meet."

She gives him an amused look. "Or one of the dopest *skateboarders*. Full stop." She turns to smile at me. "Queenie, it's so cool to meet you. Webb never shuts up about you."

Really? Because he hasn't told me a thing *about you*, is what I want to say. I don't understand why he didn't mention her. We hadn't texted a lot in the weeks before he got home, but I thought it was because he was busier than normal. With his skating—not a girl. But I make myself smile back at her, because she's Webb's...whatever. He likes her.

"It's really nice to meet you, too," I say as Webb slides her door closed and walks around to the other side of the van.

Blythe is chatty, and I feel like I could ace a quiz about her entire life by the time we get to Webb's house. I know that she's from Davis, a town up in Northern California near Sacramento. I know that she's our age and she's not yet pro, but she likely will be in the next year. I know that she has an old English sheepdog named Pickles and she hates living in a small town and that she is obsessed with Webb. She can't keep her hands off him; when we were in the van, she was always reaching her hand forward to rub his neck or touch his shoulder, sometimes resting it there for minutes at a time.

We go to Webb's place because Blythe wants to lie out by the pool. I really want to go home, but I feel like Webb will know something is up if I do. And I don't want him to know how upset I am—how foolish I feel for not knowing he's been dating someone for two whole months. He's had so many chances to bring it up; did he not tell me because deep down he knows how I feel about him? I flush at the thought. I've worked so hard to not let him know.

Webb's parents are still at work, so we have the house to ourselves. He takes Blythe on a tour, holding her hand as she skips ahead of him. I stay behind.

When they meet me out back, Blythe has changed into a tiny blue bikini. Oh. She wasn't kidding about the whole pool thing. We slide into three chaise lounges. At least Webb is wearing a T-shirt and shorts; I feel silly still wearing my school clothes.

"God, I love L.A.," Blythe says, stretching her arms to the sky. She looks over at me. "So, Queenie. Tell me everything about you, like—oh! You have to tell me about this witch thing."

My eyes widen so much I'm surprised they don't pop out of my head. Webb *knows* there's one thing I don't want him telling people about me. He's known that forever, but he let it slip with someone he's been dating a couple of months?

I punch him in the arm so hard my fist throbs.

"What the *fuck*, Queenie?" He rubs his arm.

I stand up quickly, walking around to the other side of the pool so I won't have to look at him.

Webb follows.

I don't turn around even when he stops right behind me. "Why would you tell her?"

"I…I don't know. I guess we were talking about our friends back home one night, and I told her all about you and it just sort of came up."

"You told her about Becca?" Everything pauses; even the birds seem to stop singing as I wait for him to respond.

His silence is my answer.

Becca went to school with us and lived up the street from Webb. We were a tight trio in elementary, but something happened when we got to sixth grade. Suddenly, halfway through the year, Webb and I weren't cool enough for her. She started blowing off plans and sitting at a different table in the cafeteria. We hadn't done anything to her; nothing had changed. But Becca wanted to reinvent herself at our new school, and Webb and I weren't part of the plan.

I think we would have been able to handle it if she hadn't started that rumor. She told people that Webb was hooking up with his teacher—even though we were twelve, even though Webb had never hooked up with anyone in his life. We knew for a fact that Becca had spread the rumor because earlier in the year, Webb had confessed his crush on Ms. Solomon, and we were the only ones he'd told. Becca promised to keep his secret, but she seemed jealous—mad, almost, when she said Ms. Solomon wasn't even that pretty.

The rumor blew up so much that Webb and his parents had to have a meeting with the administrators and Ms. Solomon. He said it was the most embarrassing thing that had ever happened to him, and even though the rumor wasn't true, the damage was done. It took weeks for everyone to stop teasing him, and I don't think some people—students *and* adults—ever believed it was just a rumor.

Webb steps in front of me and dips his head to make eye contact. "What happened to Becca wasn't your fault."

"We don't know it wasn't."

He sighs. "Look, I'm sorry. Blythe is…she's got a lot of energy, but she's real cool, Queenie. I want you to be friends."

Friends. After what happened with Becca, I've been wary of making new friends. It's hard for me to trust people. I'm friendly with my field hockey teammates, but I don't tell anyone my secrets except Nia and Webb. It's easier to only worry about two people betraying me.

And now Webb has done exactly that.

"Stop telling people I'm a witch."

"But you are," he says with a shrug. As if it's the most common fact in the world.

"That's nobody's business…and one spell doesn't mean I'm a witch. It means maybe I channeled Big Queenie."

"Uh-huh. Whatever, Your Highness."

I stare at him. "Do you really not get how what you did was shitty? Just because you have a girlfriend, you can't—" My voice breaks.

Webb touches my arm. "I'm sorry. For real. I shouldn't have said anything."

He sounds sincere, but what if he ends up spilling more of

my secrets? What if everything between us is now between me and him and Blythe?

"Will you come back over there if I promise nobody will bring up the *W* word?" he pleads. "Now or in the future?"

I look over my shoulder. Blythe is lying all the way back on the chaise, sunglasses tipped toward the sky.

"Fine," I say, and he shows me his dimple.

After dinner with my family and homework with Nia, I shut myself into my bedroom and lock the door. Then I slide onto my stomach, reaching under the bed until my fingertips touch the shoebox.

I stay on the floor, leaning against my bed as I open the box. There's not much inside: mostly a few old pictures of Webb and me and Becca—at birthday parties and sleepovers and playing in one of our backyards. I stare at a photo of just Becca and me. We're sitting on her front stoop, eating Popsicles. We're maybe six or seven, our stained lips spread wide, showing off our gap-toothed grins. She was a generous friend; she always let me have the last grape Popsicle, even though it was her favorite flavor, too.

In the corner of the box, there's a hair tie: a piece of elastic with a blue bow on the end. Becca left it at my house, and it must have gotten shoved under my dresser. I only found it a couple of years ago, when we moved my furniture to put fresh paint on the walls. I stared at it for a long time, wondering if I'd feel some connection to Becca when I touched it—I didn't. Still, as much as I hated her at one time, we were close for so long. I'm glad to have something tangible to remember her by.

I slip the spell book from beneath the pictures. Before I found it all those years ago, I wouldn't have imagined a spell book could look so plain. In movies, they always seem to be glowing from within, the pages turning themselves and the cover decorated with some elaborate script between the gilded edges. But it's just a composition notebook with Big Queenie's handwritten pages inside. I discovered it when I was eleven years old, while looking through a box of her old stuff at Grandma Anita's, and sneaked it into my bag so I could look at it in secret.

There were spells for all sorts of things: how to make someone fall in love with you (and out of love with you), how to change your appearance, how to find a lost object, how to ward off negativity... There were so many packed in the book, it was overwhelming the first time I looked through it.

I accidentally left it lying out one day, and my nosy sister found it and told our mother. I'll never forget the pained look on Mom's face as she sat us down in the kitchen that evening. She told us that the women in our family are thought to possess magical powers, but that we don't talk about it.

"Magical powers?" Nia said, glancing at me to see how I was taking the news. She was thirteen then, two years older than me, and she acted like most things that I said and did were dumb, but she still counted me as her ally in the family. "Like witches?"

Our mother exhaled through her nose. It came out sounding like a scoff. "Yes...like witches. Big Queenie believes in it. I don't."

"Why don't we talk about it?" I asked, definitely not believing what I was hearing. Could those spells in Big Queenie's loopy handwriting actually mean something? They weren't just silly kid stuff?

"Because some of us don't want to find out if we have them...the powers." She shifted uncomfortably in her seat.

Mom is usually so calm and controlled; I can't remember her ever being so unnerved. "It can be dangerous for someone who doesn't know what they're doing. Or someone who doesn't have the best intentions."

"But..." Nia paused, tracing a finger around the gray circles on the pale yellow place mat. "This is the first time we've heard about this. We don't even talk about it to each other? To family?"

Our mother shook her head.

"Does Dad know?" Nia asked.

"Yes." Mom sighed. "But I asked him not to bring it up with you two."

"Why?" I asked again, though I sensed she was about three seconds from clamming up for good. "I mean, why don't we talk about it?"

"Because sometimes being black is hard enough, Queenie," she said, her voice not angry but tired. "We were the first black family to move in on this block, and I don't want to give people a reason to question us."

My parents moved us here a long time ago, when Nia was five years old and I was three. We're still the only black family on the block, but we're no longer the only people of color, and we're friendly with a lot of our neighbors. I think Mom and Dad must have been really nervous about integrating the street, though. They talk about moving into this house like it was yesterday.

Nia wrinkled her nose. "So, white people get to be witches, but we don't? That doesn't seem fair."

Mom stood up from the table, shaking her head again. "Girls, we're done talking about this. Queenie, throw that thing away or return it to your grandma, but I don't want to see it again." As she left the kitchen, I heard her muttering,

"I cannot *believe* Big Queenie would leave that laying around at Mama's…like she wanted you to find it."

Nia gave me a funny look. "What are you going to do with it?"

"I don't know," I said slowly. "What would you do with it?"

She glanced warily at the book. "I'd get rid of it."

"Aren't you curious? About if we have the powers or whatever?"

She paused for so long I wondered if she was going to answer me. Finally, she said, "Yeah, kind of. But not enough to mess with that stuff. It's weird."

"It's not weird. You just don't know enough about it."

"Neither do *you*," Nia said before she left me alone in the room.

Like our mother, she wanted nothing to do with our family magic. But I did. And nobody followed up with me about returning the book, so I kept it.

And I tried out a spell on Becca to make her weak.

It sounded too simple, and I doubted it would work. I needed a piece of her clothing (I had a T-shirt she'd left here after one of our sleepovers), and a piece of her hair (I'd been worried about that one, but there were a couple of strands clinging to the shirt), and a photograph (there were plenty). I assembled everything exactly the way the spell said to, then I chanted the words written out in all caps. They weren't in any language I'd ever heard, and I felt silly, and I had to do it in my closet so no one else could hear, but I did it.

And it worked. Becca died a week later.

I couldn't stop wondering if I was responsible for her death. Would she never have gotten sick if I'd never opened up that spell book? Was she going to die anyway? I wasn't even sure if my powers existed, let alone if they were capable of killing someone. I didn't want to hurt anyone… I just wanted Becca to feel as helpless as Webb did.

I don't know why I never threw the book out after she died. Maybe I was worried about the power within the pages—what it would do to me if I tried to destroy it. Or maybe I wanted to show that, despite its existence, I could stop believing… just like my mother. And just like Grandma Anita, until Big Queenie saved her.

I thought Blythe would leave after a few days, but nearly a week later, she's still in L.A.

And Webb doesn't seem to be tired of her. I can easily track where they are by going online. I hadn't noticed her in his pictures while he was traveling because they were always in groups. But now that she's here, they're both posting new pictures every day: selfies of them hanging at the abandoned zoo in Griffith Park, riding the Ferris wheel on the Santa Monica Pier, eating burgers at the Apple Pan.

Once, he texts just as Nia and I are getting ready to head to Grandma Anita's. I ask if he wants to come with us. He says he can't, but that he's going to get over there soon. I wonder if he'll bring Blythe.

"You need to get your shit together," Nia says, looking over at me from the driver's seat. "You look like somebody died. She's just a girl…they'll probably break up soon."

"You haven't seen them together. They're nowhere near breaking up." I look down at my hands. "She says things like, 'I love this guy!' in the picture captions."

"Does she write out love or use a heart?"

"L-O-V-E. I think it might be the real thing, Nia."

"It's puppy love. Nothing serious."

I finally agree to go to a party with Webb and Blythe,

thrown by some skaters they know from the road. They're a little older, college age, but the party doesn't seem much different from the ones I've been to, besides the better variety (and quality) of alcohol, and the fact that everyone seems to be wearing sponsored gear. It's a Sunday night, but my parents are more lenient about me going out on school nights when Webb is home. And I wasn't completely truthful about where we were going.

I stick close to Webb and Blythe, observing them as they move through the crowd. Webb is popular with everyone, and again, it's strange contrasting his easy confidence with the way he carried himself after the rumor. He used to avoid looking everyone in the eye, and now people won't stop approaching him, wanting to chat.

"He's really great, huh?" Blythe says, following my gaze to Webb. He's across the room, talking to a guy with a shaved head and small black plugs in his earlobes.

I startle. I didn't hear her walk up.

"Yeah," I say after a moment. "He is."

I feel her eyes on me, and there's a pause before she speaks. "You two never went out?"

"No. Just best friends." I swallow hard. Can she see that I want more?

"He cares what you think." When I finally look over, her hazel eyes are serious. "A lot. So I hope we can be cool, Queenie. I'm sorry about what I said that first day. It was stupid, and I was trying to impress you with how much I knew about you and—"

"It's okay," I say quickly. "I know you didn't mean anything by it."

"You promise?"

"Promise." I hold up my beer, and a couple of seconds later she smiles, clinking the rim of her plastic cup against mine.

Later, I go out back to get some fresh air, trying to decide if I should call a car to go home or wait for Webb. When I came back from the bathroom, he was leaning over Blythe's shoulder, whispering in her ear, his arms wrapped loosely around her waist. I immediately walked outside, annoyed at having to see them together and then mad at myself for being annoyed.

The door opens, and when I turn around, Webb is standing there. "Here you are. Thought you might've left."

He joins me, sinking into the rickety wrought-iron chair next to mine. "Having fun?"

"It's okay." I shrug. "I don't know anyone besides you two."

"That's what I love about these things. It's not the same old people we've known since we were six."

"I guess."

"What's wrong, Your Highness?"

"Nothing." I gaze into the deep darkness of the backyard.

"Not true."

"I haven't seen you much since you've been back," I say, finally looking at him. "I know you have a girlfriend now and things are different, but…I missed you, too. And I wish…"

"What?"

I shake my head. I don't want to say it out loud because it feels whiny. But this is big, him having a serious girlfriend. And I can't stop wondering why he chose not to tell me until it was time to meet her.

He won't let it go. "You wish she wasn't here?" His voice is soft, but that doesn't make it any easier to digest his matter-of-fact words. He must know how I feel about him. Why else would he think that?

"I wish I'd known about her. Why didn't you tell me you had a girlfriend?"

"I don't know. Because…sometimes these things that start on the road don't work out. I wasn't sure she liked me enough to come visit." Webb cracks all the knuckles on one hand before he continues. "And…because I was afraid you'd be mad that I don't have as much time for you."

I look at him. There's something else he's not saying. Grandma Anita says Webb is too stupid to see how I feel about him, but I'm not so sure that's true anymore. I feel it in the air, and he's not saying it.

Because I know you have feelings for me and I didn't want to hurt you.

And that he won't say it, that he's not being completely honest with me—it makes tears come to my eyes. I turn my head so he won't see them, but it's too late.

"Whoa, whoa, hey." He touches my knee, and when I don't face him he gets out of his chair and crouches in front of me. "Queenie, come on. You know you're my number one person."

I nod, even though hearing him say it doesn't make me feel any better. It doesn't change the fact that our feelings for each other are uneven.

"I don't know what I'd do without you," he says.

Webb slides his thumb across my wet face, and I turn my head to look at him. He leans forward at the same time to kiss my cheek. Then his lips brush against mine by accident and everything stops.

We look at each other for what seems like hours, our lips so close I can feel his breath. He swallows hard, and I expect him to retreat, to apologize and run inside so he can be with

Blythe. But he takes my face in his hands and he kisses me. *Really* kisses me.

Webb's lips are soft and his mouth is warm and he tastes like beer. I close my eyes and kiss him back. *Really* kiss him: leaning forward to be as close as I can without making him topple over backward, running my hands slowly up and down the muscles of his back. I knew I liked Webb, but I'm not sure I realized how much until this moment. And now that the moment is here, I don't want it to end.

But he snaps out of it, pulling away and backing up a few feet on his bent legs before he stands up straight. He runs a hand over the top of his Afro, shaking his head. "Shit. Queenie, I—shit. I'm sorry. I gotta—"

And then he does go inside. He doesn't run. He stumbles, really, leaving his beer next to the empty chair.

I sit by myself for a while, gently touching my fingers to my lips. For a moment, Webb was mine. And it was strange and wonderful and wrong all at once.

The kiss is all I think about the next day. I'm barely present at breakfast, at school, and on the ride to and from there with Nia.

I keep going over what happened, replaying the moment from every possible angle. It's obvious he didn't plan the kiss, but had he wondered for a while what it would be like? Or did it just hit him while we were sitting there, so close and alone for the first time since Blythe arrived? Will this change things with them? And if it does, what does that mean for us?

My phone rings just as Nia pulls onto our street. I smile when I look down and see Webb's name. He rarely calls, so what happened must have meant something to him. I don't want to be the reason he breaks things off with Blythe, but I can't help hoping the kiss made him look at me the same way I've been looking at him for a while now. I hope he can't stop thinking about it, too. About me.

"Hey," I say in a voice that makes Nia raise an eyebrow. "How's it going?"

"Queenie."

Normally I love hearing him say my name, but there's something off about it this time. He's breathing heavily, like he's close to hyperventilating, and there's something I don't normally hear in his voice: panic.

"Webb? What's wrong?"

"It's Blythe."

Oh. Shit. She found out about the kiss and broke up with him. And now he's mad at me.

"I'm sorry," I say. "If you need me to talk to her—"

"Queenie, she's hurt."

"What?"

Nia pulls into our driveway and stops the car, staring at me.

"We were over at the skate park in Venice, and these fuckers were talking shit to her, telling her she should get out of there because it's for real skaters. And she can usually handle that shit, but then they dared her to do a trick and she never should've tried it—it's too hard for, like, a lot of pros—but they just kept fucking with her, and she wanted to prove herself and—"

"Where is she now?"

"In an ambulance." His voice shakes.

"Where are you?"

"Standing on some street in Venice…near the beach. We took the train down here. I don't— Queenie, I need you."

I've never heard Webb sound so scared in his life. Not

even when he broke his leg attempting a complicated trick of his own.

"I'll come get you," I say, looking at Nia. "I'll be there as soon as I can."

We pick up Webb and drive to the hospital, and I tell Nia she can leave because none of this has anything to do with her. But as much as we annoy each other at times, Nia is a good sister. She tells me to go in with Webb while she parks the car.

Webb is beside himself. He can't sit still, and on the ride over, he kept asking if Nia could drive any faster. At the front desk, we find out that Blythe is in critical condition and we can't see her. Webb nearly crumbles.

I lead him to a couple of empty chairs. He plops down with a hard thunk, as if someone else is controlling his body. I perch on the edge of my seat and wrap my arms around him, but he shrugs me off. As if he doesn't know me at all.

I sit back and try to swallow down the hurt. This isn't about me or us right now.

"Have you called her family?" I ask.

He nods. "When the ambulance came. It's just her mom. She's on her way."

"I'm sorry, Webb. I wish there was something I could do." I hate feeling so helpless.

He stares straight ahead at nothing for a while. Then he turns to me, eyes wide. "There is something, Queenie."

I understand right away, and my head starts shaking. "I can't."

"What about Big Queenie?"

"She's in Europe."

"Then it has to be you." He moves so close to me, his knees

dig into the side of my leg. "That's what you guys do, right? You're healers?"

"We don't *do* anything. Big Queenie is the only one who can..." But even as I say it, I wonder if it's true. I've never tried to heal anyone before. I've never used my magic for anything good—only on Becca, and I stopped after that.

"Queenie, please. If there's ever anything you could do for me—" His breath catches and he stops, staring down at his lap. When he looks at me again, his eyes are glassy with tears. "Please...can't you try?"

I don't know what time it is where Big Queenie is, so I let out a breath of relief when she picks up after a couple of rings.

"Big Queenie?"

"Little Queenie?" She's the only one who calls me that, and I don't mind. I am named for her, after all.

"Where are you?"

"I'm in Milan." She sounds tired. "And it's very early in the morning... Is Mama okay?"

"She's fine. I'm calling because..." I glance at the guy standing a few feet away from the hospital doors. He looks like he's waiting for a ride. I move away a bit. "I need your help. Webb's friend—*girlfriend*—is in trouble. She had a skateboarding accident, and now she's in the ICU and he's really scared."

"Okay, slow down." Her warm voice is soothing. "Take a deep breath, then tell me again—everything you know about her and the situation."

I tell her we don't know exactly what happened yet since the doctors won't give details to anyone who's not family, but that Webb overheard the EMTs saying she had a head injury and there was the possibility of internal bleeding. I tell her Webb said that, for a few moments, he wondered if she was dead.

When I finish, Big Queenie pauses for so long I wonder if she's still there. But then she starts moving around, shuffling things in the background, and I think maybe she's looking for a spell.

"This is the first time you've tried to use your powers since—"

"Yes." I swallow. "Since Becca."

"Okay, sweetie. First things first: Do you believe you have powers?"

I look around, as if her voice is being amplified by a speakerphone. "Yes," I whisper.

"What was that?"

"Yes," I say, louder.

"You have to. If you don't believe in it yourself, Queenie, your intentions will be fruitless."

I forgot that Big Queenie talks like a spiritual guide, but I don't even care. I just want to do what I can to help Webb.

I was there when Big Queenie used her powers on Grandma Anita. There were no crystals, no chants. But there was a current that ran through the air, an energy that I felt, too, as much as I didn't want to admit it. My aunt was calm and completely focused on Grandma Anita, her eyes closed and her slender brown fingers hovering over my grandmother's body. She didn't say a word, but her hands moved over different parts of Grandma Anita, spending a long time in the places where the cancer had spread.

Besides my grandmother I don't personally know anyone she's healed. Big Queenie lives up in Oregon when she's not traveling. But sometimes we video chat, and in the background I can see the cards and letters she gets from people who are thankful for her services. That has to be proof that she's good at what she does.

Big Queenie tells me about different chants and spells, and says that if I want to try crystals I can go to her friend Kiera, who lives in the Valley and whom Big Queenie trusts wholeheartedly.

"I have to tell you," my aunt says, "I've tried it all, and what works best for me is focusing all my energy on the task. Letting go of the negative and distracting forces in my mind. Clearing out the noise. Focus, focus, focus. Truly believe in the energy you're putting out there."

"I put the wrong energy into Becca," I almost whisper.

"Oh, sweetie. Do you know how many kids play with spells and Ouija boards and all of that? As soon as your mama told me you'd found the book, I should have talked to you."

"It's not your fault, Big Queenie."

"And it's not yours, either. I don't want you to keep blaming yourself for something that you didn't understand."

I feel a little better when I hang up, but not so confident that I can harness the powers Big Queenie is so sure that I have. I wasn't lying to her—part of me believes they exist, but I don't know if I'm strong enough to make them work the way I want them to.

My stomach twists into a knot when I look up at the looming brick hospital. The last time I was in one, I was visiting Grandma Anita. But I can't help thinking about Becca being taken to the hospital, too. A couple of days after I cast the spell, she stayed home from school. Webb and I marveled at the fact that it had worked, imagining Becca weak from a stomach bug or the flu. It turns out she had pneumonia that never cleared up.

Nia and I wait with Webb until Blythe's mother whirls into

the hospital: a tall black woman with bloodshot eyes and her daughter's high cheekbones. It will be a while before Blythe can have visitors besides family, which means there's no way I can try to help now. Webb says his mom is on the way and that we should leave—he'll call me when he knows something.

"Queenie?" He touches my wrist as I stand.

I look down into his tired, confused eyes. "Are you sure you don't want me to stay?"

"I'm fine. But—what I said earlier...?"

"I don't know, Webb. I— Call me when she can have visitors, okay?"

I barely sleep at all that night, keeping my fully charged phone on the pillow next to me.

In the morning, Mom takes one look at my face and lets me stay home from school. I fall asleep for a couple of hours after everyone else leaves for the day, but I jump out of bed when my phone rings and answer without looking at the screen.

"Webb?"

"She's in critical but stable condition. Visiting hours start in a bit." His voice is shaky but hopeful. "Are you at school?"

"I stayed home."

When I don't say anything else, he clears his throat. "Can you come down here, Queenie?"

"Won't her mom wonder why I want to visit? I barely know her."

"I'll figure it out. Just get here. Please?"

I go. Webb has told Blythe's mom that I became close with her daughter while she's been in L.A. I don't know if her mother believes it, but I'm allowed to go in and visit Blythe—for just a few minutes, declares the strict nurse who leads me down the hall.

The room reminds me of Grandma Anita's, with beeping machines and thick electrical cords and blinking lights everywhere. I close my eyes for a second, reminding myself that this isn't Grandma Anita. It isn't Becca, either. I wish my heart would stop racing; it's pounding so hard it feels like it's going to fly right out of my ribs.

Blythe is lying motionless in the big hospital bed. I stop when I get closer. Webb said she had a head injury, but they aren't sure how severe. She's unconscious. Her head is bandaged on one side, and her right arm and leg are in casts. There's a tube in her nose. I can't believe this is the same girl who was just drinking beers with me and posting endless pictures of her and Webb exploring Los Angeles.

I walk tentatively toward her, holding my breath. I wonder if I should have gotten the crystals from Big Queenie's friend or written down the spells she mentioned, but she didn't seem convinced they would help. She made it sound like everything Blythe needs is already in me.

"Hi, Blythe," I whisper, even though she can't respond. "It's me, Queenie."

My hands are sweaty; I wipe them on my jeans. Then I crack my knuckles. I look at the clock. The nurse will be back any minute. I have to start now if I'm going to do this.

I get as close to the bed as I can. I close my eyes like Big Queenie did, and hold my hands above Blythe. I start at her head, searching for the same energy that my aunt conjured, trying my best to focus only on the task. But my hands are shaking. All I can think of is Becca and how she never left the hospital. How she was in a room just like this because of me.

I feel stupid standing like this, but I let my shoulders relax and my hands hover closer. And I feel something. It's not strong, but it's there. An invisible spark that keeps flickering in and out of the air, like a lantern that won't quite click on.

I move my hands to her head, letting the energy guide me. It's still flickering, but it never disappears. It gets stronger as my hands move above the bandaged spot. I hold my breath because I *feel* something. If I can just hang on to this, maybe I can help her. Webb would be so happy. He would understand how much I care for him and—

The spark dies. My hands go cold, and that feeling—that energy—leaves me. I'm back in the present with the beeping machines and a motionless Blythe.

Shit.

I try again, but it doesn't come back. I lost it. And I can't help wondering if maybe I'm a failure when it comes to using my powers for good.

Webb is pacing in the hallway. His eyes widen when he sees me.

I shake my head. "I don't know if I can do this."

"Come on, Queenie—"

"It's not some moral conundrum," I say. "I don't know if I can *actually* do it. I couldn't focus. I kept thinking of Becca and—" I stop because I don't want to say that thinking of him distracted me, too.

"Becca had congenital heart disease—that's why she died from pneumonia. Her body was already weak." Webb puts his hands on my shoulders. "You didn't kill her, Queenie. Even if the spell worked…you didn't know she was born with that. You didn't give her heart disease."

"You really think so?"

"I know so. And I've told you that before," he says.

He has. Maybe I'm just desperate, but for the first time, I think maybe he could be right. If I didn't have the power to heal Blythe, why would I have the power to inflict harm on someone?

"I should go," I say, my throat stinging. "I'll try again tomorrow."

Webb comes over after dinner.

He doesn't call, and I'm pretending to do homework with Nia when the doorbell rings. I don't look up from my world history book, and Nia silently gets up to see who it is.

She comes back with Webb in tow. He opens and closes his mouth a couple of times, and everything pauses as I wonder if he's going to tell me that Blythe died.

"Everything okay?"

"Yeah," he says. "It's...the same. I just— My parents are treating me like I'm five, and I need a break from the hospital, but I don't want to be alone."

"We have some food left over from dinner."

"That'd be good," he says. "Hospital food is shit."

I start to heat up the leftover pork chops and roasted vegetables, but he takes the plate from me and says he'll eat it cold. I sit across the table while he wolfs it down. If I've barely slept, Webb hasn't closed his eyes in days. They are so tired, the whites of them so crisscrossed with red, that I wonder if he'll fall asleep here at the table. He scarfs down the rest of the leftovers, but he still looks hungry, so he polishes off a big bowl of ice cream, too.

"I'm so tired, Queenie," he says in a low voice. "I'm so, so tired."

"You can sleep in the guest room. There are fresh sheets."

"I don't want to be alone," he repeats.

"Okay." And I want so much to be able to turn off my feelings for him. But I can't help wishing that he was asking to stay in my room because he wanted to continue what we started at that party and not because he's scared about Blythe.

Webb kicks off his shoes and immediately crawls into my bed. I start to ask if he needs anything, but before I can speak, he's already snoring. I finish my homework beside him. I look at his chest rising and falling, at his curly eyelashes pressed to the tops of his cheeks. I smooth a hand over the side of his neck. He doesn't stir and I pull back my hand. I don't let myself look at him again.

In the morning I wake to find him bent over, tying his shoes on the other side of the bed.

"Are you going to the hospital?"

"Stopping by home first," he says. "I gotta shower."

I sit up, pulling the covers to my chest. "I can come by later."

"Okay," he says. But he doesn't sound like he thinks it will make a difference.

He's almost to my door when I speak again.

"Why did you kiss me?"

His shoulders drop. "Queenie..."

"You're my best friend. I deserve to know."

He turns around, not quite facing me. He looks at my window, but the blinds are still drawn tight, shutting out the sun.

"I guess I got caught up in the moment." His voice softens. "We were drinking and—part of me has always wondered what it would be like, you know? You and me."

I inhale deeply, waiting for him to go on.

"That kiss was...it was great," he continues. "But it was wrong. I—I love Blythe. I know it hasn't been that long, but I do. And that was selfish, to kiss you. I love you, too, but just as friends. I'm sorry, Queenie."

The silence is awful. It's not often I don't know what to

say to Webb, but this is one of those times. We both stay frozen until I let out a long, audible breath. I'm not surprised by what he said. I just wish I didn't have to hear it.

"I'll be by after school," I finally say.

He nods and leaves my room without another word.

Webb looks even worse when I get to the hospital.

He's losing hope, and him not having total faith in me makes me doubt myself. What if I can't save Blythe? The thought of letting him down makes me want to walk away. But I know I'd be mad at myself forever if I didn't try to help Webb.

Blythe is still unmoving in the room full of machines, and it still makes me uncomfortable, but I feel more clearheaded than the last time. As quickly as I think of Becca and Webb, they disappear from my mind. This is about trying to do some good with what I've been given. Because as much as I want to will away my powers, I don't think they're going anywhere.

Focus, focus, focus, Big Queenie said.

I breathe in all the air I can, imagining the calm of Big Queenie and her healing hands.

"Hi, Blythe," I say in a strong, clear voice as I approach her. "I'm sorry about what happened. You didn't deserve any of this." I pause. "So, I'm here because—what Webb told you is true. My family…we're healers. *I'm* a healer and…"

I want to round out the sentence with something meaningful or poetic, like Big Queenie would, but there's nothing else to say.

It's time to *do.*

I close my eyes. My mind is clear: of regret for the past and disappointment in the present and concern about the future. There is no negative energy in me or in this room. Just hope—and more belief in the power within me than I've ever had.

I hold out my hands over her head, and the spark appears instantly. But this time, it stays. Strong and steady and growing. I feel the current in the air, unimpeded by my doubts. I put all my faith, all my energy into healing Blythe.

Not for her fans or her mother and not even for Webb.

I do it for me, because if I don't accept all the parts of myself, how can I be who I really am? I've spent all this time worrying about the damage I may have caused instead of focusing on the good I could do.

The current spreads as I move my hands, and I feel it inside me, too. It feels right, what I'm doing.

Under my hands, Blythe stirs.

★ ★ ★ ★ ★

THE MOONAPPLE MENAGERIE

by Shveta Thakrar

...[W]alk among long dappled grass,
And pluck till time and times are done,
The silver apples of the moon,
The golden apples of the sun.

—"The Song of Wandering Aengus,"
William Butler Yeats

STIRRED BY AN ENCHANTED BREEZE, A RING OF trees laden with autumnal fruit shivered and began to rain down their fey bounty: apples with skin the rich gold of afternoon sunshine, apples with skin silver as the moon's brightest face. But rather than plummet to the earth, these apples soared through the air and departed the clearing, shining heralds of the Moonapple Menagerie's latest production.

Though she had watched Sabrina cast this spell four times now, ever since their coven had formed as many summers ago, Shalini still loved it. Only those adventurous enough to eat the edible invitations—the dreamers, the poets and artists, those bored and searching for something more—would get the details of the upcoming performance. With one exception, their little coven never knew who it would be. "Works better than any flyer."

"I still want to eat one," Sabrina told Shalini and Gabrielle as the three of them settled over the grassy hill in their animal forms—Sabrina a barn owl, Gabrielle a fluffy fox, and Shalini a gleaming green-black serpent—and gazed up at the vividly painted open-air stage. "Or maybe five. I bet they taste like fairy tales."

"I almost did," Gabrielle confessed, the orange-red of her soft pelt the same color as her flowing hair in human form. "I was really hungry, and my sandwich looked boring, so I was *this close* to eating a golden one." Sabrina swatted at her vulpine nose, and Gabrielle yelped. "But I didn't! Why do I need an invitation to my own party?"

Madhu rolled up on her red mobility scooter, which she'd decorated with stickers and rhinestones. Even the crutches nestled in the back had been woven through with bits of feather boas. Madhu herself wore shimmering silk salwar kameez in all the shades of her peacock aspect, along with a matching feather crown that set off the medium brown of her skin. "I finished our costume designs! Just wait until you see."

"You guys, you guys!" Bianca came scampering down the hill, layers of black frilly skirts and ornate necklaces flying behind her. With her purple-tipped hair and rainbow highlighter on her pale cheeks, she looked like her animal aspect should be a unicorn rather than the black cat it actually was. "The emotion's going to be amazing! Wait until we're fighting the mermaids. It'll feel like it's really happening."

"You did it!" Shalini bared her fangs in a grin. Normally they staged classical dramas from around the world, with spells going back generations through each of their family lines, the formulas preserved in bottles and books. But this year, the coven was trying something new. Shalini had written an original play, which meant they had to make everything up from raw magic.

"The spells are in my rings, ready to go, just like Gabrielle's." Bianca held up a hand to display the poison rings that contained spells like smoke, waiting to be dispersed.

Sabrina fluttered over to Bianca's shoulder, then used a wing to pat Bianca's head. "I knew you'd figure it out."

Bianca gestured in the direction of the bone palace not far from the Moonapple Menagerie, where a yakshini and her sisterhood of strange creatures dwelled. "Do you think she ever eats the apple?"

Each summer the coven sent one invitation to the bone palace in thanks for the yakshini allowing them to host their theater in her woods, and each summer the mysterious nature spirit failed to respond.

Shalini pressed her lips together. Everyone in the coven had seen the bone palace and marveled at the grace of its whorls and scalloped arches, but only she had ventured into the foyer. Only she knew for certain that the previous years' apples sat untouched on a marble table. "She probably has better things to do."

She did wonder, though, what a yakshini could possibly do with her evenings that made even the prospect of luminous fruit and outdoor musicals seem dull in comparison. Maybe their next play could be about that—if Shalini could get this one right first.

"Costume time!" Madhu waited for everyone to take human shape, then cast a light cantrip and tossed a handful of flower petals into the air. The petals transformed into illusions of fine gowns that settled firmly over the other girls, so Madhu could measure and adjust and snip as necessary before spell-sewing the real garments into being. "Shoes and jewelry are coming as soon as I get these altered," she promised, a virtual pin already in her mouth.

But even Madhu's gorgeous new designs couldn't distract Shalini from the fact that the play wasn't finished. Her coven sisters trusted her enough to go ahead and announce production. They believed she would come up with the perfect ending before opening night, just a week away. For now, they had been rehearsing with a placeholder conclusion.

While everyone else gushed in delight over Madhu's creations, Shalini fretted. Her friends were counting on her, but her creative well felt as dry and stale as week-old cake. What if they were wrong? What if she *couldn't* do it?

Shalini wished there was a spell for silencing the doubts in her head. Some things, though, you had to do without your sisters.

That was why she would never tell them she'd petitioned the bone palace for help.

That night, Shalini rested on the edge of the stage, bathed in the soft silver-white glow of the full moon. Legend held it wasn't the same moon as outside the woods, but one hung by a human woman and the yakshini of the bone palace. The human had mosaicked the moon together from wishes ungranted, dreams unspoken, and milky moonstones, and in return, the yakshini had welcomed the woman into her strange sisterhood.

Was it true? Shalini couldn't say. Still, she loved the idea of it, and she often drank up the moon's intoxicating radiance, stirring it into her thoughts and letting it illuminate her heart. The storytelling spell worked with any light, but there was something special about the softness of moonbeams.

Shalini hoped, her hope fierce and bright, that the moon would light her way now. She turned and let her eyes skim over the blue-and-green theater walls. Gabrielle had been so proud when she'd finished painting the gold and silver apples and the winding yellow ribbon inscribed with the last four lines of the Yeats poem that gave the Moonapple Menagerie its name. Together, the coven had put on three successful performances here. Her play would be the fourth—Shalini would make sure of it.

After chanting a quick mantra to the goddess Sarasvati, divine patroness of the arts, she opened her jewel-encrusted journal to a blank page.

Shalini's play was about a group of intrepid explorers on a quest. They would travel through the ocean, an ice dragon's crystal cave, and the night sky to return a bracelet of shining stars that had fallen from the heavens. They would battle mermaids and makaras and nagas and sea witches, sometimes through fighting, but mostly through clever wrangling of words and wit. It had promise.

But what Shalini didn't know, and what she'd been hoping to discover before anyone else realized she didn't know, was the heart of this story. Why did it matter if these explorers got the starry bracelet back to the apsara who'd lost it? What was at stake? To find the ending, she had to figure that out first.

When she wrote, Shalini reached deep into the fertile field of her imagination, digging until she found the roots of her story, then grafting branches grown from many different seeds onto the plant—and sometimes undoing the grafts—and finally pruning until she reached the desired shape. Sometimes everything fell into place, and inspiration surged, effortless, from her brain to the pen, producing a faerie tree like a sunset, with leaves in pinks and purples and oranges and reds. Those times felt like soaring through the cosmos on wings that would never tire. Other times, all that work resulted in a misshapen, rotting mess only good for firewood, and she couldn't grab the lighter fluid soon enough.

This play was fast veering into firewood territory.

The rest of the coven had already gone home. She should be having dinner with her family, too, eating the masala khichdi her dad had made. Yet how could she worry about eating when she had to fix this?

Her coven was the best thing she'd ever had. Her throat ached at the thought of losing it.

The others were all so sure of themselves, so comfortable in their roles. Sure, they groused sometimes about the work being hard, but they did it. As set designer and stage manager, Gabrielle knew how to translate the vision in her head into beguiling backdrops that drew in even the most jaded of viewers. Madhu combined fabrics and gemstones in ways that made magic tangible; she even sold some of her outfits to a local consignment shop. Sabrina, a self-proclaimed karaoke junkie, channeled her love of music into songs that made the listener sob and snicker all at once. As director, Bianca gathered and guided these various bits and pieces into a cohesive production that still managed to feel as fey, as unrestrained, as a patch of sky-blue roses from a folktale.

And then there was Shalini. What did she do besides try to make up stories? In fact, until this year, she hadn't even done *that* much. The others had encouraged her while she honed her craft, insisting that being able to create stories was magical, and she would get there soon enough. She had to justify their faith in her.

Now she cast her spell. The moonlight should be plucking the words from her mind and writing them on the page. But if she didn't know what was supposed to happen, the spell certainly didn't.

The empty page taunted her. *Impostor. Phony. They'll throw you out when they see what a fake you are.*

She slammed the book shut.

Crunch.

Shalini's head jerked up to see a churel a few feet away, gleefully taking a second bite of a silver apple. Her heart didn't just skip a beat; it nearly did a handspring right out of her chest. The churel was emaciated, with a hideous, piglike face; long, sagging breasts; tangled gray hair that screamed for a pair of scissors and a sharp comb; and backward-facing hands and feet. This last in no way interfered with her noisy enjoyment of the fruit.

"So this is the Moonapple Menagerie, hmm?" the churel observed between smacks. "It's charming enough, I suppose. In any case, it will do."

Shalini had never seen a churel in real life, but knew they were created when a woman died at the hands of her in-laws and hungered for revenge on the men in her former family. Did the churel think Shalini was part of that family? "What will do?"

The churel shot her a look of disdain. "You requested help. I am here to help you."

"You're from the bone palace?" Even though desperation had driven Shalini to the door of the yakshini's abode, she hesitated now; asking for aid felt too much like cheating. It was what someone would do when they couldn't make their own words, and she didn't want anyone else's words.

"You're a quick one, I see." The churel shoved a pearl into Shalini's hand. "This amulet will let you reach forward in time and locate the ending your future self will write."

Shalini broke into a delighted smile as she considered the pearl. To take her own words from the future—well, that was as far from having someone or something else write her ending as she could get. All she'd let herself picture was an extra dose of inspiration, but this was even better. Her own words with the struggle to find them already behind her…

"Oh, tell the yakshini I can't thank her enough! We'd love to finally see her this year."

With her fingers curled around the pearl, Shalini could already see herself leaping past the remaining days of mental thrashing and flailing to the moment when she wrote "The End" and meant it. She joined hands and minds with her future self, and her own precious words began to appear in her thoughts—

The churel snatched the pearl away, scratching Shalini in the process with her thick, yellowed fingernails. "We haven't settled on the price."

Shalini gaped muzzily at her, dazed with loss. The words had been right there. Right there!

"You will put me in your production—in a role of my choosing. This is hardly the theater I would have selected for my dramatic debut, but one must work with what she's given."

Shalini replayed the churel's words. She wanted *what*?

"As I said, I must approve my role in your production. There are distinctions your kind would never grasp about mine." The churel's unnaturally long black tongue skimmed her lips as she reached for Shalini's book. "Let me see that."

Shalini tried not to look as horrified as she felt. "Okay, wires must have gotten crossed somewhere, and I'm really sorry about the mix-up, but we don't have a role for you." Her finger trembling, she pointed to the delicate loops of moonlight calligraphy from prior spell castings. "The play's al— It's already written."

The churel stared at her with red-burning eyes. "If that

were true, I would not be here now." She scoffed. "Where was this dithering when you were tearfully pleading with anyone who might listen? Are you fool enough to believe such aid comes for free?"

"Why do you even want this?" Shalini asked. The churel had to see how absurd it was.

"The speck of slime masquerading as my husband kept me from my calling while I lived." The churel's smile was the stuff of a horror novel. "But now *you* will fix that."

Shalini didn't dare grimace at the churel—for who was to say whether her wrath was limited to her family?—so instead she scowled at the moon. This was *not* the inspiration she'd asked for.

"Come back tomorrow during the day," she said at last, not knowing what else to do. "We make our decisions as a group."

"And why would I do such a thing? If my offer fails to interest you, I certainly have better ways to spend my time." The churel pivoted on her toes, leaving Shalini clutching her useless journal. She'd come so close... Future Shalini had written exactly the right words, and now Present Shalini was about to lose them forever.

The coven would kill her. But at least this way, the play would be done.

"Fine!" she called after the creature, hating herself. "You can be in our play. Just...just give me that pearl."

"Surely. Tomorrow," the churel said, then lurched away before Shalini could protest.

No one had slept well. Shalini dreaded confessing the bargain she had made, Sabrina had come down with yet another migraine, and Gabrielle and Madhu had both had nightmares.

Even Bianca seemed out of sorts. "Blame the full moon," she said, rubbing her eye and smudging her kohl liner.

Oh, I do, thought Shalini. The dew-studded beauty of the morning felt like an affront as she guzzled a steaming mug of tea. She'd lain awake fantasizing about the pearl, and by the time dawn had painted the sky pink, she'd convinced herself the churel wouldn't come back. Her demand had been a whim. She was probably already off chasing down the men who'd wronged her, and Shalini would never see the pearl again. She would never be able to mine the genius words of her future self.

But just in case, she decided to test the waters and share her "dream" with her coven sisters.

"Is anyone else thinking what I'm thinking?" Sabrina asked, once Shalini was through. "That this is like our own weird little version of *Snow White*? We're the wicked stepmother who sent out the poisoned apple—"

Madhu toyed with one of her red-and-purple kundan earrings. "Wait, doesn't that make us the bad guys? I'm not sure I like where this is going."

"Our apples aren't poisoned, though," Bianca pointed out, "and there's no magic mirror on the wall."

Gabrielle nodded. "Aren't we more like the helpful dwarves, if anything?"

"And the only thing that needs to be rescued is the play," said Sabrina. "Okay, so it doesn't map exactly onto the original. Call it a really twisted retelling, where the tired tropes of good and evil get subverted in super disturbing ways."

"Oh, absolutely," said Bianca. "Shalu's writer brain is clearly using the language of fairy tales to work out her fears."

Gabrielle smoothed down her long white dress and lay back on the grass. "But if you think about it, it's weird the yakshini *hasn't* sent someone to check us out. I mean, it's not like we don't invite her every year."

Shalini very carefully kept her eyes lowered and her face still.

Bianca reached over to pat her shoulder. "Dreams don't mean anything. You'll figure out the ending."

Guilt churned and churned in Shalini's stomach. If the churel didn't return, she would have to admit to her friends that she'd failed to finish the play, that even now—less than a week before opening night—she had no clue how it ended. If the churel did reappear, Shalini would have to admit that she'd sold them out. Which was worse?

She smiled weakly. "Just a stupid dream."

At exactly quarter to eleven, the churel appeared—wreathed in, of all things, foxgloves—the same flowers already arranged in a crown on Gabrielle's head. The freckled magenta blossoms looked absurdly out of place woven into the churel's scraggly locks, but she didn't seem to mind. "Boo," she said, making everyone jump.

Just like that, the "dream" became a nightmare. "Um, so, everyone, guess what? It wasn't actually a dream, and I did say she could be in the play if she gave me the pearl," Shalini blurted. "And look, here she is!"

"You did *what*?" Sabrina demanded. The others just stared at her, eyes and mouths round. Shalini cringed.

"Shalu..." Madhu pursed her hot-pink lips.

"I've read your script, and I will play the apsara," the churel announced, blithe as a butterfly.

"You stole my book!" Shalini cried. The journal she'd been holding when the churel walked away the night before was now in the churel's clawed hand.

"I would hardly choose my role sight unseen!" The churel's eyes flashed the color of sacrificial blood, and Shalini recoiled. What had she done, entering into a bargain with this treacherous creature?

Trailing gray and green skirts and filmy sleeves, Bianca made her way to Shalini's side and took her arm. "Could you excuse us for a minute?"

"If I must, but do not dally." The churel casually bared her rotting teeth and mimed shredding flesh with her terrible claws. Shalini wanted to crawl right into her serpent skin and disappear into the grass for good.

Once out of the churel's earshot, the coven exchanged a five-way glance of alarm.

"Shalini, what were you thinking?" It was a good thing Sabrina wasn't in owl form, because her voice suggested she would have gone straight for Shalini with her talons. "We can't put her in our play!"

Madhu's brow crinkled. "I just got you all fitted. Now I have to outfit a demon, too?"

Too miserable to answer, Shalini only listened, her shoulders slumped. No one met her gaze. They were going to throw her out; she knew it.

"I think we need to give her the part," Bianca argued. "Or at least *a* part. Nobody wants this, but wouldn't it be much better to have her on our side? Or at least not against us?"

"Bianca's right," Gabrielle put in. "I'm not happy about it, but we're stuck. That creature's not going to take no for an answer."

"This sucks, and I'm sorry," Shalini said. "But you don't understand. I was never going to finish the play. Now, thanks to this pearl, I will, and it'll be all right. It'll be better than all right; it'll be *good*."

Bianca looked over then, her mouth turned down with disappointment, her gaze heavy and sad. "Why didn't you trust us? You should have told us."

"Yeah." Sabrina's eyes narrowed, and she folded her arms across her burgundy velvet blazer. "You really should have."

"We're a team. It's our play, too, and you didn't even ask what we thought," Madhu said, worrying a rhinestone on her scooter. "What if she ruins everything? What if she hurts us? How could you do that?"

"I'm sorry," Shalini repeated, but no one answered. Hot, desperate tears formed in her eyes, and she forced them down. Where was the magic spell to fix *this*?

The others shared a meaningful stare. Then Bianca led the coven back to where the churel waited. "Have you settled your foolishness amongst yourselves?" the churel asked.

"We discussed it, and we're not sure you fit the part," Gabrielle said, obviously trying to sound diplomatic. "But there are plenty of other roles you'd be great for."

"I could see you as a sea witch," Sabrina added. "You've got the hair for it."

"Nonsense," said the churel. "I come with my own cosmetics." As they watched, she turned into an apsara, her splendor so great it mesmerized: thick, glossy black hair; wide, seductive brown eyes; a willowy hourglass figure draped in yellow silk; and an ornate gold coronet. "The role is mine."

A bracelet of twinkling stars tumbled down from the heavens to land at the churel's newly delicate and forward-facing feet. The bracelet from Shalini's play. Great—now she was even usurping Gabrielle's role as stage manager.

"Your story is acceptable, if a bit tame," continued the churel-turned-apsara, "but you must work on the dénouement. Where is the pathos? The pain? The murder?" Her white teeth shone like the bracelet on the grass. "What is a drama without blood?"

"Everyone's a critic," muttered Madhu.

The book reappeared in Shalini's grip, and she flipped it open. The churel had made arcane, illegible scratches on almost every page. Yet the longer Shalini squinted at them, the more she could decipher: *Unrealistic character motivation; no jewel thief would EVER behave like this. No, no, no—even an ice dragon must be complex. I snored through this entire scene. Cut!!!*

It wasn't enough that she was going to get kicked out of the coven. That horrid creature had *critiqued* her play, too!

The weight of everyone's eyes pressed down on Shalini like an anchor, keeping her submerged in her shame and guilt and unable to breathe. "How dare you? You think you can just barge in here and take over our play?" she shouted, no longer worried about offending the churel. "You can keep your stupid pearl! *And* your stupid bracelet. I'll write the ending on my own."

"Shalu, no!" Gabrielle and Bianca called together, but it was too late.

Shalini had already bent down and grabbed the bracelet. She moved to fling it at the churel, and everything dissolved into a sea of blues and greens.

The band of explorers, bearing the starry bracelet, embarked on a quest to restore it to its rightful owner. In the oceanic realm, they eluded wily sea witches and fled carnivorous mercreatures while singing naughty ballads astride the backs of seahorses. "You claim the poor young merprince only hungers for your love? On the shoreline he will eat you once you've taken him above! You think the sweet young mermaid simply wants to hold your hand? You may kiss her, you may court her; still she'll stab you on the sand!"

Eventually Gabrielle's poison rings clicked open, releasing tendrils of magic like smoke that altered the scenery. When the mist dispersed, the band found itself in the crystal cave, where they battled jewel thieves, outwitted gemstone queens, and answered riddle after riddle from a greedy ice dragon.

Icicles hung like melted prisms in the monster's lair where its hoary breath had frozen the ceiling. Their long points reflected the dragon's iridescent white scales as it lumbered back and forth. "What is blue as a flower, bright as a flame, and dark as a shadow, yet has no true color of its own?"

"The sky," said Gabrielle, weary at this seventh riddle.

"Fun as this has been, we really need to get going." Sabrina treated the dragon to a smile sharper even than the icicles, then pushed past its bulk into heaps of coins, ingots, crowns, and loose jewels. "Come on."

Shalini stumbled over a stray goblet and threw up her hands to catch herself. The dragon caught sight of the starry bracelet on her wrist. "Give that to me!" it shrieked, spraying the air with ice.

"I don't think so." Ignoring its chilling breath, Madhu poked the dragon with one of her crutches until it keened and shrank away.

Bianca's poison rings opened as the explorers sang a song of victory, and the scene changed.

The band now stood in a village shrouded in misery and darkness. To light their way, Sabrina unleashed a bottle of fireflies in pink and green and orange. A few even perched among her sable curls. Unfortunately, the villagers had been cursed to live forever in the gloom, and even the fireflies' gentle luminescence hurt their eyes—never mind the starry bracelet. Furious at the intrusion, the villagers dragged the protesting explorers to a prison cell beneath the earth, where their light would never shine on anyone again.

"Sir," said Bianca to the surly guard, "we understand we've trespassed and caused harm with our light, but could you at least tell us how the village became cursed in the first place?"

The guard merely grunted.

She tried again. "It sounds like a sad and terrible story, one that would hurt my heart."

"Hearts!" grumbled the guard. "It was hearts that led us here. We gave ours up, we did, to force that stingy ice dragon to hand over its treasure. But something went awry with the spell, and it plunged us into this everlasting night. A fine waste of our hearts!" He stomped out, locking the cell behind him.

Once he left, Bianca divulged her plan. "Okay," she said, "he's not going to help us, and we can't break out of here—but we *can* sneak out. It'll just have to be in disguise."

Shalini as a serpent and Gabrielle as a vixen dug a tunnel in the dirt that led into the open air, and the others followed them out as owl, peacock, and black cat. Singing a song of escape, they rushed into the night, but at the border of the village, beyond which sunlight spilled golden motes like music, Gabrielle paused.

"I know it's not our problem," she said, "but I still feel bad for them. Everyone deserves a second chance." And she set down a packet of light-tree seeds for the day the villagers might choose to reclaim their lost hearts.

The band of explorers, having resumed human form, hurried over a diamond bridge and into the night sky, where the apsara waited. Per the placeholder climax, she would shower them with gratitude, and the story would end.

Yet a successful quest with no real stakes, no real struggle, left the story hollow. And a hollow story, as Shalini knew, was no story at all. It was the threat of losing something vital that gave a good tale its substance—that made it *true*.

The apsara, draped in gold-and-sapphire silks, with sultry jasmine blossoms dotting her long braid, held out her hand for the bracelet. "You found it!"

The veil separating the churel's reality from theirs suddenly lifted, and there the coven stood, onstage on opening night. Gabrielle's expert lighting left them nowhere to hide. Beyond the lights, Shalini spotted an audience frozen in mid-gesture: Madhu's and Sabrina's boyfriends, Gabrielle's girlfriend, Bianca's sister, her own mother—and even the yakshini from the bone palace, next to a man whose face had contorted in terror.

Her stomach knotted in on itself. The churel was going to humiliate the coven sisters before everyone they cared about.

"Well," said the churel-turned-apsara, "I stand corrected. Your script was serviceable until now, even appealing in its way. But how will you end this story?"

The other explorers—Shalini's friends—stared at one another, clearly mystified.

"Tell me what you would do, child." The apsara's luscious face was ripe with malice. "Would you trade your friends for your deepest heart's desire?"

"I don't care about your pearl." Shalini glared. Now she did hurl the bracelet at the creature, who plucked it out of the air and pulled it over her wrist.

"It is not the pearl I mean, but the security you yearn for." The pearl appeared in Shalini's hand. "That, at least, you've earned."

Shalini eyed it warily. In its subtle glint, she saw the conclusion, what the audience would see: the apsara challenging her to choose between her friends and a glittering future. Shalini, of course, chose her friends. The end.

No, not the end. Her throat tightened. It felt pat. Too easy. Something was missing.

The apsara shaped her tapered fingers into lotus mudras, as if she truly were the celestial dancer she played. "Surely you must have noticed you scarcely gave yourself a role in your own play? How little you trust your friends or yourself, always certain they will cast you aside."

It was true. Madhu had subdued the dragon, Sabrina had led the way into the village, Bianca had devised their way out of the prison cell, and Gabrielle had been the one to offer hope. What had Shalini done but just tag along?

"That you wanted to be in the flow of creation is no bad thing. That you do not trust others to understand your personal battles—that is another story, if you would pardon my wordplay." The apsara chuckled, apparently amused by her own attempt at wit.

Shalini clutched the pearl in her fist and prayed for an ending that would erase this entire night. Her friends would never understand. *They* all deserved their places in the coven.

"You know, churel," said Gabrielle, coming up to stand beside Shalini, "I liked you. I mean, you showed up wearing foxgloves!" She gestured to her own foxglove flower crown. "But now you're tormenting our friend."

"I'm waiting for you to turn into a bat and fly out of here," Sabrina informed the apsara. Her dress of ink-and-ebony satin rustled as she advanced. "Anyone can be beautiful and put on makeup, but there's no concealer good enough to cover up an ugly heart."

"You think your friend so pure?" the apsara asked, her head tossed back in mirth. "Has she told you how she could not finish writing this script without my help? How she lacked the courage to tell you the truth?"

Bianca frowned, a distraught sylph in her dawn-rose silks and ivory lace. "She did tell us, actually. A little later than she should've, but she did."

"You could erase all this, child," the apsara purred at Shalini. "All you need to do is trade me these friends for the spell to grant your desire. They will not be harmed. You simply will not see them again. They need never know your shame."

Shalini made herself lift her head high and face her friends. The audience didn't matter. The churel didn't matter. Even the play didn't matter. Only they did. "I promised you I could finish the play in time. And you trusted me, and I blew it, and I'm so sorry." She swallowed hard, then added, "I failed you."

Bianca bit her lip, while Sabrina raised her brows, making the ring of crystals around her eye twinkle. Madhu toyed with one of the lavender-and-indigo roses growing out of her raspberry salwar kameez. Gabrielle turned away, so all Shalini could see of her was her fox-colored hair and the bell sleeves of her mauve velvet gown.

They were waiting for her to do something, but what?

"Yes," said the apsara. "*There* is the blood, the sacrifice, the pathos." She waggled her head, her long tresses spilling around her in a waterfall, her silky sari glistening, and her jewelry sparkling from ankle to earlobe.

Shalini looked at her coven sisters, who were murmuring together. But it was Madhu who addressed her. "You can still fix it, you know. It's not too late."

She fought to hide her grief. How? How was she supposed to fix this?

The apsara preened. "Are you ready to learn the spell to

remove self-doubt and erase this unfortunate incident? After all, you do not belong here, per your own belief."

It would hurt, knowing the coven would forget her, maybe even replace her, as soon as this spell was done. But Shalini couldn't leave the play unfinished, and she definitely couldn't embarrass her friends like this, right?

She studied their huddle, the way they had already shut her out. No. She'd done it to herself. She knew that. Her heart punched at her rib cage.

"You don't trust yourself to end the play properly, so what holds you back?" the apsara asked. Her voice mesmerized: all Shalini had to do was give up her coven for good, and the churel would fix everything. Truly, what other choice did she have?

The coven turned as one to hear her decision. All she saw in their faces was hurt. The same hurt in her heart.

At last, she realized what she needed to do. What her friends were waiting for her to do. It was high time to revise the story she'd been telling herself.

Shalini reached up and touched the crescent moon above them, the one that had been mosaicked together from unsaid wishes and dreams. "I do need to fix this. But not that way."

Pearl in hand, she reached into herself—past, present, and future—and cast the storytelling spell.

The audience unfroze, then vanished. Now the band of explorers stood once more in the nocturnal realm of shining stars and dangling moons, of astral palaces and moonlight lotuses, where the apsara rested on her throne. She reached for Shalini. "You will give me the bracelet, and I will take you all into my service. I've needed new attendants ever since some of mine burned out. Stars have an annoying tendency to do that."

Shalini glowered at her. "We came all the way here to bring you your bracelet, and this is how you thank us?"

"On the contrary; you should consider it an honor to serve me." The apsara extended her hand again. "Now give me my bracelet."

Shalini refused, and the apsara's serene expression cracked at the edges. "Give it to me. That's why you came here, is it not?"

"You can't control us without it, can you?" It was just a theory, but Shalini grinned when the apsara gasped. Then the apsara pounced, delicate as a panther, at Shalini, who slipped into her serpentine aspect. The bracelet clamped in her powerful jaws, she undulated over the dark ground to safety.

"The stars, I think they're in the bracelet!" she called around the mouthful.

Her companions also switched to their animal shapes, then crowded around her. Together, using teeth, talons, and claws, they severed the bracelet's cord. A handful of stars scattered and fell to the earth like smoldering pearls, while others, extinguished, returned to the sky to be rekindled.

The apsara wailed, but there was nothing she could do, and she knew it. "Get out of my sight," she hissed.

"Gladly," said Shalini.

And so the explorers, crooning one final song of completion, exited the starlit stage: a strut, a slither, a prowl, a flutter, and a pad down a grassy hill and into a ring of trees laden with apples with skin the rich gold of afternoon sunshine, apples with skin silver as the moon's brightest face.

The seawater curtains closed on the stage to ecstatic applause.

"I knew you'd come through." Bianca beamed. "We all did."

"But next time," Madhu said, "maybe trust us enough to tell us what's going on earlier, so we can help?"

Sabrina nodded. "And so we don't end up with churels hijacking our play?"

"I promise," Shalini said, and she hugged them all.

"You really thought we would kick you out?" Gabrielle bumped her vulpine nose against Shalini's scaly cheek. "Silly girl. Have a little trust, would you? In us, and in yourself?"

Shalini nuzzled her back. The pearl couldn't have helped her if she didn't already know how to tell the story, and of course she wouldn't be part of the coven if she didn't have something to offer. "I will."

When the curtains opened again, Shalini and her coven, now in human form, took their bows, along with the churel. The audience whistled and clapped. The cast gave a second bow, then exited stage right.

"That definitely wasn't what they were expecting," Sabrina said, cackling wildly, "but I think it's safe to say they loved it!"

"I think you're right," said Gabrielle. "Even the yakshini!"

"I'm so glad your mistress came to see this," Bianca told the churel. "I think she might have liked it."

"Especially your beautiful sari." Madhu winked. "Made of the best spell silk."

Shalini laughed. "Thanks so much for being part of this. It wasn't the plan, but I couldn't have done it without you." She offered the churel the restrung bracelet of stars. "What will you do now?"

The churel fastened the bracelet around her bony wrist and smirked down into the audience at the terrified man the yakshini held captive. "I believe I have a long-overdue date with my...husband, shall we say. What about you?"

Shalini opened her journal and pointed to the moon. "Next summer's just a year away. I've got another play to write."

★ ★ ★ ★ ★

THE LEGEND OF STONE MARY

by Robin Talley

EVERYBODY FOR MILES AROUND USED TO REmember the story of Mary Keegan's curse, but you wouldn't know it now.

Mama says folks here in Boyle's Run forgot about Mary on purpose. Grandma says they all got too busy looking after their own behinds to worry about stories from the olden days. Fools, Grandma always says, this town ain't made up of nothing but fools.

To be honest, I didn't used to think that what happened to Mary had much to do with me, either. I knew our family came from Mary Keegan's line—you couldn't grow up in the same house as Mama and Grandma and not know that—but even so, some story from another century never seemed to matter as much as the stuff that was happening right now.

Like school, and why everybody there always looked at me funny. Or Karen, and why looking at her made me *feel* funny.

That all changed on Halloween night, 1975, though. The first time I got to see Mary Keegan up close.

Even though she wasn't far from where we lived, I'd only ever caught one tiny glimpse of Mary before that. Practically as soon as I could talk, Grandma made me swear never to go anywhere near the old statue of Mary in the woods. But one night in fifth grade—it was Halloween that time too, actually, now that I think about it—I got in a big fight with Mama and climbed up on top of our greenhouse to sulk, and I saw the faint outline of Mary's statue over the treetops to the south.

Mama and I had fought that night 'cause I'd tried to sneak out. I wanted to go trick-or-treating like everybody else, but Mama told me to stay in and weed the flowers.

Well, if I wasn't going out, the last thing I wanted to do was work in our stupid greenhouse. Instead I climbed up on the roof right as it was starting to get dark. When I looked off to the south, the tip of Mary's statue was just barely poking out above the pines.

A weird feeling thrummed under my skin like an itch. Like it was pulling me to her, even though the trees were so thick all I could really see was a dark, blurry shape rising up from a small clearing. Even so, the crowd of people snaking through the woods toward Mary was clear as day.

I asked Mama about that later, and when she tried to explain, that was when I finally understood just how much the folks around here really had forgotten Mary Keegan. If they'd remembered, they never would've let the kids go out there.

See, most folks around here—the ones younger than our grandparents, anyway—don't know who the statue is even supposed to be. All anybody sees when they go out there is a creepy statue of some lady. To them, Mary's grave is nothing but a place where you probably won't get caught getting up to whatever you might want to get up to.

Stone Mary, they call her. Or *Stoned Mary*, if they're trying to be funny.

But I've never been allowed to go out there with everybody else on Halloween. It'd be disrespectful to our ancestor for me to trample over her grave like that. Besides, Mama says, why should I want to go out with dumb kids who think our family is a bunch of weirdos?

I never answer when Mama asks me stuff like that. She always thinks I don't want anything to do with the folks in town, just like she doesn't. She figures I *want* to spend my days with her and Grandma, weeding the plants and making change for the out-of-towners who come from all over to buy our rare orchids and chrysanthemums. She can't imagine any reason I'd rather be hanging out on the smoking block with Karen Rogers and Suze Payne and the rest of the junior girls, waiting for football practice to end and driving up to the water tower to get high.

I think Mama figured out some of it, though. 'Cause when I told her Karen got me a job working at the Hardee's out on Route 22, Mama didn't even seem all that surprised. I thought she'd tell me to quit, but she just rolled her eyes and said I'd best be careful dealing with townsfolk.

Well, as far as I could tell she was making a whole lot out of nothing. So when we were finishing up our shift that Halloween night, Steve Boyle and Becky Callahan started talking about going out to see Stone Mary, and I got that weird thrummy feeling again and said I wanted to go, too.

Steve whooped and said he'd always known I was a far-out chick, and Becky went into the bathroom to fix her makeup.

"You sure?" Karen whispered to me, when Steve went

over to the ice-cream machine to make himself a cone. Halloween wasn't a night when too many folks wanted a burger, so we'd had the Hardee's to ourselves for most of the dinner shift. It would've been a shame if *nobody* got to have something tasty. "I thought we could go to the railroad tracks. It's quiet out that way at night."

Now, Mary or no Mary, a trip out to the railroad tracks with Karen sounded pretty nice to me. I was getting along better with folks at school by then, but after what happened with Joey Leary, I was still being careful not to get *too* close to any one person.

But if there was anyone I wanted to bend the rules for, it was Karen. She and her parents had only moved down here from up north the year before, so she had no idea my family was any different from anybody else's.

That wasn't the reason I liked her, though. There was just something about Karen. Something I couldn't put a name to.

One night a few weeks before Halloween, the two of us had driven out to the railroad tracks and sat on the edge of the bridge, talking and smoking. Mostly, she was smoking and I was talking. Complaining, as usual, about my mother, and how she was never going to let me out of her sight long enough to live my own life.

"It's as if she thinks she can keep me in that greenhouse forever," I said, while Karen puffed her cigarette and drummed her nails on her knee. All night, she'd been acting antsy. "I told her I just want to be normal, like everybody else, but she acts like it would be the end of the world."

"Look, Wendy, there's something I should tell you." Karen stubbed out her cigarette and started twisting her mood ring around her finger. Then she turned to look at me, her wavy brown hair spilling out across the shoulders of her peasant blouse.

I sucked in my breath. It was kind of startling, having the full force of those dark brown eyes on me. "Okay."

"I didn't come here to—" Karen stopped, even though I hadn't said anything. I realized too late I was staring at her lips, thinking about how they looked in the faint bit of moonlight shining off the creek below the railroad trestle, and I forced myself to meet her eyes again. "I, um. I really like you. And the truth is I haven't been—"

I'm still not sure exactly how it happened—and believe me, I've replayed it in my head a million times since then—but before she could say anything more, we were kissing.

Which was a bad idea. I knew it was a bad idea. I didn't know all that much about how normal folks were supposed to act, but I *did* know normal folks didn't do stuff like that. Besides, I liked Karen, and I didn't want things to get complicated between her and me. For Keegan women, when things started getting complicated, bad stuff wasn't far behind.

So I was going to pull away from the kiss. Really, I was. But then Karen pulled away first.

I tried to act like I wasn't crushed. Like none of this was a big deal at all. I laughed and mumbled something about my breath probably smelling like cheese, and Karen laughed too, and then she started trying to get me to sing along with Elton John on the radio, and soon we were both laughing harder than ever.

But it wasn't really funny, because I couldn't stop thinking about how much I liked Karen. Or about the last time there was someone I really liked. It was different that time, but... maybe it wasn't quite as different as I wanted it to be.

We couldn't have been more than eight. Joey Leary was my best friend—or at least, he said he was—until the day he tripped me on the playground out back of the church.

I fell and landed in a mud puddle, messing up the new dress Mama made me. I cried and cried while Joey and his friends laughed about how he'd tricked that weird little Wendy Keegan girl into thinking he liked her, then shown her what for.

I'd cried all that night on Grandma's lap. Three days later Joey got stung by a bee, and his face swelled up like a sponge dipped in water. He was dead before they could even get him to the hospital down in Hopewell.

After that, the minister said I wasn't allowed on the playground anymore, and people started calling me a freak. It's not as if folks in town had ever exactly been nice to me, since everybody knew I was a Keegan, but after Joey they didn't bother hiding what they thought anymore.

It lasted years. Guys would try to trip me in the cafeteria, and girls would snicker behind my back at the lockers. Teachers wouldn't call on me in class, and I learned to skip gym on the days when they were picking teams for kickball. It was better to hide behind the dugouts with the stoners than to get picked last.

Something strange happened a year into high school, though. The stoners got to be cool. And, somehow, so did I.

Just like the stoners, nobody's parents ever wanted them to have anything to do with me. A lot of folks seemed to think I was like one of the rare flowers we grew in our greenhouse. Exciting and dangerous all at once.

All I had to do was play up how different I was—not *too* different, not *weird* different, just a *little bit* different—and suddenly, people started talking to me again.

And then Karen moved down here and sat next to me in English, and all at once I had an actual, real-life best friend for the first time since Joey. As far as Karen knew, I'd always been cool.

It was different with the others. With Becky and Suze and all the rest, I had to work not to remember what they used to say about me. Steve's dad, Reverend Boyle, was always after us to "forgive and forget," but as far as I could figure, forgetting was a lot easier than forgiving.

I knew I didn't have anything to do with what happened to Joey—I was clear on the other side of town when he got stung, and how was I supposed to know he was allergic anyway?—but even so, I'd been careful since then.

I liked hanging out with my new friends, but I didn't get to know anybody *too* well. I'd already decided I'd never go around with boys the way Mama and Grandma used to do. I didn't especially *want* to go around with boys, so that helped, but still, I figured the closer you were to somebody, the easier it was for them to cross you. And what if somebody else wound up dead right after they made me mad? No, thank you.

So, as much as I wanted to go back to the railroad tracks with Karen that Halloween, it seemed safer to keep my distance.

Besides, that feeling was thrumming harder than ever in my chest, telling me it was time for me to see Mary. It was way past time, in fact.

"Nah, I want to go see Stone Mary," I said as Steve came back with his ice-cream cone and a fresh cigarette.

"I'm not so sure about this," Karen said, shifting from one foot to another in her platform sandals.

"Yeah, I don't know, y'all." Becky stood in the bathroom door, a fresh coat of blue shadow shimmering on her eyelids. "Last time we went out there Carl Molloy tried to look down my shirt and said the ghost made him do it."

"Stop your bitchin', Becky." Steve blew out a stream of smoke, then stubbed his cigarette out in one of the customer ashtrays. "You've never been on Halloween. It's totally different then."

"It's just some statue." Karen rolled her deep brown eyes. Even exasperated, she still managed to look gorgeous. "A statue's not gonna be any different on Halloween than any other night. It's not as if you really believe that dumb story about it coming to life."

"Well, maybe I believe the other one." Steve waggled his tongue at Karen like the guys in KISS. "About how if a girl touches it, she's guaranteed not to get knocked up that night."

"Gross." Karen shoved Steve in the chest. He laughed and tried to grab her hand. I felt like shoving him too just then.

"Okay, but look, y'all." Steve opened the cash register and started counting out the singles. "Mike Delaney called, and he said everybody's going to the woods tonight. If you girls want to go see a movie instead, go for it, but you'll be the only ones in the whole drive-in."

That did it for Becky. Besides, it wasn't like she had much else to do that night.

See, there's not much in our little podunk town anymore except the railroad station and the bottle plant over by the creek, but during the Civil War, Boyle's Run was booming. Everybody around here did everything they could to support the Confederate cause, whether it was fighting, or working in the armory, or growing food for the troops.

Everybody except Mary Keegan. So far as anybody around here knew, she never lifted a finger to help the Confederates through the whole war. Instead she and her little daughter spent the war doing pretty much what they'd always done—keeping to themselves in their little house out in the woods, growing their garden, and acting like they were better than the rest of the townsfolk.

That's what they all used to say, anyway. They said other things, too. That Mary's daughter must be a bastard, since nobody'd ever heard of Mary having herself a husband. That it was awfully peculiar how the crops out by Mary's house always did so well, even in the years when everybody else's gardens were suffering from drought or bugs or cold. That she was so quiet, so secretive, she might very well be a Yankee sympathizer.

The folks of Boyle's Run suspected Mary was up to all sorts of mischief, but they never once seemed to guess she was a witch.

As the war went on, things kept getting worse for the South, and the harder things got for everybody, the more the mutterings about Mary and her daughter grew. By 1864, folks were shivering through the harshest winter of the war, and pretty much everybody knew the South was done for. Still, though, soldiers were out in the fields getting shot, and the women and a handful of men were stuck here, trying to cobble together enough food to feed their families.

And folks started saying to each other that the queer woman out in the woods, that Mary Keegan, must have an awful lot of food stored up. Everybody had seen how her garden had thrived that summer, even when everybody else's got done in by the blight.

So one night—the coldest night of the year—folks stormed Mary's little house out in the woods. When she heard them coming—they were hooting and hollering, the way men like that still do when they've had more whiskey than's good for them—Mary pushed her daughter out the back window and told her to run fast as she could to a friend's house in the next town over, while Mary stayed behind to face the mob.

They banged on her door and demanded she turn over her food stores. Now, the truth was, Mary didn't have much stored, but the mob wasn't about to believe that. They tore her little house apart. And when they couldn't find the barrels of food they'd come for, they set fire to what was left of it.

Mary had no choice but to abandon her burning house and run out into the cold. Nobody in all of Boyle's Run would take her in, of course, and she couldn't very well run to the same house where she'd sent her daughter—the mob might follow her and kill them both.

And so that night, Mary Keegan froze to death. One of the men who'd been part of the mob found her a few days later while he was hunting, deep in the woods. It was just as cold as it had been all that winter, and Mary was frozen solid, in the same position she must've been in when she died—kneeling on the ground, one hand raised up in the air.

The men buried her right where they found her. They didn't bother to mark the grave. They figured nobody'd ever cared enough about Mary Keegan to want to visit her while she was alive, so there was no reason for that to change now that she was dead.

That'd be the end of the story, if it hadn't been for what happened once the war was over.

Remember what I said about Mary being found with one hand lifted up to the sky? Well, folks may not have figured out she was a witch before, but they started to get that idea clear enough once the other men started coming back from the war. 'Cause right about then, things started going real, real badly for Boyle's Run.

First came the flood. Now, this was in 1865, when the

South was already ruined from losing the war. That summer there were five long days of rain in Boyle's Run, and on the last day a flood came raging up from the creek, sweeping away everything in its path. Most of the town's livestock drowned, and plenty of its people, too. Even the armory, which the Yankees had forgotten to burn, was carried off into the water brick by brick.

Still, the folks of Boyle's Run were determined. They rebuilt the town, albeit at only half the size it'd been before the war. They told themselves they'd rise up from the waters like Noah.

The year after that, though, a fire swept through one hot summer night. In the worst of it, one of the men working the bucket line—it happened to be Cormac Boyle, the son of one of the town fathers, and the man who'd led the others out to Mary's house that cold winter night—looked up and saw a shape rising out of the fire, clear as day. The outline of a woman, kneeling, her hand held over her head.

As they worked to rebuild the town for the second time, Cormac told everybody what he'd seen. That was when folks started talking about Mary Keegan again. Now they started saying she was a witch, and that her last act before she'd died had been to lay a curse upon the town.

They kept saying that, too, in the years that came after. Especially when something bad happened.

And bad things happened an awful lot in Boyle's Run. Floods and fires. Tornados, and even hurricanes. Outbreaks of measles and typhus and yellow fever.

If a dog went mad, it was 'cause Mary Keegan's spirit had gotten into it. If a baby died in the cradle on a chilly night, it was 'cause Mary Keegan had crept into his window and sucked his breath away.

Well, some of that's pure rubbish, but Grandma says some of it's not, either. 'Cause no matter what you believe, there's no denying that our family—the Keegan family—has been spared the worst of it.

When Mary's daughter—she was my great-great-great-grandmother—came back after the war and built herself a house out in the woods, she missed the worst of the floods and the fires. She never took sick, either. In fact, of all the women in our line—'cause Mary's daughter wound up having a daughter of her own, and her daughter had a daughter too, and so on and so forth—none of us ever got any of the illnesses that've always been passed around Boyle's Run faster than the collection plate at First Methodist.

When Grandma was a girl, some folks decided enough was enough. They figured it was past time they sought Mary's forgiveness. Maybe that, they whispered among themselves, would break the curse.

So they went deep into the woods and found the spot where they believed Mary Keegan had knelt that night. They hired a carver to make a beautiful statue in the shape of a woman kneeling, one hand raised up over her head. They perched the stone carving right on top of Mary's unmarked grave and put a shiny metal plaque at the bottom in her memory.

Back then, Grandma and her mama lived in the same house where she and Mama and I live now, only a couple of miles north of that spot in the woods. Grandma's mama was the one who built the greenhouse out back. Our family still has the gift for plants that Mary did, even if nobody in town will buy from us.

But Grandma says folks never said one word to them about that statue, or the curse, or forgiveness. Even if they're trying to apologize to a dead woman, folks in these parts will never speak to the real live Keegans if they can help it. They figure we still throw out curses willy-nilly on anybody who wrongs us.

I don't know the first thing about casting curses, and neither does Mama. To tell you the truth, though, I'm not so sure about Grandma. See, my grandfather—he was one of the Fitzpatrick boys—died in a bicycle crash a few months before Mama was born. That was a week after Grandma caught him running around with one of the Callahan sisters. I've never thought it wise to ask how his "accident" came about, but either way, the men who get mixed up with Keegan women never stick around, for one reason or another.

Anyhow, Mary's statue is still out there, and even though the little metal plaque has rusted so bad nobody can read it anymore, the curse seems to have died down for the most part. Sure, bad stuff still happens in Boyle's Run from time to time—there was that fire that leveled the new Town Hall when I was ten, and lately, there've been more and more tornados—but folks seem to figure that's just the usual bad luck that happens everyplace. Hardly anybody seems to remember why they put up that big stone carving in the woods to begin with.

At first, that night at Hardee's seemed just like any other Halloween. We finished breaking down the registers and cleaning out the grills, then changed out of our uniforms. We stuffed half a dozen paper bags with leftover fries, and Steve locked the doors behind us just as a crack of thunder sounded in the thick clouds overhead.

We all piled into Karen's car. Karen kept giving me these strange looks while she drove, like she was mad at me for not wanting to go to the railroad tracks with her, but there was nothing I could say with Steve and Becky there.

And when we were halfway to the woods, I started to feel really funny. At first I thought it was just 'cause I was worried about Karen being mad, and 'cause the stories Steve and Becky kept telling from the back seat were so weird. They didn't know the first thing about Mary Keegan, that was obvious, but it seemed they'd heard plenty about Stone Mary.

"I bet we'll see some action tonight," Steve said as Karen pulled her Dodge Dart onto the highway. It was fifteen minutes to midnight. "They say when the weather's all spooky like this, Stoned Mary wakes up. And when there's something serious coming, like a tornado, its eyes open and glow red."

"That's a load of bull." Karen blew smoke out the window and glanced at me again. She didn't look as mad this time. She looked...kind of worried, actually. "There are tornados two, three times a year lately, but have you ever met anybody who's seriously seen that thing's eyes turn colors?"

I tried to listen, but the closer we got to Mary's corner of the woods, the funnier I was starting to feel. Almost like I could hear another voice in my head.

This one didn't belong to any of my friends, though. It was weird and whispery, and it was saying something I couldn't understand. The same word, over and over.

"Yeah, I know." Now Steve was acting like he didn't believe the stories any more than Karen did. "It's like how they say if you climb on the statue at night, the ghost will haunt you for the rest of your life. But I know at least three guys who've climbed up on that thing, and nobody's gotten haunted yet."

Now I could make out the word that kept repeating in my head.

Stop.

"Besides," Becky added from the seat behind mine, "the story about its eyes glowing red doesn't have anything to do with the weather. What *I* heard is that Stone Mary used to be a real lady, and folks in town hated her so much she turned to stone, and the only time its eyes glow is when one of the lady's descendants comes in front of the statue at midnight. That makes it remember it used to be alive, and then it gets mad at the town all over again and starts shooting death rays out its eyes or something. It's a shit story, if you ask me."

Karen stubbed out her cigarette in the dashboard ashtray and glanced over at me again.

Stop. Stop. Stop.

Karen was right. The stories about Stone Mary were bullshit.

Except…that last thing Becky had said…

I wanted to look at Karen again, but I couldn't force myself to meet her eyes.

The voice was practically shouting now. It was coming from up ahead of us. From the woods.

Stop! Stop! Stop!

Maybe this trip wasn't such a great idea after all.

"Mike said no grass grows in Stone Mary's shadow," Steve said as Karen passed a cigarette back to him. "It's all just dirt."

"Yeah, because people are always going out and trampling it." Karen rolled her eyes in the rearview mirror. "Have you ever been out here in the daytime? It's gross. Beer bottles and cigarette butts and burger wrappers all over. One time somebody spray-painted *Stay High* all the way down the statue's back in purple."

"You've come out here in the daytime?" I practically had to shout to hear myself over the noise in my head.

"Yeah. Actually, maybe we should wait and come back tomorrow when it's light out. You can see better then."

"No." I was still talking too loud, but I couldn't help it. "I need to go see Mary now. Right now."

The voice in my head wasn't saying *Stop* anymore. It had

faded into something harder to understand. It didn't sound angry anymore, either.

Karen pulled over behind a line of parked cars at the side of the road. Station wagons and pickup trucks and more Dodge Darts. People from school were climbing out of them, wading into the mess of empty bottles and trash that lined the side of the highway.

The woods loomed high on either side of us. Above us, the clouds were thicker than ever and moving fast. There were no stars. A few pairs of headlights were all we could see by.

My knees were bouncing on the bucket seat. I had to get out of this car. I *needed* to get to Mary.

"Hey, y'all!" Ricky Fitzpatrick shouted as Karen shut off the engine. He was leaning against the side of a wood-paneled station wagon, lighting up a joint. "You just closed up Hardee's, right? Didja bring any fries?"

"Yeah, man. Trade you for another one of those." Steve jogged up to join him, Becky trailing behind.

I checked my watch. Five minutes to midnight.

Everybody seemed to be hanging out by the cars or drifting toward the trees. I could see the beginning of a path there. It wasn't a trail, the kind hunters or hikers used. It had been trampled over the years by kids trooping in.

It was the path I'd seen from the greenhouse roof that night. The path that led to Mary.

I moved toward it so fast I nearly tripped over a broken bottle. I scrambled up, ignoring the offered hand of some guy who asked if I wanted a beer, and took off again. By the time the first bolt of lightning cracked across the sky, I was almost running.

I'd nearly made it to the trees when a hand closed on my

arm. I bit back a scream and tried to jerk away, but the hand was too tight.

"You can't go through there," a voice whispered. It took me a minute to realize the sound wasn't coming from inside my head this time. It was Karen. "You can't get any closer to her."

"No, no, I've got to see Mary," I whispered back, before I realized what I was saying, and that it was weird Karen was talking about this.

And that she was calling Mary *her* instead of *it*.

"Wait." I stopped struggling. "What do you mean?"

She sighed and motioned toward the car. "Get in. We're going home."

I looked longingly toward the path, but Karen pulled me back to the car. She looked ready to shove me into the front seat. As she reached for the door handle, I saw my chance and ripped out of her grip.

"Wendy!" Karen whispered, but I'd already left her behind, running as fast as I could.

I reached the trees and darted down the path, my tangled hair flying out behind me. The woods were crowded with people, smoking and drinking and talking and laughing, none of them in any sort of hurry. As I ran past, I heard them say my name.

"Was that Wendy Keegan?"

"What's she doing?"

"God, you know, she seems okay sometimes, but she really is so weird."

I ignored them all.

I'd almost reached Mary—I could see her silhouette through the smoke-filled air, huge and dark and looming against the trees—when Karen's hands clamped down again, grabbing me by both arms this time.

"Wendy, you can't!" she muttered urgently into my ear. "Mary's too angry!"

"She isn't, that's just it!" I hissed back, not even sure where the words were coming from. "Let me *go*!"

"I *can't*!"

"I don't *care* if you think I'm weird!" I wasn't even bothering to keep my voice down. I fought, trying to wrench away from Karen, but she held on tight. "Or if any of them do! Mary needs me!"

"If you go anywhere near Mary Keegan's grave we're all dead!"

I stopped fighting. My heart thundered in my throat. "What did you say?"

"Come here." Karen dragged me off the path and into a grove of trees, out of sight of the others.

"What are you talking about?" I whispered. My chest heaved. That newspaper photo of Joey Leary's face flashed through my mind, pulsing in time to my heartbeat.

"It isn't safe for you to be out here." Karen finally let go of my arms and shoved her hair out of her face. She looked around us in every direction, trying to make sure there was no one close enough to hear. Her eyes were wild and frantic. "Your mom must've told you that, right?"

"What do you know about my mom? Or Mary Keegan?" I fought to keep my voice low. I could still feel Mary pulling me to her, but if what Karen said was true... *Joey Leary. Remember Joey Leary.*

Another crack of thunder sounded, louder than before.

"We have to get out of here." Karen's eyes kept darting around. She looked ready to jump out of her skin. "You can't be anywhere near her at midnight."

"I'm not going anywhere until you tell me what the hell this is about."

"Look, I..." Karen sighed. "I haven't been honest with you."

"Yeah, I figured that much out." I shoved my hands into the pockets of my jeans.

"I tried to tell you the truth before. That night, when we—at the railroad tracks. But I didn't—I couldn't..."

She trailed off, and I stared down at my boots. Now, instead of worrying about Mary and Joey Leary, I was worrying about that kiss.

Maybe it hadn't meant what I thought it had at all. Maybe this whole thing had been some sort of mean prank, like the kind kids used to play on me at school. Like when Mike Delaney kept stealing all the erasers out of my pencil case every time I got up to go to the bathroom until one day I started crying in the middle of Arithmetic.

"Wendy." Karen put her hand on my arm again, but it was light this time. "I'm—my whole family—we're witch hunters."

That was definitely not what I'd thought she was going to say. Grandma had told me stories about witch hunters, of course, but they were the same stories other grandmothers told about boogeymen in the closet, or monsters that hid under your bed if you didn't eat your vegetables. Witch hunters weren't *real*. "You can't be."

"We are." Karen nodded, her face solemn. "That's why we moved here. We were up in Salem until my parents heard there was a curse down here in Boyle's Run that was still active. They decided I was old enough to get an assignment of my own this time, so they asked me to get to know you at school, to see if I could find out anything about your family. Only I didn't count on how I'd— Wendy, I'm so sorry."

I nodded, dully. I should've known better than to think Karen was really my friend, much less anything more. And now I'd betrayed Mama and Grandma without even knowing it.

I tried to think if I'd ever told Karen anything her parents could use against us. Probably. All I ever talked about was my family and how much they frustrated me.

A *witch hunter.* How could I have been so stupid?

"I don't know what you're talking about." I turned away, saying what Grandma had taught me to say if somebody point-blank asked me. "There's no such thing as witches."

"I'm so sorry." It was obvious Karen didn't believe me, not even a little. "If I'd known what you were really like, I never would've— Anyway, I told my parents you're not dangerous, but they said we have to investigate anyway. There've been reports of weird deaths here. Something about a suspicious bicycle accident, and cars that go off the road south of your greenhouse every few years. But I know *you* would never want to hurt anyone—which means you can't go anywhere near that statue of Mary Keegan tonight."

I turned to look through the trees toward where Mary stood.

I couldn't just leave her there. She was too lonely.

"My mom said the curse has been mostly dormant for the past couple of decades," Karen went on, breathless now, "but people are starting to forget why they put that statue out there in the first place, so it's starting to activate again. If any one of the Keegans goes where that statue can see you, the curse will come back in full force. Mary's still too angry at this town to let it go."

"She's not angry." I stretched up on my toes. I could just barely see the tip of Mary's outstretched hand. "She's sad."

"What?" Karen blinked at me. "How do you know that?"

I shook my head. There was no way I could explain, but I knew it as well as I knew the queer shape of a ghost orchid, or the bike route from our greenhouse to the front door of Boyle's Run High. I could feel the deep, powerful sorrow running from the ground where Mary Keegan had knelt on that cold night, flowing up into the statue that marked her grave.

"She didn't ask for all this to happen," I mumbled. "The family curse was too powerful. She thought she could stop it, but it was out of her control."

"Okay, look." Karen kept twisting her mood ring around on her finger, her voice quavering. "My parents have been studying the Keegans for months. They said if any of Mary's descendants gets near her grave, a voice will tell her to stop. It's the last warning."

"I know. I heard it." That thrumming feeling coursed through me, like a wave powerful enough to split my skull in two. It was nearly midnight, and it didn't matter what Karen said. I had to get to Mary. "But she's not telling *me* to stop. She's trying to make the *curse* stop. She didn't want to hurt this town any more than I wanted to kill Joey on the playground."

"Any more than you wanted to—" Karen's dark eyes widened. "Wendy, *what*—"

The rain started all at once.

The skies opened up, the water landing on the hard-packed earth like a never-ending drumroll. Behind us, Becky and Carl squealed and ran toward the shelter of the trees.

"I have to go." I pushed past Karen. "I have to see Mary."

"You can't! Wendy, wait!"

I jerked away from her and ran faster than I'd ever run in my life.

Someone else called my name, Becky maybe, but I ignored her and charged down the trampled path. There were people everywhere, shouting and holding their jackets over their heads.

The rain pounded down on me, too, but I barely felt it. All I could feel was Mary Keegan's grief.

"Mary?" I shouted. I was getting closer, my feet thrashing through the mud. There were voices behind me, people from school calling out as I ran past, but it didn't matter. "I'm coming! Wait for me!"

Something slammed into my shoulder. A moment later, it was thumping down, as fierce as the rain. Hail, big icy rocks of it. To my left, someone screamed, but I never stopped running.

Then—there she was.

Mary.

I spotted her first out of the corner of my eye, when she was no more than a shape between the trees. Then I came to the clearing and all at once she was in front of me, opaque stone gleaming in the rain.

She was bigger than I'd expected, a lot taller than me. She would've looked frightening if the sadness pouring off her wasn't so strong. Her face was solid and dark, with no more than a tiny glimmer of red light. She bent, kneeling, one arm stretched up to the sky as though summoning the storm.

Which, of course, she was.

"Mary!" I had to scream to hear myself over the howling wind. "It's me, Wendy Keegan! Your great-great-great-great-granddaughter!"

Nothing happened. Mary stood, silent, the rain pouring all around us.

"You meant to forgive them, didn't you?" I shouted up into

that silent stone face. "You wanted to stop the curse? Well, how about I forgive them for you?"

Mary didn't answer. But the tiny glimmer of red light grew.

It was her eyes. They were opening.

There was some truth to the stories after all.

I closed my eyes and tried, with all the strength I had, to forgive.

I started with Joey Leary, and the friends who'd laughed with him—Steve and Carl and Mike and all the others.

I forgave them.

I forgave the girls who'd smirked at me at the lockers, too. I forgave my grandfather for running around on Grandma, and the customers at the greenhouse who'd tried to cheat us the winter I was seven and sailed over the Route 22 guardrail on their way home.

I forgave Karen, for not telling me why she'd sat next to me in English that first day, and for everything she hadn't told me since. And for anything she might do in the future, too, if I let her get close.

Nothing she could ever do would deserve the kind of punishment the Keegan curse doled out. Mary had known that, too.

Last of all, I forgave Cormac Boyle and the rest of the men who'd chased Mary out into the cold. And I forgave Mary, too, for not being able to stop the curse herself.

I fell down on my knees. And in that moment, I *was* Mary, kneeling on that very spot.

I raised my hand into the air. I could feel the wind blowing and the hail raining down, and I tuned out every voice in the trees behind me as I repeated in my mind the same word Mary had said that night.

Stop, I told the wind and the rain and the curse and all the powers greater than me. *Stop. Stop. Stop!*

"Wendy."

I forgive them, every one! I never meant to hurt them!

"Wendy, it's over."

It was Karen's voice, but I didn't dare move.

"Listen to the sky, Wendy. It's done."

I listened.

The hail had stopped. The wind, too.

The rain went on, but it wasn't pounding anymore. It was drizzling. A regular autumn rain. The hurricane wasn't coming tonight.

Karen's hand gripped mine, and gently, she lowered my arm.

She was right. It was over.

I climbed to my feet, slowly, carefully. Karen was standing across from me, her dark hair soaking wet and plastered to her head, her eyes wide. Rain ran down her face in rivers.

Beyond her, I could see the others. Faces staring. Fingers pointing.

And I didn't care. I wasn't angry at them, not anymore, but I was done acting like some version of myself they wanted me to be.

I met Karen's eyes. She touched my hand.

She knew more about me than anyone else in the world, and she was still here.

"I don't know what you just did, Wendy Keegan." Karen smiled. "But I think it was something good."

★★★★★

THE ONE WHO STAYED

by Nova Ren Suma

WE SHOULD HAVE GUESSED ANOTHER GIRL would find our fire. If we'd had our eyes on the night, casting through the thick tangle of trees to that particular stretch of woods, we might have known she was coming long before she made her way to us. We could have stopped what sent her running.

Instead, we were consumed with what brought us to the woods in the first place. The moon was full, white and pulsing. The time was approaching midnight. Summer warmed our skin already, before the fire even reached full roar. Our eyes were contained to our circle, our ears filled with the noise made by our own bodies. We weren't thinking of another.

All the while, the girl was gaining ground. She didn't know it herself, but she was in our path. She would come upon our circle within moments. She'd come crashing through the break in the gray birch trees, where the maple bent to let in stars and sky, and there she'd freeze at our ring of faces rippling in the glow. She'd be shaking with fury, slick with fright, and we would be hungry to be so raw again, so new, to taste that rage, ignite it to flame and wear its ashes. She held so much power. She didn't even know.

At first she was only a flashlight bobbing in the darkness. Erratic, frantic blooms that made the tree arms monstrous, that confused the moon and made it seem so far away. At some point, she lost the flashlight, and then only her fumbling noise could be made out. Thrashing through the branches, stumbling over tree roots, skidding down the slope, and picking herself up again, the wounded-animal sound of her cries.

By this point we had heard her. We couldn't ignore the clamor of her approach as she reached the fringe of trees. Besides, there was something she carried that each one of us, from darkest to bright, from hardest to most uncertain, could recognize. The storm inside her could fill this whole wooded grove and take us over. She was coming. Were we ready?

"Do you hear that?" the quietest of us said.

No one had to answer. We all heard, and we were all thinking the same thing.

"Not another one," the tallest of us said.

The coldest of us kept still and made no comment, her bare feet close enough to stoke the flames. The warmest of us smiled. Her teeth glinted in the night.

The one of us with the worn scratches all up and down her arms felt a song surging inside her as the girl got closer, and the one of us who had the most tender heart felt it also and let the tears rain down her cheeks.

"This time, it'll be different," one of us said. "This time we won't let her run."

★ ★ ★

Mirah Rubin sensed she'd be different by morning. She expected a big night, but she couldn't have guessed how it would change her, or in what irrevocable ways. All she knew was that when Jayson Turner said to meet him by the bend in Old Fork Road, there where the path into the woods beckoned with a black and bristling gap, she said yes. She said yes faster than her finger could tap it out. She said yes and wore new underwear for the occasion, chewing off the tag with her teeth.

Her flashlight had a fresh set of batteries, and a hammer hit hard inside her chest. Jayson Turner was a senior and had never been seen with her in person, eye to eye, except when he'd pushed past her in the hallway the last day of school, when his arm brushed her arm and left a blooming swirl of intention and heat. Mirah was about to be a sophomore in a short stretch of weeks, but he sought her out. He waited all summer, for school to be long over and about to begin again, before he said he wanted to meet, now, at last, tonight. An invitation like this might never come again.

To her parents—overworked, short on the water bill and short-tempered because of it—she said she was suddenly invited to sleep over at Natalie's. To Natalie and the rest of her friends, she said nothing, not yet. She felt the cool flush of night as she stepped out into it. When she looked up at the moon it was full—a pale circle against black—and she wondered if that meant anything. Maybe good luck. Then she didn't think of anything besides crossing the backyard as fast as she could. She didn't want to keep him waiting. She scaled the fence and leaped the drainage ditch. She headed for the shortcut field that would get her to Old Fork Road. Jayson Turner had asked her to meet him at the bend. He said he'd swing by in his car and pick her up there instead of in front of her house. Jayson Turner said that, which meant not only did he remember their shared moment in the hallway (that electric touch, her arm on fire for almost an hour afterward), he knew where she lived.

If Mirah could have stopped to take a picture of this moment, to remember this feeling and keep it forever, she would be a blur of color, a litter of flowers, a pile of smiling faces with dancing, drunken hearts instead of eyes.

Our hearts were in our throats. We remembered nights like she was about to experience. Our blood pounding, our bodies slick with sweat under our summer dresses before we even had to run. For some of us, it was decades ago, the memory gauzy with distance and gone gray, but for others of us it was recent, still in our rearview. For the youngest of us, it felt like yesterday. We remembered, but we had no way to rewind the night and warn the girl. If only we could have been watching, perched in the highest tree at the edge of that field she used as a shortcut. We would have waved our many arms to her. We would have bird-called from every set of lips and pitched acorns, pocket debris, and stones. If we had to, we would have jumped to ground and risked broken limbs.

We say this with conviction, but we also know what it's like to have no idea what's coming and to want to meet it anyway, no matter what anyone says. To ignore warning signs, to believe the best in people. A truck hit each of us, one after the other, and it's still on the road, now heading for this girl.

The shyest of us lost her virginity in the back of a green Dodge and lied for years, to herself and to anyone who'd listen, to say she liked it.

The loudest of us came home from the trip to the county

fair, where she spun around in the teacups and visited the fun house, and afterward she didn't speak a word out loud for six months.

The angriest of us, the one cradling the most fire, the most seething fight, wouldn't acknowledge anything that happened between the year she was seven and the year she turned eleven and her uncle moved away. Whole gaps of her childhood lie in wait under wool blankets or are buried beneath sea level in dank caves. Yet she does remember. She has always remembered. That's the point.

We used to be little, and soft. We used to say yes before we even heard the entire question. We used to think we had no recourse for making someone's heart ache like ours have ached, for resetting the balance in the universe, for striving for the thing we're not supposed to want but we still do want: revenge.

We are different ages, from different parts of town, from different schools and families and decades. Some of us have, and some of us have not. Some of us are beautiful. Some of us make the cashiers in the supermarket cringe. But all of us were girls once, in some way or another, back before we found each other. Before we realized what we had inside us. Before we knew what we could accomplish together. Before we yelled into the night and demanded it remember our names.

The thing is, we couldn't have stopped the girl if we tried. There she was, had we known to part the branches and peer out of the woods. She was on the side of Old Fork Road, waiting for the first peek of his headlights. She'd reached the bend.

Mirah waited, as instructed, at the bend in the road. She stood there and she waited for the sound of his car, the sight of his headlights, but it was taking Jayson Turner forever to show up. When her feet started aching, and she cursed herself for wearing the wrong shoes and such an uncomfortable, wriggly, snappish skirt, she found a large rock to sit on where she could see the road and where it could see her. She checked her phone every other minute, even with the volume up, and she watched for cars from either direction. She wondered why he wanted to meet *here*, of all places. Alone in the night, she started to do a lot of wondering. She kept her back to the trees.

It was after a full twenty-eight minutes had passed, and after her eyes had adjusted to the stretch of darkness, when she noticed the two white sticks. They formed a cross, and they carried a name: Alison. She remembered Alison, a girl a grade ahead of her in school. This must have been the roadside shrine that marked where she got hit, at this bend, near where the overgrown path opened into the darkest knot of trees. Mirah hadn't realized it was so close to her house.

The shrine was a year old and not yet forgotten like other roadside memorials for other classes' accidents long past. It was fresh from last summer, though not too fresh. The white paint was growing moss. Rotting gas-station flowers were scattered on the ground. Mirah tried to remember all she knew about Alison. Had she been on the softball team? Did she have an affinity for overlarge sweaters? It could be, if Mirah's memory served, that they used to ride the same bus route, because the high school and the junior high got out at the same time and the buses were shared. Alison would sit in the first three rows with her friends, and she never ventured to the back, where the rowdiest of the boys held court. If a younger kid sat beside her, Alison even smiled and shared her seat. That was pretty much all Mirah remembered of her. That, and the faded facts of her accident last August.

People said she ran out of the woods, probably drunk—the rumors were insistent she had to be drunk—and straight into an oncoming car. No one knew what she was doing drinking alone in the woods. They did know that the impact of the car sent her sailing, and the shock at her sudden appearance sent the driver in reverse. No one blamed the driver. It was a blind bend, a deliriously drunk girl. No one looked to the woods for answers, and it didn't occur to Mirah that it could be anything else.

While Mirah waited for Jayson Turner to show up, she got to her knees and crouched closer to the shrine. She wasn't praying; she wouldn't do a thing like that. She was only curious. Only looking.

The shrine was simple, made with barely any effort, just the two sticks and Alison's name painted on it. A Mets cap was perched on the ground, weathered and surely crawling with insects. It had probably once sat on Alison's unwitting head.

What a stupid girl. If she'd kept safe to the side of the road and crossed where the trees cleared, the car wouldn't have even hit her.

Mirah considered saying a few words, but nothing came. She knew this wasn't a grave, yet still she searched the dirt with her fingers until she found a smooth, small pebble that felt right. She heard the sound of a car approaching, so she did it quickly. She chose a spot on the arm of the cross and left the pebble behind. For Alison.

Then she scrambled back to a visible spot in the bend.

We don't speak the name Alison to one another or even to ourselves—though we didn't know her name that night, and some of us spent weeks not knowing. Once we learned it, we spent a long time trying to dislodge it from the tense ridges of our brains, until we realized she would forever be among us, even if she didn't choose. So we mouthed her name into our mirrors without using sound. We wrote her name on slips of paper that we drowned in water, then air-dried, then tore to pieces, then burned.

Alison was the first girl to find our fire. She came out from the trees on a summer's night a year before this one. The way some of us remember it, she was down on her knees crawling, but others remember she was quick on her feet. She was slippery. Twice she escaped our arms, and three of us had to hold her down.

"What's she doing? Why won't she stay still?"

"Did she bite you?"

"Get her! Get her legs!"

We lost track of who was saying what. We can only imagine how frightened she was by the sound of us all around her.

Once we had her, we tried to soothe her. We said, "You're safe. You're with us." But she didn't stop thrashing. We asked her, "What happened to you? Where were you? Why were you running?" But she didn't have coherent answers. Did we frighten her, with the blood and earth and unidentified smears decorating our chests, our faces, the palms of our hands? Did the fire seem too sinister? Did the way we were dressed, or mostly undressed, upset her? Or was it the way our combined weight kept her pinned to the ground?

She was crying openly at this point. It's a thing we try not to remember.

The most panicked of us tried to explain who we were. The kindest of us attempted to cover her with a cloak—long and thick enough to act as a blanket, mottled with leaves and twigs and stinking of fire smoke yet still warm—but she must have thought she was getting smothered. She wormed away and batted at us with her torn fists and kicked at us with her scratched legs. Something had done that to her before she reached us, something in the woods, and the most timid of us worried we'd been the ones to awaken it.

"No," we said, circling her, our arms reaching out to try to grab a limb, "we're not going to hurt you. You're safe here with us. Stay."

She didn't stay.

She took one last look at us and bolted through the trees in the direction of the road, and there was nothing we could do to stop her. She didn't hear us calling her. She made it out at the bend, where Old Fork Road had the vicious turn and no sign to slow, though when we attempted to scry for her all we saw was a bright light that hurt our eyes and all we heard was the whispering judgment of the forest.

The car ended her life, but we drove her to it.

We didn't speak her name, but we would not forget it. It was Alison Darby Chance—a few of us searched out her house after and peered through the window at her grieving mother; the guiltiest of us attended her funeral. We could have helped her. We could have healed her and protected her and filled her up to bursting. We could have offered her a way to live forever and wear the pain of what happened like a crown of venomous snakes around her head so no one would ever dare hurt her again.

"What do you want most in the world?" we would have asked her.

That was the question each of us was asked, upon joining the circle. Intention.

And she would have opened her mouth for the first time to speak a word to us and not scream, and her teeth would catch the firelight, red as her tongue, and our toes would curl in delight when she said it, though we'd been warned against wanting the very same thing.

"Revenge," she would have said, had she stayed.

The oldest of us would have been on her right side, and the youngest of us would have been on her left, and both would have reached out to let her feel the raw power coursing through us from hand to hand to hand.

Mirah lifted a hand to the approaching car and waved. She wore the widest smile. "Jayson?" she called, but it wasn't Jayson Turner. It was some random car passing on the road. When Jayson Turner finally did pull up, she had almost abandoned her perch on the rock and gone back home. She'd almost convinced herself that a ghost was walking, coming from the forest to check what flowers were left at her shrine, and she'd almost run off in fright to avoid it. But her head was only making stories. Her eyes were only making the darkness dance. When the headlights came fast around the bend, she felt every inch of herself bristle with energy and possibility. This car slowed. Here he was, Jayson Turner, downing the lights and parking on the side of the road beside the field. Here he was, stepping out. Jayson Turner.

Only, when he emerged from the car he had too many legs.

It seemed there were more of him than there should be. She'd thought this was a date, that he was taking her with him to a party, but had she misunderstood and was it something else?

The darkness confused her, and her flashlight didn't help it make sense. He hadn't come alone. Here was Jayson Turner, and here also were two of his tallest friends.

There were things she told herself to make sense of this, and there were other things best kept submerged. It was a party, she told herself. A senior party. Jayson Turner was the designated driver and giving his friends a ride…though she didn't understand why they weren't in the car anymore. Why they were crossing the road to where she stood with her back to the woods. Why all three of them were coming toward her.

"Wait, where's the party?" Mirah said. She didn't want to get poison ivy, and if she'd known they were going in the woods, she would have worn sneakers with socks and a pair of jeans.

"It's in here," Jayson Turner's friend said.

"Can't you hear it?" said his other friend with what seemed like a smirk.

Jayson Turner nodded at the trees, and then they were all looking, the three boys and Mirah herself, trying to separate the party sounds from the vast patch of unbroken darkness.

She pitched her ears toward the trees, she strained herself seeking music and laughter and the beckoning sounds of an event not worth missing, one she would be seen at on the arm of Jayson Turner. A wild and unforgettable night that would shift her position in the universe, just in time for the school year to start. How she wanted to find that in there, how she ached for it. Yet all that came back to her ears were the crickets and the branches rustling, the howl of an animal, the bristling dance of the trees.

She turned back. Jayson Turner covered his mouth and said something to his friends.

"Wait, wait," Mirah said, because she wanted so badly to believe, wanted it more than she'd ever hoped to know if there was a God who could answer each and every question (and she had so many questions), more than she wanted her parents to suck it up and stay together, more than she wanted her grandmother to come back to life the way she used to be before she fell face-first down the cellar stairs.

"I hear it," Mirah said. "They're in there. I hear the party. I do. I hear it. Let's go." Before Jayson Turner could change his mind and leave her there all alone at the bend in the road, she led the way toward the trees.

The woods here have seen many things over the decades, and they've kept hold of it all. Only a sparse few nights that passed under these branches could curdle the blood. There have also been bird-watchers and camping expeditions, Girl Scouts counting flower species and collecting bugs, mud-spattered children chasing frogs in the creek, couples slipping into zipped sleeping bags skin to skin, drunk teenagers laughing and laugh-crying and vomiting in the brush, wandering hikers panicked about being lost, not realizing all along they were half a mile from civilization, people singing to themselves or arguing with themselves or standing very still in the center of it all, appreciating the sound of rustling leaves. All this swept up together in the memory of the place, as if it were happening at the exact same time, layer over layer over layer, time melded together to form one moment, the girl from the summer before and the girl from the summer not yet finished wearing the same face and screaming the same screams.

There was no party.

We'd been in the woods for hours—we came almost every Saturday night—so we knew that already. Soon Mirah would know it, too.

Mirah thought she knew Jayson Turner from watching him at school, from what she'd heard trickled down from other girls, from what he said when he'd texted her, but she didn't, not at all.

She did say *no*, and she did say *stop*, but her only witness was the blanket of night all around her, eyeless and armless and too helpless to do a thing.

After they left her, Mirah did nothing for what seemed a long time. Then she sat up. She had the flashlight in her hands, and she didn't know how it got there. She had lost her phone and her shoes, and she couldn't feel her feet. When she started running, it was without a plan or a direction. She thought she might never stop; she thought her body not capable of stopping. She stumbled and she fell and she picked herself up and she kept going because out there in the wooded distance she saw a light flickering, a fire, she smelled the smoke, and the only thing she was conscious of knowing was that she should run toward it. Half of her wanted to be found and taken home, and the other half of her wanted to run straight into the fire and feel the flames.

She was the second girl to find our fire, but we wouldn't let her get away like the last one did. She came when it was so close to midnight, and that couldn't be coincidence.

She found us. We said this into her matted hair and into her mashed ear. *You found us.* She didn't put up a fight when the strongest of us led her into the circle. *You found us.* When the leaves were placed. *You found us.* When her blood was taken and dripped into the bowl. *You found us.* The water and the oil poured. *You found us.* We asked her the urgent questions (like where she lived, like who we should call), but she wouldn't answer, so we asked others.

Once she knew the after, she wouldn't mind. The fire turned more furious, the frenzy faster, our voices one voice, our power growing roots in the dirt and reaching high into the night air as if it had been stitched together from all of us and we from it.

She looked up at us like a soaked and startled doe who carried the arrow between her eyes.

She didn't recognize us as sisters yet. She may not have known we were even human beings, a few of us practically still girls ourselves. In the daylight she would see us for who we were, and we would let her: Her neighbors and the people she passed on the streets of town. The librarian. The former prom queen. The gas-station attendant. The ballet teacher. The outcast who hung around outside the convenience store. The artist who painted the murals on High Street. The girls' soccer coach. The scientist. The salutatorian. No one would suspect we shared these nights together, or what we could do.

The most careful of us kept the girl cradled, so she wouldn't skitter away. The one of us who was most skilled at calming leaned in and lent a soft voice to her ear. Some of us kept close, and others of us kept our distance. All we knew was that she had stayed this time, she hadn't gone running for the road, and now we would help her, we would hear her, we would avenge her, if she wanted us to. Most of all, we would offer her what we had and let her in.

The moon cast down its light onto all of us. We would tell her what was possible. How we could inspire accidents with four-door sedans or speeding bicycles. We could constrict airways. We could stifle the beat of fatty hearts from all the way across town. We could also do smaller things, like broken fingers and crushed egos, like fumbles and failures and debilitating bouts of the flu. We could do good in the world, too, like calm red rashes and stop night terrors, like show someone lost she was not alone. There were enough of us to do anything. As for Jayson Turner and his friends, they would never be able to hurt anyone else again. That, we could surely do.

"How is it so bright?" the one of us called Mirah said. The moon had grown along with us, and she was looking up at it.

She didn't understand she'd done it. We all had, and we were only getting started. She didn't realize that all her roaring, living, breathing anger could create so much light.

★★★★★

DIVINE ARE THE STARS

by Zoraida Córdova

MARIMAR MONTOYA KNEW THEY WERE ALMOST at Rancho Divino when the air thickened with the rot of unturned earth and wilted wildflowers.

She'd returned to western Colorado twice in the last five years for funerals—days after her parents died and she went to live with Tía Parcha at thirteen, then two years later when Tía Parcha met an untimely fate, just like the rest. Five years and nothing had changed in these lands—not the unyielding sun, not the hungry earth, and not the tire-eating road that led all the way home.

"That's as far as this piece of crap-o-la is getting," Chuy said, putting the dusty red jeep in park behind a neat row of cars off the side of the road. Gaston's Mustang was at a hasty angle, Enrique's Lamborghini was covered up with a tarp (typical), and Tatinelly's pink Beetle was sandwiched between two sedans.

"How the hell did Tati get that thing up here?" Marimar asked.

Chuy pulled out a pack of American Spirits and slapped them against the palm of his hand. His brown eyes rolled to the back of his head before turning to his cousin. "Maybe her magic isn't completely gone after all."

They sat in the car for a little while longer, the windows rolled down just enough that the wind whistled around them and dry leaves made their way between the cracks and onto Marimar's lap. She'd been away from the city for sixteen hours and already green things—no matter how near death they were—found their way to her. As always, her power was stronger the closer she was to Rancho Divino and away from the smoke and iron of the city. She held the leaf to her nose and wished she had a book so she could press it.

"Do we *have* to go?" Chuy asked one last time. He turned the rearview mirror to make sure his thick, meticulously groomed dark hair was in place.

"You've asked that six times since we left New York and the answer is still yes," Marimar answered, opening the door and taking the first of many steps toward Rancho Divino. She was barefoot, digging her toes into the dirt like worms.

Chuy side-eyed her, his full mouth smirking around a cigarette burning as quickly as his nerves. His eyes were drawn back to the mirror, back to the road where another car was jostling its way up the hill to fill the empty space behind their jeep.

"Ugh, Dirty Diego got an invite, too?" Marimar asked, slamming her door shut.

"The vultures descend even before the body is cold." Chuy shook his head but marched on beside her, pulling out a white invitation bleeding black scrawl, his thumb tracing his grandmother's shaky letters.

Come collect. Me muero. I'm dying.

When Marimar was little she used to run across the hills trying to wake the fairies that lived among the twisted gardens. Rosa Divina liked to tell stories of the winged creatures that protected the ranch with their otherworldly magics born right from the stars. Rosa Divina promised that if Marimar used her power, if she showed potential, she'd wake the fairies. But no matter how much she tried and tried, Marimar's power would not spark, and she never saw any—there were too many bugs and dragonflies in the way. So Rosa Divina never had to keep her promise. Marimar always believed that her own lack of potential was the reason Rosa Divina didn't take her in after her mom died.

As she marched down the winding road, arm in arm with Chuy, Marimar fought the urge to sprint into the tall grass fields and search for the winged beasties. But if the fairies had once protected the ranch, they were long gone by now.

At the sight of the family home Chuy lit his second cigarette.

"This is depressing," he said. "I remember it being bigger."

Chuy wasn't wrong, but memories make things grander and more beautiful when you want to think fondly of them. At the end of the road, nestled at the junction of surrounding hills, the ranch resembled a toy house. Marimar imagined picking up the whole house between her index finger and thumb and shaking it against her ear to listen for the rattle inside. If she closed her eyes she could picture everything within its walls. The floorboards that groaned in the middle of the night, as if the wood was still alive and trying to stretch free. Tall glasses of candles that covered every available surface, rivers of wax melting into every crack it could find. Great open windows that let in the sweet smell of grass and hay and flowers. Fat chickens and pigs Marimar and Chuy tormented while their mothers, Peña and Parcha, tended to the gardens around back.

Back then the ranch was palatial. Their own private world among the sky and mountains, and Rosa Divina was the queen of it all.

"Do you think she's really dying?" Marimar asked, batting her hand at a dragonfly that kept buzzing around her cheek. "Maybe it's like the time she pretended to be sick so that my mom and me would move back home."

Chuy puffed out his cigarette smoke, and it took on the shape of a bird, batting its wings toward the heavens. He smirked at his cousin. "Or like the time she said if my mother didn't get married she'd wither away to dust."

"Or like the time she caught you and the farm boy."

"And then you and the farm boy's brother."

"Why is it always the end of the world with this family?"

Marimar shrugged because she didn't have an answer. She had never thought of her grandmother as mortal. The Grand Rosa Divina couldn't die. Could she? But then why else ask every living relative to gather in the family lands, handed down from generation to generation since 1857? And come collect what? The lands were to go to the eldest daughter—Peña Montoya. But Marimar's mother was dead, so the next in line was Enrique.

"Why is everyone standing outside?" Chuy asked. The final stretch of the road was steep, the wind reaching out like hands and pushing them the rest of the way. When they were little they'd race and roll down. Now they were trying to keep their equilibrium, feet dashing until they landed in front of the ranch, where two dozen of their closest and most distant relatives were standing around. Aunts and uncles and cousins they hadn't seen in years, some only from faded photographs, watched Marimar and Chuy approach.

Marimar walked up to the house, a swarm of dragonflies now trailing around her. With every step her heart descended into the pit of her stomach. Her childhood home was nothing like she remembered it, and even though she was expecting some wear and tear, she was not ready for this.

Dark green ivy and vines crept between the wood panels, through shattered windows, all consuming, as if devouring the house back into the ground. Roots broke through the porch like tentacles, wrapping around the door handle to shut the way in.

And if Rosa Divina was still inside, it shut her way out.

"Grandma?" Marimar beat her fist against the door, and a splinter lodged itself into the tender side of her palm. "Gran—"

"We've tried that," Enrique said, stuffing his fat hands into his trouser pockets. He was Rosa Divina's only son, which made him Marimar's uncle. But he was a mere ten years older than her, and hated being called anything that made him feel like he was aging. "But please, tell us what the City Dwellers would do that we haven't tried for hours."

Ever since she was little, he'd found a way to silence her, remind her that she was just as ordinary as he was. Maybe it was distance and time, but she wasn't afraid of him anymore.

"Shut up, Enrique," Marimar growled, trying to grab the root that kept the door from opening. Meanwhile, the dragonfly pests attempted to land along her arms, her wrists, the baby hairs that stuck out of her ponytail.

Enrique chuckled. "Praise the saints, you finally have a backbone."

Marimar tried to look through the windows, but they were clouded with layers of dust. The vines shook, as if shivering in the chill of the setting sun.

"What should we do?" Tatinelly asked, her voice like the susurration of leaves on the breeze. "This little one's starting to get hungry."

The years had been good to cousin Tati. She placed her hands on her pregnant belly and found a smooth boulder to sit on while they waited. Her husband—a small, thin man with sunburnt patches all over his arms—tried not to stare at the growing gathering.

"Didn't she hide keys inside the apple tree?" Chuy asked.

"The orchard is withered," Enrique said dismissively, but stuck out his chest, asserting command of the situation. He seemed to grow taller as the rest of the family turned to him and only him for a way into the ranch.

Marimar couldn't even keep track of the people who kept coming down the hill and settling around the front steps like human debris. She made a mental note of the Montoyas from California, the Montoyas from Spain and the Montoyas from Mexico City. All of them checking their watches, tapping their feet, sucking their teeth. All of them ready to collect whatever prize was allocated to them and run.

Only Chuy and Marimar stood off to the side, forever and always slightly too different from the rest of their clan, just like their mothers.

"Isn't it weird," Chuy told her, "to think that we're all related?"

"Cats are related to lions."

Chuy lit up another cigarette, his hands trembling now. "Which ones are we in this scenario?"

Marimar wasn't sure which one she'd pick, but it didn't matter because Enrique was walking away from the group and marching around back. She nudged Chuy, and they followed him.

Lion, Marimar thought. *We're the lions.*

Enrique was in the small shed behind the house. The shed was in better condition than the ranch since it wasn't covered in vines. But when he opened the door, it came right off the hinges. He threw it off to the side, sweat making his light-brown skin shiny.

"Puta de su madre, I can't wait to sell this slice of hell," he said between expletives as his hand closed around what he was looking for.

"I thought your mom washed the curses out your mouth," Chuy said, and when Enrique jumped, he smiled.

"What are you doing?" Marimar stood her ground as Enrique slung a rusted axe over his shoulder.

"I'm tired of waiting. That old witch has made my life miserable since the day she realized I'd never carry any of her godforsaken superstitions."

"They're not superstitions," Marimar said, anger licking at her skin right down to her bare toes.

Enrique barked a bitter laugh. "Keep telling yourself that. There's an evil here. That's what got my sisters. I'm sure as hell not letting it get near me or mine."

Chuy flicked his cigarette butt on the ground and whispered in her ear, "For the sake of the world I hope he's sterile."

"Come," Marimar said, and pulled her cousin along after their uncle.

The crowd of Montoyas parted to make way for The Grand Rosa Divina's heir. He wielded the axe high over his head as he marched upon the door. The sun was a bloody red thing sinking behind the clouds, streaks of furious pinks and oranges creating the illusion of fire.

"Stop!" Marimar shouted, but Enrique did not listen, and he brought the axe down on the roots that kept the door shut. The vines ripped, the roots twisted, but the axe was like a fist against solid brick. Enrique couldn't stop now, so he kept hacking away at a root that petrified with every strike.

"It'd be easier to burn it to the ground," Chuy said, looking down at his lighter. The cherry of his cigarette lit up the angles of his face.

When she was a little girl, Marimar wanted magic to be real. She wanted to conjure spirits from the ether like Rosa Divina. She wanted to pull gold right out of the earth, meld it with her bare hands just as her great-grandfather had once done. She wanted to speak to the stars like her mother, before the stars stopped speaking back and she wasn't strong enough to bear the silence. The magic left all of them, little by little. When it was gone, there was nothing that could fill that void, and the fate of the Montoyas always ended in early graves. So, instead of grabbing hold of the last threads of that magic, they forgot it. Those who could outrun the curse left. Those who couldn't never got far.

But Marimar didn't want to forget. She wasn't sure if magic was a curse or a blessing, but it was part of her. As twisted as Rosa Divina was, she survived in a world that didn't want her and she survived the magic that claimed the lives of her family. *Come collect. Me muero.* That's what Rosa Divina sent to every family member standing outside this house. Marimar was sure that not one of them had announced themselves. It was all by brute force and shouting and banging that they tried to get inside.

"Stop!" Marimar shouted, and this time, even the mountains trembled with the sound of her cry.

She made her way through the dark, and pushed Enrique aside. She stood in front of the door. She heard the night, an incandescent whisper that only happened when she was home. She heard the stars.

"I've come to collect."

At her words, the roots gave way, relinquishing their hold on the door. The house released a deep sigh that shook the entire structure. Dragonflies and lightning bugs flitted in the dark open hall, their hazy glow illuminating the foyer. Floorboards peeked beneath layers of dirt, which must've come in with the roots and vines that broke through like stitches.

Marimar didn't wait for the others. She knew Chuy was right behind her, and he was all she needed. They went right for the living room, where The Grand Rosa Divina liked to sit and drink mezcal by the fireplace and watch the sun set behind the mountains.

The old witch was right where she always was. Her warm brown skin cracked like the parched earth around the house, and her hair was braided into a crown around her head, still regal. Those bright brown eyes crinkled with a knowing smile. Marimar felt her own heart spike with relief and terror combined.

"Gran," she gasped.

"Oh my saints," Chuy said.

"It's not polite to stare," Rosa Divina told them, her voice strong and raspy as ever. It was the rest of her that needed some getting used to.

The Grand Rosa Divina was covered in vines—they grew straight out of her flesh like extensions of her veins, they wrapped around the high-backed upholstered chair that faced the fireplace. Rosebuds the size of pearls bloomed from the branches sprouting out of her skin. And her feet had turned into thick brown roots that tore through every part of the house and dug straight back into the earth.

For a long time all Marimar wanted was to get away from the ranch. Away from the constant reminder of her mother. Of the whispers of the night. Of the magic that teased like flint on steel but never ignited. Now all she wanted was to pick up a broomstick and sweep away the layers of dust and decay that gathered in every corner of the house. Snakes nestled around the fire, having found their way through the holes Rosa Divina's roots were driving through the walls. Silvery spiderwebs glistened, stretching entire arachnid cities along the banister, up the stairs, and across the ceiling. Chickens and pigs still ran around the house, but they were slower than Marimar and Chuy remembered.

"How long do you think it's been like this?" Chuy whispered as they carried brooms and trash bags down the hall.

"I'm not sure I want to know," Marimar said.

As the rest of the family filled the house with their overnight bags, Marimar and Chuy cleaned up the living room as best they could. Three of the younger Montoyas brought every table and chair they could find. If Rosa Divina couldn't move, then they would build a dining room around her.

For people who didn't want to be there hours ago, they moved quickly. Tatinelly brought flowers from the yard by the bushels, making centerpieces that masked the smell of dirt clinging to the wallpaper. The Mexico City Montoyas started in on dinner, and the Spanish Montoyas claimed dessert. The California Montoyas made their way to the basement to find anything to drink themselves through the dinner.

"You could lend a hand," Marimar told Enrique.

He took a seat across from his mother, where her bottle of Oaxaca mezcal and a single glass were just out of reach. He poured himself a drink without offering it to his mother first, and sat back. "You're looking well, Mother."

"And you look positively mundane," she said, then turned her head to Chuy. All it took was a *look* from her ancient eyes and Chuy ran off somewhere, only to return moments later with a glass he was polishing with the hem of his shirt. He filled half the glass and handed his grandmother the smoky drink.

"Come on, Mother," Enrique said, his hands dirty from holding the axe. "Do we have to sit through this? The place is a mess. We all know I'm next in line for the land. Just—where is the paperwork?"

The Grand Rosa Divina looked at her son. She knew he'd slithered out between her legs, but even then she could not recognize him. He was untouched by the stars. When she looked into his eyes she saw no love—only hunger and greed.

"Upstairs. Second drawer on my nightstand."

He took his drink with him, bypassing two Montoyas who clutched chickens by their necks in each hand, feathers leaving a trail toward the kitchens.

"Tatinelly," Rosa Divina said.

"Yes?" Tatinelly and her husband were wide-eyed, their fear acrid sweat from their pores. They approached, both resting a hand on the pregnant belly as if their fragile bones could protect that child from the world.

Rosa Divina held her hand out. "Puedo?" *May I.*

"Of course," the couple said. "We'd be honored."

Rosa Divina placed her free hand on the top of the belly and closed her eyes. Marimar wondered what those old ears picked up. Could she hear the stars? Were they whispering now? Why couldn't Marimar hear them inside the house? Rosa Divina's hand grew a single white rosebud in the thin flesh where her index finger met her thumb. The old woman took a deep breath and a bigger drink of mezcal.

"A girl. Excellent. Be *good* to her," Rosa Divina said. "Let her run free."

"Thanks, Gran," Tatinelly said. "I'm sorry I don't get to visit more."

But Rosa Divina dispelled the apology with a wave of her hand and the blooming rose that withered into dust seconds later.

When Tatinelly and her husband left to help in the kitchens, Marimar took the seat in front of her grandmother and drank straight from the bottle. They said nothing. They never needed to. Marimar simply reached out and placed a hand on one of the roots jutting out from her grandmother's foot.

"Why did you do this?" Marimar asked as glass broke and pans clashed in the kitchens. "*How* did you do this?"

"I didn't. We become what we need."

"What does that mean?" Marimar asked.

But Rosa Divina's brown eyes were cloudy and graying with sickness. She simply sat back and listened. The stomping feet of children, the drunken laugh of cooks, the sizzle of meat, the rattle of silverware, the buzz of a dozen dragonfly wings. And beneath all of that, a series of heartbeats. Each one with its own unique rhythm of wishes and hopes and dreams. Chuy gasped and dropped the plate in his hand because, now, he could hear them.

"I knew the stars chose you, too," Rosa Divina said.

Chuy took his grandmother's hand and placed it against his wet cheek. Marimar tried to remember the last time she saw her cousin cry, and remembered sitting at the top of the hill as they both called out to the stars and were answered with silence. Why did they choose him now? And her heart twisted with a selfish desire—*why not me?*

"What's the meaning of this?" Enrique shouted from the stairs. He held a fistful of papers in his hand and waved them in front of his mother's face. He held a finger to Marimar's temple like a cocked gun. "Her? She's a child!"

"Marimar is eighteen, aren't you?"

"I am." Her heart beat louder than the others, but only Rosa Divina and Chuy could hear the change.

"This land belongs to *me*," Enrique said. The other Montoyas were emerging from every room of the house and gathering in the living room. "Why do you think we all came here? For your lies about some great destiny? For your drunken stories about the past? You're a damn rose bush, Ma, and everyone is acting like it's just another day. I'm not leaving without what's mine, and *this land* is rightfully mine."

"Nothing is yours!" The Grand Rosa Divina shouted. "The world wasn't made for you. The world was *made*.

"I didn't call you here to give you jewels or to watch you fight over a bit of dirt. I called you here to see which ones of you would show up and why. Come collect what's left of our magic, our stories, because when I'm gone, what will you have?"

"I'll have peace," Enrique said, angry tears streaming from his hungry eyes.

"That's enough of you," Chuy said, and this time, Enrique remained quiet.

Rosa Divina sat up as much as her legs would allow and stood. At first, she wavered, her round body attempting to balance on the roots that devoured her legs. When she was steady, she poured the last of her mezcal. Her arms and fingers slow like branches in a summer breeze. She turned to her family and raised her glass.

"All you have is each other. Listen to the stars. Listen." The earth rumbled. "Now, go."

Half the Montoyas ran back out of the ranch and into the night. Others stayed behind to help, or to gather what they could. Silver, pigs, goblets, books—anything that could be carried. Anything that could be sold.

"What's happening to her?" Tatinelly asked.

"Gran," Marimar pleaded. "I don't understand. What are you doing?"

"I'm not doing this," Rosa Divina said. "I am becoming what I need."

The Grand Rosa Divina Montoya stretched higher and higher. Her legs became the base of a thick tree trunk, roots undulating through the floorboards like rivers carving their way through stone.

"Go," Marimar told Tatinelly. "Go!"

"I'm not leaving you," Chuy told Marimar, and grabbed her hand. She never doubted.

Marimar held her grandmother's fingertips until she was too tall to hold. Rosa Divina's arms stretched outward, bending into branches. The house shuddered around them, and then the door slammed. Enrique stood there with a candelabra in hand, the blue flames burning fiercely at the wicks.

"You always were her favorites," he said. "Now you get to be buried with her."

"No!" Chuy shouted as Enrique threw the candelabra onto the couch, and it caught like wildfire. It wasn't enough. He knocked over every candle on the tables, the fireplace mantel.

Marimar looked up at her grandmother once more. There

were so many things she wanted to ask. Why now? Why this? Why her?

"Don't let the magic leave you," Rosa Divina told her.

"I won't." It was a promise. And in that moment, she felt it. The familiar pull of the night, the whisper of the earth.

Those times her grandmother had told her to find fairies in the hills, to listen to the stars, Marimar had always come home defeated. But now she knew she hadn't been listening. Now she knew they had been with her all along. The dragonflies shimmered with light, with the magic of stars and the wild and the mountains. They surrounded Enrique, their tiny arms and legs crawling all over his face as the roots extended over him, around him.

"We have to go!" Chuy shouted, pulling his shirt over his mouth.

He grabbed Marimar by her wrist and pulled her. They had always protected each other the way their mothers couldn't. They climbed over the roots in their path, over their uncle's still body and toward the open front door. The fire raged behind them, eating through the furniture, the walls, the floor. Burning through everything except the tree.

Do you think she's really dying? Marimar had asked.

The Grand Rosa Divina couldn't die.

What was left of the Montoyas was a scattered few. They stayed there until the fire died and the sun rose. The stench of rot and decay around the house was replaced with smoke. If they closed their eyes they could imagine themselves sitting around an autumn fire pit, the kind of family that was bonded by blood and roots and magic.

Bathed in morning light, the house was nothing but a pile

of ash around a great tree with branches that reached for the heavens.

"Look!" one of the Montoyas said, her bloodshot eyes wide. She pointed at Chuy.

A rose the size of a quarter bloomed bright red between his clavicles. He wasn't the only one. Tatinelly lifted her shirt, revealing the pearly rivers of stretch marks across her belly. She had a rose growing out of her belly button.

"I guess we collected more than our lives," Tatinelly's husband said, his laugh refreshing in the aftermath.

"Not me," Tatinelly said, smiling at her swollen belly. "The little one."

They watched as the breeze carried away the ash, leaving nothing but the tree, surrounded by hundreds of dragonflies.

Marimar repeated her grandmother's words over and over. This was all hers. She was still barefoot, and she still couldn't tear herself away. It was the crackle of Chuy's lighter that brought her back to the present. She hugged the rest of her family as they began their journeys back home. But she and Chuy were already home.

"Look at that," he told her, smiling with all his teeth as he pointed to her hand.

On the inside crook of her hand, at the base of her index and thumb, was a rosebud, small and delicate and not yet bloomed.

"We become what we need," Marimar said, and though the stars were hidden, she knew they were listening.

★ ★ ★ ★ ★

DAUGHTERS OF BABA YAGA

by Brenna Yovanoff

ONCE, MY DOWNSTAIRS NEIGHBOR MAYA FOUND this CCCP shirt for five dollars at the thrift store. She wore it under her blue flannel until her grandma Ludy saw.

We were playing Dachshund Dash on our phones in that dark triangle under the front stairs, and Ludy came in with a little wire shopping cart and some onions in a bag and saw us there, and her face was dry and wrinkly, dotted brown like an apple doll, but right then, she turned the color of cream.

She stood over us with her bag of onions, yelling for us to stand up, and were we animals? She could still remember the Soviets.

We were only in the eighth grade and didn't really know what the letters on the shirt meant. We stood there in the front hall, in the place near the stairs where the carpet was sad and lumpy like there was a mouse under it, while Ludy shouted. She kept stamping down the lumpy place with her foot, pointing at that stupid thrift-store shirt—the hammer and the sickle. It was a flag for a country that wasn't even a country anymore, just a bunch of bad memories the grown-ups only talked about when they thought we weren't paying attention.

Before, I'd always thought the picture on the flag looked like the sky in a little kid's drawing. Like a moon and a sunset. Like a golden Cheshire smile. I had barely thought about it at all.

But to Ludy, it was a harvest blade on blood, because symbols mean things.

Maya hung her head and looked at the floor, but I kept staring at that one yellow star.

If this were a story, it would be me who wore the shirt. I'd be the main character, and not talking about some girl from my building who called me a pizda on the bus once and moved upstate last year and who I don't even talk to anymore.

But the skinny yellow moon on that T-shirt is not about me. Anyway, my grandma lives in Newark.

I'm not telling you this because I think Maya was supposed to have magically known better, or that I'm better than her, or that I wouldn't have done the same thing if there was a really good deal on a T-shirt I didn't understand. I probably would have.

Just that even in our most-told stories, sometimes the grandmas don't know how to tell the really bad parts. We grew up not understanding a lot of stuff, and the year before, Maya had started spelling her name with a *y* instead of a *j* because otherwise no one knew how to say it.

This is not about that. This is a story of what happened later, when the Kolbe charter school closed and we all got bused to St. Constantine instead. I'm not saying the thing with the T-shirt was some kind of portent or anything. I'm just telling it so you'll understand where it is I come from, and where all those other, shinier kids didn't.

The thing about where I live is that no one is actually from there. Everyone's family came over at different times and in different ways. We all just ended up in the same place.

You probably think I'm saying that in a metaphor way or something, but I am literally talking about Chauncey Heights. It's a pretty good neighborhood, even though it's not a nice one. We don't all go to the same churches or know the same language, but we have a lot of the same food and the same stories. We know how to fold the dough for uszka even if we're not Polish, and we know the words to each other's jumping rhymes and to stay away from Damian Michnicki the day after Easter because he will hide behind the dumpsters to throw water on you and try to smack you in the legs with a branch. We mostly understand each other's rules, is what I mean.

My Easter's on a different day than Damian's, but I know how it is to have a church that's not like on TV. Church of domed roofs, church of bells, of red eggs and backyard chickens and my grandma digging holes in the garden to put a little statue of Saint Joseph facedown in the dirt.

My dad says the reason the old ladies all wear saints medals and come in to buy their beef tongue from him instead of at the ShopRite is because they miss home. Also, it is sometimes hard to find beef tongue at the ShopRite. He says that red eggs on Easter are only pious gestures, and holy water to bless the house is purely superstition. There are no witches, no magic, just a way of trying to touch a place they can't go back to.

It doesn't matter.

I was still raised to bury saints in the yard.

The problem with whether or not boys like you is, you can't always tell.

I think about that whenever Tyler Strauss leans his elbow on the science table and stares at me. I think about boys a lot. About how hard I worked to make myself pretty. How sometimes now I wish I didn't.

"Stony, you have got legs like a starving-ass chicken," Gina diSario said in the locker room in seventh grade. That was a long time ago, before the whole lower floor at Kolbe got flooded and they canceled PE. "The way you look is like some kind of walking-around ladder."

And I made sure to laugh, because the thing you do in moments like that is, you laugh. I was even proud of myself right then for knowing how, but now it makes me think of something my grandma told me once. Americans smile too much, she said. They smile all the time, for no reason. Stojonovskis are better at knowing the geography of our own faces. We only smile when something makes us happy.

But like I said, that was back in seventh grade, before my chicken legs got unchickeny and my butt got noteworthy. And now we go to St. Constantine instead, and I have hips for days. I smile like a toothpaste commercial. Just like everybody else.

"I *am* American," I told my grandma.

It was true, too—I could say the names of the presidents and knew about Pokémon and all the words to "Livin' on a Prayer" and the Star Spangled Banner. I knew that when you colored a Halloween picture for the Fall carnival, you colored the devil red.

Just like I know that sometimes it's easier to let the girls at school call me Stony, instead of butchering my name. I know that sometimes boys look at you because you have hips, and not because they care what you think about anaphase and metaphase. That even though you can say all the bosses and underbosses and consligliere s on *The Sopranos* in order of episode and importance, they really just want to see you naked.

And so that's how I knew that Tyler Strauss could be looking because my legs do not look like a ladder anymore. Or he could be looking because he heard from Dave Kapowski that I let him feel my chest at the Washington game, which is only like 70 percent true. (I did, but I was wearing my puffy vest, so I'm not sure how much it counts). Or he could be looking because I look like the kind of person who knows the periodic table and all the bosses on *The Sopranos*.

But that last part, probably not.

The boys at St. Constantine are a kind of bad I'd never met before. Noisy, grabby assholes who pull out their halos when the teachers walk by. I smile at Tyler anyway, because I made a wish on my fourteenth birthday and then the wish came true. I got a butt and I got pretty and learned to straighten my hair, and now everyone calls me Stony, and sometimes, I just want to bite a hole in the world. I wish I could stop smiling at things I hate. Sometimes I wish I never learned.

The me that smiles is the good one. The one who does the dishes and works the register at the shop and makes my mother happy. Smiling-me is never any trouble, but I like it better in the kitchen with my father.

He doesn't believe in magic, but we both like *How the Universe Works* on the Science Channel. We put together catering trays and talk about our favorite parts like we're making a list of new saints. Saint Newton, Saint Copernicus, Saint Nikola Tesla. Saint the Hubble Telescope.

I pretend they're a prayer to bless me, a charm for luck. The sacred mysteries didn't stop being mysterious just because the world changed and got fast internet, and there's magic in the little things, even if my dad doesn't see it. It's there in the secret lives of girls, most of all. The way we smile and straighten our hair. We do magic every single day. We have to.

Paint your nails silver and your heart sort of turns silver, too. Your claws and bones and teeth are steel. And so, when Maya called me a pizda on the bus that time, I cursed her. Later, I was sorry. That big, unruly kind of magic only really happens when I get mad.

I drew nine circles nesting inside each other, took a drink of my dad's Luksusowa, and spit it on her school picture. Bit a piece of butcher's twine until I broke it.

Later that same week, I heard from Darcy in 3F that Maya was washing her hair after swim practice and it all fell out. Everybody said it was something bad about her skin, or else some kind of gland, but I knew better.

With silver nails and the right kind of smile, you can bite through anything.

Harmony Jessup is really weird.

She always looks comfortable and messy, like she just woke up, and when she sat down at my table in the cafeteria my first week at St. Constantine, I was surprised, but not completely. The thing with Harmony is, she kind of just does what she wants.

"Are you a witch?" she said, peeling the lid off a little cup of pudding.

I figured that she meant the green, warty kind from cartoons, with pointy hats and brooms. My kind was nothing like that. The stories I knew were all about what's right and fair. Baba Yaga and her chicken-footed house. Her punishments for the wicked. I was just a girl with rainbow-snake leggings and silver glitter nail polish.

"What? No." And I rolled my eyes just in case. "What are you even talking about?"

Harmony leaned on her elbows, shrugging this cool little shrug. "Katya S. says you got a ninety-eight on the trig test last week. The only ones good at trig are suck-ups and witches, so you gotta to be a witch."

That made me laugh, slumping in my chair. "Yeah, well. I'm not."

"Okay," she said. Then she looked up. She had that kind of face that looks a million years old and like a little girl at the same time. "I am."

I was eating cold shashlyk, leftover from our pre-season Jets party, biting it straight off the skewer. The meat felt just the right amount of tough between my teeth.

Harmony didn't seem to care about me eating leftovers with my hands, which was nice. Anyway, what she was doing was weirder.

She took the top off her sandwich and started pulling it apart into separate layers on the plastic bag. Then she got out a Coke and a thing of Cheetos. "You know that superhero test?"

I shook my head, sucking the burned place where the wooden stick tasted like smoke. "Like they take your blood or something?"

She laughed and threw a piece of lettuce at me. It hit my shoulder and tumbled down onto the table. "You give somebody a choice for magical powers and then test their personality by what they pick. You say you want to fly, it's supposed to mean you have a hero complex—like Superman or something. But if you say you want to be invisible, it means you're all about the villains. Invisible people are up to some nefarious shit."

I threw the lettuce back at her. "That's how you know a dude invented that question."

Harmony smiled. She was wearing this dark, shiny eyeshadow, layered on thick, like magic marker. "How so?" She said it softly, like here was the real test.

"It's some high-level bullshit, is all. Thinking people only pick the secret one because they want to do bad things."

She nodded and leaned closer, and all of a sudden her eyes were big and bright and lit up like planets. "*Right?* I mean, think about all the ways you could figure out how to do good! How cool would it be to go around messing with the bad guys where no one can see you?"

That hadn't been what I meant. All I meant was that sometimes you pick invisibility so some asshole in a snapback and track pants doesn't scream at you about bjs out the car window when you're walking to the bus. You pick invisibility because it's halfway through English and you got dressed in the dark because you still share a room with your sister who sometimes works doubles, and you just realized you wore the leopard bra and now it's showing through your shirt and you can't go home to change. You pick it because for your fourteenth birthday, you got a pair of hips—and yeah maybe you wished for that, maybe you even like it. But goddamn it, don't you sometimes just want to move around in the world without everybody making a big thing about it?

Harmony was still talking about heroes, about all the good you could do from the shadows. "We should start a secret club, go around and avenge things."

"Avenge what?"

"Whatever you *want*," Harmony said. "Pick your grievance." Like it was a fast-food order or a fan of cards that she was holding out for a magic trick.

But I didn't know how to do that. It was impossible to pick a grievance out of all the bad, wrong shit that happened every single day. The big ones are the kind nobody can do a thing about, and the little things seemed too little to get vengeful over. How could I be mad about Jackson Preaker telling me I smelled like cabbage? It was just nothing.

The real things all belonged to someone else. I could feel it sometimes when the ladies in the butcher shop talked about the Cold War, the discotheques they went to when they were my age, and how they stayed out all night with their friends, listening to Madonna and George Michael on black-market cassette tapes. How the moon was the entire sky and they played the songs so many times the tapes wore out and sounded like they were coming from underwater. Played them until all the singers sounded drowned.

The crack in their voices makes all the petty bullshit at St. Constantine feel like nothing.

I wanted to make Harmony understand that. That I was worried anything I'd do or pick would feel small. If I could do righteous magic, I wanted it to be big.

If I could do righteous magic, I would make it so the Petrova sisters would always have beef heart when they wanted it, and not ever start to cry when they talked about cassette tapes.

The day I stopped rolling my eyes about secret heroes and started believing in them was the day after Wyatt Carlson broke up with Katya R., and then called her a slut all over school even though that's a two-person activity and it's not exactly like he just fell in there accidentally.

But he was going around St. Constantine with his pack of golden grinning wolves anyway, acting like she was a weather event or some piece of really bad luck that just happened to him.

It was after last period, when all the kids with cars had already gone home and all the raggedy ones were standing around in the municipal lot, waiting for their buses. Wyatt was alone, sitting out on the edge of the big cement planter by the pickup lane, waiting on some of his douchebag friends to finish up with football.

We were leaning on the bench for the city bus, and Harmony elbowed me and jerked her head in his direction. "Watch."

She went and plonked down next to him in that way she had. When he looked up, she gave him a really good smile. Then she scooted closer, and I pretended to be busy with my phone. Sometimes you can do that, even when you're wearing a vintage spangle disco top and leggings covered in cartoon sharks. Even when you are hard and toothy and silver to the core, sometimes that's just a second kind of invisible.

Harmony leaned in and put her hand on his arm, very kind. It looked weird, because no one I knew really wanted to be kind to Wyatt Carlson. He is purely the worst.

"Hey, Wyatt," she said, and there was a sweet, steely edge in her voice that made a shudder run up my spine. "We need to have a talk."

Wyatt frowned. He looked at Harmony's sleepy smile. He looked at her hand.

"The reason no one likes you," she said, and she said it gently, "is because you're a piece of shit."

Wyatt stared down at her, blank as blank, but a muscle in his jaw was twitching.

Harmony gave him a floppy little shrug. "And I know you think it doesn't matter. That you're going to keep getting everything you want, that everybody's just going to keep handing it over. But they're not." She leaned closer, and now her voice wasn't gentle at all. "You're going to graduate, get drunk and old and sad, and you're going to find out that the girls you conned or bullied into touching your dick in high school won't want to do it anymore. They'll be too wise and too smart and like themselves too much to even get near you."

He kept looking at her, his big, meaty hands opening and closing. I knew it was meant to make her nervous, but even as he did it, there was something in his face, like deep underneath, he was afraid.

"Wyatt," she said, looking at him with that certain angelic angle of her head, that smile. "This is the very best things ever get for you."

You could see the exact second when something changed inside him. Even if everything she was saying hadn't been true before, it was true now. I thought he was going to shout at her or hit her and got ready to throw my phone at him, or at least yell for the liaison officer.

But he didn't, and after a second she got down off the planter and came back to me.

The thing about witches is, all the ones in movies and cartoons and stuff are wicked. You learn to recognize them—draw them with their pointy, pointy hats, then paint them green. Know them by their brooms, wands, warts.

Harmony wasn't any of that. This was better.

It's a double-edged thingy, being a butcher girl. This is a fact.

The other girls all make faces, and boys like to tell you that you smell like cabbage, but you know they're actually saying something else, because you never wear your kitchen clothes to school. You do your laundry, wash your hair, and if you smell like anything at all, it's something sweet and sharp and secret. Like spices and dried blood.

There are good things about being the daughter of a butcher. A good thing is if we're having a block party or a birthday, everyone always asks us to bring the cabbage rolls, and then we can all rejoice about not having to eat the soggy ones that Katya C.'s mother makes that taste like wet hot dog.

A bad thing is that even if I'm not in the mood and I didn't volunteer, I am always in charge of anything nasty.

The day we had to cut up baby pigs in science lab, everyone at my table looked at me and didn't say it. They didn't have to. They just sat and waited for me to pick up the knife.

The pig was different from the ones at the shop. The skin was weird and rubbery and wet, and the stuff dripping off it smelled like chemicals. I made a face when I poked it with the blade. I had to press hard to cut the belly open.

We took notes and studied them, these pale little piggies, digging with our fingers and pinning them like pretty collages with the insides showing, the outside peeled back like a strange kind of flower, and then Lucas Hayes threw up.

He did it quietly, over the side of his lab table, but there is really no good way to be the boy who throws up in science in front of everybody. That's just the rule, and even if you didn't know before, everybody knew it after.

I was sorry for him, but in this *whatever* way. I figured that at least it was over. The other boys would laugh, and then he could leave and go to the nurse's. I really thought the fact that it happened would be the worst part.

But it wasn't, and the next day, all those big beaming golden boys were following him around making puking noises.

At Kolbe, the teachers would have called down thunder on something like that. It wouldn't have been allowed. It wasn't allowed at St. Constantine, either—they had one of those zero tolerances—but that kind of thing only works when someone knows how to catch you. The anointed douchebags in their halos never got caught at anything.

It took a week for me to understand that they weren't going to stop, and that no one who could make them stop was ever going to see. They would keep dishing it and Lucas would keep taking it, they would just keep looking golden. And that to me was almost worse than that they did it in the first place.

The way they thought it was so funny was sort of normal—people are assholes, that's not a secret. The thing that made me bite my pencil and wish for a metal spine was that they *could* do it, and keep on doing it forever.

And Lucas was basically nobody, right? Already half a ghost. He was one of those skinny, worried boys with dirty hair who never really looked at you. I didn't know him, is what I mean. But he was nice. I had two classes with him, and the first week I was at St. Constantine, he waited and held the door for me when I was carrying a War of the Roses diorama. I know that sounds like such a little thing, but Lucas Hayes held the door for me. No one else did.

He still came to class, because he was the kind of person who always came to class, and the other boys still followed him around, because for them, nothing ever got boring. And Tyler Strauss was always the one who started it.

Lucas sat with his head down and his neck red and didn't say anything, while Tyler pretended to stick his fingers down his throat until the rest of them joined in, and Hailey Clarke and Riley Whitley howled. Then Tyler would look at me across the table in science, leaning on his elbow and making this face that I don't know how to explain—one part satisfied and two parts hungry.

"You shouldn't be so mean to him," I said, when it had been nine days and the jackass circus had been going on so long my ears were starting to feel hot. "It's not like he could help it."

Tyler grinned his big TV grin, the kind that always seemed to be nudging you to go along with it. "That's what makes it funny. Anyway, come on, it's not like it matters. It's just Lucas."

I stared back at him and tried to think what Harmony would have done. She would have told him it was cruel to laugh at someone for what they couldn't help and that no one is *just* anyone. That he better get ready, because one day something bad or embarrassing would happen, and everyone would see him the way he really is, small and weak and pitiful, and then they'd make mean, stupid fun of him when it would have taken less effort to be kind, but he was so backward and messed-up that kindness might actually feel worse.

Harmony would have had some kind of truth to curse him with, but all my words were wrong.

The only truth I had in me was *You'll be sorry.*

"I know my grievance," I said to Harmony. We were eating lunch together by the trophy cases, under the student government banner, because she asked me to and none of my friends from Kolbe had second lunch. Also, I was still thinking about how she'd handled Wyatt. Also, I really did like her.

She nodded, tipping her head back and smiling her sweet smile at the ceiling. "I knew you'd have one eventually. This place is full of them."

In truth, though, I didn't have just one. The grievance was bigger than a single person. I made a whole goddamn list.

There were three kinds of names on it. The ones who did

the following and the puking sounds, the ones who did the laughing, and the ones who laughed and pretended not to.

Back when I made Maya's hair fall out, it had been a stupid, angry thing, half an accident almost.

Well, okay not really.

Maybe it was more that I was tired. I was over it, and I wished she would be punished for calling me a pizda, not because I was even so mad at her, specifically—it was a popular word at Kolbe that year, because it meant the same thing in like nine different languages—I was just *mad.* Mad at Maya, and mad that the meanest, most hateful thing that someone could say was just another way of pointing out that you were a girl.

This time, the magic was cool and slow. I was a poison night-flower blooming on black, not righteous, but vengeful.

I was so much angrier.

Here is what I did.

I wrote their names on a piece of butcher paper that I tore off from the big roll at the shop. There were fifteen people, printed in red felt pen, and Tyler was at the top.

At the bottom, I made a circle, because the oldest deepest magic is a story, and all the best stories are a circle. I folded the paper nine times, then poured out some pork blood from the jug for pudding and dipped my fingers in to seal it.

Because if I'm any kind of witch at all, this is the kind I'll be. Tough but fair, monstrous but just. No enchanted spindles or poison apples, only names and blood. A witch with the power to fly through the night in the bowl of a mortar, a house that walks on chicken feet, a fence of bones, a skull with magic fire shining out its eyes.

My witch is furious and ferocious. She doesn't grant wishes. But if you do what she says and treat her right, she just might help you. In the stories, there's always a catch, though, right? The catch is this—her way of helping is *her* way. Sometimes the way she helps you is by raining fire on all your enemies.

On the outside of the paper, I wrote this sentence, this sacred mystery—not a prayer, but a promise:

The moon is full, and even the stars are scared of me.

Some of them noticed the smell before they looked. Some were smart enough not to open their lockers. But not very many. Most people will always want to see what's inside, even when they shouldn't.

The way butchery works is, not every part is valuable. You have the expensive cuts, roasts and chops and loin. Those go in the glass case in front, lined up for the customers in tidy rows like a meat garden. Then you have the tougher cuts for stew or sausage. And after that, you have the cheap parts. Leftover bits for various nefarious things.

Feet, hearts, livers. Tongues and lungs and kidneys. There are a lot of bits.

Everyone got the honeycomb tripe and the livers. Webby, lumpy clusters of beef kidneys. The tongues were for the ones who laughed the loudest, the maws were for the snickerers. All the things these gleaming hoodlums in their haloes wouldn't even touch—sheep's eyes and pigs' feet.

Jackson Preaker got snouts and lungs, the better to tell girls they smelled like cabbage.

Since Tyler Strauss did the most and the worst of everything, he got the head.

The fruit of my work did not look good. It was slippery and oozing, buzzing with flies.

But the smell was even more spectacular. After all night in the school with the furnace on, the junior hall was pretty ripe.

Riley Whitley, who was on varsity debate and could text in class without getting in trouble and who always shrieked in pretend horror and actual delight whenever someone made fun of Lucas, got some of the gooshy stuff on her sneakers, which had started the day white. I stood on the steps by the soda machines and laughed, while Riley screamed and screamed. I kind of wished it was like those explosions you see in movies, all billowing and gold, so I could walk away from it. The screaming was aces, though. It was pretty good.

The vice principal called me in. After all, I was the butcher girl. But you could tell she didn't know how to talk about organ meat, or even ask the right questions. They were never going to prove it.

"I don't understand," she said, not like she was talking to me, though, just shaking her head. She was still stuck on how someone got fifty pounds of sticky, bloody parts into the school. Got all those parts through fifteen combination-locked doors.

But it wasn't that hard. Not when you have steel in the blood.

Harmony does her magic in the soft white space between what *is* and what *could* be, but my punishments are never done in whispers. And I believe in the hallowed saints of science, sure—Newton and Copernicus and Tesla. Saint the Hubble Telescope. But I believe in magic, too. The really big stuff that mostly happens when I get mad.

Harmony waited outside the office. When I finally came out, she grabbed me. Her fingers pinched too hard, and I looked at her hand until she dropped it. I wondered if we were going to have a problem.

"You're supposed to be invisible," she said. "You're supposed to be the hand moving behind the curtain."

I raised my eyebrows. I didn't laugh at her, but *come on*.

I was wearing this really slick pair of jeans—metallic silver like a space robot or a gallant knight—and my hair was loose and long and very thick, even though it was always getting tangled on purses and seat belts and most of the girls from my neighborhood had cut theirs short in middle school because they said it looked old-fashioned. And maybe Harmony was sweet and sly and secret, but that's just not my style.

I stood under the student government banner, waiting for her to do her trick, hit me with the truth. All the sharp, reproachful things she could have said. *Stony, you are a bad disaster, a rageful monster, a battering ram. A Craftsman hammer when all you need is a scalpel.*

And those things would have sounded right to me. They would have been true. I wasn't sure I cared, was all. The sound of Riley Whitley screaming was still aces.

Harmony put her head on one side like she was staring into me, measuring all the way down. Then she nodded. The bell rang for second lunch, and she gave me that small floppy shrug and hooked her arm through mine.

We are the clever daughters. We are the witch-girls. That's all you need to know.

When Harmony smiles, the world melts. People's secret futures open in front of her like doors. She decides you're a hero, you become one. She decides you're a villain, or a slimy asshole loser sitting on a big cement planter, you become that instead. Her best weapon is the truth.

When I smile, though…

When I smile, I'm not smiling. I'm showing you my teeth.

I was born to bury saints in the yard.

★★★★★

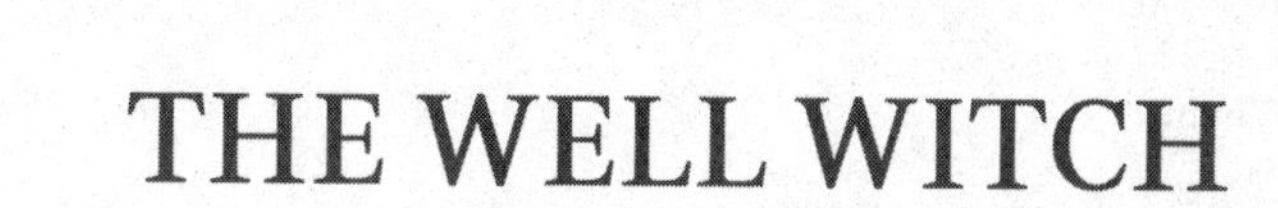

THE WELL WITCH

by Kate Hart

Texas, 1875

"THERE A MAN ABOUT THIS HOUSE?" ASKED the stranger.

Elsa eyed the group of men. Few dared to live on the Llano Estacado, the high desert prairie lands of the Texas panhandle, and after three years alone there, she feared very little. She had a healthy respect for the usual dangers: sunstroke, starvation, snake bites, wolves. But men were the most unpredictable animals, and those that found Elsa's oasis were usually lost both in geography and life, looking for directions, land, or, worst of all, wives.

She always showed them on their way, but she did not care to provide otherwise. "I live here alone," she replied. No sense in hiding the obvious. Possession was nine-tenths of the law—possession of a gun, anyway—but as she could only hold two of those at a time, she was forced to use less lethal weapons.

The stranger crossed the line where her green island met

the surrounding sea of rippling bleached grasses. "I'm Delbert," he said, swinging a leg to dismount. Up close, wrinkles and a grizzled beard aged him beyond the other two. "This here is Roy." Roy lifted a moth-eaten forage cap to reveal a nearly bald head. "And Zeb."

Zeb touched the brim of his cowboy hat. "Pleased to make your acquaintance, miss..."

"Elsa," she said.

Delbert stared around the property. She watched him take in the inexplicably verdant landscape, the flowering bushes around the house, the fact that the house was made of wood when no tree could be found for miles. Beyond, the prairie stretched out of sight, punctured only by sagebrush and low cactuses.

When she offered no explanation, Delbert cleared his throat. "Any chance we could get a bit of water?" He gestured at the canteen hanging from his horse. "Ain't seen a drop since round about the Canadian."

"Well's over yonder," she said, pointing behind the house. It was impossible the men had made it that far without water, never mind that the river was north and she'd watched them approach from the east. They were either more lost than they realized or terrible liars, and neither boded well.

"How'd you find a well all the way out here?" Roy asked as he dismounted.

"Just lucky." It was true—Elsa did feel fortunate to live with her humming awareness of what flowed beneath the ground. But with water more precious than money on the Llano, it didn't do to go advertising her abilities.

She stepped into the shade of her porch while the men filled their canteens. Roy guzzled straight from the bucket until he began to retch. "Worthless fool," Delbert said. He fanned himself with his black felt hat, similar to the one Elsa herself wore. "Reckon we could stop off here for a day or two?"

Elsa studied them. All three carried revolvers in Army-branded holsters, but they wore plain clothes, their faces dusty and sunburned. She didn't ask about their travels—the less she knew, the better—but they wouldn't get much farther on the piles of soap they were riding. "Until your horses are recovered," she said finally. With all the grass on the Llano, their animals should have been healthy, which meant they'd either been ridden hard or neglected, and Elsa approved of neither. "My home is my own," she said, "but you're welcome to bunk down in the barn."

Barn was a generous term. The structure was cobbled together from the remains of a sod house and some adobe additions, the roof just tall enough for a man to stand. "It's not much, but it's clean." Catching the look of distaste on Delbert's face, she couldn't help adding, "And the mule sleeps warm. His name is Otis."

Delbert opened his mouth, but Zeb shushed him.

That evening, Elsa served the men cornbread and beans, though her supplies were running low. The Army companies no longer needed guidance to find water, and they rarely came to the oasis anymore without her father's wares to buy. With the bison hunted close to extinction, neither the buffalo hunters nor the Comanches were available for much trade, either.

Elsa had been making do with her garden and some hunting, but she couldn't grow coffee or sugar or cornmeal. She dreaded the days-long trip into town. Its small main street of clapboard storefronts made her feel trapped, the saloons and whorehouses held no interest, and shopping was a chore:

the Anglo storekeepers tried to cheat her, and the Hispanos distrusted the German accent she'd gotten from her mother.

As much as she disliked visiting town, having strangers on her property was far worse. Despite a gorgeous sunset blazing pink and orange on the horizon, Elsa ate dinner alone to avoid conversation. Few were likely to guess that the haven was of her making, but coveted land was a dangerous place to live. These men didn't seem in the market for property, but she knew the house's existence alone would make them curious about its interior, and its unusual landscape only made that worse.

The inside was an oasis of another kind, filled to the low rafters with treasures gathered from her father's travels. A stuffed bird with brightly colored feathers looked down from a metal cage, procured on a trip deep into Mexico. An enormous brown snake coiled around the cage and stretched across the roof beam to the far wall. A collection of skulls clustered in the front corner, including one large creature with three horns and a strange neck frill. Her father had traded with others who'd brought back beadwork from the frozen lands up north, beautiful silk gowns from beyond the great waters to the west, and shells the size of Otis's head.

A tall clock taken from an overloaded wagon train still kept time, and it tolled over the empty mesa every hour. When it struck nine, she lay down to sleep, but the men stayed up passing a bottle. The incessant wind carried their voices through her window. "That girl's hair's mighty strange," Delbert said.

"It's black," Roy said. "Nothing strange about that."

"But there's gray in it, and she ain't seen more than twenty summers."

"Silver," Zeb corrected in a quieter voice. "It's shiny like metal. Or water."

The other two teased him for having taken notice, but Elsa was flattered, though she stiffened again when Delbert spoke. "Think she's Mexican or Injun?"

Someone spit. "She's brown, either way," Roy said.

"She could just be browned from the sun," Zeb pointed out. "Don't reckon it makes much difference, though, do it?"

Elsa had to agree. She couldn't have given her pedigree if asked. Comanchero traders like her father were named for their best customers, not their heritage. Most were descended from a combination of white Spanish settlers and soldiers and the local native tribes—Comanches as well as Apaches, Kiowas, Pueblos, and others. Elsa spoke English, Spanish, and some Comanche, and she let visitors assume as they pleased.

"Oh, it makes a difference," Delbert said, "but beggars like us can't be choosers."

"Delbert," Zeb said reprovingly.

"I meant for provisions." The scorn in Delbert's voice made her glad she'd left him to sleep with the mule, though it seemed unfair to Otis. "I got no inclinations of *that* kind."

Be that as it may, Elsa thought, *I'll still be keeping my guns at hand.*

"Where d'you think her people are?" Roy asked.

"Date on her momma's grave says ten years gone," Zeb said. "Nothing on her daddy's stone, but he can't be gone long, seeing as she's still in her blacks."

Elsa was impressed, if disconcerted, by his observant nature. Otis had indeed been her sole companion since her father had failed to return from his last trip.

"But how'd they end up here in the first place?" Roy persisted.

"Maybe her folks was Comanche," Delbert said. "They're the only ones could survive out here."

Her parents had certainly been survivors. Her father, Domingo, had found Marta, Elsa's orphaned teenage mother, beside a broken-down wagon on the Santa Fe Trail. He took her along on his trade route, where her ability to find water immediately, rather than wandering about searching, made him the fastest Comanchero around. When they'd realized a baby was coming, Domingo had parked his carreta and set up a trading base at the best well Marta could find along the cart road.

"Comanches, hell." Roy took a swig from the bottle. "She'd be sleepin' in a tipi if so."

Elsa almost smiled. A tipi would have been a far sight cleaner than the sod house Domingo originally built. Dirt had rained into their hair and eyes and food, no matter how much newspaper Marta tacked to the ceiling. Once her mother stabbed a rat straight through the muslin that covered the walls.

"Tipi makes more sense than a cabin," Zeb said. "Must have taken months to haul that wood."

Weeks, anyway. That rat had been the final straw. Marta told Domingo that unless he built a proper house like the one she'd had as a child, she'd dry up the spring she'd created and move them all to town. He'd headed east the next week and returned with a wagon of lumber.

"Mighty strange," Delbert said around a lip full of fresh tobacco. "Not as strange as all the green around it, though."

Elsa strained to hear their replies. Her father had warned her not to expand the oasis, but it provided her only comfort after her mother's death. Creating a gazing pool seemed the best way to honor a water witch, though Elsa had to admit that she might have gone overboard with the flowering vines on the trellis.

Fortunately, the men didn't seem to suspect anything more than luck. Roy mumbled something about how the earth was a curious place, and Zeb snorted. "It's full of wonders, I'll agree. For instance, I'm wondering if y'all will ever pipe down so I can sleep."

"Zeb's cranky," Roy said. "Must be time for his beauty rest."

He and Delbert mumbled a little longer, but Elsa didn't catch anything worrisome. Still, she decided, tomorrow she would move the lock from the privy onto her cabin door. It wouldn't keep out a determined man, but it should discourage a curious one.

The grandfather clock clanged another hour, and she settled down into the feather mattress that had been traded for several buffalo hides. The last thing she needed was a man about the house. She was comfortable in the small museum of her parents' lives, and hoped her rude barn guests would soon leave her in peace.

"Surprised you ain't wearing pants, as much man work as you do 'round here."

Elsa shrugged at Delbert, ignoring his sneer. "Skirts make relieving oneself with modesty much easier."

His cringe satisfied her, and made Zeb chuckle. "We cooked bacon, Miss Elsa—would you like some?"

She had not offered the men breakfast, and felt chagrined by his generosity. "Thank you," she said. "My meat stores have gotten rather slim of late." She paused, then went on. "Perhaps you know—has General Mackenzie caught Quanah yet?" Young chief Quanah led the last remaining band of free Comanches, and he'd been trying to hold off the Army's advances by holing up down south in Palo Duro Canyon.

Delbert laughed. "His band been at Fort Sill since June. Had to give up. They barely made it through the winter after Ol' Bad Hand Mackenzie slaughtered all their ponies last fall."

Elsa kept her face a mask of composure, but Zeb's was unmistakably marked with grief. "Well. I suppose I won't count on them for trade then," she said. She often wished her family had never helped the Army survive on the Llano, but even her father, who knew well that the Americans never kept their promises, had not guessed their capacity for savagery.

"Them Co-manch ain't the only ones with dead horses." Roy slapped his hat against his thigh as he emerged from the barn. "Mine's croaked and Del's ain't far behind."

They followed Roy into the barn, where, sure enough, his gray mare lay dead. Delbert's gelding was also on the ground, taking shuddering breaths, and Zeb's horse stood with its head lowered between its front legs. "Hey, Bitty," Zeb said, rubbing her spotted flank. "It's alright."

"Now what're we gonna do?" Roy asked. "Worthless damn Injun ponies."

Delbert spit on the dead horse, which made Elsa gasp. "Indian horses with US Army brands?" she demanded.

"They're all stolen back and forth," he said, as if she were not intimately acquainted with the practices of the area. "Damn. We gotta get moving somehow. How far to the closest trading post?"

Elsa didn't inquire about their hurry, but phrased her reply carefully. "Unless you can find folks willing to sell, and there aren't many, you'll have to go to Fort Sumner."

Roy blanched, confirming her suspicions. She wondered if they were criminals or just Army deserters on the lam. "That's at least a week's ride," Zeb said, "one way."

"How far is Santa Fe?" Delbert asked.

"Twice as far," Elsa said. "Assuming you have good weather and can find water." She wasn't sure she'd bother giving them that help.

Delbert punched his hand. "We ain't got two weeks," he growled, as if their problem was her fault.

"Gonna be longer than that," Roy said. "Zeb's horse ain't exactly up to the trip right now."

Zeb studied Bitty for a minute, then turned to Elsa. "I hate to impose," he said, "but there's nothing to be done. If you'll have us a little longer, we'll get Bitty nursed back to health, then I'll head...somewhere, and get us fresh mounts."

Elsa sighed. Few men could survive the Llano on foot, and these three were certainly not up to the task. "Fine," she said, resigned. "But you'll have to earn your keep." She looked at the dead mare. "And you can start by burying that horse."

Delbert turned away, and Roy followed, grumbling, but Zeb nodded. "We'll be much obliged."

The next two weeks passed slowly. Elsa was used to doing—and dressing—as she pleased, but the men's presence meant no baths on the porch or dips into the spring. The men were always in her space, save the sanctuary of her cabin, and even there she felt watched. The worst was surprising Roy by accident one dark evening in the privy. She'd seen nothing of importance, but his face flamed for days.

He should have been embarrassed by his shabby work around the homestead. Zeb accomplished twice as much in half the time, while Delbert stood about and gave orders, later taking credit for work he'd only watched. Roy's horse had passed hours after Delbert's, and when both were buried, she'd assigned the men all the tasks she never managed to get to: repairing the fence on Otis's paddock, digging a new irrigation path to the far edge of the garden, fixing a hole in the roof of the barn.

"It don't rain out here," Roy said. "Why bother with the roof?"

"Because when it does rain out here, it comes down in sheets," Elsa said. "Take your pick of which to sleep under."

Roy and Delbert gave in, but their resentment was growing, especially once they ran out of whiskey. Every evening at dusk, they sat about her front porch, glancing surreptitiously at the cabin door. She wore the key around her neck and never let on what wonders hid inside, but the clock's hourly chime couldn't be missed.

"How the devil did you get a grandfather clock all the way out here?" Roy asked one night after dinner.

"I didn't," Elsa said.

Delbert snorted. He'd long stopped accepting her evasions as answers. "Well somebody did."

"My father found it abandoned on a wagon trail," she lied. Admitting he was a trader would only make them wonder about his inventory.

"And he hauled it on horseback?"

"On a wagon." She changed the subject. "Zeb, Bitty is looking better today."

Zeb turned from the porch rail, where he'd been watching tuft-headed prairie chickens settle down for the night. "She's gaining weight back. Glad you had that feed stashed away."

Elsa had sacrificed some of Otis's winter stores. Getting these men out of her life as soon as possible was worth it, and she trusted that Zeb would replace the feed when he returned—assuming he returned at all. The man was mighty helpful and his patient manner pleased her, but even honest men could die.

She'd liked to learn more about him, but questions invited more of the same, and she didn't care to reciprocate. Besides, Delbert seemed to be enjoying his fictional future role in the cattle ranch he'd invented as their reason for passing through. He would, of course, be quite important. His claims that Charles Goodnight planned to start a similar enterprise nearby, however, gave Elsa pause. Goodnight was already well-known as a cattle baron, and with the Comanche threat removed, she feared it would only be a matter of time before her oasis was absorbed by larger claims.

"Well," she said, before the subject could come up again, "I'm ready for bed. See you in the morning, gentlemen." They accepted the dismissal, Zeb tipping his hat in farewell, and she waited until they'd reached the barn before unlocking the door to the house.

The first rays of moonlight shone through the windows, casting most of her strange possessions into shadow. Even within the safety of her walls, she felt conspicuous, as if the slightest noise would draw unwanted attention. Every creak in the floorboards made her cringe. Below them, a tributary ran underground from the spring, rising into a small pool beneath her kitchen. She opened the small trapdoor and inserted a tall, curved pipe, feeling the familiar tingle in her hands as they drew water up into a basin.

Face washed, she filled a tin cup and silently pushed the remaining water back down the pipe. But as she carried the drink to her bedside, unpinning her hair with the other hand, her elbow bumped a huge pair of flat antlers. They knocked into a pile of metal contraptions, which fell over with a deafening crash and hit a lantern, shattering a glass pane that sliced into Elsa's arm. She yelped, dropping her tin cup onto the floor with a final clank as she clamped a hand to the wound.

A moment later, someone knocked at the door. "Miss Elsa?" Zeb called.

Blood seeped from beneath her fingers. With help, she could bandage it without making a mess of everything, but he'd have to come inside for that. *At least I haven't stripped to my underclothes yet.* "Are you alone?" she called.

"I am," he said. She unlocked the door and let him in. "What happened?"

"I broke a lantern." She held out her arm, still pressing against the injury. "There's a spare sheet in the cupboard there—will you tear off a piece?"

Zeb jumped to obey, but halfway across the room, he let out a muffled screech.

"It's stuffed!" Elsa said, realizing he'd spotted the snake. "It's not real!"

He put a hand to his heart and hurried to the cupboard while she used the leftover basin water to clean up the blood. Then she sat on the edge of the bed and let him wrap her arm. "How does that feel?" he asked when he finished.

"It stings," she admitted, "but I'll survive." Stronger than the pain was a bittersweet grief—the last time she'd touched another person had been a goodbye hug with her father. "You make a fine doctor," she said, surprised by her desire to keep Zeb near a few more minutes.

"I bandaged many a wound in the Army."

He tried to keep his eyes cast down, but Elsa knew he was dying to see. "Go ahead," she said, laughing. "Look around." She wondered what he must think, not only of the bizarre collection, but of how it amused her to arrange it. A black top hat sat upon a blue wig made of horsehair, which sat atop a small stone bust of George Washington. A pair of gold horseshoes and a child's doll made of cornhusks hung on a post beside a frame that housed winged insects stuck with pins. Stacks of books tottered in the far corner, organized by color to create a rainbow.

"This is...quite a room," Zeb said at last.

"My father was a Comanchero," she said. "He always brought gifts home."

Zeb nodded. "How long has he been gone?"

Her face flushed in the dark. She should have abandoned mourning clothes a long time ago, but replacing them either meant a trip to town or sewing a dress from blankets, so she'd made do with clumsy alterations. The frayed hems and too-short sleeves were suddenly embarrassing. "About three years," she said.

"That's a long time to be alone."

"I don't mind." *Or didn't. Until now.*

He studied her. "My father was a shopkeeper, back in Tennessee. His collections weren't quite this impressive, but he had a fine selection of rare coins and postcards."

Elsa smiled. "Tennessee is a far piece. The Army brought you here?"

His own smile faltered. "Partway," he said, and lowered his voice. "I was stationed at Fort Sill."

"I suspected as much," she said. He raised his eyebrows. "When I asked about General Mackenzie. You seemed..."

"Never did have much of a poker face," he said, shaking his head, and his voice dropped to a whisper. "I couldn't stand it. He made us kill those horses and leave those people behind to die."

Elsa reached out without thinking, placing her hand on his forearm. She couldn't tell if it was the injury or the connection that made her skin feel warm all over. His eyes avoided hers, so she took the opportunity to study him—the brown beard, slightly lighter than his shaggy hair; the crooked nose, maybe broken in childhood; the abrupt change from tan to pale skin underneath his collar.

He looked up. "All those women and children, and now the ones that lived the winter are stuck on that reservation in the Wichitas, trying to survive on rations that ain't worth the bugs that's mixed in 'em… I done a lot of things for the Army that I'm proud of, but a lot more that I ain't, and when Del said he and Roy was leaving…" Elsa tightened her grip and he looked down. "Anyway, ma'am," he said, staring at her hand. "If they come looking for us, you won't be at risk."

"I'm well-known to the Army," she assured him. "They've drunk from my well often. But I appreciate your help." It was unexpectedly hard to let go of his arm.

Zeb stood up. "I'm happy to be at your service," he said, and took another glance around the room. "Miss Elsa…"

"Yes?" she prompted.

His eyes went to the key on its leather necklace string. "Don't tell Del and Roy what's in this house," he said. "Don't tell 'em any more than you can manage."

"There's little of value here," she said. "Or rather, it's only of value to me."

He frowned. "All the more reason they'd take it."

She studied the fine buttons on his shirt, wondering if they'd come all the way from his father's shop. "I hope your future and theirs diverge soon."

"Oh, they will," he assured her. "Just as soon as I get 'em clear of you. I'd planned to lose them in this wild country and head on to Santa Fe before this horse business happened."

Elsa paused. "Bitty's recovering well. You could take off anytime you like."

"Not 'til I get 'em clear of you," he said again, and held out his hand. He pressed his lips to her wrist when she obliged. "I may not be a good man, but those two are downright bad, and I won't leave my problems here for you to solve."

He let go of Elsa and closed the door quietly behind him. It was several more hours before she could sleep.

After that evening, the mood on the homestead changed. Delbert and Roy hadn't eavesdropped on the conversation—they lacked the stealth to get within fifty feet without Elsa hearing them—but they grew antagonistic toward Zeb. Though Elsa gave the orders, they pretended Zeb was their taskmaster, making constant snide comments about his eagerness to please "the missus."

Zeb, meanwhile, worked from dawn to dusk. He ignored their comments in his direction, but met any slight toward Elsa with increasingly sharp rebukes. There weren't enough supplies for him to make her bacon again, but every morning at sunrise, he shared his dwindling coffee stores and some quiet conversation with her on the porch.

Elsa felt both disconcerted and touched by his gestures. It had been years since someone had cared for her, but aside from fetching him water at the hottest part of the day, she wasn't sure how to reciprocate without making things worse. She wanted to invite him inside for dinners, but just loaning the man a book had done plenty. "Look at the city boy!" Roy'd called, spotting Zeb reading one evening. "Whoo hoo, he's a fancy one!"

Delbert spit to the side. "What'cha reading, fancy boy?"

Zeb held up the cover as if his answer mattered. "Captain Marcy's guidebook."

"Well," Roy said, glancing at Delbert for approval. "Ain't you…fancy."

"Can't hurt to learn up before I try this trip on my own."

Roy's eyes narrowed. "You'll be leavin' soon then?"

Zeb put the book down. "I reckon Bitty's as ready as she'll ever be."

"Tomorrow?" Delbert clasped his hands behind his back. "Or the next day?"

"Tomorrow morning, I was thinking."

Elsa listened from inside the house, feeling choked. Tomorrow was at least a week later than she'd hoped, and yet…it felt too soon. "Zeb," she said, stepping outside. "Are you sure?"

He stood. "No time like the present." He turned to Delbert and Roy. "I'd appreciate if you'd put together your extra supplies for me. Canteens, matches, whatever you can spare. I'll pick up replacements when I reach the fort."

Elsa touched her throat. The fort. She'd been wondering if he'd take that risk. "Zeb," she whispered, when the other two had walked away. "You've got to go on, to Santa Fe."

"There's just as much Army there," he said in a low voice. "I got to take the risk if we're gonna get these boys movin' on."

Elsa swallowed hard. "Come inside for a moment."

He looked around, checking that Del and Roy were out of sight, and followed her. The house was sweltering behind the closed shutters. "If you should…want to stay…" she began.

"No," he interrupted. "They can't stay here."

"But once you've returned," she said. "If *you* should…care to stay on a bit, here. With me."

His eyes widened, and for a moment, she thought him frightened. Then he smiled. "Well. I'd be delighted to stay on." Slowly, he reached for her hands, holding them between their bodies. "For as long as you'll have me, I reckon."

A smile spread over Elsa's face, too. "Delighted," she repeated. But the reality of their situation couldn't be ignored. "I'll make a map of the watering holes. I know them all, for a hundred miles or more."

"How?" he asked. "You said you'd never been farther than—"

"Never mind that. For now, you just…you just come on back to me quick as you can."

"I tell you what," he said. "Once I've been gone a week, leave a candle in the window. Then I'm sure to find my way. I promise."

Elsa appreciated the sentiment even if she doubted he could ensure its veracity. "I'll keep a light on." She squeezed his fingers. "Even if I have to burn the whole place down."

"Let's hope it doesn't come to that."

"A poor joke," she admitted, then scowled. "I can think of better ways to deal with Delbert and Roy, anyway."

He frowned. "I wouldn't leave you here alone if I thought they'd hurt you. Despite their many flaws, they're generally opposed to violence against ladies."

"How chivalrous. So my virtue is not at risk?" Elsa asked, trying to lighten the mood.

Zeb cleared his throat. "Well. Roy is no threat, given an, um…unfortunate injury."

"Oh?"

"Let's just say he hasn't enjoyed the company of a woman in quite some time."

Elsa wasn't sure whether she felt sympathy exactly, but his embarrassment about the privy made more sense now.

"And Delbert is…somewhat picky."

Elsa cocked an eyebrow. "Meaning?"

"He prefers his women on…the paler side."

The insult would have stung under other circumstances,

but given the situation, she said, "Well, he's a bit old for my tastes, so thank the Lord for small miracles."

Zeb laughed and took her face in his hands. "Believe me when I say, you're the most beautiful woman for hundreds of miles."

"I'm the *only* woman for hundreds of miles," she pointed out, but let him press his lips to hers regardless.

Watching Zeb ride away was one of the worst moments of Elsa's life.

Her mother's death had been slow, a disease consuming her from inside while Elsa and Domingo could do nothing but watch. When her father died, it was much the same: Elsa watched the horizon with dwindling hope, until winter arrived and blew away all chances of his return.

Now Zeb disappeared into the distance, and Elsa watched until he was nothing more than a mirage. The flutters of first love were all mixed up with the twisting nausea of fear and abandonment. She wanted to stay at the porch rail until he reappeared, but survival on the Llano didn't allow for flights of fancy.

So she forced herself away and found the other men lounging on the shady side of the barn. Roy lay on the grass, leaning back against his saddle, while Delbert sat on the fence cleaning his rifle. "Gentlemen," she said, nodding in their direction.

"Ma'am," Delbert said, with more than a hint of sarcasm.

"Deer often venture out to the escarpment for feed this time of year," she said. "I wondered if you two might be so kind as to see if you can rustle us up one." It was still hot, but fall was getting on, and she'd need stores for winter if she was going to survive the Llano's blizzards.

Delbert spit, narrowly missing his own knee. "Well, the thing is, Roy and I got other plans for today."

"Oh?" She put a hand on her hip. "And they are?"

Roy, chewing on a stem of grass, tipped his hat back to reveal his eyes. "You're looking at 'em." Del laughed as Roy pulled the hat back down and crossed his arms as if to nap.

"Well," Elsa said. She couldn't force them, but if they thought she'd be making their dinner tonight, they'd be mighty surprised. "Enjoy your day then." She headed back toward the house.

"Wait," Roy called, and she slowed. "We got a proposition for you."

She turned. "Our agreement was chores for the length of your stay."

Roy smiled, the stem moving to one side of his mouth. "Zeb made that arrangement. But Zeb's gone now, ain't he?"

"He'll be back," Elsa said.

Delbert jumped down from the fence. "You better hope so."

Elsa squashed a flicker of fear. "What's your proposition then?"

"Well," Delbert said. "It seems mighty suspicious that a lady like you could live out here so long on her own. Seems you must have some kind of riches hidden inside that house."

Elsa was surprised this question hadn't come up sooner. "Who would I trade with? Have you seen anyone wander by?" Delbert raised an eyebrow and she huffed. "Do you think I eat beans for dinner every day by choice?"

He shrugged. "Well then. That means the Army ain't likely to visit soon, which brings us to option two. Which ain't an option so much as an order."

"I don't take orders from you," Elsa said.

“You do now,” he said, patting the rifle.

Elsa cursed herself for sending one of her guns with Zeb, and leaving the other inside. He’d seemed so sure she wouldn’t need it. She couldn’t believe he’d known this was their plan… which meant he’d misjudged them, a possibility that was no more comforting. “What is it you want?”

Roy made a show of shining his handgun on his woolen pants. Elsa wished it would misfire and take whatever his previous injury had left behind. “Figured it’s about time you show us ’round the place.”

Elsa straightened her back. “As I said, you’re welcome to the barn, but my home is my own.”

Delbert gestured toward the house with the rifle. “Not anymore.”

Fury and terror burned inside her like twin torches, but Elsa turned stiffly and proceeded up the path, the men following on her heels. At the door, she stopped and took a deep breath. “I fear you will be mighty disappointed—” she started.

Roy pushed her. “Just open the damn door.”

It swung wide, bright sunlight slicing into the room. Roy whooped as the glint from the horseshoes blinded him, but his elation turned to irritation as he inspected more closely. “What is this mess of metal?”

She shrugged. “Old traps, mostly.”

Delbert sifted through a stack of cigar boxes, casting each aside as he found seashells and stones instead of jewels. “Where d’you keep the good stuff?” he demanded.

“This is all there is,” Elsa said. Her revolver lay near the washbasin, and she tried to edge closer without their notice.

But Roy whirled around and caught sight of her goal. “You stay where you are.” He stomped across the floor and held both weapons pointed at her chest. "Don't reckon you'll be needin' this little six-shooter anytime soon."

Elsa forced her panic down. Her knives were out of reach, and Delbert removed her machete from the wall, swinging it sarcastically. "Nothing but a heap of junk." He spit on the bearskin rug. Its white fur didn't even register as strange, much less valuable.

"You're a mighty big disappointment, Miss Elsa." Roy took the top hat from George Washington and used it to replace his own. "We was planning to pack your riches onto the mule and head to Mexico."

Delbert turned to the pantry and picked through its contents, taking whatever food appealed to him. "But now you're stuck with us." He held out a jar. "How you feel about pickles, Roy?"

"Rather eat 'em than be in one."

They both cackled. Elsa watched them pick over her supplies, taking more food, the matches, most of her candles, several dishes, and all the silver. The books, of course, were left untouched, but the buffalo robe, her box of tools, the traps, and an Apache bow and arrow all went out the door.

Fine, Elsa thought. *Let them humiliate me. I can survive just fine without their help, certainly until Zeb gets back.*

Delbert set his spoils on the porch. "Roy," he said, "go fetch that wood."

Elsa watched Roy walk to the barn and return with an armful of planks torn from Otis's stall. "You get on inside then, Elsie," he said, dropping the wood and wiping his face.

"Inside?" Her mind raced, wondering whether they planned to steal the mule or light a fire.

"It's only fair," Delbert said, pulling a handful of nails from his pocket. "If we're not allowed in, I don't know why you should get out."

★ ★ ★

Elsa sat on her bed, listening to the men laugh as they nailed her door shut. Her shuttered windows left the room stiflingly dark. They were small enough to keep out predators, but now she felt like cornered prey.

When the hammering stopped, she heard Del muttering, then Roy yelled, "Damnit!"

She peeked through the shutters to see him dancing around, holding an injured hand. Delbert was laughing as he put the pin in one of the traps. He placed it gingerly below the window, looking up to wink at her visible eye.

Captured, she thought. To what end, she wasn't sure. "Delbert!" she called. "What if I need to use the privy?"

"You got a bucket?"

She paused. "I suppose."

He lifted the rifle. "Better learn to use it."

Delbert was smart enough to ignore Elsa's questions, but Roy was easily annoyed and eager to prove himself clever. "Why bother feeding me?" she asked the third day, when he slid the daily bowl of corn mush onto the windowsill. "Seems a fool way to starve a woman out."

Roy snorted. "Can't get those horses with you dead."

Elsa studied the tin cup of water he'd provided, not knowing she had makeshift plumbing. "You think Zeb will just hand them on over when he sees me held hostage?"

"If he comes back, you'll play along, or you'll both end up in the garden with your momma."

Elsa resisted the urge to toss the water in his face and snapped the shutters closed. *Two weeks*, she told herself. *Two weeks and Zeb will come back.*

The chances of Del and Roy leaving peacefully with the

horses seemed unlikely now, but she wasn't sure she had any alternative but to wait them out. She'd already bruised her shoulders trying to open the door. Without a saw, it would be difficult to widen a window or the trapdoor, and the noise would draw the men's attention. Even if she did escape on foot, they'd quickly catch up to her on Otis. She might could steal him from the barn...if only the men weren't sleeping in shifts to prevent it.

She'd underestimated them. She wouldn't make that mistake again.

Taking stock of her remaining provisions, she figured that with careful planning and small portions, she could survive with full strength until Zeb came back, possibly a week more. But if something happened to him...or if he chose not to return...

Well. No point in deciding which was worse.

She knew it was weeks too early, but just in case, she used her flint fire starter to light a candle in the northwest window.

In the morning, she watched in helpless fury as Roy and Delbert harvested her entire garden. They tied Otis to a porch rail in sight of her window and tossed the stalks and stem to the mule, laughing as his stomach began to bloat. For days after, they left him outside while expanding their own space inside the barn. The answer to "what if Zeb doesn't return" became apparent: Delbert and Roy were preparing to winter over in the oasis.

At least we won't starve immediately, Elsa thought, but it was little comfort. Gathering sufficient stores for herself was challenge enough; the men knocked off early every afternoon and would never be able to provision all three of them through the winter.

Elsa struggled to keep herself occupied. She did daily chores as best she could, sweeping the floor, making the bed, even giving herself sponge baths at the basin. She emptied her bucket commode out the southeast window, where the wind was most likely to blow the smell away. Throughout the day, she checked on Otis, always comforted to see him alive, if not well cared for.

But her brain still raced from anger and despair to frustration and boredom, each feeling as dangerous as the last. Wild scenarios played out in her mind—Zeb arrested, murdered, caught in a hailstorm, swept up by a twister.

She kept a tally of marks on the windowsill, counting down the days, impatient for two weeks to pass, and terrified they wouldn't bring Zeb with them. But stir-craziness still snuck up on her. One moment, she was gazing around the cabin, thinking of her parents. The next, she was furious. Treasures! What use were they to her now? She crossed the room and kicked a drum made of cowhide, earning herself a warning shout from outside.

On the eighth morning, she began to sort her belongings according to a new perspective. The bone awl from a beading kit could be repurposed as a different kind of tool. The beautiful carved cottonwood dolls might have to fuel the wood-burning stove, though it hurt her soul to consider. Few things would serve as weapons, and many were cruelly useful for travel. She put those under a blanket, out of demoralizing sight.

That afternoon, she lay on her bed with arms extended, attempting to test her powers. Try as she might, she could only move small trickles around, not the tidal wave she needed to drown her enemies. She spent the entire next day trying to create a sinkhole in the main path, but only managed to twist Roy's ankle with a small hole.

If only I could summon more than water, she thought, remembering a similar despair years ago. *If only I could summon Zeb home.*

By the day when fourteen candles lay spent beneath the windowsill, Elsa's mind was beginning to melt. The heat alone was cause enough, but if she opened the shutters, the men would come taunt her until she closed herself in again. Her stomach gnawed constantly, but she didn't dare let herself eat more than one day's rations. She'd read every book in her stack at least twice, rearranging the tomes by author, by title, by size. She'd patched every hole in all three of the dresses she owned, but her thread supply was small, and the brownish light that came through the shutters made sewing difficult.

Otis began to bray the panicked call he made when wolves were nearby. Elsa's heart jumped into her throat, knowing wolves wouldn't circle in broad daylight. She ran to the window and saw him snubbed to a post near the barn.

"No!" she screamed.

A shot ran out.

Shaking, she closed the window and sat on the floor for hours until, to her horror, her stomach growled. She leaped to her feet and fashioned a mask from a handkerchief, but nothing could block out the scent of Delbert and Roy cooking her best friend.

After nightfall, a noisy pack of coyotes came to pick the mule's bones. Their caterwauling drove Elsa from her bed, where she'd been lying all evening, face covered with both arms. The noise awoke something frantic, consumed her with the need to escape. She dropped to her knees at the trapdoor and tore at the floorboards, desperately trying to widen the space. When blood dripped from her fingernails into the spring below, she grabbed the bone awl to pry at the wood.

By the time the coyotes wandered away, her energy was gone, too. But the larger hole soothed something in her mind, something she couldn't quite make herself examine yet. Exhausted, she realized her candle was out, and raised her shaking arms to light another. But the drawer was empty. She'd never bothered to keep much of a supply—the darkness had never troubled her before.

Lighting the last lantern wick instead, she collapsed into bed and uneasy dreams.

Her days became a mindless blur. When the wind blew hard enough to cover the noise, she scraped at the floor with the awl. When it broke, she dismantled the birdcage and fashioned new tools that made the work much quicker.

At night, all of her wooden possessions served their duty as beacon fuel, as did the bird's feathers and the cornhusk dolls. She tore her extra clothes into strips, but they smoked and smoldered instead of providing a flame. The books burned too quickly, singing her hand as she beat out the flames before they consumed the cabin.

Roy and Delbert jeered at her. "He ain't coming back," Roy yelled from the darkness. "Zeb's long gone and he ain't interested in a skinny thing like you."

"You ain't in love now, are you?" Delbert heckled. "You don't really think that white man's in love with *you*?" They both cackled.

Elsa paid them no mind anymore. In the deepest corner of her heart, she dreaded that what they said was true, but life on the Llano had taught her that survival always came before feelings.

She added the horsehair wig to her pile, which made her realize she'd overlooked another asset. Digging through her father's old belongings, she found his straight razor, brought it to her head, and quickly lopped off both her braids, adding them to her burn pile. Next she planned to try the feather mattress. It wasn't as if she'd been sleeping anyway. Then she'd have to break apart her cupboard, burn her shelves, and if pressed, the mantel, too.

But not the walls. The walls were her captors, but also her protection.

Unless.

Stricken by the idea that had simmered for weeks, Elsa went to the southern window. Roy and Delbert sat in their usual place, playing cards. They were obviously hunting enough rabbit and prairie chicken to keep their stomachs content. Her own gave a painful twist, but she'd die before admitting to them she was hungry.

She was going to die, regardless. When their stores ran out, they'd stop bringing her the tiny rations they provided now. She'd have to get out.

She couldn't keep waiting for Zeb.

But she would leave a light on like she'd promised. If she had to burn the whole thing down.

Elsa spent her last day sitting perfectly still, staring at the memories she'd be leaving behind.

No. The memories she'd keep. Only the items would be abandoned.

Night slipped more slowly than usual over the mesa, hiding the grasslands inch by inch until it enveloped the house.

Outside, Roy and Delbert began their usual taunting. "Not lightin' that candle tonight?" one called. She could no longer tell their voices apart. They had ceased to be people to her, just specters haunting a nightmare. One began to sing a cruel song about a wife left behind to mourn a husband gone to war. "He ain't coming back for you," the other called.

He doesn't need to. I'm coming to find him.

She threw back the shutters for the first time in weeks. "I got a new proposition," she yelled. The singing stopped. She felt their eyes on her. "I propose," she said, voice splintering, "that y'all enjoy yourselves in hell."

Both men jumped to their feet, guns pulled. Elsa didn't hurry. They couldn't get through the door any easier than she could. Taking careful aim, she clicked the flint against the steel, sending a spark into her braids on the windowsill. From there, she caught the clothing scraps she'd soaked in lantern oil. Then the mattress. The cursed front door. The walls.

As the men crashed against the house, she gathered her travel supplies from under their blanket, then lowered herself through the floorboards into the pool she'd driven underground hours before. Crawling on her belly, she emerged behind the house with the torch she'd prepared, lighting it from the flames already shooting outside. Roy and Delbert didn't notice as she raced for the barn. The sod and adobe wouldn't burn, but the wooden supports and mule feed would consume all they'd stored inside.

"Get to the well!" she heard one yell. "The barn's on fire!"

Elsa stuck to the perimeter until she reached the corner of her oasis, then turned back to tell it goodbye. The cabin was already half gone, the barn not long behind it, the yard so brightly lit that she could see her flowers wilting. Her mother's handmade gravestone reflected the flames, and she pressed her fingers to her lips. "Goodbye, Momma. Tell Daddy I love him."

The grandfather clock gave a final clang as the roof of the house caved in. She pictured her stuffed snake writhing in its second death.

"Hurry up with that bucket!" one voice yelled.

"The well is empty!" the other shouted back.

Elsa turned and set off northeast, hoping her love was just lost and not gone. The constant wind blew the fire south. She brought nothing but the water along behind her.

★ ★ ★ ★ ★

BEWARE OF GIRLS WITH CROOKED MOUTHS

by Jessica Spotswood

JO IS HALFWAY DOWN THE STAIRS WHEN THE vision strikes. She stumbles, her feet scrambling on the steps, hands clutching at the banister. The words scald her throat—prophecies always want to be spoken aloud—but she swallows them back, bitter as black tea. Her lips tingle and burn, her vision swims, and then—

She is somewhere else, somewhere not-here; she is descending another staircase, a grand wooden affair that curves as gracefully as the prow of one of Papa's ships. Her hand rests on the banister, but it is not her hand as it is now; it is older, wrinkled, with blue veins lining her thin skin like rivers. An enormous sapphire anchors her ring finger and dread anchors her heart. Four blue-eyed girls are gathered in the hall below. They are waiting for her.

"It's happening again, isn't it, Grandmother?" a blonde girl says. Dimly, Jo registers that she *is Grandmother, that the girl's ocean eyes*

are like hers, like Eleanor's and Georgiana's and their mother's before them. They are the unnervingly blue eyes of a Campbell witch.

"We have to find a way to stop this. I won't stumble over any more cousins washed up dead on the shore." A girl with dark curls and apple cheeks plants her hands on her wide hips.

"If one of us has gone mad, she won't stop till she's the only one left standing. Not unless we stop her." Josephine feels fond of this small, angry, bespectacled girl. "That's what happened last time, isn't it?"

"And," the sour-faced blonde says, looking straight at Josephine, "the time before that. Once the madness starts, only one Campbell witch will survive in each generation. Isn't that right, Grandmother? That's what the Book says."

"The Book is wrong." Josephine's hand trembles on the banister, and she makes a conscious effort to stop it. She cannot betray any weakness, any regret for her deception. These girls will smell it on her like blood in the water. "My sisters—they ran. They may still be alive because of it. I altered the Book. Recorded their deaths, so that no one would look for them."

She expects an explosion, a flurry of accusations that does not come.

"They left Mercer's Cove?" The blonde frowns.

"They left you*?" the apple-cheeked girl asks.*

The girl with spectacles crosses her arms over her scrawny chest. "I wouldn't be sorry to see the back of any of you. But we have a better chance of surviving if we work together."

The fourth girl—tall and willowy, and silent up to this point—steps forward, her fists clenched at her sides. "I'm not a murderer, no matter what any of you might think. I'll stand beside anyone who's willing to stay and fight."

These brave, foolish children, *Josephine thinks. They are enormously powerful, clever girls, and yet they are still so terribly, terribly* young. *They have been spoon-fed warnings not to trust one another by doting, oblivious fathers and by damaged, unforgiving aunts who still wear the scars of the last generation in their eyes and on their lips and scored into their hearts. But they don't believe it. Even when presented with the truth, they think they will be the ones to change the curse. To not only survive, but to do it* together.

Josephine has lived a long time now, but she's never seen a Campbell witch able to choose sisterhood over sovereignty. It's not in their nature. Herself included.

She stares down at the sapphire ring on her finger. By all rights, it should have been Georgiana's. She tries to summon up the memory of Georgiana's face, but it's murky, as though her sister is lying at the bottom of the sea.

For all she knows, that may be true. She has not seen either of her sisters for almost forty years. They could be long dead—but she would know, wouldn't she? She would feel it?

Her hand trembles again on the smooth wood of the banister. For nearly half a century, she has been the matriarch of the Winchester family, the richest and most powerful woman in Mercer's Cove.

But she would trade it all to be able to remember her little sister's smile.

Jo breaks to the surface, gasping. For a moment, frantic, she still cannot picture Georgiana's face. Her mind is empty except for the feel of the glossy wood beneath her palm, the heft of that sapphire ring on her finger, and the dizzying panic that pulls at her like the tide.

"Jo? Jo!" There. Georgiana: a riot of soft brown curls framing a heart-shaped face. A pink rosebud mouth and freckles across the bridge of her nose that *will* persist, despite Elle's potions. Georgie wraps a long arm around Jo's shoulder and shepherds her down the stairs, across the hall, and into the parlor.

"Are you hurt?" Georgie settles next to her on the rose-velvet settee.

What have I done? Jo raises her hand—now smooth and

freckled and empty of adornments—to her dismayed mouth. *What will I do?* That sapphire ring—it's meant for Georgie. Nathaniel Winchester let slip to his sister, Alice, that he intends to ask his grandmother for her sapphire betrothal ring, and of course Alice told Elle, and Elle told Georgie, and Georgie's been floating around the house like the cat who ate the canary ever since.

Georgie waggles her fingers in front of Jo's face. "Did you knock your head?"

"No. Just give me a moment." She has to think. Why was *she* wearing Nathaniel's ring? How is that possible? He's never given her a second thought, nor she him.

"That's a relief," Georgie chatters on. "No broken bones, no concussed head this time. Why must prophecies happen so often on the stairs?"

"It's a between place," Jo says faintly. That's what Mam told her. Doorways and stairs.

"It's damned dangerous is what it is," Georgie swears, then looks delighted by her own daring. Papa would box her ears if he heard. *She is still so young*, Jo thinks. Only sixteen. No older than the girls in her vision. Girls who were...Jo's *grandchildren*. And her great-nieces.

Georgie takes Jo's hand. "Was it a bad one?" she asks, more sympathetic. Georgie is their summer storm cloud, quick to anger, quick to tears, quick for it all to pass. She's been desperately in love half a dozen times, but those feelings flared hot and bright and were extinguished at the first perceived slight. This time, with Nathaniel, the flame has burned steadily for nearly six months.

But Jo knows the staircase from her vision. Knows that ring. Her gift has shown her many things, but it's never shown her anything like this: her own unfathomable future. She never expected to have one.

In the vision, she wore Nathaniel Winchester's ring. She descended the staircase of the Winchester mansion; she was the matriarch of a new line of witches. She *survived.*

But at what cost? In her vision, Jo married the man Georgie is in love with, a man with whom Jo has only exchanged pleasantries about her health and the weather. Her sisters had left Mercer's Cove. They had not seen one another in almost forty years.

"It's nothing," Jo lies, her mind spinning.

"It doesn't seem like nothing. You're pale as milk," Georgie insists, stubborn as always. "Shall I fetch you some tea?"

"The Book," Jo says. She needs to see it. Run her fingers over the names.

"What do you need that old thing for?" Georgie stands and lets go Jo's hand to smooth her bell-shaped pink skirts. She looks the height of fashion with her puffed gigot sleeves and the pale silk sash around her waist. "Whatever you saw, put it out of your head. We're not going to be like the others."

As if it were that easy. As if they could just *decide.*

"Do you want to help me or not? Get the Book, Georgie," Jo snaps.

Georgiana's bow-shaped mouth twists. The flame in the oil lamp leaps. The fire jumps and crackles in the hearth, throwing shadows onto the gray walls. Jo draws back from the sudden heat as Georgie marches from the room. A moment later Jo hears her slippered feet pounding up the staircase. Jo takes in a deep, shuddering breath. Her little sister is getting more powerful. If Jo were to cross Georgie, she isn't sure it would go well for her.

And Jo's visions are not always, strictly speaking, *true.* They are mere slices of time, possibilities present and future. They show her what could be, elsewhere and else-when. But humans are funny creatures, and their choices always play a role.

Except, it seems, for Campbell witches. Their fate seems locked in stone.

Georgie returns and tosses the large, square book roughly into Jo's lap. "There," she says, slumping into Papa's high-backed chair. "It hasn't changed."

Jo opens the Book. It smells of ink and dust. Their family tree spiderwebs through the yellowed pages: the history of the Campbell witches. It and the poison cabinet concealed in another volume were the only possessions Mam brought with her when she fled Scotland. Names and dates of birth and death are written in a variety of hands—precise copperplate and shaky scrawls and looping script. It is not so remarkable on first glance, but upon close inspection, a careful reader would note three irregularities:

First, no Campbell witch bears only sons, or finds herself barren. Each woman who lives to maturity births at least one daughter. Second, next to every daughter's name is one of five words—*water*, *air*, *fire*, *earth*, or *spirit*—the nature of her elemental gift. Third, there are not very many years between birth and death for these daughters. Most Campbell witches do not live beyond five and twenty. Only one in each generation survives to old age.

It has been that way since the beginning of the Book, over two hundred years ago.

In every generation, one Campbell witch goes mad and murders the others.

It has always been so. Will always be so.

That's what Mam taught them. What the Book and her own experience taught Mam.

Jo's first clear memory is of her mother leading her through the poison garden, pointing over her shoulder as Elle toddled behind them. "You mustn't grow too fond of her, nor this one, either," Mam had warned, a hand on her high, round belly. "We have power that most women can't dream of, darling, but love—that's a luxury Campbell witches can't afford."

"But you love Papa," little Jo had pointed out.

Mam had shrugged. "Men are different. Campbell witches, like you and your sisters—you cannot trust one another. You cannot survive together." Her blue eyes had narrowed. "But it's not so easy surviving apart, either."

Mam had fled Scotland as a girl, but whatever she ran from gave her nightmares. She would not speak of her own sister, or her cousins (dead, according to the Book), or of the terrible burns on her back that no amount of salve could heal. When Jo was fourteen, Elle twelve, and Georgie only ten, Mam dove off the cliff behind the Winchester mansion and straight down into the furious sea.

Her death only drove the three sisters closer. Despite her warnings; despite her awful, clever tricks to set them against each other; despite their many differences, Jo and Elle and Georgie do love one another. Three headstrong, motherless, mundane girls might not have got up to much trouble under the lenient watch of their ancient housekeeper and their father, a Portuguese pirate turned shipwright. But these girls are hardly mundane. Between Jo's prophecies, Eleanor's proficiency with poison, and Georgiana's flare for fire, their fights have become downright dangerous.

And now this baffling vision. Jo runs through it again and again in her mind, sinking deeper into the settee, the velvet soft through the thin blue muslin of her dress. Georgie grows bored and picks up her novel, absently petting one of Papa's liver-spotted hounds as it lounges by her feet. Outside, the clouds collect on the late-afternoon horizon.

What had Josephine told those blue-eyed girls?

My sisters—they ran. They may still be alive because of it.

An unfamiliar feeling washes over her. For once, it isn't the dread of knowing the future and being unable to stop it. How many visions had she had of Mam, all wet black skirts and dark hair tangled with seaweed, her body battered on the rocks below the cliff? How many times has she foreseen fevers and flu and fire?

Mam ran, and—for a time, at least—she survived. Till she was two and thirty. Jo pages through the book in her lap, doing the calculations in her head. That was unprecedented for a second Campbell witch. But Jo and Elle and Georgie—they're strong. Their love for one another *makes* them strong.

Jo glances over at her little sister. The future she saw is a sharp fork from the present. She does not see it happening without her intervention. If she chooses that future—decides for both of them—Georgiana might never speak to her again.

But, estranged, they might all live. *It's not so easy surviving apart, either,* Mam had warned. But that doesn't mean it's *impossible.*

There are a number of complications, of course. Chief among them, Jo cannot do this alone. She will need assistance. She'll need Elle.

An hour later, she strolls into Eleanor's bedroom. "Elle, we've got to talk. It's impor—"

She stops mid-sentence when she finds her sister in her four-poster bed, astride a sailor. At least, Jo assumes from his thick black beard and the tattoos spiraling up his muscled arms that he is a sailor.

"A bit occupied!" Elle tosses over her shoulder.

Jo's face flushes. "Good Lord, Elle. You could have locked the door."

"You could have knocked!" But Elle sighs and clambers off the sailor, wrapping herself in a sheet. The man catches Jo's eye and winks. He really is quite handsome, all golden skin and dark chocolate eyes. "I'm afraid my sister is quite determined that her business come before my pleasure, Rafael. Could you remove yourself to the dressing room?"

"Of course, love." He saunters into the dressing room adjacent, though not before offering Jo an eyeful of every inch of his anatomy. She supposes she could have dropped her eyes to the floor. But she's never seen a naked man before, and frankly she's curious. If she is to be married—if her scheme is successful—her wedding night will be much sooner than she thought.

While Jo is ogling Rafael, Elle slips into a green silk dressing gown. "What is so important, sister?"

"Must you be so free with yourself?" Jo asks, mortified. "What would Papa say if he knew you were entertaining a sailor in your bed?"

Elle gives her an arch look. "I imagine he'd say I'm taking after Mam. What, you don't think she sampled his wares first? She meant to start a new line of Campbell witches, didn't she? She'd want to ensure her husband was virile enough for the task."

Jo sits at Elle's dressing table. "Does Alice know you're still dallying with sailors?"

Something flickers over Elle's face. "Alice and I have come to an understanding."

"Which entails you acting like a trollop?" The harsh words are out of Jo's mouth before she thinks them through. She came to ask Elle a favor, after all. But she likes Alice Winchester. Unlike most of the other girls in town, Alice has always been kind to her.

"I'll let that go, just this once, because I know you're fond of Alice," Elle says evenly. "As it happens, Alice's father has arranged her marriage to Emma Colchester. Alice shall be Lady Colchester next spring. It will be announced in a fortnight, at the Winchester ball."

Elle—fierce, unstoppable Elle—looks suddenly brittle as china, as though she might break into a thousand pieces at any moment. *Oh, Elle.* Jo hadn't seen that coming at all.

"Can't you poison Emma?" she asks. "We could make it look an accident."

"I offered." Elle tenderly strokes a pink-and-white leaf of elephant's ear. Beneath her touch, it shivers and grows. "Alice does not wish it."

"Alice is too good by half." Jo does not mean it as a compliment.

"A rich viscountess." Elle moves on to the heart-shaped leaves of a young arrowhead plant. "I cannot compete with that. Lady Colchester is beautiful, and titled, and very powerful."

"Not as powerful as you," Jo points out.

A smile crawls slowly across Elle's face as she looks down at her plants. Those harmful to the touch are sequestered in her greenhouse or the poison garden, but Jo knows that, ingested, these could cause severe ill effects. "It does bring me some small comfort, knowing that I could poison the bitch in a heartbeat." She turns back to Jo. "But enough about your poor, lovelorn sister. You came to ask me a favor, I think?"

Jo checks to be sure the dressing room door is shut tight. It is, but she keeps her voice hushed nonetheless. "A poison and a potion."

Elle sprawls at the edge of her bed, her dressing gown open

to mid-thigh. She is utterly unselfconscious in her own body in a way that Jo never feels. "For?"

"I…would rather not say," Jo hedges.

Elle shakes her head, her long dark hair tumbling down her back. "You know I won't give you anything without knowing what it'll be used for, and on whom."

"I want a love charm of sorts. Something to make a man feel…romantic." Jo flushes.

Elle runs her palms along her down blanket. "I'm intrigued. How romantic, exactly? I'll need to know the particulars. Are you looking for a dance or two, or—" she waggles her eyebrows "—something a bit more scandalous?"

"I need him to kiss me," Jo explains. She might be the eldest, but she suspects she's the only Campbell sister who's never been kissed. Georgie has allowed her suitors a few liberties, and before Alice, Jo caught other men sneaking out of Elle's rooms. "Perhaps more than once. Enough to compromise me, but not enough to cause a real scandal."

Elle's blue eyes go wide. "You're the subject? Jo, darling. You don't need a potion to make a man kiss you. You've just got to give him a bit of encouragement. I can show you how. You're a pretty girl… If you didn't look so sour all the time—if you relaxed your shoulders a bit, and smiled like you can't see straight into a person's soul, then—"

Jo isn't interested in this cataloging of her flaws. "He's in love with someone else."

"Oh. That is trickier." Elle frowns. "Is he the faithful sort? Never mind, it doesn't matter. I know just the potion. He won't be able to keep his eyes—or his hands—off you."

"Perfect." Despite the ignominious beginning, this is going rather well. "I'll let him compromise me, and then—being a gentleman—he'll have to propose, won't he?"

"If he's a gentleman." Elle frowns, obviously disappointed. "But the spell won't last forever. Are you sure this is what you want? To trap some poor fellow into marriage? He might come to resent you, especially if he's in love with someone else."

"It doesn't matter." It's worth it to ensure a future where she survives, and her sisters are safe, even if she doesn't know where. A future where Jo is rich and powerful and respected... nay, judging from the look in those girls' eyes, *feared*. She allows herself a small smile.

"And the poison? For the girl, I presume?" Elle is frighteningly clever sometimes. "What did you have in mind?"

Jo's smile fades. "Something to make her sick. Just enough to miss the Winchester ball."

"Poor girl. That's the event of the whole spring." Elle clucks her tongue. "Who is she? For that matter, who's the man lucky enough to be my future brother-in-law?"

Jo sets her jaw. "Nathaniel."

"Nathaniel who? Nathaniel *Winchester*?" Elle asks. There is only one Nathaniel in town: Alice's older brother, the handsome only son of the richest family in town, and—

The penny drops. "*Georgie's* Nathaniel?"

Jo nods, her stomach sinking but her eyes resolute.

"I won't do it." Elle stands, hands on her voluptuous hips. "I won't poison my little sister so that you can steal her sweetheart." She begins to pace the room like a restless cat. "Why would you ask me to do something so cruel? Are you in love with him?"

Jo shakes her head. "No. It's not like that."

"Then for heaven's sake, Josephine, tell me: how is it? What would possess you to do something like this? To flounce in here and ask me to help you do it? Georgie loves him. It might be just puppy love, it might be something real and lasting, I don't know. But she deserves the chance to find out. She deserves to have what Mam had with Papa, before..." Elle swallows, and Jo knows they are both remembering those last years with Mam, when she drank whiskey in the poison garden all day and paced the cliffs all night. "I'll never get to have that. Not with Alice. You don't even want it. One of us should be so lucky, don't you think? Why would you take that from your own sister?"

"I saw it, Ellie. In a vision." Jo's voice catches. "A vision where I was *old*."

Elle looks at her for a long moment. Then she goes to the dressing room and holds a murmured conversation with Rafael. He emerges, dressed in a black waistcoat, shining black boots, and fawn-colored pants that taper from ankle to knee. "Another time, love," he says, before kissing Elle plumb on the mouth. She returns the embrace, then shoos him out the door.

"All right." Elle fixes Jo with her blue stare. "You've got my undivided attention. I think you'd better tell me about this vision."

A fortnight later, Jo sits at Elle's dressing table again. She watches in the gilt-edged looking glass while Elle styles her hair into artful curls topped by a ridiculous feathered headdress. She is wearing a pink silk organza evening dress, inlaid with imitation-pearl beads. Its low décolletage shows the top of her breasts, which Elle has padded and plumped to great effect. A white sash accentuates the smallest part of her waist, made smaller by Elle's ruthless cinching of her corset. White gloves stretch from her fingertips to just below her elbows. She is beautiful.

She is miserable.

I'm doing this for Georgie, she reminds herself. For all three of them. But she isn't sure her little sister will understand that. She hopes that Elle's poison will work, because if Georgie finds her with Nathaniel, she may be in real danger. Just last week she went down to the deserted beach at night and watched as Georgie transferred fire from the oil lamp to her palm, and then practiced aiming fireballs among the waves.

Elle eyes Jo critically. She reaches out, tweaks one of her curls, and smiles. "You look lovely." She reaches for a small vial on her shelf.

"Are you sure this will work?" Jo asks.

Elle raises one eyebrow. "Do you doubt my skill?"

"No." Elle learned poisons at Mam's knee. She inherited Mam's garden and has only improved it in the last few years. "Only my own charms. People will think Nathaniel's taken leave of his senses, to throw Georgie over for me."

"He's a man, isn't he? They'll believe it easily enough," Elle jokes.

A knock sounds on the door, and a chill runs up Jo's spine. What if something has gone wrong? Shouldn't Georgie be asleep by now?

"You see? *She* knocks," Elle hisses. Then, louder: "Come in!"

Georgie enters, her cheeks flushed, wearing a dressing gown. "Why aren't you dressed?" Elle asks, feigning ignorance.

"I'm not feeling well," Georgie says. "I'm sorry, Elle. I know tonight will be difficult, with Alice's engagement being announced publicly, and—"

"Oh, don't worry about me," Elle interrupts. Guilt flashes across her face. "Are you feverish? You look a bit feverish. Do you want me to stay home with you?"

Jo gives her a sharp look. She needs Eleanor at the ball. She can't do this without her. Is Elle having second thoughts?

"No, there's no reason both of us should miss all the fun." Georgie yawns like a sleepy kitten. "It came on all of a sudden. I feel so hot and sleepy, I can barely keep my eyes open."

"Here, let me..." Elle rummages through her collection of vials and hands a small one to Georgie. "Put a dab of this on your forehead and your wrists, and it should help you fall right to sleep. Shall we ask Mrs. O'Brian to bring you some tea?"

"No, I'll just have a little lie-down." Georgie yawns again. "Give Nathaniel my regards?"

Seeing her so soft and sleepy, guilt stabs at Jo. When Mam hadn't slept in too long, or when she'd had too much whiskey, she could be mean. Georgie bore the brunt of it; she was too young to understand why sometimes Mam was bright and playful, and other times she was spiky and silent, as dangerous as one of her plants. Jo used to bring Georgie to the nursery and read her stories till she fell asleep, the weight of her feeling like home.

When Georgie's footsteps patter away down the hall, Elle turns to Jo. "I feel rotten. This breaks our old promise."

When Mam died, they vowed they'd never use their magic against each other. That they would never fall into the trap of other Campbell sisters.

"I know." Jo frowns. But she can't see any way around it. Georgie is too headstrong, too in love, to hand Nathaniel over to Jo on the chance that the vision is true. Jo is gambling a great deal: her sister's love, her future, her very life. "Will she ever forgive me, do you think? What if it were Alice?"

Elle smiles, with teeth. "Thank your lucky stars it's not."

Jo shivers, glad that Georgie is less bloodthirsty. "But you're willing to sail away tomorrow?"

"Better not to see her become Lady Colchester." Elle's lower lip wobbles the slightest bit, and then she straightens her spine and sets her shoulders. "I sail at dawn with Rafael. We'll have such adventures. Perhaps I'll follow in Papa's footsteps and become a lady buccaneer."

Her forced cheer makes Jo's heart ache. "Will you write me?"

"Of course. And my letter for Papa is beneath my pillow. Make sure he reads it, will you? I hope he'll forgive me for running off with a sailor and ruining his reputation. You becoming Mrs. Winchester—and sister-in-law to a viscountess—ought to help." Elle takes a deep breath. "I've left a letter for Alice, too. I'd be much obliged if you would deliver it discreetly."

"Of course." The tightness in Jo's throat threatens to overwhelm her. Tears prick at the corners of her eyes. This isn't goodbye, not yet, but… "I'll miss you," she blurts out, and Elle grabs her hand.

"Don't cry. I'm not gone yet!" Quick as lightning, Elle pricks Jo's finger and squeezes, letting her blood fall into the small vial. "There. Don't second-guess it now, Jo."

Jo nods. "There's no other way."

Mine, Jo thinks, as their carriage winds up the hill toward the Winchester mansion—as the white-columned house comes into view through the windows—as Papa hands first Jo and then Elle down onto the carriage box. As she walks up the grand, curving staircase to the second-floor ballroom, neighbors milling around in their finery, she cannot help but feel a sort of avarice that is new to her.

Jo knows what the people in Mercer's Cove say about her family. That her mother was a drunk whose death was no accident. That her father's smile is still a tad too piratical. That Elle is no better than she ought to be, and dangerous besides, peddling all those potions. They say Jo herself is odd, given to fits where she goes slack-mouthed and staring.

Of course, none of that keeps the fine townsfolk from stopping by the back door to purchase fortunes from Jo and tinctures from Elle. Elle makes salves to heal burns and plasters to heal coughs, love potions to catch husbands or wives, herbs to prevent babies, and—when she is convinced it's warranted—the occasional poison. Still, the people of Mercer's Cove call her a witch and little better than a whore. They deem Jo strange and spooky.

Only Georgie escapes their censure. Adorable, apple-cheeked Georgie, whose penchant for fire is far more easily concealed than Jo's prophecies. And Georgie is far more circumspect than Elle.

Jo thought she didn't mind it anymore. But tonight…tonight she notices how ladies put their heads together and whisper when they see Elle. How they draw their wide satin skirts aside when Jo gets too close, as though her oddness might be catching. How they smile with their mouths and avert their eyes.

When Jo is Nathaniel's wife—when she is the Winchester matriarch—no one will whisper about her anymore. Not so loud she can hear them, anyhow.

The thought sends satisfaction rushing through her.

Is this choice as altogether altruistic as she would have herself believe?

Jo's doubt grows as she stands among the wallflowers lining the ballroom. As she waits for Elle to slip the potion into Nathaniel's rum punch. When they arrived sans Georgie, he inquired after her health and anyone with eyes could see how smitten he is with their little sister.

Now, as Jo watches, Mr. Winchester—the tall, silver-haired heir to a shipping fortune—announces Alice's engagement to Lady Colchester. Alice is tall and graceful in a cream satin dress with ruched chiffon at the broad, sloping neckline. She takes Lady Colchester's gloved hand in hers, her head bowed demurely as her betrothed leads her into a waltz.

Jo glances across the ballroom at Elle, who looks as though she'd like to drink a whole cup of poison. Soon enough, though, Elle whirls across the room and claims a dance from Nathaniel. And when she relinquishes him, Nathaniel makes his way across the crowded ballroom and asks Jo to dance.

He is very tall, with a shock of dark hair and kind brown eyes. He dances well, accounting for her missteps with ease. Jo finds herself wondering what it might be like to be with him in the way that Elle was with Rafael. She wonders if he would be graceful in the marriage bed, too.

They are quiet, but it's a companionable silence. Jo glances up and catches his eyes on her décolletage. She's never had a man so openly admire her figure before. Of course, there is not usually so much to admire. She hopes that Elle hasn't given him more of the potion than she ought. It is the sort of thing Elle might find amusing.

Jo considers him thoughtfully beneath her lowered eyelashes. He has nice hands, she decides, with long, elegant fingers. What would they feel like against her skin? Should she let him take liberties, beyond a kiss or two?

"You're flushed. Are you warm?" Nathaniel asks. "I hope you're not catching Miss Georgiana's fever."

"Oh no, it's just the crush of people," Jo lies.

Mam told them that Campbell means *crooked mouth* in Gaelic. That Campbell witches lie as easily as they smile.

"Would you like to go out on the terrace?" Nathaniel asks, and she nods.

This is all a lie, she reminds herself. Still, it feels nice to have him guide her through the crowd, one hand on the small of her back. Hundreds of candles light the ballroom, and flowers lend their sweet heady scent to the candle wax and the briny sea air that drifts in through the open French doors. Nathaniel propels her outside, onto the terrace that overlooks the sea. The moon is waxing tonight, shining down on the dark water.

"Shall we go into the gardens?" Jo asks. She needs to get him alone, where no one will see the scandal about to unfold. Where no one will notice how he's looking at the odd older sister of his intended. "I've always been fond of your statuary."

Nathaniel leads her down the staircase. "Do you know I once thought to study art at university? To go off to Paris and paint?"

"Truly?" Jo cannot imagine it. He seems so...respectable.

"Truly. Father would have none of that, of course. Called it a childish delusion. My responsibilities are here, with the shipping business. With my family." They are behind a hedgerow now, at the entrance to the rose garden. "You're the eldest, and with your mother gone—you must have a keen understanding of family responsibility."

"I do," Jo says. That's why she's doing this, isn't it? For her sisters? It feels more selfish now. She lets herself believe the lie for a moment—that she is beautiful, that this moment has not been carefully engineered. She looks up at Nathaniel through lowered eyelashes and shivers at the cool breeze coming off the sea.

He moves closer, and Jo can feel the heat from his long, lean body. She lets herself stumble on the uneven bricks of the path. "Oh!" she laughs, high and nervous, and he catches her with both hands, his touch warm on the bare skin between her sleeves and her gloves. Even when she's righted herself, he does not let go. He runs one finger along the dip of her elbow, and this time when Jo shivers it's not from the cold.

She has arranged to trap him, and yet she is the one who feels caught, pinned in place by the desire in his eyes. They are not brown, she sees now; they are hazel, with flecks of green and gold. His hand trails up the curve of her neck and comes to rest gently on her cheek. "Josephine," he murmurs in wonderment. "How have I never noticed it before?"

"Noticed what?" she whispers.

His mouth is only inches away. "How lovely you are," he says, and then his lips meet hers. Jo returns the kiss with an unpracticed eagerness that surprises them both. He teases her mouth open, his tongue darting inside, and Jo finds that she likes kissing quite a lot.

Nathaniel moves his mouth to her ear, and it is only then, as he murmurs endearments, nibbling on her earlobe, his hand cupping the side of her breast, that Jo comes back to herself. She pulls away, thoroughly compromised—and thoroughly shaken by how much she's enjoyed it.

Nathaniel reaches for her again, but she sidesteps him. Her gloved hand comes to her mouth in dismay. What has she done? This was meant to be a lie.

For him, it is a lie. He had no choice in it.

She took away his choice. He might not know it, might attribute it to the rum and the moonlight, but Jo will always know.

Behind them, the sea pummels itself against the shore. Against the cliffs her mother dove off in the dead of night to end her nightmares once and for all.

"My God." Nathaniel seems to realize what's happened all at once. "Josephine, I— You must think me a cad. I never intended—"

"No," Jo says. "It's as much my fault as yours."

He shakes his head. "A gentleman must control himself, no matter how tempting he finds a woman."

"Jo? Jo?" It's Elle. She turns the corner and gasps when she sees them together. "Mr. Winchester, what are you and my sister doing out here in the dark, alone and unchaperoned? Jo, you look a fright." She fusses with Jo's curls, with her feather headdress.

"I'm perfectly fine, Elle. It's nothing," Jo says. She wishes she could take it all back.

"It's not nothing. Did anyone see you leave the ballroom together?" Elle asks.

"I—" Nathaniel swallows. Hesitates. Then squares his shoulders. "Your sister's right. I'll speak to your father at once, Josephine."

"You intend to ask for her hand in marriage?" Elle asks. Jo holds her breath.

"There is no other honorable choice," Nathaniel says. He squeezes Jo's hand, his touch there and then gone, and heads for the stairs.

"I believe Papa's in the billiards room!" Elle calls helpfully.

When Nathaniel is gone, it's quiet save for the soft rhythm of the surf against the shore. "We did it," Jo says finally. "I'll be Mrs. Winchester."

"How *could* you?" a voice cries from the darkness, and Georgie steps out from behind the marble statue of an angel.

She is wearing her black riding cloak, with the hood up. Her face is in shadow, but the tears on her cheeks catch the moonlight. Jo's heart splinters at the sight of them.

"Why, Jo? You don't even *like* Nathaniel!" Her voice breaks, and the sound slices through Jo like shards of glass.

"I had a vision," Jo says. "A vision where we all survived. You and Elle left Mercer's Cove. I stayed, and I married Nathaniel."

Georgie stalks closer. "Your visions aren't infallible. They are *possibilities*."

"Even a possibility—that's more than we had before," Elle explains. "The Book says—"

"Mam said—" Jo starts, at the same time.

"Mam was mad. I wish we'd thrown that damn Book into the sea after her." Georgie whirls on Elle, her black cloak flaring out around her, her hood falling back. "You helped her. You kept this from me."

"You never would have agreed to let her have Nathaniel," Elle says. "I wouldn't."

"You're damned right I wouldn't," Georgie swears. In the house on the hill, the candles flare higher, brighter. "So you took away my choice. You took away *his* choice, too. You must have used a potion. He never would have touched her otherwise."

Her laugh stings, but Jo knows it's the truth. The kisses, the caresses—they were all false. "Georgie—"

"You're using him. He's a good man, Jo. An *honorable* man. He deserves better than this. Better than *you*. And so do I. You betrayed me. Both of you. *Together*." Above them, the candles in the ballroom leap higher and higher, throwing strange, macabre shadows of the guests.

"Georgie, calm down!" Elle pleads.

It's too late. In the ballroom, the candles have caught. Guests begin to shriek. The band stops playing as fire begins to crawl up the wooden windowsills and catch on the rose damask curtains. Jo imagines it dancing up the pastoral wallpaper.

"Calm down?" Georgie shrieks. "How dare you. That tea you brought me this afternoon… You *poisoned* me, Elle!"

Her little sister's ire has always been quick to rise, but Jo has never seen Georgie like this. The waxing moon makes her strong, and her anger makes her magic flare. Above them, the flames leap from the second story toward the roof. Their neighbors pour out the terrace doors, down the steps and into the gardens.

"It's my fault. I saw myself here," Jo tries to explain. "I saw myself on the staircase, wearing his grandmother's ring, the sapphire one that—you know the one. I was old. I had *grand-children*. But you and Elle were still alive. We hadn't seen each other in years; you'd both gone away. Don't you see? I had to intervene, to make the vision come true. But I couldn't—I couldn't ask you to give up Nathaniel."

"So you took him." It is a strange and eerie thing, to see lightning without the rush of rain or crack of thunder. It cuts through the clear night sky, and Georgie aims it true. It connects with the gray-shingled roof of the Winchester mansion.

"Georgie, stop!" Jo cries, panicked. "Please. Nathaniel's still inside."

"Alice!" Elle screams, and runs for the stairs.

"Elle, no!" Jo darts after her, but Georgie grabs her wrist and wrenches it, hard.

"We're not finished," she growls.

Jo watches as Elle pushes her way past their neighbors, up the steps and straight into the burning mansion.

"If something happens to her—or to Nathaniel—"

"It's on your head." Georgie's angry blue eyes reflect the flames. "This is all because of *you*. I can't stand to be in the same house as you. The same island, even. I'll catch the night ferry to the mainland. That's what you wanted, isn't it? For me to be so heartbroken that I'd leave Mercer's Cove? Well,

I'll go. But I'm not broken, and I wouldn't count on it that I'll stay gone."

Georgie draws her cloak back up over her brown curls. There are a thousand questions Jo wants to ask. Where will she go? What will she do? Does she have enough money? Can she ever forgive them?

But she doesn't ask. She knows she doesn't deserve the answers.

The next morning, Jo is sitting slumped at the kitchen table when Eleanor stumbles in, still dressed in her bottle-green velvet evening dress. Her dark hair has tumbled down around her shoulders and she reeks of smoke. Her right hand and arm are wrapped in some kind of poultice to treat her burns.

Jo starts as though she's seen a ghost. "You were supposed to be on a ship hours ago."

"I can't leave her," Elle says.

Alice, she means. Nathaniel and Alice were both injured trying to make certain everyone had gotten out safely. Nathaniel broke his leg leaping from a second-story window after the grand staircase became impassable. Alice's back was burned when falling debris caught her beautiful cream dress afire. It would have been far worse if Elle hadn't rushed to her side and beat out the flames.

The mansion is in ruins. Alice and Nathaniel were both taken to Lady Colchester's estate, just outside of town, to convalesce. The physician was called, of course, but Elle had rushed headlong after them with her own tools. Jo had assumed Emma Colchester would throw her sister out on her ear, and that Elle would be somewhere in the midst of the Atlantic by now.

Her panic rises at the strange calm on her sister's face.

"What about Rafael and your grand adventures? What about Europe? You'd throw that all away because of some misplaced guilt?"

Elle smiles. "I love her, Jo. If any part of me wasn't sure before, when I saw the house afire and knew that she was still inside, I—"

"What about Lady Colchester?" Jo interrupts, desperate.

"She genuinely cares for Alice, I'll give her that," Elle says grudgingly. "She has agreed to let me look after Alice until she's well. After that—we'll see. Engagements can be broken, can't they?"

Jo's stomach plummets to her slippers. "You can't stay in Mercer's Cove. If you stay, it will all be for nothing! I'm betrothed to a man who doesn't want me, and Georgie hates us, and—I have to at least know you'll be safe, Elle. We can rebuild that house. The staircase. God knows the Winchesters have the money. But you've got to—"

"No. Not even for you." Elle shrugs one shoulder.

"It's all wrong," Jo says miserably. "This isn't what I saw at all."

"Maybe we can't fight our fate," Elle suggests.

"I refuse to believe that." Jo is uniquely situated to fight fate. To see it coming and bend it to her will. She chose her sisters over everything (*her sisters...and wealth and power*, a small voice inside reminds her). But they refused to make the same sacrifices. Elle chose Alice. In the heat of her anger, Georgie chose revenge. And now Jo feels farther away from them than ever.

You cannot survive together, Mam had said. *But it's not so easy surviving apart, either.*

★ ★ ★ ★ ★

LOVE SPELL

by Anna-Marie McLemore

I THINK I FELL IN LOVE WITH EL ACÓLITO THE first time he gave me communion. But I can't know for sure. I had flinched from his touch so many times, sure God would strike me down for wanting the boy placing la hostia on my tongue.

The priests have ways of giving us communion without touching us, and the acolytes too. It's an art as delicate as slipping the red shell off a nutmeg seed. La Virgen Herself must guide their hands. Their fingers never graze our mouths or nick our tongues.

But la Virgen did not steady this boy's hands. I imagined Her in the transept, bright with stained-glass light, laughing without sound as his fingers brushed my lips and we each shuddered back as though we might burn each other.

La Virgen may be our Mother of grace and mercy, but She is also more mischief than our priests will ever admit.

If the other girls and their mothers didn't notice el acólito's fingers on my lips, the pressure of his nails soft as the vein of a feather, it was because they were not watching the acolytes. They were watching our newest priest. A younger one, no older than twenty-five, with a back muscled enough that they could see the hint of it through his cassock, and eyes that shone purple in full sun.

I had never cared for him, this violet-eyed man they call the handsome priest.

I cared for him even less when he slapped el acólito's hand so hard he almost dropped the chalice.

La hostia caught in my throat. Even soaked in wine, it felt dry and hard as cornmeal. I looked up with my eyes but did not lift my chin.

El acólito looked so chastened, like a little boy caught reaching toward a blue flame, that I felt my weight sink into the kneeler.

"Don't you know anything?" the handsome priest scolded, at a whisper. "We don't bless witches."

My aunt has a saying about women like us: Find the right bruja, and you're half done.

The Villanueva sisters can bring down any fever, resting their hands on a hot forehead until they know the right green leaves to break the calentura. For susto so bad it's worth driving a day to cure, my tía recommends a woman three hundred miles away, rumored to be so old no one knows when, or if, she was born. And my second cousin makes a little fortune off gullible tourists, but she also knows how to cure more than a too-heavy handbag.

My aunt and I don't cure susto or pneumonia, or rid children of their nightmares. Our gift is for lovesickness.

"Can you get rid of it?" the lovesick always ask when they come to our door.

"Yes," my tía says, so long as they can stomach the cure.

(It's our great misfortune that my tía will take anything as payment. A bag of purple potatoes. Jewelry kept from the lovers who left. Leeks so recently dug up that sand still flecks the bulbs. If she insisted on money, we'd have the roof fixed. From a distance, her home has the look of a child's dollhouse left in an attic, charming in its sloped roof and arched windows, but forgotten long enough to sag under age and wear.)

Our art isn't amnesia; we leave that to the Sandovals down the road. No one who visits us forgets the objects of their love. You still know who they are, and that, once, you felt a love for them that wore off like a fever. They become whoever they would've been to you if you did not love them. A friend. An acquaintance. A pretty neighbor whose name you may or may not be able to place.

"What are you doing out there?" my aunt asked from the kitchen window.

I was standing under our Harrow pear, the sad, blighted tree that hadn't given fruit in two seasons. But I loved it. I loved even its withered branches and sickly leaves, always red and orange as though frozen in autumn.

I caught my aunt's look. *Just leave it alone and let it die in peace*, her eyes said. To her, all my watering and pruning was as useless as trying to grow corn from empty husks.

She flapped her hands at me to join her inside.

A young woman had come to us holding a wedding dress, the skirt wide but limp as a pierced balloon. My tía and I already knew who she was. We'd been expecting her. Her pendejo fiancé had left her at the altar the weekend before.

Her family was still eating the leftover pigs-in-a-blanket. They'd brought the five-tiered cake to the retirement home three towns over, and donated twenty pounds of silvered almonds to the church.

The young woman held out the dress to my tía. "Can you cure me?"

My tía put a hand on my back and pushed me forward. "She can."

"Now?" I whispered to my aunt.

I had watched her give many lovesickness cures. I handed her the matches, added the smallest pinches of ash to the water, mixed the remedios for the heartbroken to drink. But I had never made one myself.

I worried that getting a good look at me would make the woman run. I wouldn't be seventeen until fall, a world away from my aunt with her silver braid. Wisdom crinkled the corners of her eyes, while my right temple wore a sprinkling of acne so persistent I'd gotten used to hiding it behind my hair. No lovesick heart would trust a girl who still needed witch hazel.

But the woman held out the wedding dress. Without meaning to, I opened my hands and accepted its weight.

Sometimes, my tía tried to talk her pacientes out of the cure. Love should be driven from the body only if it will destroy all else, she often told them.

"Once it's gone, it's gone," she warned.

But she did not try to talk this woman out of it. When her novio took off with half their wedding gifts in the back of his Camaro, the women in town made the sign of the cross out of gratitude. The loss of fine sheets and silver was worth getting rid of this man who considered the voices of women chatter, meaningless as the clicking of a barn windmill. I thought I felt the very earth under us sigh in relief as he crossed out of our town's limits.

The woman hadn't just brought the wedding dress so she could clutch its satin. We needed a little of it, a piece stained and starched by tears she had cried for that man.

She held her back teeth tight as I ripped a scrap from the hem.

My aunt looked on as I burned the cloth. The flame swallowed it up, and when the ashes cooled I added a tiny pinch to a jar of water. My aunt had made me practice this a hundred times. The motions of my fingers had to be careful and precise, especially with the ash. The line between cure and poison is always fine, and walking it takes all the skill and gift I have in me.

Making a remedio meant listening both to my own don and all I had learned from my tía. Always, the cure had to be drawn from the lovesickness itself. A few drops of honey; their wedding cake would have been pastel de miel. Lavender; she'd tucked sprigs of it in her shoes and into her hair the day he left. Guajillo chile, her favorite kind; she would need to get her bite back to heal her own heart.

The woman held out her hand, knowing what we needed last.

Your blood is sick with your own love, my tía always said. *A little bit of the sickness helps make the cure.*

It was the same reason we needed something that held their tears.

I lifted a needle from the ones we'd boiled in water and held in the blue flame of the stove that morning. The woman did not flinch when I pricked her finger, or when I held her hand over the jar, the red twirling into the grayed water.

I handed her the remedio. She shuddered. They always do at the sight of the dull water, tinted faintly with their own blood, that they must now drink.

But she drank it.

Later, when we were cutting back the wild mint, my tía said, "You are ready."

I tossed a handful of leaves into the burlap bag. I had learned the lovesickness cure under my aunt's watch. I could not imagine keeping my hands steady without her. Not now, not in fifty years. "Don't say that."

"That's you letting your fear speak for you." She tucked a spray of bluebells into my braid. "If you let fear be your voice, you will never have sure hands."

My aunt has a saying about men like the handsome priest: The only thing that bothers them more than brujas who ignore God is brujas who enter His house.

She did not go to church with me. So she had not seen el acólito cringing with the shame of having his hands slapped just after he'd washed them with holy water. She had warned me that if I went to service I was a fool, and that if I tried to take the Eucharist, I was a fool twice over.

That Sunday, with el acólito's fingers on my lips, I understood my aunt's warning. And when I heard the whispers trailing after me like a wedding train—*she has nerve, doesn't she? You know her tía's pear tree doesn't give fruit; la Virgen Herself blighted it*—I knew I would not go back.

Instead I knelt with my rosary each night, el ave maría and the Twelve Truths of the World on my lips. I said my prayers to God, who I believed still wanted me, even if the men who took up His name on Earth never would.

My mother had warned me, before she and my father let me come live with my tía to learn about my gift. She warned me that, especially in small towns, people believed in our remedios when they needed us and called us sorceresses when they didn't.

"They'll stab you in the back, cariña," my mother told me. "One day they'll drag you into the middle of town and cut your throat, all of them screaming you're a witch."

"If they stab me in the back, I'll be dead before they cut my throat," I muttered as I packed my clothes.

But I listened. I kept to my aunt's house and to short errands in town.

I only slipped once. It was that summer, a night my heart felt so emptied, so untethered from the weeks I'd gone without taking la hostia, it was as though my body went looking for it. I sleepwalked right out of my aunt's house and into the road.

My aunt's house melted into my dreams. The colors she painted the rooms—dark green, deep gold, rich blue—became the shades of the land and sky in autumn. The smell of her kitchen, the jars of marigold petals and rosebuds, transformed into a night garden. The wooden stairs were rocky ground, so that when my feet touched true ground outside, my sleeping body could not tell the difference.

I woke startled, hissing like a cat. I flinched at how the wet earth had crawled up the backs of my pajama pants, sticking them to my legs. The wind whipped the ribbon off my braid, my hair flying free.

The shriek of an engine tore through me. My heart flinched with fear and recognition. My feet found traction on the rough wood of railroad ties, but then lost it, so fast I thought the wind had hands.

El acólito, out of his white robe with the white cord for a belt, now wore the jeans and duck-cloth jacket of any other boy out at night.

El acólito, who did not have his fingers light on my lips but his hands tight on my waist.

The acolyte, who had just pulled me out of the way of the late train.

Even as a girl used to hearing *bruja* whispered at her back, the smallest things could still embarrass me. And now, even with this boy's hands on me, even with my pulse still hard in my throat, I felt the odd shame of realizing what pajama pants I was wearing. Red hearts on a pink cotton background. My mother had bought them for me to make fun of how I drew hearts on everything. The edges of my notebooks were crammed with them. I couldn't leave a note for my tía without adding a heart to the corner. My mother called it a funny habit for a girl learning to cure lovesickness.

When the acolyte and I both got our breath back, when the last freight car had screamed past and the rasp of metal faded, he slackened into politeness. He stepped back, dropping his hands from me and asking if I was all right.

Even with the formal posture, he still wore that shamed look he'd gotten from the violet-eyed priest. I didn't know why. There was no one out here to see us.

"I'm sorry," he said. Odd words from a boy who'd just kept my own dreams from killing me.

He lowered his head, more than he needed to for our small difference in height, and I understood he was not embarrassed that the church had seen him scolded.

He was embarrassed it had happened in front of me.

The idea that he cared what a bruja thought of him was like the brush of his fingers against my lips. It was the whisper of the pear tree's leaves the first season it flowered and greened.

I had been near enough lovesickness to know better. But

I brought el acólito into my aunt's house, both of us silent as we passed her door.

He let me take his clothes from him for the night. Not all of them, but enough that he showed himself to me. He told me how his mother had given him a girl's name when he was born. That girl's name had never truly been his, so his mother named him again. She decided that just because she was wrong the first time did not mean she shouldn't christen him the second, this time with a boy's name. A name that suited him.

"Adrián," he told me. His proper name, the boy's name his mother had given him.

He told me this as he took my clothes from me, as though these were things he needed to see all of me to tell.

After that, Adrián brought communion to me and my tía.

I wondered how hard the violet-eyed priest would slap him if he caught him smuggling la hostia from the church. Adrián brought it to my aunt's kitchen, adorned not with somber cloth but with ristras of bright chiles, where the blood of Christ would be an inch of Tempranillo from a bottle forgotten the night before.

My aunt took communion, but always with a laugh, as though she were obliging this boy.

"I don't believe God hides Himself behind an altar rail, or in bread," she said one Sunday as he unwrapped la hostia, blessing it on her kitchen table. "But I will take it, if it will make you happy."

Adrián gave his own obliging smile. "It will."

"And you don't worry over giving communion to an old witch?" she asked.

"No." His laugh was soft as he lifted la hostia from the cloth napkin. "I don't."

My tía never said thank you. Or, she did, once, by shoving one of our live chickens at him, a red-brown one with a few tail feathers as blue-green as a peacock's. She did not ask if he wanted it. She only thrust the hen into his arms and said, "She gives good eggs, and she won't peck you much when you come for them."

The chicken—I had named her Gertrudes the summer before—squawked and flapped as Adrián adjusted his grip on her.

"Show our guest out," my tía said.

I led Adrián to the front steps.

"I'm sorry about my aunt," I said once I shut the door behind us. "She's not just humoring you, I promise. She does believe."

His shrug was slow. "Faith comes in as many forms as the faithful."

"You sound ready for Holy Orders."

He laughed. I was glad he took the compliment the way I meant it, that I thought he could one day match the wisdom of the old priest, or the kind spirit of the short priest. Not the fury and judgment of the handsome one.

"Thank you," he said. "But the priesthood, it's not for me."

"You don't see yourself in the cassock?"

"I see myself married."

He looked at me with the same clear stare as when he gave me la hostia. But there was no altar rail. And I was not kneeling.

I had only tasted his mouth once, that night a few weeks earlier. But I remembered it as well as the taste of a communion wafer.

His look was so unbroken and unguarded that it held for only a few seconds before we both shivered away.

"I mean—" he caught on the words "—one day."

I took in a breath of the air between us, hoping there was some trace of him on it.

Adrián held Gertrudes out to me. "This seems as good a time as any to give you back your hen."

Gertrudes flapped again.

"You'll take good care of her, I know it." I eased her back into his arms, calming both her and Adrián. "All I ask is you don't cook her. She's a good layer."

"I wouldn't cook a hen you're fond of, even if she didn't lay. But I don't want to take her from you. She's yours."

"Don't you know anything?" I asked, my voice laughing but hard. "Never refuse a gift from a witch."

I couldn't pretend I hadn't meant the echo. I cringed hearing myself mimic the handsome priest.

The light went out of Adrián, his shoulders slumping as though the fault was rightfully his.

He nodded his goodbye.

I let him go.

And because I could not go after him, I filled a notebook with a thousand pencil-drawn hearts.

I said nothing to my tía about how Gertrudes was my favorite. She knew, and if I had mentioned it, she would have smirked at me.

She did anyway, that night as we fired her cast-iron pan on the stove.

It was a smirk I read easily, just as she wanted me to.

I may have given him your favorite hen. But you gave him your heart.

June opened into midsummer. Redbud blossoms gave way to the blue-purple flowers of the chaste trees. And every Sunday, Adrián came.

But we spent only the one night together, that first night. I did not take his hand again.

"You'll stay for dinner?" my aunt asked each week.

"Thank you," he said. "I should get home, though."

The third time she asked, I followed Adrián toward the door, wanting to confess that the moment of him setting the host on my tongue was never enough.

But my tongue, still missing the taste of his, would not speak the words. There was not enough of him left in my mouth.

"She means it, you know," I told him instead. "My aunt. She's not just being polite."

He turned his face to me.

"You should stay," I said.

"I'd better not," he said, with a sadness I did not understand and did not have the courage to ask after.

That night, I filled a hundred more pages with hearts drawn in pencil.

If he had been a novicio, I could have driven him from my dreams so much more easily. I could have told myself he would never be mine because he would never belong to any girl.

But when Adrián left his acolyte's robe behind, it would be for a wedding ring, not a cassock. He would take a vow of marriage, not abstinence.

The reason I did not bring him into my bedroom again was as familiar to me as the Hail Mary: boys like him, boys who served as acolytes, did not marry witches.

Boys like Adrián sometimes loved witches, even considered marrying them. But when it came time for any public declaration, they always faltered. Boys who spent years at the altar in white robes could not bring themselves to tell their mothers and their churches that they loved a bruja.

Love, however, had little to do with any of it. It was fear that drove their hearts. Fear of the priests who might slap their hands. Fear of the mothers who lowered their eyes and shook their heads when their sons disappointed them. Fear of a God they imagined watching them, the shadow of His disapproval on their bodies.

I wanted to remember nothing but the deepening brown of Adrián's eyes as he told me he wanted to marry one day.

Instead, I remembered how boys like him were raised to count girls like me as daughters of the Devil.

No one taught these boys to hear the voice of la Virgen. Our Lady spoke for us when no one on this earth would.

Three Sundays later, my tía let me sleep. She usually got me up as the sun was just spilling orange into the upstairs bedroom, so I could check the hens for eggs.

I ran outside at the sound of her truck's engine turning over.

"Where are you going?" I asked, yelling over the diesel's purr.

Her weathered hands gripped the enormous wheel. "The nursery."

"For what?" I asked.

"We're getting a new tree."

I surveyed the yard, crowded with the row of apricot trees, the chicken coop, an herb garden that sprawled all the way to the road. "Where're you gonna put it?"

My tía set her sights on the pear tree. "We're taking that damn thing out."

"No," I said, as though my tía's house and land were mine.

"It's blighted," she said. "It's not getting better."

The flick of her hand toward the sick tree hurt as badly as if she'd tossed aside the seeds we saved from her heirloom tomatoes. I'd planted that Harrow pear with my tía the first summer I visited her, my small, chubby hands packing the dirt around the base. The sapling's leaves had been bright as wet grass, and the sky had deepened to blown-glass blue by the time we finished.

Now that the blight had taken hold, half the Harrow pear's leaves had withered to red-brown, and the edges of the rest had turned wine-colored. Its spindly boughs and sparse foliage made it look stuck in early winter. For all we could do for the lovesick, we couldn't help the dying thing in my aunt's yard.

I retied the ribbon on the waist of my pajama pants, my red hearts on pink cotton. I could not bring myself to get rid of them even though they reminded me of a boy I could not have. Since the night he'd first touched me, I'd filled three notebooks with drawn hearts.

"What if someone comes for a remedio?" I asked my aunt. "When should I say you're coming back?"

"If someone comes for a remedio," she said as she drove off, "then give it to them."

I couldn't argue. Marisol had called late last night to say she'd seen the woman with the wedding dress in the center of town, hooking her feet onto another man's bar stool.

I sank into my tía's sofa with a bowl of cereal. I wasn't making huevos motuleños just for myself.

The first knock at the door was earlier than usual. The lovesick didn't often come in the morning. They came late in the afternoon, when the way the light slanted made them so sad they couldn't carry it, or in the evening, when no one would see them at the back door. I figured it was Marisol with morning gossip, so I didn't bother slipping a bra on under my shirt, or rubbing the splash of milk out of my pajama pants. I wanted Marisol to tell me she'd seen the woman with the wedding dress kissing a man twice as handsome and a hundred times kinder than the man in the Camaro.

But when I opened the door, Marisol wasn't there. Neither were the Villanueva sisters, or Señora Delgado, or any of the other curanderas.

I crossed my arms over my chest, wishing I'd at least thrown on jeans.

"I'm looking for your aunt," Adrián said. It sounded like a question.

I dropped my arms from my chest and braced a hand on the door frame, wondering if he would look away.

He didn't.

"She's gone for the day," I said. "What do you need?"

The smallness of his laugh made it sound even sadder. "What do you think?"

The back of my neck heated, remembering all the hearts I'd drawn that summer.

The way my mother told it, girls always held on tighter than boys. A boy moved on while the girl still scribbled her first name with his last.

Did Adrián want the love he had for me gone so much he couldn't even wait for it to fade from his boy-heart? And if he had really been lovesick over me, wouldn't he have stayed some Sunday when my aunt offered him a place at our dinner table?

"Fine." I waved him inside.

He handed me a folded strip of cloth, deep pink as roselles.

The ribbon that had fallen out of my hair that night.

I stilled the twirl of heat in me as fast as it rose.

"Where did you get this?" I asked.

"I didn't get it anywhere," he said. "I kept it that night."

I took the ribbon and held it tight to my palm. That night always came back to me like the layers of a perfume. The smell of the trees in the dark, the soap and dust of his jacket, the train's rusted metal on the cold air.

But a new scent drifted off the ribbon.

Salt.

Not the kind from a jar.

The kind a boy had let fall onto a hair ribbon.

I owed my life that night to a boy who took walks alongside the railroad tracks when he couldn't sleep. I could at least give him the remedio.

There was nothing else for a bruja and a boy worthy of an acolyte's robe. His mother hadn't given him a proper boy's name just so he could love a witch.

I burned the ribbon, and flicked the smallest pinch of the ash into water. I added things that might remind him of me. A lemon blossom off the tree that shaded our front walk, the bud purple and cream. A splash of leftover wine like the kind he blessed when he gave me communion. I stirred it with a teal feather, one Gertrudes had shed last summer and that I had cleaned and kept.

Adrián held a groan at the back of his throat. "I have to drink that?"

I twirled the feather's vein through the water. "No cure worth having is pretty."

He cuffed up his sleeves, knowing what came next.

"Why wouldn't you ever stay?" I asked, because now there was no reason not to.

"You never seemed to want me to."

The feather stilled in my hand.

Of course I wanted him to.

His stare opened, as though waiting for me to tell the truth.

Yes, I wanted him to stay. Every time.

And I wanted him never to stay, because then I would become another bruja who had gotten her heart broken by un acólito.

He offered his hands, holding them palms-up in front of me, as though I could have my pick of his fingers.

I held a clean sewing needle over the pad of his ring finger.

He nodded at me. *Go ahead*, his face said.

But I couldn't make my hands do it. Not when I felt the hot glow of his heart warming the needle like a live coal.

In the bright trembling of my fingers, I heard a whisper, soft and blue as la Virgen's veil.

She would not let me take from this boy that which was already mine.

Adrián's love was not a small, discrete thing I could draw from him like a lost jewel. It had grown tendrils and brambles. It had encircled his heart like morning glory over a brick wall. Like moonflower vines crawling and wrapping around everything they could reach.

The sound of green things filled the kitchen. Leaves rustling in harsh wind. Shoots breaking up through spring ground.

I checked the shifting light from the window.

The green of the Harrow pear filled the frame. It loomed and grew, breaking out of its two-year winter. The branches burst with health and new greenery. The blighted leaves fell away, and the wind took them. A million little white petals speckled the boughs, showing up on the dark wood as quickly as snowflakes. Red-gold fruit formed like water drops and weighted down the branches.

Those dozens of new pears left me silent except for one breathless laugh.

Adrián followed my gaze to the window. "Wasn't that..."

I nodded.

He'd seen it shriveled and blighted. He'd seen the sand-colored leaves clinging to the branches. He'd prayed over it, asking God and la Virgen to touch the boughs. Now it stood bushy and clover-green, so heavy with fruit the branches bowed.

I pushed his hair out of his face and put my mouth on his.

In the fearless way he believed, in the brazen hope he kept in his heart, he was as much brujo as I was bruja. That pear tree, green and alive, was as much his doing as mine.

I wondered how many hearts in this town held magic inside them. Knew it. Feared it. I wondered if this was why they shunned us, if we brujas reminded them too much of something within themselves.

The scent of pears slid in through the cracked window. It slipped between our mouths, Adrián's lips close enough to touch mine as he breathed.

I spread my hand over his shirt, feeling the thick fabric underneath, and I wondered if my fingers spanned wide enough to cover his heart and the veins that held it.

The sun lit up the Harrow pear, casting shadows on his body and my hands. It filtered through the leaves and blossoms. It caught in the drops of water that jeweled the pears. That tree, once blighted, now held every season we ever saw. The countless five-petal blossoms. The green of deep summer. The weight of fruit in fall. Everything but the winter we'd known for so many months.

I came back to church that Sunday. My aunt did not. I didn't blame her. Even the Harrow pear, in its full greenery, could not match the weight of being turned away from the altar rail for so many years. She stayed home, planting the sapling tree she had brought home with her, a mate for the now-living Harrow pear.

So that Sunday, I walked the length of the nave alone.

Adrián gave me la hostia with a sureness that scared the violet-eyed priest from slapping his hand. He blessed me in front of the congregation, and in front of the priests who had trained him to turn away witches. He gave me what he was meant to refuse me, and in doing so, he declared the way in which we belonged to each other.

I took the host, to show Adrián's mother that I was a bruja with heart enough for her son.

That afternoon, Adrián and I would walk through town. The main streets, not the back roads. He would wear his white robe and cord even as a bruja kept pace alongside him. We would bring communion to my aunt, who knew there was at least one acolyte behind the altar rail who would bless her.

And that night, I would untie the white cord from around Adrián's waist. I would take him from his white robe. I would slide into his hands the soft weight of a new pear.

As I thought of these things, I caught la Virgen in the corner of my vision. Beneath Her blue veil, She cast Her eyes to the church floor. But Her lips held a small smile, as though She will always see the love we carry in our hearts long before we understand it to be there.

★ ★ ★ ★ ★

THE GHERIN GIRLS

by Emery Lord

Nova

ON THE LAST NIGHT NOVA IS HOME, SHE COOKS out on the back patio. Steak kebabs with spicy eggplant and mushrooms. Honey-roasted corn and grilled bread with burrata.

Nova eats slowly, watching her sisters laugh around the fire. The flames reflecting in Willa's glasses. Rosie's hair draping past her shoulder, tiny buds from the greenhouse tucked into the braid. Nova remembers that Rosie taught herself to do this at some point, plait her hair like a feudal maiden. But sometimes it feels like Rosie was born just knowing how to look like Rosie.

Sometimes it feels like Nova will never stop being relieved to see Rosie here at home, safe and happy. It was two years ago this very weekend that Rosie moved out. It was her choice—Nova knew that. But it felt like Rosie had been stolen away into a dark kingdom.

As they're finishing up, a little shadow snakes his way into their circle. *Cats should be scared of fire*, Nova thinks.

He slides up against Rosie's leg, nudging at her, and Nova shakes her head. "The black cat is just…not going to help with the rumors, Rosie."

"Oh, like anything ever helps with the rumors." Rosie scratches a line down the cat's nose, and he closes his eyes happily. "Don't listen to her, Gnomey."

The cat has lived here for over a year now, ever since Rosemary came home. They've had cats at the farmhouse before, of course, but none that came inside every night to sleep at the foot of Rosie's bed.

"I still can't believe you named the cat *Gnome*," Nova mutters.

"He named himself." Rosie picks him up protectively. She sits between Nova and Willa, her natural place as middle sister. There are always three Gherin girls born to a generation: one to support you on each side.

That, as much as anything, is why Momma always spends the fall equinox with her own sisters—this year, in the Cotswolds. Nova comes home from New York to be with Willa and Rosie. Day and night in equal balance; sisterhood in balance. Daddy, bless his heart, is visiting his brother in Denver this weekend. Always quietly supporting his girls, even if it means giving them some time alone.

"I couldn't eat another bite," Willa announces.

"Oh no?" Nova holds out one hand. "So you don't want snacks for the movies later?"

Nova's last night home for equinox is always a fall movie marathon, mostly witch films—their little joke. Willa lays her palm on Nova's, smiling innocently.

"Espresso brownies, eh?" Nova laughs a little. "*And* toffee ice cream?"

"Oooh," Willa says. "Yeah."

"I used the last of Momma's cocoa on the kebabs."

"I can run out," Rosie says. "You need jalapeños for Daddy's meat loaf anyway."

"Oh, that's right." Novy considers this. She's had her fill of Grander, Wyoming. Last time she went to get groceries, a girl from high school said hello and then: *I'd heard you buzzed your head.* That just about summed it up. Grander: where you can move two thousand miles away, and people will still hear about your damn haircut. "And more peanut butter, if you want me to make that sauce for noodles before I go."

"You don't have to prep meals for us," Willa says. "We can do it."

Well, they can make deli sandwiches and pick up take-out, anyway. Rosie is too dreamy-eyed for cooking, prone to burnt-black edges and fire alarms. And Willa, well. Willa thinks cooking seems too fiddly when frozen pizza tastes so good.

When they're all done, Nova douses the fire pit, and it gives off that satisfying sizzle. Around any given bonfire, she thinks of being twelve, the year her history class touched on the Salem Witch trials. Every face in that room craned toward her, awaiting reaction. *My mom's an herbalist and a doula and a massage therapist*, she wanted to scream. To this day, half those kids' parents shuffle into Momma's sunny parlor for appointments. Some weep on her table, worn-out by pain. Momma kneads their backs and coos, "It's okay now. Let it out."

When Nova asked her mother if they were related to the Salem witches, Momma smiled at her three girls. "In a way, you're related to many women who have suffered for misunderstanding and fear."

Nova liked the idea of interconnectedness, without a clear explanation. Willa, their little National Merit Semifinalist, needed data. But there were no textbooks on the Gherin family women, just a few cracked leather journals with generations of handwritten notes. In middle school, Willa charted out a family tree—the taxonomy of their gifts. The three of them, and Momma, were listed as *Tactile*. Momma could soothe, but only by touch. Sometimes that meant calming colicky babies; sometimes it meant helping heartbroken people finally cry—releasing their buried feelings was ultimately soothing. Over the years, she'd discovered this to work, temporarily, on burns and bug bites.

Nova could sense what specific food would taste best to people in that exact moment. Rosie knew what plants needed to thrive. It made her a nurturer in all the good ways, but it also made her try to fix things she could not fix. Like broken boys who would break her, too, if they could. And Willa, well—she could feel every nuanced emotion with just a brush of skin on skin.

They used to be jealous, Nova and Rosie, that Willa's gift had so much heft. Nova loved cooking anyway, and being able to comfort people with it was a bonus. Rosie's gift turned her plant-raising into useful herbal medicines and bath products. But Willa had access to information, whether she wanted it or not. Sometimes she did not.

The Gherin girls never called it magic, even though they tried to hone and utilize each talent with care. After all, was perfect pitch considered *magic*? An eidetic memory? No, they were simply unusual gifts.

Nova gathers the last of the dishes and closes the patio door behind her.

"Anything else, Novy?" Willa calls from the front hallway. "Cocoa, jalapeños, the good peanut butter, and ice cream?"

Nova visualizes the aisles, wondering if she has supplies to make a rustic vegetable tortellini. She likes to leave her family stocked up—it assuages the guilt a little, as she flies the miles and miles back to New York. "Maybe I should come."

"Just stay," Rosie says. "In case anyone calls."

"What's that supposed to mean?" Nova frowns. Rosie's room shares a wall with hers. And for all three nights Nova's been home, he's called on his walk from the restaurant to the subway. For no reason. Just to check in. Nova likes the sound of his voice.

"Nothing, nothing!" Nova can hear Rosie smiling. They both know that this—whoever Nova has been talking to in the evenings—will become worth telling someday soon.

Rosemary

Willa drives because she can now and because Rosie likes to sit shotgun with the window down. They soar Daddy's truck down the back roads with the radio up.

The trees have put on their yellow dancing dresses. Fall air. And this time, Rosie is going to breathe it in.

Last fall, she was still standing on shaky ground. After a bad winter, she'd grown back parts of herself in spring and summer, letting the sunlight hit her face. She spent hours in the greenhouse, spritzing and repotting. Clipping back dead leaves.

She had replanted herself where she belonged, but she

needed water and light and air and nutrients. Most of all, she needed time.

That was a year ago, and she's strong now. She feels strong in her classes, a year deep into a botany degree. She feels strong riding horses with Daddy on the weekends. Driving to Cheyenne with the girls from her department for ice-cold beers and dancing. Just dancing to dance. With no one's permission; with no one's approval.

The grocery store is still bustling. As always, the girls get a few sidelong glances. No one *really* believes they're witches—not with any fervor anyway. But they do wonder. The way you wonder, as a child, if your stuffed animals talk when you're not there. You *know* they don't... Right?

The rumors about hexes are, of course, fabrications. Gherin girls are raised to rely on karma, that slow and steady mare.

Up near the checkout, Rosie pauses, breathing in a change in the atmosphere like a whiff of ozone after the rains. And this feeling...it's familiar. Nearby. A tug on gravity so slight that no one notices but her.

She glances around, eyes scanning.

And the linoleum floor falls out beneath her feet.

Why would he be here? Why?

Is she imagining it? For months after she left him, she'd startled at every young blond man in her peripheral vision. Even after she heard that he'd moved.

He's carrying a case of cheap beer, his high school football buddies following behind him with chips and bags of ice.

He always was both handsome and pretty, somehow, that dark blond hair kept in a knot at his crown. Jawline cut close around his full lips. And that same beat-up denim jacket, a thrift store find just tight enough to highlight biceps.

Vain. He was always vain about his looks, though he pretended it was effortless. She'd seen it after she moved in with him, the careful dumbbell reps, the mirror glances.

Rosie can't think—at least, not in words. The images flash, a reel of their greatest hits. The month they were both obsessed with that dumb pop song, playing it over and over in his truck. His fool's gold hair hanging loose as he got up from bed. *No.* His icy silence. "Forgetting" to pick her up from work. His anger, how it pulsed like a heartbeat.

Wyatt.

Wyatt, Wyatt, Wy, Wy, Why?

Why does a small, warm relief rush in—the vindication that she's wearing mascara and her best jeans? God, she hates that. She hates that, after everything, she craves his approval. She has since the moment they met. On his first day in school, he—this Army son with a face like an oil painting—settled down next to her in the cafeteria and said, "Hey," as if picking up a conversation they'd left off in another life. It wasn't until after the bell rang that he held out a tanned hand. Elegant fingers, Rosie thought. Long but sturdy. She wanted a glimpse at his love line. "Wyatt, by the way."

She clasped his hand, a touch that jolted up her arm. "Rosie."

"Rosie," he repeated. Trying it out in his mouth. Maybe knowing, even then, that he'd say it a thousand more times.

He is in the grocery store, of all places. In a town where he no longer lives.

Now they stand a few yards apart, eyes locked.

She walks toward him. Or does she? It feels like the tile itself slides her into his orbit.

He steps toward her, too, drawn away from his group.

"Rosie," he says quietly. Reverently, she thinks. Just the one word. He has the smallest smile on his face.

"Hey." She pushes a loose piece of hair behind her ear. Tries to return the smile so she looks relaxed, and not like her heart is a rusted motor whirring to life. She means to ask what he's doing here. Her hands tremble.

His eyes skim down her body, drinking her in, gulping. "You look good, Ro. I guess that's cliché to say."

She wants to snatch her name from his mouth. Only people who love her get to call her that. Instead, she lifts one shoulder. "When have I ever disliked clichés?"

Hadn't she loved when he played guitar for her? Hadn't she worn his football jersey knotted at her waist? *I know it's stupid*, he'd said, pressing the soft mesh into her hands. *But all the other guys' girlfriends wear them.* And Rosie, well, she'd felt so pleased to be claimed by him, to wear his name on her back.

He'd been right that it was stupid.

"What are you doing tonight? I'm staying with Dev—we're having people over. You should come." He runs a hand through his hair, casual as can be.

"Yeah, maybe. Why not?" she says, wanting him to be impressed with her nonchalance. To see that she is unbroken.

Why not?! she thinks. *Because he sank his claws into your soul so deeply that the puncture wounds bled for months. And, in this moment, you'd reopen them if he so much as nodded toward his truck.*

"Will!" Wyatt says, eyes finding her over Rosie's shoulder. "Hey, look at you!"

When Rosie turns to look at her sister, she finds Willa with eyes narrowed. Novy always looked at Wyatt like that, like slats of blinds, snapping near-closed. The Gherin girls couldn't read minds, not like people whispered about anyway. But Rosie could so clearly hear Willa wanting to reply: *Hello, Satan.*

"You're a junior!" he is saying. "Right? Man, how did that happen so fast?"

"Right. Crazy."

"You should come over, too! House party at Dev's," he says.

"That's nice," she says, in a tone that suggests it is not nice at all. Why can Willa—her *little* sister—be as cold as he deserves, while Rosie flounders politely? "But Nova's home this weekend. So we better get going."

Willa reaches out a hand. Rosie will not take it. She puts her arm through Willa's, her sweater a buffer between them.

"Well, if you change your mind…" Wyatt says. "Try to stop by. It's been too long, Ro."

"Okay," Rosie says, looking back with a smile.

Stop it! a base part of her brain screams. *No more smiles, no more trying.*

Once they're in the truck, Willa exhales. "*God*, that was weird, him being there. Right?"

"I mean, not really. He's back in town visiting friends." Rosie hears herself defending him, even in this tiny thing. She forces herself to think of Gnomey, waiting for her at home.

Those are the last words they exchange in the truck.

Willa

The whole ride home, Willa worries that Rosie is sitting in the passenger seat, remembering the good times. Willa is remembering the bad ones.

On graduation day, he gave her sister a simple rose gold ring.

"It's not an engagement ring," Rosie explained, her hand splayed out for Willa and Nova to see. "Just a gift."

So romantic, Willa thought.

Nova blinked at the woven band. "I thought you liked yellow gold."

Rosie pulled her hand back, scorned. "It's rose gold. Like my name."

She moved in with him in September, the day after fall equinox. Two towns over. They'd both commute to the local college.

Rosie and Nova had a blow-up fight. Novy said moving in with a guy before turning nineteen was the most Grander, Wyoming, thing that Rosie had ever done. Rosie shrilled back about Novy's snobbishness. *You only support me when I make the same choices you would make!* Rosie cried. *But I'm not you, Novy!*

Rosie loaded all of her possessions in his truck as Momma sat on the back porch. Willa had helped, cheerful and naïve, with arms full of boxes.

Daddy kissed Rosie's cheek and whispered, so that Wyatt couldn't hear, "You come home anytime, Rosie girl, okay? Day or night."

Willa waved as they drove off, blissful as newlyweds. When she turned to go in, Daddy had his back to the road, one hand gripped over his heart.

Weeks passed. In the greenhouse, leaves went dry as paper, curled up at the edges. Petals drooped like too-loose silk.

Rosie rarely answered her phone. Didn't stop by. She returned texts by saying she'd call later, but if she did, it was brief and blandly cheerful. Glib explanations of all the housework and decorating they'd been doing. She dodged concrete plans by chirping, "Yeah, maybe! I'll let you know."

She never let them know.

Willa twisted off the cap of Rosie's homemade jasmine lavender shampoo, trying to hang on to the realness of her.

Later, they heard she deferred her admission to the university. They heard she was still working at the florist's shop, but also waitressing late at night. Willa didn't know till later that Momma would drive to the gas station near the diner some nights, just to see Rosie move from table to table.

One night, Willa exploded at the dinner table. "We should just go *get* her!"

"That's not how it works," Momma said quietly. Daddy looked like he was going to cry, right there over the nice roast that Novy taught them to make.

"Why *not*?"

Momma exchanged a look with Daddy, unreadable. "Rosemary is an adult."

At the time, Willa thought her mother was trying to point out that it was normal—healthy—for an eighteen-year-old to move out of her parents' house. That they'd all do well to remember that Rosie was her own, not theirs.

After, though, Willa heard it differently. Heard her mother reminding herself that Rosie was legally an adult, that they couldn't just go and *take* her back. That, in trying to, they might drive her closer to him.

It lasted six months.

Six months that, later, Rosie, wouldn't talk about.

On the day the first crocus bloomed, Momma stopped scrubbing midway through a pile of dishes. The plate clattered into the sink, and she rushed outside, Willa on her heels. She thought maybe Novy had caught an earlier flight.

But it was Rosie, sitting in the passenger seat of an old sedan, driven by a middle-aged woman Willa had never seen. But Momma had seen her before. Another waitress at the diner.

Rosie stared up at the farmhouse.

Momma ran to her, splecks of mud flicking across her long skirt.

Rosie got out of the car, sheltering a scrawny black cat in her arms. Willa couldn't tell, in that moment, if Rosie was protecting the cat…or using the cat as protection between herself and the rest of the world. Momma wrapped an arm around her middle girl, murmuring, and Willa hurried to get Rosie's bags.

"Thank you," Momma told the woman driving. "I can't… I just. Thank you."

"I've been with a few real pieces of shit myself," the lady said, shaking her head. "'S hard to leave. Real hard."

"Can I give you some cash, for the drive over from—"

"No, no," she said. "Rosie's a good girl."

"Thank you. *Thank* you," Momma said, emphatic. Then she turned in to Rosie. "Come on, baby. You did good."

"I don't know what I did wrong." Her mouth was pale and dry. What kind of winter had done this to Rosie, Willa wondered.

Momma's voice was a fierce whisper. "You did nothing wrong, my love."

Rosie slept for two days. Willa brushed her hair, but Rosie shifted to avoid Willa's hand touching her skin. Daddy read to her even when she fell asleep, stories about seven generations of one family, about magic and the real world intertwining. Willa sat outside the door, listening to his voice.

Finally, Rosie let Momma rub her hands and feet. She wept and wept—onto her eyelet pillowcase, onto the cat's fur. Sometimes it sounded like howls. For weeks, she barely spoke. The most noise Willa heard her make was tsking at the cat.

Now, in the passenger seat, Rosie is silent, and Willa worries what happens once they get home. There is no Momma to soothe her. No Daddy to take the night shift with his gentle presence. *Novy will know what to do*, Willa reassures herself, pressing into the gas pedal. Novy always knows what to do.

Nova

The autumn wind snakes up to the porch, and Nova pulls her sweater tight. She stares at the road from town as if her sisters will manifest right then, like they won't show up if she blinks. Willa texted her from the grocery store: He's here. It was perhaps the fastest Nova has ever typed a response: Get her out of there.

Oh, Rosie girl. Would she cry and rage and feel it? Or would she be sunken-in and wispy, floating away like smoke?

Nova hadn't been here when Rosie came home last year. Nova arrived the next day and walked right upstairs, leaving her bag in the foyer. Momma and Willa warned her that Rosie didn't want to talk, didn't want to be touched, didn't want to cry. *She's processing*, Momma said. But when Nova knocked, Rosie's voice said, quite clearly, to come in. She was sitting up in bed, staring out the windows at the paddock and toying with the ends of her loose hair.

"Hey," Novy said, her voice thin with sorrow. "Oh, Ro. I'm so sorry about all this."

Rosie turned, eyes narrowed. "You always hated him. Don't pretend to be sad."

"Rosie." She knelt beside the bed. "I'm not pretending. I'm just sad for a different reason than you are."

Novy was sad because her sister had become a gambler. Rosie trudged home to him every night, joylessly asking to be dealt in. She offered more and more pieces of herself on the green felt table, believing this one—no, really, this one—

would win him fully. And so here she sat, curved inward and seeming impossibly smaller than when she started.

Rosie pressed her face into her hands, though no tears would come, and Novy climbed onto the bed beside her. Rosie let Nova cradle her, as Nova had on the day she was born. In the hospital photo, Nova looks so careful with her delicate baby sister.

"It's okay," Nova crooned. "Everything's okay now."

Later, Novy would get up to make her banana-walnut muffins, heavy on the cloves, and some mint tea.

Now, Nova runs her own hand over her hair—until she hears the tires down the lane, grinding against pebbles in the dirt.

Rosemary

Rosie jumps out of the truck, staring at her older sister waiting on the porch. "Novy? Everything okay?"

Nova says, "What is he doing in this town?"

Rosie is genuinely befuddled, as if her older sister is revealing a long-hidden clairvoyance. She turns to Willa, who looks away. "You texted her?"

"I panicked, Ro! I thought you might go with him."

"Oh, my God," Rosie says, throwing her hands up. "Honestly, the both of you. I was fine. I'm fine."

"Didn't he move away?" Nova demands.

"He's visiting! Staying with a friend! Jesus! What is wrong with you two?"

Willa takes a deep breath in, perhaps to mediate between them. Instead, her voice carries on the wind, yelling. "Do you remember the day I visited you at that house, Rosemary? *That's* what's wrong with us."

Rosie's chest constricts—a gasp or a sob, she can't tell.

"I can take care of myself, and it's *shitty* that you don't trust me to." Rosie pushes past them. She clutches the bannister up the stairs, replaying his face in her mind. His eyes, locked on her mouth. It feels, as always, like an old cartoon, like the sight of him pounds her upside the head with a wooden mallet. She's woozy, with images of him spiraling around her vision.

He was here. He was right down the road. Why had she been *nice* to him? Rosie has spent a year being strong, feeling so capable. But he must have known she'd crumble in his presence. Why else would he have strolled right up to her, with that easy smile? She'd moved out of their house over a year ago without a word, fleeing after he left for work. She must be weaker than she thinks, because even he could see it.

Rosie can remember the fallout. She can remember all the times he was moody—punishing her with silence. All the times he made her feel like she was to blame for everything bad in his life. She remembers sitting in the empty bathtub of their too-small house, sobbing with the fan on so he wouldn't hear. Because he wouldn't comfort her. He'd be angry that she was making things harder.

And God, that time he showed up to the diner to yell at her. She remembers that.

I know you're feeding that goddamn stray when I'm not home, Rosemary.

He'd convinced her that her sisters didn't *get* her. Not like he did. *They don't have your best interests in mind. They hate me for no reason. But we don't need them*, he'd said.

So why can she still feel the happy memories, pooling inside her like warmth? How good it felt on the good days. Him teaching her to throw a spiral in the front yard, patient and laughing. Opening up about how horrible his dad was.

That explained a lot, you know? He didn't have a role model for how to treat a woman.

She slams the door behind her, though she can already hear her sisters' feet on the hardwood floors. The first sob comes like a hiccup. The second, a cracking open. Her knees bend, easing her to the floor beside the bed. *For goodness' sake, Rosie,* she thinks, furious at herself. *You'll be no good convincing them that you're fine if you cannot act fine.*

"Ro." Nova pounds a fist on the door. "Open it."

The doors in the house don't lock—never had. But the girls have a rule between them, for doors and for emotional boundaries: never barge in unless it's an emergency.

"I'm fine," Rosie calls. Honestly, can't they ever understand when she just needs some quiet?

"Rosie," Willa says, her voice breaking. What had she yelled outside, about the day she came to the house? God, Rosie had dragged her into such a mess. "Ro, come on. Please?"

"Fine."

They stare. Rosie is clutching her midsection like everything inside of her is going to spill onto the floor.

"He poisoned everything," she whispers. "He ruined me."

"You are the furthest thing from ruined," Novy says.

Willa frowns. "But we agree that he's a snake."

They help her onto the bed and squeeze in beside her.

"Of course I remember that day you came to the house," Rosie tells Willa. "I should have apologized for it a long time ago."

"What day?" Nova asks.

When Rosie nods, Willa takes a deep breath in, about to go underwater.

Willa

Four months after Rosie moved out, Willa took a bus to the next town over, then walked two more miles in the icy Wyoming winter.

She hadn't believed Novy that Wyatt was bad news. She had chalked it up to Novy's protectiveness of Rosie, to her cynical nature. Willa thought Momma was exaggerating when she muttered, *There is a darkness in that boy.*

But now Rosie wasn't returning her texts or calls anymore. Momma assured them that Rosie was okay, though Willa had no idea how she knew. At first, Willa worried. Then, she got angry. At Wyatt for whatever part he played in this, and at Rosie. How could it be so easy for her to walk away?

Willa's nose was pink and runny by the time she knocked on the door of the one-story brick house. She didn't even feel the chill. She'd beat down hell's front doors to get to her sister, even if Rosie didn't want her there.

She glanced around, looking for clues. In the soil that should have been a garden, a black cat blinked at her. The door pounding hadn't scared him off, apparently. He sat still as a decorative gnome.

"Rosemary! It's me!"

Rosie pulled the door open, her arms hidden by an oversize sweater. "Willa! What are you…? Are you okay?"

Willa kept her face hard, looking at Rosie for…evidence. Of what, she didn't know. Temporary insanity. Illness. Something. "Well, great. You *are* alive. Good to know."

"Of course I am! I'm fine!" Rosie said, almost convincingly. Something was deeply *off.* Willa's blood sang with warning.

"Well, that's just great, Ro!" Cold wind hit Willa's watery

eyes, making them ache. "But I'm not. Everything is falling apart, and you're *nowhere*."

Rosemary stood there in the doorway of that house, looking shocked. Who had she become, holed up in this place?

"I'm so sorry, Will. Wyatt's phone broke, so he's been using mine. He must not have seen your messages."

Willa's cheeks burned with what he might have seen in those messages. Heard in her voice mails, increasingly upset. "But why wouldn't you call me? I haven't seen you in *months*."

"I'm sorry," Rosie said, sounding small. So very small. "I didn't know you were—I didn't know."

"Okay, well. Now you do. And I know you're not dead. So, great." Willa turned on one heel, marching off the porch.

"Wait!" Rosie stood there, a tremor running through her bony shoulders. "Please don't go. It's just so much harder than I thought, okay?"

This took Willa back a bit. It seemed like an admission. "What is? Being a grown-up?"

Rosie held her hands up, open-palmed, as if cupping the whole world—the air and the bare trees and the pearl clouds above. "Everything. Momma and Daddy made it look so easy."

"So, *leave*, Rosie," Willa pleaded. "Come home."

"Oh, Will." She ran a hand over Willa's hair. "I love him. But I love you too, okay? For always. Will you please just come in?"

"Am I allowed?" Willa asked. When she'd asked to visit before, Rosie had told her Wyatt didn't want company until the place was looking nice. *Company*, Willa thought. Is that what sisters are?

Rosie shrugged feebly.

They wound up at the little kitchen table with two cups

of tea. Rosie didn't offer up a house tour, and Willa didn't ask. The kitchen and living room were outdated and beige but impeccably neat, filled with secondhand furniture Rosie had spruced up. But there wasn't enough light. And no plants. It was inconceivable to Willa that Rosie could even breathe without flat green leaves, spiky ferns, without bunches of herbs in the kitchen window.

"Where are your plants?" Willa twisted around, wondering if perhaps the light was better at the back of the house.

"Wyatt has allergies," Rosie said.

To...all plants and herbs and flowers? Willa frowned. But wasn't Rosemary equally allergic to the taupe, lifeless house?

"Is that your cat out front?" Willa asked.

"Not mine, exactly," Rosie said, wrapping her hands around her teacup. "So, tell me what's going on. Everything is falling apart—that's what you said."

Willa covered her face with one hand. Maybe, just maybe, she could offer up this earnest, painful part of herself. And maybe Rosie, in turn, would do the same—tell the truth of what was going on in this house. "Well, I'm in love with my best friend, and I'm not sure why it feels like dying."

"Ha!" Rosie said, a burst of total recognition. "Oh, Will."

"I'm serious."

"I know you are. So...Ingrid?"

Willa nodded. "I don't know when it happened. But now, it's like...when she texts me, it feels like a lightbulb flips on inside of me. Like something physical gets bright and buzzy. Sometimes, if we're talking late, I can't sleep because I feel like I could float above my bed."

"Yeah," Rosie said, pained.

"But she's my best friend, and I feel like it isn't right to think about her in that way."

"Well," she said. "Can you help it?"

No. And it hadn't always been like this. She and Ingrid had been inseparable since seventh grade, when their schools merged and so did all their ideas and hobbies and inside jokes. Ingrid was guileless, quick to announce how she felt. The summer she went to sleepaway camp, Willa hugged her and accidentally felt her friend's sadness at leaving, her nervousness about fitting in, her fear that Willa would find another best friend while she was gone. But Ingrid had already *told* her all those things. What a pair: a girl who could feel hidden emotions and a girl who never bothered to hide them.

But something had shifted in that easy comfort. Earlier this year, Willa found herself looking away shyly when Ingrid complimented her. Willa started wearing long sleeves all the time, for the moments when Ingrid linked arms with her. She wanted to protect her friend's privacy. She wanted to protect her own pride, too.

"Do you think she feels the same way?"

"Sometimes I really do," Willa admitted. "I think…if I wasn't getting some undercurrent of feelings from her, I wouldn't still feel this way?"

"Mmm." Rosie nodded.

"But other times, I'm sure that I must be reading into it. She's never talked about girls before."

"Yeah, but have you?"

It was a fair point. "She did date a guy last year. And I think she really did like him."

"Well, maybe she's like Novy."

Novy's biggest relationship in high school had been with a girl, but in college, with a boy. She was never one to have faraway crushes with longing looks. She fell as she got to know someone, when they made her laugh and proved they could show up. It wasn't like that for Willa; at least—it hadn't been so far. Only girls had ever given her that happy, woozy feeling.

"Did you ask Novy for advice?"

Willa snorted. "Yeah. She said, *I dunno, Will, ask if she wants to make out.* Very helpful."

Rosie smiled sadly into her hand. "I miss her."

"Me, too. Both of you."

"I'm right here," Rosie said.

Are you? Willa wondered.

Rosie studied Willa's face. "I know you wouldn't, but is it tempting to touch her? To see how she feels about you with no risk?"

In some ways, of course. Willa feared that confessing her feelings would make Ingrid uncomfortable. And, at the mere touch of a hand, Willa could know how Ingrid felt without risking their friendship. But of course there was a risk. Because Ingrid wouldn't be able to hide her disgust or disinterest, if that's what she felt. She could break Willa's heart without ever knowing. "I'd never violate her privacy like that."

Wyatt came in just then, Rosie startling a little at the sound of the door.

"Hey, babe!" Rosie called. "Guess who's here."

Wyatt turned the corner with a tight smile. "Willa! This is a surprise. You came all the way from Grander?"

"Sure did." Willa wanted it to sound like it wasn't hard. Like she could do it any old time she wanted, when he wasn't expecting her. "Easy trip."

"Well, nice to see ya. Sorry the place is such a mess. I was hoping we'd have it looking nice for company."

Willa glanced at Rosie, whose smile was stretched so taut. Like it would snap.

"I think it looks great. And I was just going," Willa said.

Her smile, however, was genuine. Because she was going to get the last thing she came for.

She hugged Rosemary and walked toward the door.

"Take good care of her," she told Wyatt. And she shook his hand, though she basically had to lift it from his side. It was such a weird thing to do, but Willa didn't care. Means to an end.

A dust storm of feelings rushed in: his scalding resentment toward Rosie—God, it was like he *hated* her. His suspicion about why Willa was here. And this…this *self-righteousness*, as if he had been wronged. A pride that all his feelings were justified.

Willa dropped his hand and spun to Rosie, eyes full of tears. "Ro."

"I'll call you soon," Rosie said, chipper, but that was for Wyatt's benefit. Her eyes bore into Willa's with absolute fury. Willa had broken Rosie's trust in one touch.

Nova

"That's why you left," Nova says. She'd wondered, and been too scared to ask, what finally made Rosie walk away. She was afraid the answer would compel her to lace a pan of spicy enchiladas with arsenic and leave them at Wyatt's front door. "Because Will knew how bad he was?"

"I stayed for fifty-four more days," Rosie says quietly.

After a long while, Novy sits up from the bed. "I'll put the kettle on."

Rosie is staring into nothing, the same milky-eyed gaze she came home with after that horrible half year in that horrible house. "Tea won't make it not true."

Of course it won't, Novy wants to snap. Tea doesn't *fix* anything. It's just comfort you can hold.

Three minutes. That's how long it takes the copper kettle to boil. And it's the time Nova needs to compose herself, to cool down. Sometimes she stares at the kettle and imagines that it's her anger—not the stovetop burner—that creates the steam. She transfers the heat, releases it.

She wishes that Rosie could sip the tea and feel anger blooming inside her chest, as red and bright as hibiscus.

Novy waits for the tea to steep, remembering an argument she had with Rosie like watching ghosts. The signs were right here, just before Rosie moved in with him.

He has a temper. Novy had kept her tone even, as if stating it casually.

Rosie pushed off the counter. *He hasn't had an easy life. You don't know anything about him. There's a lot going on.*

Okay, Novy said. *But none of that is your fault.*

Rosie told her later, after everything, that she did know that his temper wasn't her fault. But sometimes, she didn't help matters, she added. Sometimes, she just didn't know how to be a good girlfriend to him. She misread his moods. She clicked through options like tumblers on a lock—listening as he spoke, kissing him meaningfully, staying in another room to give him space. But a combination that worked once didn't always work the second time.

Nova felt relieved, in that moment, that she had cut her hair off. What that boy did to her sister made her want to tear it all out.

The kettle whistles, and Nova reaches for it.

She still isn't entirely sure why she shaved her head. Those idiot kitchen bros, that's what she thought at first. They were either hitting on her or talking down to her like a little sister.

Maybe she thought, on some level, shaving her head would break the connection: *I am not your sister or your girlfriend or your mommy.*

Or maybe…maybe it was because college spent with a boyfriend had made so many people assume. They were wrong, and she wanted them to second-guess.

In her peripheral vision, Willa flies past like a spirit, a blur of color on her way to the study. She emerges with a stack of Momma's notebooks. Some are ancient, with cracked binding—passed down through generations. Others are newer and jammed with leaves of paper, handwritten by great-aunts. All of their relations, documenting how these powers seem to tick.

Willa drops the notebooks to the counter with an unceremonious thud. Her eyes are full of furious tears. "You should have seen him, Novy. Looking at her with that cocky smile. How *dare* he? And what if he stays here? What if he moves back?"

She flips through the pages, not gently. "We have to know someone. There has to be a gift that can hurt him. Or that can make Rosie forget. *Something.*"

Nova stirs the tea, giving Willa a moment. Finally, she says, quiet, "It doesn't work like that, Will. There aren't shortcuts for this. You know that."

"Then I want to curse him. Isn't there, like, voodoo or something?"

"That is not ours." Nova's jaw clenches. "You know that, too."

But Nova holds out one hand for her sister to take. Willa grips it, eyes closed, and Nova knows she can feel the fury and despair. Nova, in turn, makes a note to brew more tea—chamomile for Willa, with honey.

Willa pulls her glasses off, drops them on the counter. She

rubs her eyes hard enough to smear her mascara. "What then, Novy? What?"

"I don't know." She wraps one arm around her sister. "I just don't know yet."

Later that night, Novy stares up at her ceiling. When her phone rings at 1:17, she knows whose voice she will hear.

"Hey," she says, settling back into her pillows.

"Hey, kid." Sometimes she hates it, the way he calls her that. He's only a few years older. But other times, when she's feeling cramped inside being the eldest sister, it's nice to think that someone sees her as the younger, less burdened person.

"How's the restaurant?" she asks.

"Same. New roasted chicken special, good stuff. But Holmes, that dumb asshole, nearly cut his thumb off tonight. You gotta come home," he says, as he has every other night. And then he qualifies it with some restaurant talk, to make it clear he wants her home for work. "This temp can't slice radishes for shit. Thick as a coin. I'm like, 'C'mon, man. They should be so thin I can see through them.'"

"That sucks."

"No kiddin'. But you're back tomorrow, right?"

"I was supposed to be. But my sister, she um—"

"Which one?"

"Rosie. She had this bad boyfriend, a year or so back..."

"I remember," Hunter says. Does he? Nova remembers telling him. At the bar after work, just the two of them. She was the sickest type of homesick that week. Teetering on the bar stool, tipsy and blubbering about her sisters like a fool.

"Gherin?"

"Yeah, I'm here." She sighs, rolling over to her other side. "He's back in town. She saw him."

"Shit." Nova knows Hunter DeLuca well enough to know he's scrubbing a hand over his short hair. *"Shit."*

"Yeah."

"Well, lemme know if you stay. I'll vouch for you to Chef."

Oh, *really*. He hates excuses, hates to look bad at work. All kitchen, all the time. "Yeah?"

"Yeah."

"Well, I'll let you know." She'd never abandon Rosie—never, ever. But sometimes? Well, sometimes Nova thinks Rosie needs her to step away.

"You'll come over here? When you get home? I've been working on this breakfast empanada like you showed me, and—"

"Yeah," she says. "I'll come over."

"Okay, good. Well, seeya." The line beeps out. This is what he does most nights, nearly hangs up on her. He doesn't like parting words, trying to detangle himself from the conversation.

Nova glances at the phone now, still lit up in her dim room. DeLuca, it says. She never calls him Hunter except sometimes in her head.

She can't even remember when they exchanged numbers. Not in the first couple of months, that's for sure. She didn't trust any of them, and she was working around the clock.

She does remember the day she looked twice at him. She'd stepped into the walk-in cooler, looking for a salad dressing base she'd begun earlier. She hadn't heard him enter behind her, but there he was, tall and imposing in front of the closed door.

"Listen, you gotta give me a heads-up on what you want me to do." He was in a black sous chef jacket, bandana around his head like always. He spoke as if she'd begun the conversation, like he was being forced to respond.

"Excuse me?"

"When the guys give you a hard time. Do I tell them to shut the fuck up? Or is that making it seem like you need my help, which you don't? Do I pull them aside and say that's enough? Or does that make you feel more...separate or whatever?"

The chill didn't touch Nova's arms, just then. She studied this man, with his long lashes incongruously soft near a sharp jaw and nose, near stubble, and tried to let it sink in that he was asking her how she'd like to be supported. "Well, for starters, maybe don't corner me in a closed fridge."

"Oh." He studied their positions, how he'd blocked her exit. "Fuck."

Nova had laughed then, a little at his obtuseness but mostly at his nervous surprise. He stepped sideways.

"I don't need your help," she said. Her impulse was to thank him, but she refused it. "I'm fine."

"I know you are. You're good at this." He said this like a pronouncement, like his stupid blessing made it true. Not the years of practice and honing the talent she was born with. Not the culinary degree or the three kitchens she'd worked in before this one.

"I know I am," she snapped.

He grinned, a rare, slow-blooming thing. "The ego's good, too. Practically a prerequisite for this job."

It doesn't have to be, she wanted to yell. The macho culture, the aggressiveness and posturing, it was all so childish. Little boys on their bikes, forming neighborhood packs like the kitchen was a clubhouse.

It made her show back up after a bad night. Made her want

to head up a Michelin-starred restaurant someday and have her face in a photograph of the Top 100 restaurants.

"All right, well," he began. Truly, how was one human so bad at exiting a conversation? "You let me know, Gherin. If you need anything."

"Thank you," she replied, sincerely. "But I won't."

She'd been wrong.

Rosemary

In the morning, Rosie feeds Gnome and tends to the plants around her room. She brushes one finger against the pink-striped Calathea leaves, painted with thin strokes. She reaches for a philodendron stem, like a tiny arm extending toward a giant, deep green hand. With each new touch, she makes eye contact with the plant. Like she is asking what it needs.

Rosie can feel Nova leaning against the door frame, wondering the same thing about her.

"I'm fine, Novy," Rosie says. But when her sisters don't believe it, she struggles to believe it, too. Why can't they just *trust* her?

"Can I make you some breakfast before I leave for the airport?" Nova asks.

Rosie sets down the watering can. "No, thank you."

"Ro," Nova says, gently. "Please swear to me that you won't go over there."

"Over where?"

"To wherever he's staying." When Rosie doesn't respond, because she is *seething*, Nova adds, "I can cancel my flight, Ro. I'll stay. Just say the word."

It hits Rosie like whiplash, the comment reverberating

back again. She turns, slowly, fists clenched. "Just say it to my face, Nova. Say that this never would have happened to you."

Nova blinks at her. *"What?"*

"You knew he was poison. None of this would have happened if I had listened to you."

"No," Nova says, evenly. "None of this would have happened if he wasn't a monster."

Rosie grips her fists tighter, wanting to scream. She can read between those lines: Nova thinks Wyatt saw easy prey because Rosie *is* easy prey.

"It's not..." Nova starts again, looking frustrated with herself. "You know none of this was your fault, right?"

"That's what they tell me!" Rosie says in a sarcastic, too-chipper voice. Momma told her; the therapist she saw for a year told her.

"It *wasn't* your fault, Rosie," Nova says.

Willa appears in the doorway to referee. Rosie hates that her youngest sister gets put in the middle so often. But Novy gets under her skin. Expects too much. And Rosie pushes back.

"But it *was*, Novy!" Rosie yells. God, it feels good to yell. The feelings release with the words, loud and unshackled. "You knew. Momma and Daddy knew! I didn't. There's something *wrong* with me! Just! Say! It!"

"There's something wrong with *him*, Rosie! He's a hedge maze from hell! Momma and Daddy and me, we had a bird's eye view, so we could see. We were farther away, that's all."

"If that's true," Rosie says, "then why did I crumble last night?"

"Because you were caught off guard! It's *so* sneaky, the way he treats you."

"She's right, Ro," Willa says from the doorway. "And when

it feels like your fault...you know that's still him, right? He turned everything—everything—back on you."

"Neither of you understand," Rosie says shakily. They had no idea how much sense her own thoughts had made, when she lived in that house. What now looked like denial had felt entirely true.

"Ro." Willa enters the room, just two steps. "He fooled me, too. Even last night! I started to wonder if he was as bad as I'd built him up to be. But he was. He *was* that bad. You were so brave to leave."

Rosie glances between them, disbelieving. These are exactly the things her sisters would say to try to make her feel better. But she only wants the truth.

"Dammit, Rosemary," Nova mutters. She stretches one arm back to Willa, who touches her hand. Rosie's eyes flick between them, waiting.

"Admiration," Willa says quietly, looking up. "And anger. And protectiveness. And feeling like a failure. Frustration that she's not communicating well with you."

Rosie's eyes flood with tears. "Admiration?"

"God, Ro." Now Nova's eyes are watery, too, and Novy never cries. "Yes."

Rosie can see, even with teary vision, that she's been wrong. That Novy is on her side. That Novy has been on Rosie's side even when Rosie herself wandered away from it.

Rosie blots beneath her own lashes. "I'm sorry that I yelled."

"Oh, please," Nova says, swiping the apology away.

Rosie never yells, really, except at Nova. And she's always wondered why that is. It seems so clear now: she can yell at her older sister because Novy's love is not conditional on Rosie's behavior. The tears take over, shaking her shoulders. She sinks to the edge of the bed, and her sisters drop beside her.

"You're going to miss your plane," Rosie tells Nova miserably.

"Like I give a shit about my plane."

And that, of all things, is what quiets the static in Rosie's mind. Her sisters would kneel on the old pine floors beside her. They'd miss their flights. They'd plead with her to let them in, but they'd never, ever kick her door down. They'd whisper her name back when she'd lost it, place the missing pieces back into her hands.

What a wonder—love that powerful, but so careful to never break anything in its path.

Rosie holds out both her hands, and closes her eyes as each sister grasps on tightly. It feels as real as blood gushing out, fast and warm. Willa, she knows, can feel every facet of pain. Her distrust of herself, of others, her anger, her frustration at everyone who doesn't understand, her fear that it could happen again, her embarrassment that she still feels drawn to him, her ache at being perceived as weak. The love—the huge, reliant love of her sisters. Surely Willa must feel that, too. *And please*, Rosie begs the universe, *let both my sisters feel that I am also okay.*

When Rosie opens her eyes, Willa is looking right at her. "Nothing I didn't already know."

Nova searches Rosie's face. "How about I make cherry scones before I go?"

Nova

Late that night, in an outside borough of New York, Nova knocks on the apartment door. She rolls her eyes as Hunter scoops her up onto his dumb jock body and hauls her inside. A big dopey pit bull, Nova thinks. Roughhousing. When he sets her down, she has white flour smudges on her shirt. Her eyes find the pastry dough, rolled out thin on the countertops.

A train groans past, rattling the walls. She missed it, the city noise. Craved it. But later this week, she knows her lungs will cry for the plains, for open air and seeing all the way to where the horizon line bends.

"Your flight okay?" he asks.

"Yeah," she says. Her chest ached during takeoff, as it always does, leaving.

"And your sis?"

"Hanging in there. She's tough."

"Why doesn't that surprise me?" Hunter says, opening the fridge. "Beer?"

Nova accepts the can, cold in her hand, and tips it back.

"Don't leave again," he says. But he makes eye contact, reads her face. He has sisters, too. If they needed him, he'd swim across the Hudson in nothing but his skin. "Not for a while, okay?"

"Okay," Nova says. She weighs her heart in her palm, tests if it is enough or too much. As if it is a decision. As if any Gherin girl has ever believed she has total control of her destiny.

Later, when he's dicing tomatoes, she watches his forearms, still tanned from summer. A butcher knife tattooed down one arm, shears down the other. One for each parent's vocation. She thinks she could stand to watch his arms—lifting crates of vegetables, shifting pans on the stove, held out and waiting—for a while. Maybe for a very long while.

Willa

Downstairs in the farmhouse, Willa hears a tap on the glass before Ingrid's lavender fingernails appear under the barely open bedroom window. One long leg swings inside, then the other and her hips. Willa has a kind of low-level obsession with Ingrid's hips, the heft and bone of them.

"My whole family knows you sneak in here, you know. Just come through the front door."

Ingrid shrugs. "It seems more respectful to at least *pretend* I'm not breaking the rules."

She crawls along the bed until their bodies are aligned, and nuzzles into Willa's neck.

On contact, Willa feels that Ingrid is comforted. Contented. And a tiny bit worried. Ingrid has known for months that Willa can feel her emotions. But Willa is learning that touch can be like hearing, the difference between eavesdropping and knowing there is a buzz of sound around you.

"Rosie okay?" Ingrid asks, her voice just below Willa's ear. Willa is so helpless to the smell of her—the sandalwood shampoo, but also her skin. Can something smell soft?

Willa shrugs, fitting her legs with Ingrid's until they're entwined. "She's working through it."

Both girls stay quiet, as if listening for the sounds of Rosie's sadness, for the wails of a minor-key orchestra. But it's quiet, just now.

"Doesn't it freak you out sometimes, how badly love can break you?" Willa whispers.

"Mmm," Ingrid says.

"You could hurt me like that, you know." Willa means it, too. She handed Ingrid some vital part of herself earlier this year and trusted her with its safekeeping.

Ingrid stretches her neck long, tucking Willa's head beneath her chin. She reaches to lace their fingers together.

"No," she says, quiet. "Never like that."

The kissing that follows is interrupted by a sharp knock at the door and Rosie's voice calling out, "Will?"

"Just a sec!" Willa says, unraveling herself.

"Sorry to bother," Rosie replies. "Did Momma move the extra box of candles?"

"Hall closet!" Willa says. "Top left."

"Thank you," Rosie says, her voice already farther away. "And hi, Ingrid!"

"Dammit." Ing laughs, rolling over. "You guys know *everything*."

Rosemary

Lifting Gnomey from the bedroom windowsill, Rosie scratches the spot behind his ears. She sets him on the bed, where he happily settles into a tight circle. Little nomad cat.

Wyatt's boot connecting with his skinny little rib cage. Even that, she reasoned at the time, was her fault. Wyatt had said not to feed him.

The mangy thing goes or you do.

He'd never done that before—suggested that she could, or should, leave. Rosie imagined a black, wrought-iron fence around her life with him. Had the gate really never been padlocked?

Where did Wyatt imagine she'd go? Home, of course. To her family. They'd told her she could do that. Why had it not seemed truly possible until now? Why couldn't she see it until Wyatt acknowledged it?

So began a series of small dares. When Wyatt wasn't home, Rosie dared herself to open the door, scoop up the cat, and walk to the sidewalk, across the street. No alarm sounded. Only the singong of the spring birds, finally here. She dared herself to put a few things in a bag. Harmless—and just as easily unpacked. When a friend from work picked her up for a shift, Rosie dared herself to ask for a ride home instead. Trembling, she grabbed the bag and the cat.

She barely breathed until the house was far behind them.

She barely breathed for months after.

Now Gnome looks up at her with blinking green eyes, like a child waiting for a bedtime story. Once upon a time in a cold underworld, a boy took something from her that she can't quite name—a tangled piece between trust and innocence. But not all of it. *Not* all of it.

She'll tell her daughters someday: *If you don't feel safe enough to yell back, you're not safe enough. My babies, that is not love.* She imagines three girls—will they look like her? Like a someday-partner or like Novy and Will? Will she see Daddy and Momma in their little faces?

Rosie Gherin opens the bay window behind the ledge where she has lined up white pillar candles. The September air carries a chill, but she no longer fears being snuffed out. Rosie has fire in her blood from her ancestors, from Nova's fast, stovetop heat and Willa's smoldering coals. And some fire that's all her own.

One by one, she lights the wicks.

★ ★ ★ ★ ★

WHY THEY WATCH US BURN

by Elizabeth May

I.

THE WOMAN AHEAD OF ME BRIBED THE GUARD for chalk before they executed her. I never learned her name; it might as well have been my own. My penmanship on this stone floor is abysmal, but I'm keeping my mind occupied while the crowds roar outside for the next of us. I smell the wood burning through the small, square window now, and it makes me want to vomit.

Tomorrow, I am meant to leave. My punishment (a mercy, they say) is penance. Work. Prayer. But everyone knows women who go to those camps in the forest never come back out; what they mean is my bones are strong, and I am young, and I will not die quickly. My body makes for better labor than tinder.

For those who come to this cell after me, this is for you. A lesson:

Destroying a girl is one of the easiest things in the world.

I would have said differently, once. It's such a simple form of denial, and it goes like this: bad things happen to *those girls. Other girls*. Not *this* girl. Not *me*. I'm different.

You're only different until the day you're not.

My destruction began with words. I held the accusation on my tongue, uncertain. I fought my hesitance (because I'm different. *I'm not those girls*), that awful prophecy every woman remembers when her time comes. A prediction, based on the countless women who came before us.

But I was compelled to say his name. To speak my truth: he hurt me, he put his hands on me, he left bruises.

Liar.

My explanation was punctuated by rattling, quick exhales, but they told me to calm down. They said I was being hysterical. They spoke to me as if I were a child.

Why didn't you fight back?

Don't they understand fear? Don't they know what it looks like? Haven't they seen animals lie prone on the ground, unable to move because they just *can't*? That's what prey do when they sense a predator. It's how they survive.

What were you wearing?

Clothes. They were *clothes*. I wasn't waving a red flag at a bull; I was just existing. I felt pretty until he made me feel shame.

Flaunted your body. Asked for it. Wanted it. Deserved it.

That's not what happened. *No, no, no*. It was a complete sentence. *No*.

Whore. Slut. Temptress.

You seduced him with your clothes, your body, your sinner's smile. You cast a hex with your eyes, didn't you? That's what he said. That's what he told us. How could he resist? You're nothing but a devil. A witch intent on destroying a good man.

Here's how to fulfill a prophecy: you are a woman, you speak the truth, and the world makes you into a liar.

Then they tie you to a post, put you out into the town square for everyone to see, and light you on fire. They all cheer as the wind carries away your ashes.

Thus endeth the lesson.

II.

I have no paper or pencil, no chalk or stone floor. But I have a heart and I have a mind and these are the events and my thoughts as I would have written them.

In our camp, the priest believes that if we had instruments to write, we would use them to compose spells.

The priest, the police, and the crowd who threw stones at me tell me I am a witch. Every woman in this camp is, they say.

So if I were to cast a spell, it would involve food. Before this (before *him*. Before he ogled and touched and grasped—), I served beautiful platters to businessmen in one of the tallest skyscrapers in the City. A constant banquet of mouth-watering meals—royal *ballotine* of pheasant, beef *madrilène* topped with gold leaf, morel *soufflé* for dessert. Appalling amounts of food that I was never allowed to eat, that always went unfinished into the dumpster.

Here we eat bread, and what one of the girls calls *slop* (porridge or potatoes, depending on the time of day), and other scraps meant only to keep us upright in order to chop trees for lumber.

Ever since my trial, my stomach has ached. On the road here, the truck bounced constantly along the rough single track (all dirt, uneven from the constant rain), and I had not eaten for days. The officer drove for hours up the winding mountain, and the metal cuffs bruised and cut into my wrists. He had snapped them on too tightly (deliberately; he said I deserved worse).

"How long until we get there?" I asked quietly, leaning forward to speak through the bars that separated driver from prisoner.

The officer was silent for so long that I wondered if he would answer at all. Then, with a sneer: "Does it matter? It'll be the last day you spend outside of the camp, witch. Enjoy it while it lasts."

Judges always said we could be released if God willed it. But everyone in this country knows women who go into the forest never come back out, and it has nothing to do with God. Our labor is too valuable. They could give us more efficient ways of cutting trees, but the use of axes is our penance. The priests bless the wood and mark it with symbols to ward against witchcraft—highly valued in an age when they claim witches walk amongst us, disguised as your mother, your sister, your daughter, your wife.

Any woman, they warn men. *Any one of them at all. They're liars, not to be trusted.*

So our lumber builds men houses, furniture, and gleaming tables like the ones I once set with food. The warded wood is meant to protect them from me, from all of us. From our curses and our words and our seductive ways—but not just that.

We provide the wood that burns witches.

I suspect the ache in my stomach is not the tasteless food (truthfully, it settles like a stone in my belly), but the scent of fir that surrounds the camp. It had been that way for miles as the police truck drove up the mountain. The fog had descended, and a sight that might have looked enchanting before my stay in prison only served to make me feel suffocated. There were no houses on that road, no trucks or cars that passed—only an endless expanse of kindling. These trees are more effective than iron bars; you'd be dead before you reached civilization.

The only thing for miles and miles is the camp. The biggest building is a wooden chapel with a white cross painted on the door, and surrounding it are a few log cabins that are as small as prison cells.

One of these is for sleep, but it's a threat, too. They need only bring torches and we'll die burning just like the others. This is how they keep us in line: the illusion of freedom (pray to God, pray for forgiveness, on your knees, on your knees, *goddamn it, get on your knees*), obtainable if we remember how to be meek, how to be submissive and voiceless. *Remember how it was before?* they might as well ask. *Remember how you silently judged those* other girls*? You thought it must have been their fault, that they cast spells with their body, their eyes, their words. But when you remembered your own tongue, your own words, it was to say* no *instead of* yes.

My mind wanders like this while in prayer. I don't think of God; I keep thinking that it's my own fault for saying the name of the man who hurt me, for trying to speak the truth. *Maybe it didn't happen like I thought it did. Maybe I did something to deserve this.* But that's not my voice. It's *his*, and it's *theirs*.

The officer reminded me of him when I reached the camp.

He pulled me out of his truck and spun me around to roughly remove my handcuffs. The camp was empty then; the girls had all gone out to work, overseen by the priest and guards. The only sound in the forest had been a click of metal as the officer finally freed my bruised hands.

I caught the scent of fir and my stomach heaved. The officer grasped my arm and shoved me forward. "This way."

He showed me the cabin where I now sleep (so small, blankets on the floors, pressed up against twelve other girls for warmth), then the shed where the axes are kept. He told me about the lumber quota: meet it and we eat, don't and we starve. He told me about how I needed to pray every morning, and every night, and while I chopped down trees. He told me this wasn't optional. He told me this was a mercy granted by good men.

"The girls don't have names here," he told me, his eyes as sharp as blades. "You don't use names. You don't have names. You're nothing now. Do you understand?"

I shut my eyes at the memory from my trial. The papers called me *Jane Doe*. We were all Jane Doe until people called us worse. Then we weren't even given the courtesy of a fake name. We lost the right to freedom, to rest, to food, to something as simple and important as being called anything other than "witch" and the obscenity that rhymes with it.

"Do you understand?"

"Yes. I understand."

"Good. I'll pray for you, witch."

Then he shoved me into the chapel, and told me to get on my knees (*goddamn it, get on your knees*) and pray with him.

III.

I stole coal from the potbelly stove to write these words. After I finish, I will wipe them from the floor as if they never existed, so the priest doesn't see. He would have me killed for this part:

If I cast a spell, it would be to heal my hands.

They are a mess of blood and blisters and calluses from the hours spent with my axe chopping, chopping, chopping down trees. I want so badly to sing or hum to distract myself from the pain, but we are not allowed. The guards and the priest do not let us sing, for spells can take the form of song, and they fear we will enchant them.

This is meant to shame us into silence, I think, but sometimes I take up my axe, and I hear the ragged cadence of twelve other breaths in sync with my own and I imagine it's a song instead.

All thirteen of us, on the same breath, singing our wish for the same thing: to survive.

IV.

Forgive me for these shaky letters, but I cannot keep my hand steady.

I dropped my axe yesterday. It felt so heavy in my grip, so cumbersome that I could no longer hold it aloft. Into the soil it went, and another girl picked it up for me. She is beautiful, this girl. Her eyes are as deep and black as an ocean at night. Her hair is the same color, though I would say it looks like an expanse of moonless sky. Oh, her features are so austere, so regal, with high cheekbones beneath smooth ochre skin. When she speaks, it's with the softest lilt on top of an American accent that betrays time spent elsewhere.

She handed me my axe, and god help me, I blushed when her fingers touched mine. It was like relearning what touch felt like (before *him*, before *that day*, when it could bring comfort and not pain).

"You hold this in a narrow grip," she said in that lilt, that beautiful lilt. Like music to my ears. If she spoke enchantments in that voice, I would have been under her spell, and I would have been so willing. "It's better to spread your hands farther apart. May I?"

I started when she gently took my hand in hers. She wrapped our fingers around the handle of the axe, and did the same with the other hand. "You grip it like this, see? It gives you more control when you strike."

More control, yes. More.

Her eyes met mine, and it was as if the world suddenly tilted on its axis (*my* world, every vulnerable part of me). For a mere space between heartbeats, I lost myself in her gaze. A guard yelled at us for stopping (*get back to work!*), but I barely heard him. I only heard the rasp of her rough wool clothes when she leaned forward. A desire struck me then, small and bold and surprising: I wanted to press my lips to hers.

She smiled, as if hearing my thoughts. "See you around."

The next time I swung the axe, it splintered the wood and severed the tree in a single, powerful stroke. It felt like magic.

V.

My charcoal is less frequent now as the weather grows colder. The twelve other girls are in my cabin as I write this, pressed against each other to conserve warmth. The girl with the obsidian eyes lies in the blankets next to me, and she often murmurs with her lilting voice full of sleep.

Last night, she spoke to me as if we were sharing a dream. "Are you ever angry?" she asked, her words a low breath in the darkness. "Sometimes you say things when you're dreaming..."

I was surprised by her words. Most of the girls here talk in their sleep (nightmares, hunger, tears, *no, no, no, stop*), and our unspoken rule is to pretend we can't hear.

"Yes," I said quietly.

When I strike my axe, my rage becomes a living thing that writhes inside me, and I welcome it. Then I think of witches, and understand that there are too many people in this world who would rather see a woman burn than wield power.

I feel anger the most when I watch new girls arrive and disappear into the woods, never to be seen again. Some of them are taken by guards (the girls who struggle to hold their axes, or who become ill; the priest calls them a burden, a disappointment, and says that God has rendered his punishment). Others leave in the night to escape to civilization that I know is too far to reach without food or supplies. In the end, it is always just us. Thirteen girls; thirteen survivors.

The size of a coven.

"Good," the other girl said thoughtfully. "Anger is good. You can survive on anger. For a while I wondered if you would drop your axe and never pick it up again."

"Did you think I would?"

"I hoped you wouldn't."

I studied her features, the way her cheekbones caught the light from the dying embers of the fire. I wanted to memorize her. I wanted to be able to keep the image of her with me, always, conjured up again on a day when I need it most.

Perhaps for when I'm taken into the woods, too.

Here is how I will always remember her: She hums in her sleep. In the darkness of our cabin, I can always tell it's her beside me, because her touch is featherlight—as if she's asking for my permission. She always seems so strong, so utterly invulnerable. When she gazes at the priest and the guards, they sense a threat, and I've seen them try so hard to break her. They give her less bread than the rest of us, because she does not pray to their God. They call her a heathen.

If she's a heathen, then I'm a heathen. Their God takes too much.

"Have you ever been tempted?" I asked her.

"Oh, yes," she replied, and she curled against my side with a shiver. "But I don't listen to him."

"Him?"

"We all have someone who caused us to be here. *Him. Her.* Their names don't matter; they all fear the same thing." She leaned forward and pressed her forehead to my shoulder, her next words whispered against my skin. "You understand the truth, though, don't you? The most terrifying thing in the world is a girl with power. That's why they watch us burn."

VI.

We did not make our lumber quota this month.

As the icy days grow more numerous, it becomes harder to work. Our wardrobe is not appropriate for the hours we spend outside; our shoes have holes, and our clothes are merely scraps of layered secondhand fabric.

"You'll just have to work that much harder, won't you?" the priest said in the chapel on Sunday as we prayed. "If you feel that axe slip from your hands, remember your lessons. 'I can do all this through Him who gives me strength.' And so we shall pray for strength."

The priest likes to speak in a soft voice compared to the guards. He presents himself as humble. He tells us to work harder as he starves us. He tells us to hold on to our axes as our fingers are numb from cold. He quotes scripture to women he's already condemned to Hell.

He is the sinner who cast the first stone.

The priest has a favorite among the girls. I call her Blue, because she has the most vivid eyes I've ever seen. He gives her more bread. If he touches her in the chapel, his hand lingers too long. After prayers on Sundays, he keeps her behind as we go off to chop lumber.

The priest likes Blue because she keeps secrets well. The priest likes Blue because he thinks she barely speaks at all. He doesn't know that she prefers to speak at night in the darkness of the cabin, when we all lay together for warmth.

"I'll hurt him if he makes you stay behind again," I told her yesterday. "He thinks I'm going to Hell anyway."

He looks at Blue in a way that reminds me of my past, of leering and grasping and bruises on my thighs. I'd go to Hell for every single one of these girls if it meant they never have to endure that.

"I'll help you," said one of the other girls. Rose, for the birthmark on her freckled cheek. *The Devil's kiss*, the priest calls it. Next to the obsidian-eyed girl, she's his least favorite. "That Bible of his looks like a decent weapon."

Obsidian smiled and nodded her agreement. So did the other girls.

We were not permitted to use names, but we all had secret ones for physical features that made us stand out. Obsidian, Rose, Blue, Scar, Green Eyes, Hazel, Tall, Tiny, Curly, Red, Blondy, Porcelain. They called me Night, for my dark hair.

Green Eyes had suggested we learn our names from Before. *In private. Just because they don't treat us like we're human doesn't mean we have to do the same.*

Green Eyes wanted us to know her Before Name so badly she cried. The name her parents had given her was for a son, and she had endured a long, hard, difficult road before choosing her name as their daughter. It was hers, and now it had been taken away. This place (*them*, the people who accused us) had taken away *everything*. Our names, our lives, our identities. Our struggles.

But one girl disappeared into the woods, dragged off by the guards for introducing herself with her Before Name, and we learned it was easier this way. Safer.

And so I am Night. Green Eyes chose her new name, too.

"No hurting him," Blue said. She rested her head on her knees. In the flickering light of the cabin stove, I noticed a slight bruise on her pale cheek from last Sunday. "We didn't meet quota."

Rose wasn't deterred. "What does that have to do with—"

"It just does," Blue said with a sigh. "Shipment comes tomorrow before prayers. I need to think."

I didn't like the way that sounded. "About what?"

"Nothing." Blue shook her head. "Nothing. I'm going to sleep."

The next day, after we came back from work, we found the cabin filled with food again. Blue wouldn't look at us, and I knew what she'd done, the sacrifice she'd made. The exact thing I would have done.

She made a deal with the devil for us all.

VII.

The priest expects confession every Sunday, and I've lied every time.

It's to get off my knees, you see. They have bruises over

the bone, my skin covered in smudges of black and blue and brown.

A new girl came weeks ago, and before she disappeared into the forest, she would show the rest of us these bruises with pride. As if three hours of prayer every day (twenty-one hours a week, not counting the expectation of pious thoughts, the dinner speeches, the nighttime murmurs. An entire day spent praying to a god for forgiveness—the same god that men offer the burned corpses of witches) meant much of anything.

I thought about trying, once. Shortly after I arrived, I got on my knees and focused my thoughts on guilt, on propriety, on pretending to be this woman that they want because maybe then they'll drive me back to the City and I'll never smell wood again.

It wasn't because I believed. I just didn't want to die here.

I'm not like those girls. I'm different.

I caught myself in that terrible, destructive mantra in the middle of my fake prayer and wanted to scream. Those are not my thoughts. Those are *his* thoughts, *their* thoughts. Even when I was pretending, they were still there, those callous words whispered at the back of my mind.

They've infected my brain like a virus, like wood rot.

This time, as I entered the reconciliation room and settled on my aching knees, I struggled to come up with a lie. Through the confessional screen, I saw the shadowed outline of the priest, and I imagined his hawkish eyes on me, the expression he wore when I worked. When I swung my axe (again and again, each stroke splintering the wood with strength I never knew I had), he stared in resentment and loathing. Always. As if he hated my very existence.

I was supposed to beg for forgiveness for being a witch, but the words wouldn't leave my tongue.

Here's the truth: I want to cast spells, I want to heal, I want to destroy, I want to create, I want to use magic and rise, and rise, and rise, to my feet, into the air, and fly. If witchcraft is the voice of women rising free and powerful (to change the world, make it ours, on our feet instead of on our knees) then I wish to be a witch more than anything.

"Forgive me, Father."

I don't need forgiveness. I don't want forgiveness. You are in no position to forgive. You hurt Blue.

"For I have sinned."

I am a sinner. You are a sinner. We are human, and therefore, we sin.

"It has been seven days since my last confession."

It's truly been months and months and months, because what have I to confess? Who are you to listen? And why is it that women are believed to have introduced sin? Eve was the original witch, a woman whose curiosity changed her entire world. And you would have burned her for it.

I hesitated. My speech had been so practiced, so careful. Why couldn't I say it? I had to say *something.* None of the girls in the camp could ever come into the reconciliation room and claim to be without sin, because we were witches and we were sinners and we were women.

Don't you understand, you stupid girl, the old priest from my childhood told me once. *It is in a woman's nature to sin. You can't help it.*

"I have lied," I said. "I have given into temptation."

"Tell me again," the priest replied. "You tempted that man to sin? You cast a hex on him?"

What temptation? I'd bring him a meal, or his morning papers, or write down his meetings, and he'd grab me with a laugh as I walked by. I'd go home and try to wash the memory from my skin. He would call me sweetheart, dear, love, pet, because I might as well have been any woman—any woman at all—unworthy of a name. What hex? When did I cast it? Was it when my eyes were on the floor (meeting his gaze made me want to shrink inside my skin, minimize myself, hide), or was it in the murmured excuses I gave to leave (back to work, sir. I have so much work)? Perhaps my crime was simply the misfortune of being a female in public. Was that it? Was it my body, Father? I was born with it, and it's mine, and I thought he took it from me, but when I have my axe in my hands or when I lie down with Obsidian at night, it finally, finally, finally *feels like my own again.*

Let me tell you, Father. Let me tell you my greatest sin. If I cast a hex one day, it'll be to destroy him. And you. And this place.

"No," I told him. My voice was like steel. "No. But I wish I had."

VIII.

I was worried the guards would take me into the woods and make me disappear.

As the priest escorted me out of the reconciliation room (his grip on me was so tight that each finger left a bruise) to the main part of the chapel, the girls were still in prayer. I caught their gazes, and they all looked afraid for me.

They looked as if they might kill him for me.

When Obsidian moved as if to stand (to do what? I don't know), I caught her gaze and shook my head.

I didn't want any of them to disappear, too.

The priest took me to a solitary cabin deeper in the woods. For days, he forced me to go without food, without heat, without anything. Before he left, he told me this: *Pray. Pray to God that He should give you mercy. Day and night, witch. Nothing but prayer, until you're begging me to let you out.*

I have not broken enough to beg yet. I plot, and I wish. I write these words with my fingertip on the dirty floor, because I will not be silenced.

And because I will not be silenced, I cast my first spell: to tell the other girls I am here.

I'm not gone, I whispered to them on the wind. I swear I heard it shake the trees. *I'm still alive. They didn't make me disappear.*

The following day, a panel near the door opened, and the priest delivered food.

"You're lucky," he told me. "You don't deserve this, but someone reminded me that 'if my enemy is hungry, feed him.'"

And that's how I know it was Blue, and she made a deal with the devil again.

Obsidian has snuck out to see me every night since my spell. I hear her whisper my name and settle in the dirt on the outside of the cabin. She keeps her vigil there until morning.

Last night she came just when I felt as if I might give up hope. The priest hadn't brought food for two days, and the scent of wood made me imagine terrible things. I had nightmares of being back in my prison cell, waiting to burn.

"Night?" Obsidian's voice was like a warm breeze in winter. "Are you awake?"

I pressed my hands to the door that separated us, and imagined myself sitting next to her beneath the canopy of trees. "Yes."

I swear I felt the heat of her hands through the wood, as impossible as that was. I wanted to touch her again, wanted her to press her lips to my forehead like she did just before I fell asleep every evening.

"Porcelain is sick," Obsidian whispered. "Blue had to give her your rations."

"Good."

Not good. None of this was good. Blue shouldn't have to

be the girl sacrificed to the monster to save us all. Every one of us should take the monster's head.

"I miss you," Obsidian breathed.

I shut my eyes and pressed my forehead to the door and pretended it was her skin, still warm from my kiss. "If the priest leaves me here—"

"Shh. We won't let that happen."

Behind my lids, I saw her face. Her high cheekbones and brown skin, her beautiful endless eyes. "Say a spell for me then," I told her. "Send it into the world, so I'll see you again."

"Shall I tell you my spell?" Obsidian asked. "I say it during prayers. One day I'll snap, and I'll make them all bleed." I hear her nails scratch down the wood, her next words like a spark of fire on tinder. "Because I am a wolf, and wolves survive."

Long after she left, I whispered her words in the dark room. They were my spell now, too, repeated when I had little hope left.

I am a wolf, and wolves survive.

IX.

I am still in the solitary cabin. Obsidian tells me it has been nine days, but it feels like an eternity.

Last night, the girls all came to visit me. I heard their voices through the darkness, and they heard mine, and we told each other of the people who brought us here. Of why we are accused of witchcraft.

She is not normal enough, too fae-like, too strange.

She laughs too freely, loves too freely, uses her body too freely.

She is too assertive, too independent, strives for too much.

She is too smart for her own good, studies too much, reads too much.

She is too masculine, too forceful, too aggressive.

She is too feminine, too sensitive, feels too much.

Every woman is never enough; she's always too much. We angered someone, somewhere, for our *too muchness.*

If to be *too much* is to be a witch, then I am a witch, and we are all witches. I told this to the other girls, and I heard them all whisper back *yes*, because to be a witch means our *too muchness* serves a purpose: it gives us power.

We all whispered spells that sounded like songs, our voices freed into the darkness. Flying, flying, flying.

I hope the priest looks hard at that cabin the next time he takes a girl there. Because if he studies the door, just at the bottom, he'll find the names we carved there of our accusers.

Every one of us has someone we want to destroy.

X.

When I was finally released from the solitary cabin, the other girls crowded around me during the night as if to protect me. Obsidian is always next to me when we sleep, and we whisper words in each other's embrace. Nonsense things, because we are often so exhausted these days.

"What's your name?" I asked her the other night.

After all these months, our names remained like our dreams: unspoken, secret. They reminded us of all the things we had lost. Lives we could never have back.

Obsidian and I tried to make peace with our new names. She would tell me how she cherished the night, how she loved to gaze up at the stars and dream and wonder. *Night, my dear*

Night, she would tell me, *don't you realize the stars are most radiant then?* She would trace constellations among my freckles and name each one.

So I told her about obsidian, and how people once carved the rock to make blades and arrows to hunt, and she loved it.

And then, on other nights when the girls slept more soundly, she would kiss my lips and call me her Devi, her goddess. She would whisper a translation of the Devi Sukta from the *Rigveda* into my ear, and I would fall asleep listening to the words: *They know it not, yet I reside in the essence of the Universe. Hear, one and all, the truth as I declare it.*

But I wanted to know her true name, for her to know mine. I wanted to listen to her murmur it when she curled against me and stroked my hair and sang me another hymn.

"Vidya. My name is Vidya," she breathed against my pulse. What a beautiful name. It sounded like a spell, one for hope. Something that would make flowers grow. "Yours?"

"Faye."

She repeated my name, and took my hands in hers. Vidya pressed her lips to each cut, each bruise, each callus along my palms.

When I woke the next morning, every injury was gone, as if they had never existed at all.

XI.

It is winter now. The snow is high, and the priest and the guards cannot make it to our cabin. Oh, what a relief, to be standing on a Sunday instead of kneeling. But it's grown too cold, and the coal has run out, and so I write this again with my heart. Yet I am not despairing, you see. None of us are. We are elated.

We cast a spell for fire.

It was beautiful. You must know how beautiful it is to stand, to hold the hands of my sisters, my friends, my lover. To squeeze our fingers tight and shut our eyes, and hear our voices. Oh, our voices. They merged together as one. Our lungs swelled with air and our hearts grew with hope, and when I opened my eyes, everything looked brighter, more vivid, and we all had fire between our hands.

I understand now that magic is not for wickedness, not for the devil, not for those with cruel hearts. It's for hope. For survival. It thrives in the darkness not because it is dark in nature, but because the fire shines brightest then.

This is what witchcraft looks like: It is women holding hands, harnessing power, and changing their fate. If every woman practiced such a thing, we would learn what Eve did after she ate that apple. When she held knowledge in her hands.

We would upend the world.

XII.

The snow melted in a circle around the cabin from the heat of our magic. Flowers grew overnight, the only signs of life in an otherwise winter landscape. Wildflowers, some of them. But others are there, too: heliotrope and tulips, marigold and snowdrops, red poppies that seem more vivid than I remember. A flower bed of all seasons, all colors, blanketing the ground between the forest and front stoop of our cabin, as if to protect us from the priest and the guards whose cabins are still buried in snow.

We barely have enough food to last between us, but we aren't worried. What else can we do but take this reprieve and lie among the flowers and welcome the air on our skin? It's been so long since we've had rest.

Yesterday, as the other girls watched the clouds overhead, I pulled Vidya away with me to the other side of the cabin and we sat together among the wildflowers there.

Vidya made a crown of daisies for me, and said my name in wonder. Then she called me her Devi, her goddess, because this is still our private name, and I want to keep it, too. "You look wild," she told me, stroking her fingertips down my cheek. "Like a fairy. Would you steal me away from this place if you could?"

Her black eyes were shining and her dark hair tangled around her face, and her ochre skin glowed like fire. I called her *my wolf, my beautiful wolf,* and wished I had a hymn to sing to her. "No, I wouldn't steal you away," I said, pressing her into the flowers and twining our fingers together. I loved the heat of her, her smile, her eyes, her voice, her everything. "Let's not run, Vidya. We won't disappear like the others."

"What, then?" she asked me.

I smiled down at her. "I would follow you, my wolf. We'll all be wild together, you and me and the other girls. Just like this. We won't fear anything anymore, will we? We'll burn our path through the trees, wolves and witches and goddesses, and we'll make the world ours."

"Yes," Vidya said. "Yes."

I leaned forward and captured her lips with my own. She made a small sound, a wild sound, a wolf sound; if it had been a song, it would have been the most beautiful one I'd ever heard. She kissed me back, and I sighed against her lips. My own song.

Vidya slid her hands down my shirt, undoing buttons. When she had me bare, she smoothed her palms across my skin, my hips, my thighs, murmuring words as if in prayer. Her fingers were not frantic, but gentle. So gentle. She counted the marks on my body, the signs of my penance, and I did the same to her.

We whispered spells against each other's lips. We composed our own hymn, our own enchantment. Our bodies were the altars on which we practiced our magic.

Later, we watched the sky dim above the trees. "Faye," Vidya whispered with her lips to my temple. "Witch. Beautiful. My witch."

Long after our magic faded, we still glowed like the remnants of dying stars.

XIII.

The snow has melted, and the priest hid away in the chapel once he saw our garden. I write this from the cabin, where the guards have locked us inside.

We watched others come up over the mountain, men who drew their guns and pointed them at us. They had to bring tinder with them, because everything here is too damp to catch fire. We can hear them now, setting it all around the cabin, amongst our flowers. I imagine them trampling petals with their boots, attempting to squash our magic down, to light it aflame, to destroy it.

They intend to burn us inside.

Vidya is holding my hand as I write this, and before anything else I must tell you that I love her. She is my Obsidian, my wolf, my beautiful dark-eyed girl. She taught me how to hold an axe.

And I love the girls. My coven. Our wolf pack, Vidya is

saying with a smile. Shall I tell you our names? We are no longer secret. We are no longer afraid.

We are Vidya and Gabby, Chloe and Alice, Maria and Tasbeeh, Grace and Antonia, Cecile and Daniella, Emily and Mahira, and me. Faye.

We are thirteen. We have always been thirteen. And we are wolves, and goddesses, and witches.

Here we leave our handprints scorched into this wood, so they will all be forced to remember us, remember our names, remember what they did, and how they tried to silence us.

The other girls are calling for me now, telling me to get ready. But before I go, I must write another lesson here for those who come after us if we don't succeed, for the women who find their way into this forest and are tempted to drop their axes and disappear. I am writing this now with my heart and with my mind and with my magic where I know everyone will see:

Look at our handprints. Memorize our names.

We did not go quietly.

★★★★★

AUTHOR BIOS

BRANDY COLBERT is the critically acclaimed author of *Pointe*, *Little & Lion*, and *Finding Yvonne*. Her short fiction and essays have appeared in several anthologies for young people. Brandy lives and writes in Los Angeles. Her favorite movie witch is Louise Miller from *Teen Witch*.

ZORAIDA CÓRDOVA is the award-winning author of The Vicious Deep trilogy, The Brooklyn Brujas series, and *Hollow Crown*. Her short fiction has appeared in the *New York Times* bestselling anthology *Star Wars: From a Certain Point of View*. She is a New Yorker at heart and her favorite witch is the Evil Queen herself, Regina Mills.

ANDREA CREMER is the *New York Times* and international bestselling author of the Nightshade series, The Inventor's Secret series, and *Invisibility* (with David Levithan). She splits her time between the lakes and forests of Minnesota and the mountains and deserts of southern California. Her favorite literary witch is Morgan Le Fey.

KATE HART is the author of *After the Fall* and a contributor to the anthology *Hope Nation*. She is a citizen of the Chickasaw Nation and lives in northwest Arkansas, where her family owns a treehouse-building business. She sells woodworking and inappropriate fiber arts at TheBadasserie.net. As for favorite witches, she dressed as The Wicked Witch of the West for five childhood Halloweens in a row.

EMERY LORD is the author of *Open Road Summer, The Start of Me & You, The Names They Gave Us*, and *When We Collided*, which won the Schneider Family Book Award. She lives in Cincinnati with her family and several overflowing bookshelves. Her favorite literary witches are the Owens sisters.

ELIZABETH MAY is the author of the YA fantasy trilogy The Falconer (*The Falconer, The Vanishing Throne, The Fallen Kingdom*). She was born and raised in California before moving to Scotland, where she earned her PhD at the University of St. Andrews. She currently resides in Edinburgh with her husband and two cats. She loves quiet, heroic witches with an abiding loyalty to family and friends, like *Practical Magic*'s Sally Owens.

ANNA-MARIE McLEMORE grew up hearing la llorona in the Santa Ana winds and enraptured by stories of witches like Morgan le Fay. She is the author of *The Weight of Feathers*, a finalist for the 2016 William C. Morris YA Debut Award, and 2017 Stonewall Honor Book *When the Moon Was Ours*, which was long-listed for the National Book Award in Young People's Literature. Her latest novels are *Wild Beauty*, a School Library Journal Best Book of 2017, and *Blanca & Roja*.

TEHLOR KAY MEJIA is the author of *When We Set the Dark on Fire.* Her short fiction also appears in the anthology *All Out.* Tehlor lives in the wild woods and alpine meadows of southern Oregon with her daughter. Her favorite literary witch is Circe from *The Odyssey.*

TESS SHARPE (editor) is the author of the Young Adult mystery *Far From You* and the feminist thriller for adults *Barbed Wire Heart.* She lives in the backwoods with a pack of dogs and a cabal of slightly feral forest cats. Her favorite witch is Morgan Rowlands from the Sweep series.

LINDSAY SMITH is the author of the YA novels *Sekret*, *Skandal*, *Dreamstrider*, *A Darkly Beating Heart*, and the Saints of Russalka trilogy, and is the lead writer and showrunner for Serial Box's *The Witch Who Came In From the Cold.* Her fiction and comics work has appeared on Tor.com and in the anthologies *A Tyranny of Petticoats* and *Strange Romance Volume 3.* She lives in Washington, DC, with her husband and dog, where she writes on foreign affairs. She watched *The Craft* way too many times while growing up in Oklahoma, which was nothing and everything like the Sawtooths.

JESSICA SPOTSWOOD (editor) is also the editor of the feminist historical anthologies *A Tyranny of Petticoats* and *The Radical Element.* She is the author of the Cahill Witch Chronicles and the contemporary novels *Wild Swans* and *The Last Summer of the Garrett Girls.* Jess lives in Washington, DC, where she works as a children's library associate for the DC Public Library. Her favorite literary witch is Luna Lovegood.

NOVA REN SUMA is the author of *A Room Away from the Wolves* and the #1 *New York Times* bestselling *The Walls Around Us*, which was a finalist for an Edgar Award and was named the #1 Kids' Indie Next Pick for Spring 2015 and a Best Book of 2015 by the *Boston Globe*, NPR, *School Library Journal*, the Chicago Public Library, and *The Horn Book*. She also wrote the novels *Dani Noir*, *Imaginary Girls*, and *17 & Gone*. She teaches at Vermont College of Fine Arts and lives in New York City. Her favorite literary witch from childhood is Dorrie the Little Witch, who often wore two mismatched striped socks, like Nova does today.

ROBIN TALLEY is the *New York Times* bestselling author of five novels for teen readers: *Pulp*, *Our Own Private Universe*, *As I Descended*, *What We Left Behind*, and *Lies We Tell Ourselves*. Her short stories have also appeared in the young adult collections *A Tyranny of Petticoats*, *Feral Youth*, and *All Out*. Her first book, *Lies We Tell Ourselves*, was the winner of the inaugural Amnesty CILIP Honour and short-listed for the CILIP Carnegie Medal and the Lambda Literary Award. Her favorite fictional witch is Ursula in *The Little Mermaid*.

SHVETA THAKRAR is a writer of South Asian–flavored fantasy, a social justice activist, and a part-time nagini. Her work can be found in a number of anthologies and magazines, including *A Thousand Beginnings and Endings*, *Beyond the Woods: Fairy Tales Retold*, *Uncanny Magazine*, and *Faerie Magazine*. When not spinning stories about spider silk and shadows, Shveta crafts, devours books, daydreams, draws, travels, bakes, and occasionally even plays her harp. Wise and/or wicked women who work magic are all dear to her heart, but if she has to pick a favorite, she really likes Granny Weatherwax and daayan and the Snow Queen and Kiki and…

BRENNA YOVANOFF is the author of a number of young adult novels, including *Places No One Knows*, the *New York Times* bestseller *The Replacement*, and *Paper Valentine*, which was named a best book of the year by the *Boston Globe* and NPR. She lives in Denver, where she regularly cooks beef heart. Her favorite witch is Baba Yaga.

ACKNOWLEDGMENTS

Creating a book is always a team effort, and that's especially true for an anthology. Jess and Tess would like to thank:

Jim McCarthy, our amazing agent, for jumping into our DMs and encouraging us to take this from a Twitter conversation to a real book, and for all of his wise counsel along the way.

Michael Strother, for his contagious excitement and for initially acquiring the project.

T. S. Ferguson, for his witchy enthusiasm, insightful edits, and championing the book in-house.

Copy editor Libby Sternberg, for catching all our mistakes, and managing editor Kristin Errico, for keeping us on track.

Cover designer Erin Stein, for a gorgeous witchy cover that represents the collection so beautifully.

Siena Koncsol, Shara Alexander, Linette Kim, Bryn Collier, Evan Brown, and Krista Mitchell, for helping our book connect with its readers.

Booksellers, librarians, and educators, for getting books into readers' hands. You are amazing.

Tehlor, Andrea, Lindsay, Brandy, Shveta, Robin, Nova, Zoraida, Brenna, Kate, Anna-Marie, Emery, and Elizabeth, for trusting us with your stories. They are beautiful and fearsome and magical in all the best ways, and we are so honored to work with you.

Our patient and loving partners, who were not at all unnerved by all the revenge going on in this anthology.